THE
GIVER

THE GIVER

Based on the novel by

LOIS LOWRY

Adapted by P. Craig Russell

Illustrated by

P. Craig Russell, Galen Showman, Scott Hampton

Colorist: Lovern Kindzierski

Letterer: Rick Parker

Scanning, cleanup, and digital coordination: Wayne Alan Harold

HOUGHTON MIFFLIN HARCOURT

Boston   New York

Text copyright © 1993 by Lois Lowry
Illustrations copyright © 2019 by P. Craig Russell

Script and layout—P. Craig Russell
Art, chapters 1–21—Galen Showman and P. Craig Russell
Art, chapters 21–23—P. Craig Russell
Memory-sequence art—Scott Hampton
Coloring—Lovern Kindzierski
Lettering—Rick Parker
Scanning, cleanup, and digital coordination—Wayne Alan Harold

hmhco.com

The illustrations in this book were done in blue pencil, pencil, ink,
blue ink wash, and grey ink wash on Strathmore paper.

The text type was hand lettered by Rick Parker.
The display type was set in Priori Sans.

ISBN: 978-0-544-15788-0

Manufactured in China
SCP 10 9 8 7 6 5 4 3 2 1
4500743115

For all the children
to whom we entrust the future

1

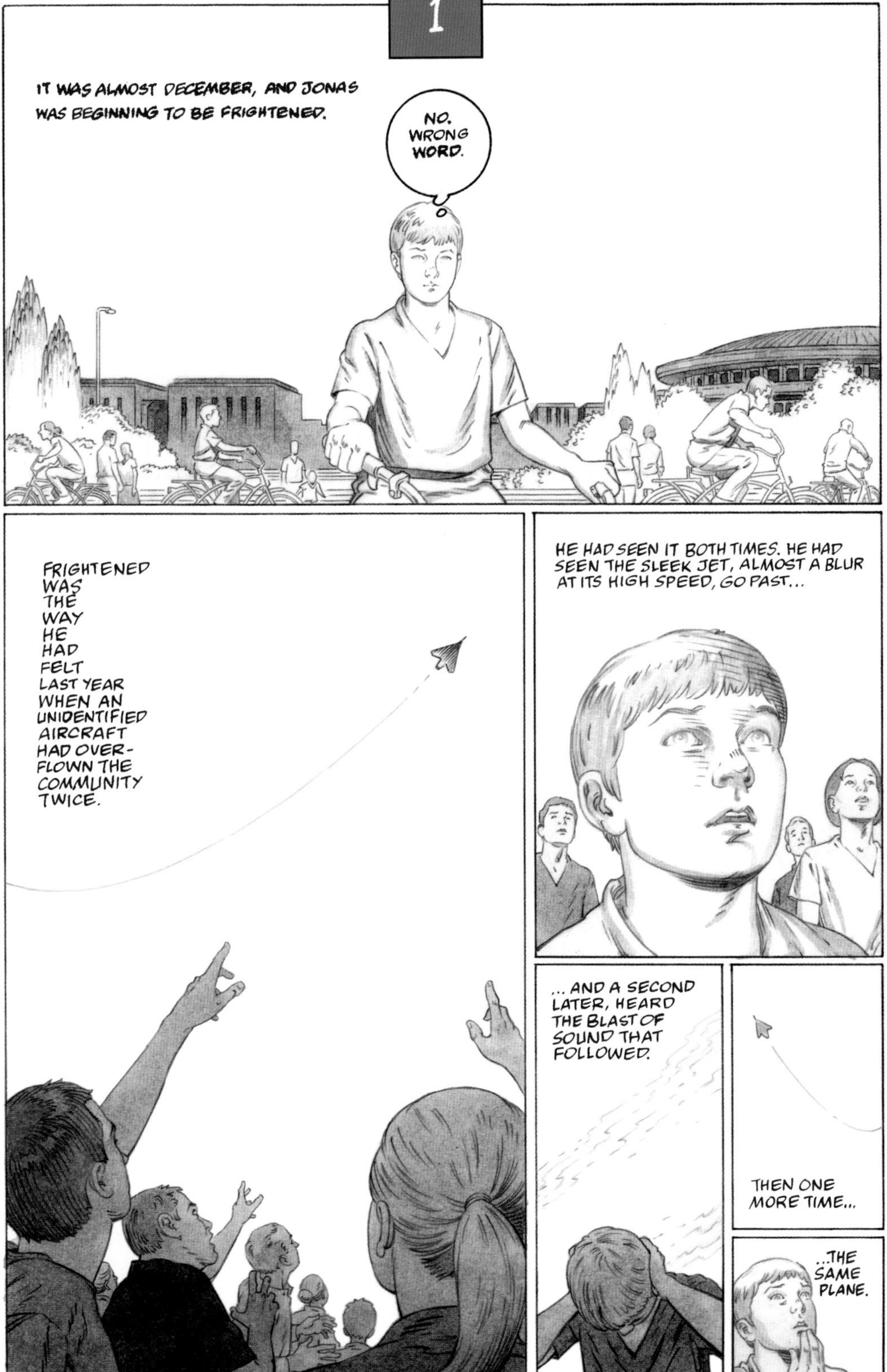
IT WAS ALMOST DECEMBER, AND JONAS WAS BEGINNING TO BE FRIGHTENED.
NO. WRONG WORD.
FRIGHTENED WAS THE WAY HE HAD FELT LAST YEAR WHEN AN UNIDENTIFIED AIRCRAFT HAD OVER-FLOWN THE COMMUNITY TWICE.
HE HAD SEEN IT BOTH TIMES. HE HAD SEEN THE SLEEK JET, ALMOST A BLUR AT ITS HIGH SPEED, GO PAST...
...AND A SECOND LATER, HEARD THE BLAST OF SOUND THAT FOLLOWED.
THEN ONE MORE TIME...
...THE SAME PLANE.

AT FIRST, HE HAD BEEN ONLY FASCINATED. HE HAD NEVER SEEN AN AIRCRAFT SO CLOSE, FOR IT WAS AGAINST THE RULES FOR PILOTS TO FLY OVER THE COMMUNITY.

OCCASIONALLY, THE CHILDREN WATCHED FROM THE RIVERBANK WHEN SUPPLIES WERE DELIVERED BY CARGO PLANES. THEY UNLOADED AND TOOK OFF DIRECTLY TO THE WEST, ALWAYS AWAY FROM THE COMMUNITY.

BUT THE AIRCRAFT A YEAR AGO HAD BEEN DIFFERENT.

JONAS HAD SEEN OTHERS STOP WHAT THEY WERE DOING AND WAIT, CONFUSED, FOR AN EXPLANATION OF THE FRIGHTENING EVENT.

CITIZENS. GO IMMEDIATELY TO THE NEAREST BUILDING AND STAY THERE UNTIL FURTHER NOTICE. LEAVE YOUR BICYCLES WHERE THEY ARE.

INSTANTLY, JONAS HAD RUN INDOORS AND STAYED THERE, ALONE.

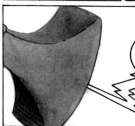

THE SENSE OF HIS OWN COMMUNITY SILENT, WAITING, HAD MADE HIS STOMACH CHURN.

BUT IT HAD BEEN NOTHING.

A PILOT-IN-TRAINING HAD MISREAD HIS NAVIGATIONAL INSTRUCTIONS AND WAS DESPERATELY TRYING TO MAKE HIS WAY BACK BEFORE HIS ERROR WAS NOTICED.

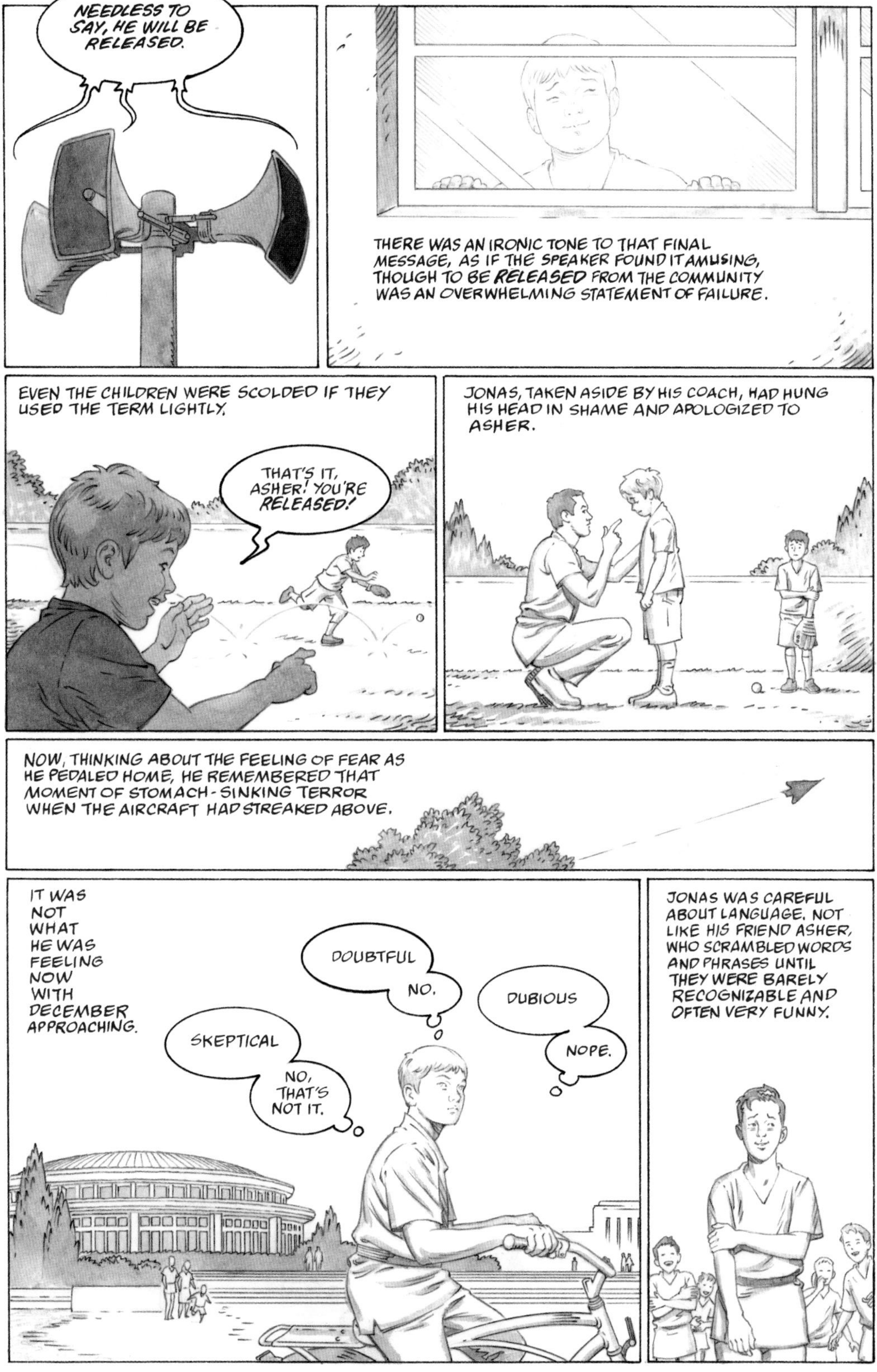
NEEDLESS TO SAY, HE WILL BE RELEASED.
THERE WAS AN IRONIC TONE TO THAT FINAL MESSAGE, AS IF THE SPEAKER FOUND IT AMUSING, THOUGH TO BE RELEASED FROM THE COMMUNITY WAS AN OVERWHELMING STATEMENT OF FAILURE.
EVEN THE CHILDREN WERE SCOLDED IF THEY USED THE TERM LIGHTLY.
THAT'S IT, ASHER! YOU'RE RELEASED!
JONAS, TAKEN ASIDE BY HIS COACH, HAD HUNG HIS HEAD IN SHAME AND APOLOGIZED TO ASHER.
NOW, THINKING ABOUT THE FEELING OF FEAR AS HE PEDALED HOME, HE REMEMBERED THAT MOMENT OF STOMACH-SINKING TERROR WHEN THE AIRCRAFT HAD STREAKED ABOVE.
IT WAS NOT WHAT HE WAS FEELING NOW WITH DECEMBER APPROACHING.
DOUBTFUL
NO.
DUBIOUS
NOPE.
SKEPTICAL
NO, THAT'S NOT IT.
JONAS WAS CAREFUL ABOUT LANGUAGE. NOT LIKE HIS FRIEND ASHER, WHO SCRAMBLED WORDS AND PHRASES UNTIL THEY WERE BARELY RECOGNIZABLE AND OFTEN VERY FUNNY.

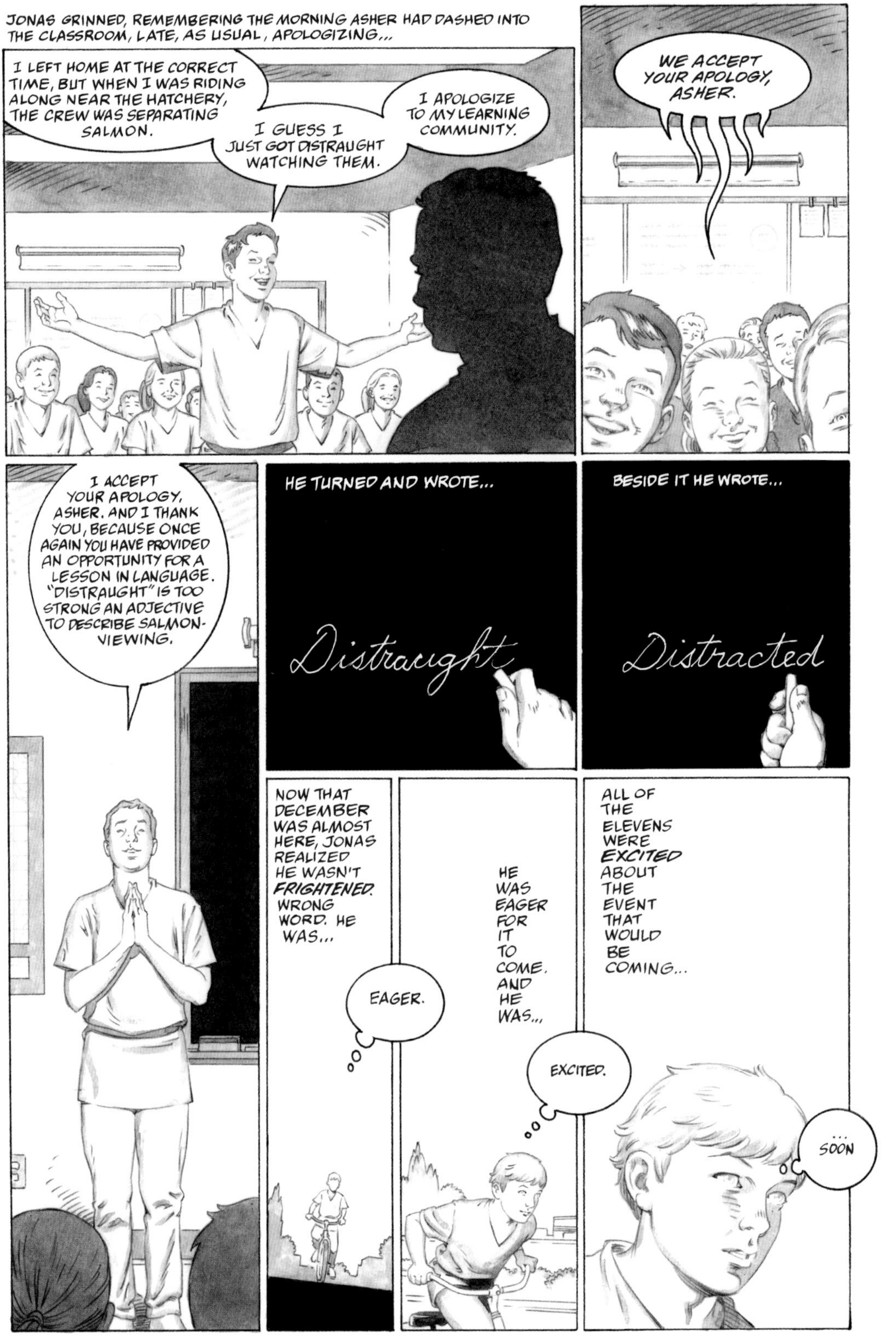

JONAS GRINNED, REMEMBERING THE MORNING ASHER HAD DASHED INTO THE CLASSROOM, LATE, AS USUAL, APOLOGIZING...
I LEFT HOME AT THE CORRECT TIME, BUT WHEN I WAS RIDING ALONG NEAR THE HATCHERY, THE CREW WAS SEPARATING SALMON.
I GUESS I JUST GOT DISTRAUGHT WATCHING THEM.
I APOLOGIZE TO MY LEARNING COMMUNITY.
WE ACCEPT YOUR APOLOGY, ASHER.
I ACCEPT YOUR APOLOGY, ASHER. AND I THANK YOU, BECAUSE ONCE AGAIN YOU HAVE PROVIDED AN OPPORTUNITY FOR A LESSON IN LANGUAGE. "DISTRAUGHT" IS TOO STRONG AN ADJECTIVE TO DESCRIBE SALMON-VIEWING.
HE TURNED AND WROTE...
Distraught
BESIDE IT HE WROTE...
Distracted
NOW THAT DECEMBER WAS ALMOST HERE, JONAS REALIZED HE WASN'T **FRIGHTENED**. WRONG WORD. HE WAS...
EAGER.
HE WAS EAGER FOR IT TO COME. AND HE WAS...
EXCITED.
ALL OF THE ELEVENS WERE **EXCITED** ABOUT THE EVENT THAT WOULD BE COMING...
... SOON

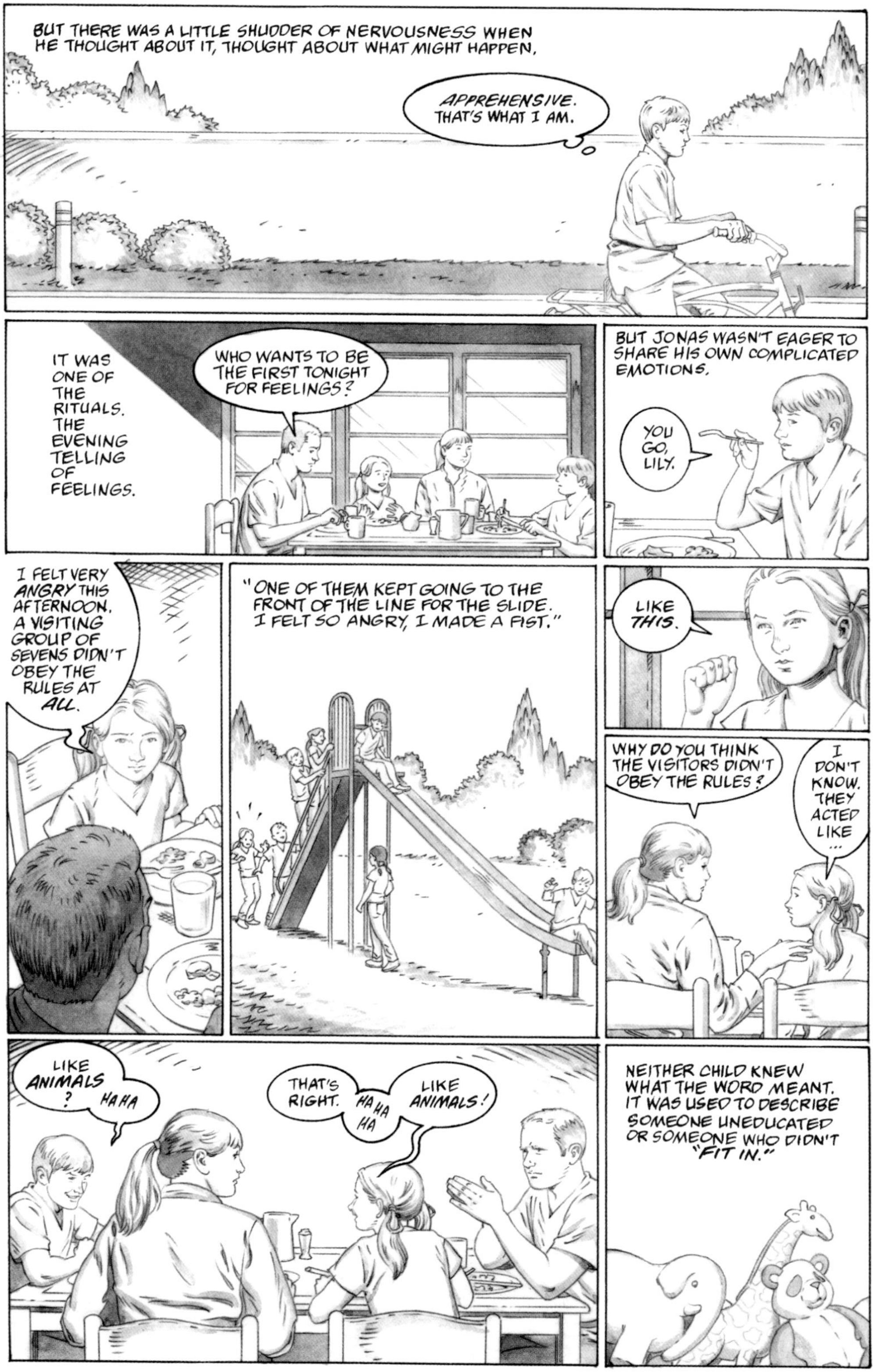

BUT THERE WAS A LITTLE SHUDDER OF NERVOUSNESS WHEN HE THOUGHT ABOUT IT, THOUGHT ABOUT WHAT MIGHT HAPPEN.
APPREHENSIVE. THAT'S WHAT I AM.
IT WAS ONE OF THE RITUALS. THE EVENING TELLING OF FEELINGS.
WHO WANTS TO BE THE FIRST TONIGHT FOR FEELINGS?
BUT JONAS WASN'T EAGER TO SHARE HIS OWN COMPLICATED EMOTIONS.
YOU GO, LILY.
I FELT VERY ANGRY THIS AFTERNOON. A VISITING GROUP OF SEVENS DIDN'T OBEY THE RULES AT ALL.
"ONE OF THEM KEPT GOING TO THE FRONT OF THE LINE FOR THE SLIDE. I FELT SO ANGRY, I MADE A FIST."
LIKE THIS.
WHY DO YOU THINK THE VISITORS DIDN'T OBEY THE RULES?
I DON'T KNOW. THEY ACTED LIKE ...
LIKE ANIMALS? HA HA
THAT'S RIGHT.
HA HA HA
LIKE ANIMALS!
NEITHER CHILD KNEW WHAT THE WORD MEANT. IT WAS USED TO DESCRIBE SOMEONE UNEDUCATED OR SOMEONE WHO DIDN'T "FIT IN."

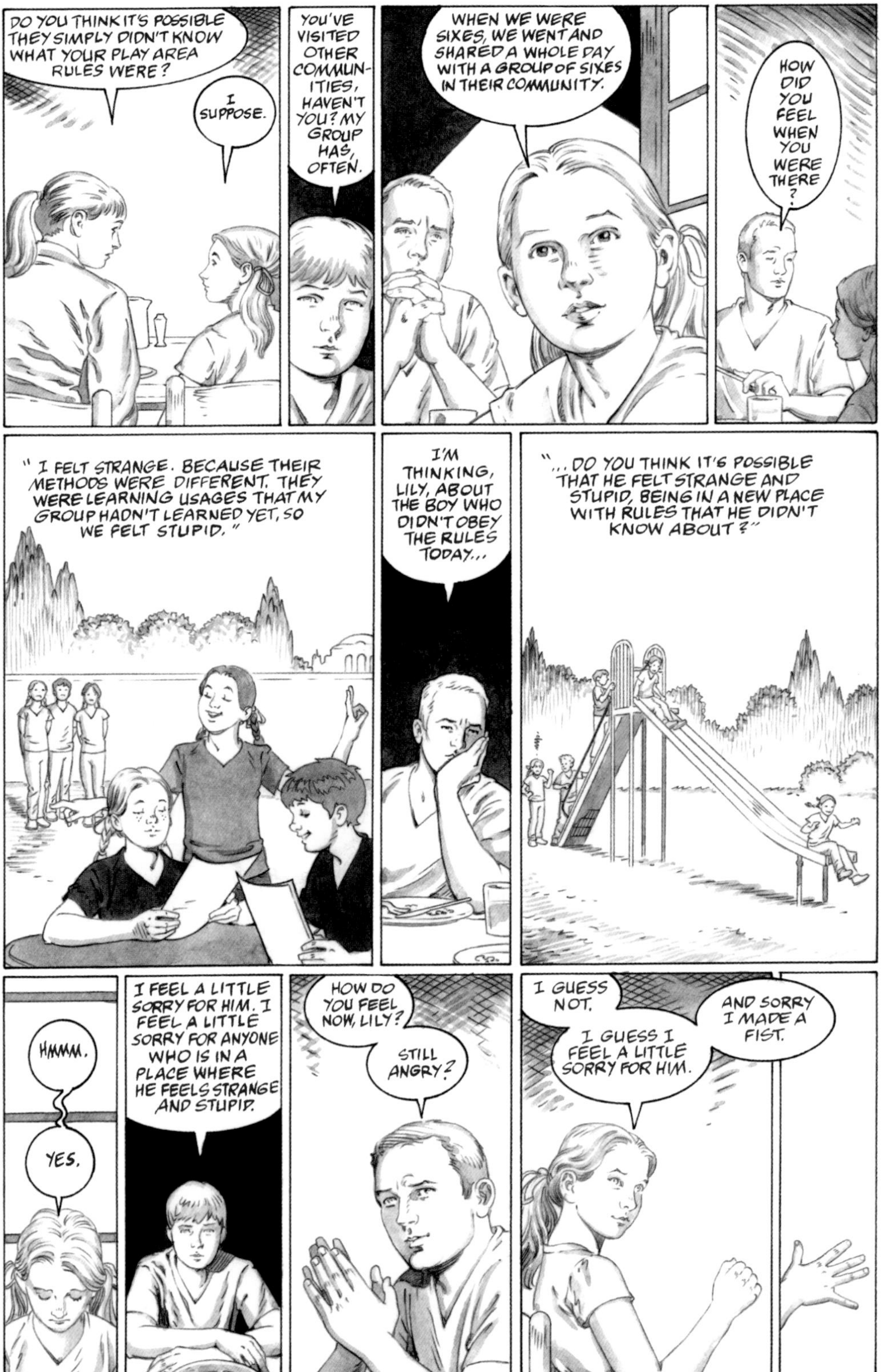
DO YOU THINK IT'S POSSIBLE THEY SIMPLY DIDN'T KNOW WHAT YOUR PLAY AREA RULES WERE?
I SUPPOSE.
YOU'VE VISITED OTHER COMMUNITIES, HAVEN'T YOU? MY GROUP HAS, OFTEN.
WHEN WE WERE SIXES, WE WENT AND SHARED A WHOLE DAY WITH A GROUP OF SIXES IN THEIR COMMUNITY.
HOW DID YOU FEEL WHEN YOU WERE THERE?
"I FELT STRANGE. BECAUSE THEIR METHODS WERE DIFFERENT. THEY WERE LEARNING USAGES THAT MY GROUP HADN'T LEARNED YET, SO WE FELT STUPID."
I'M THINKING, LILY, ABOUT THE BOY WHO DIDN'T OBEY THE RULES TODAY...
"...DO YOU THINK IT'S POSSIBLE THAT HE FELT STRANGE AND STUPID, BEING IN A NEW PLACE WITH RULES THAT HE DIDN'T KNOW ABOUT?"
HMMM.
YES.
I FEEL A LITTLE SORRY FOR HIM. I FEEL A LITTLE SORRY FOR ANYONE WHO IS IN A PLACE WHERE HE FEELS STRANGE AND STUPID.
HOW DO YOU FEEL NOW, LILY?
STILL ANGRY?
I GUESS NOT.
I GUESS I FEEL A LITTLE SORRY FOR HIM.
AND SORRY I MADE A FIST.

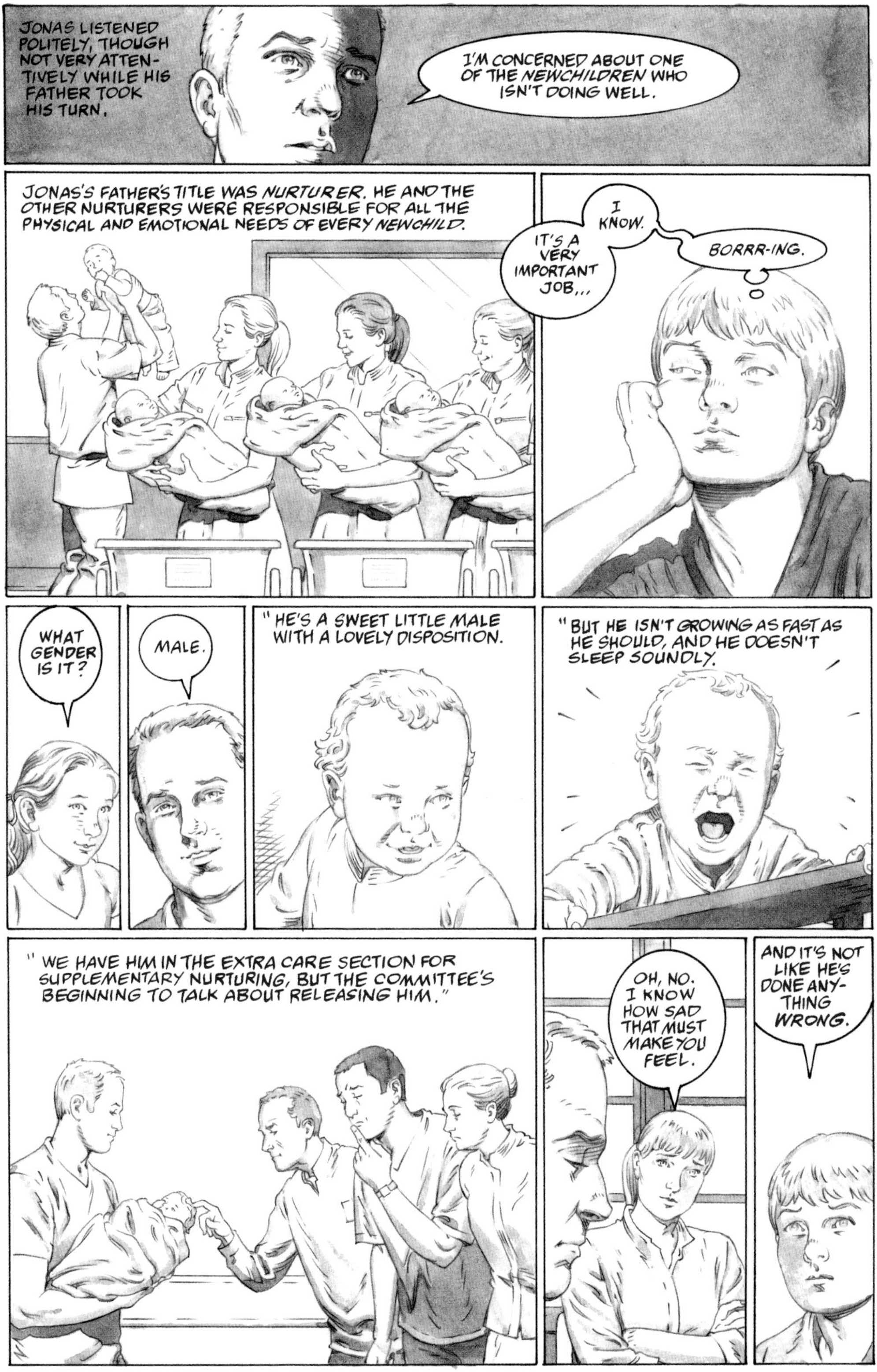
JONAS LISTENED POLITELY, THOUGH NOT VERY ATTENTIVELY WHILE HIS FATHER TOOK HIS TURN.
I'M CONCERNED ABOUT ONE OF THE NEWCHILDREN WHO ISN'T DOING WELL.
JONAS'S FATHER'S TITLE WAS NURTURER. HE AND THE OTHER NURTURERS WERE RESPONSIBLE FOR ALL THE PHYSICAL AND EMOTIONAL NEEDS OF EVERY NEWCHILD.
IT'S A VERY IMPORTANT JOB...
I KNOW.
BORRR-ING.
WHAT GENDER IS IT?
MALE.
"HE'S A SWEET LITTLE MALE WITH A LOVELY DISPOSITION.
"BUT HE ISN'T GROWING AS FAST AS HE SHOULD, AND HE DOESN'T SLEEP SOUNDLY.
"WE HAVE HIM IN THE EXTRA CARE SECTION FOR SUPPLEMENTARY NURTURING, BUT THE COMMITTEE'S BEGINNING TO TALK ABOUT RELEASING HIM."
OH, NO. I KNOW HOW SAD THAT MUST MAKE YOU FEEL.
AND IT'S NOT LIKE HE'S DONE ANYTHING WRONG.

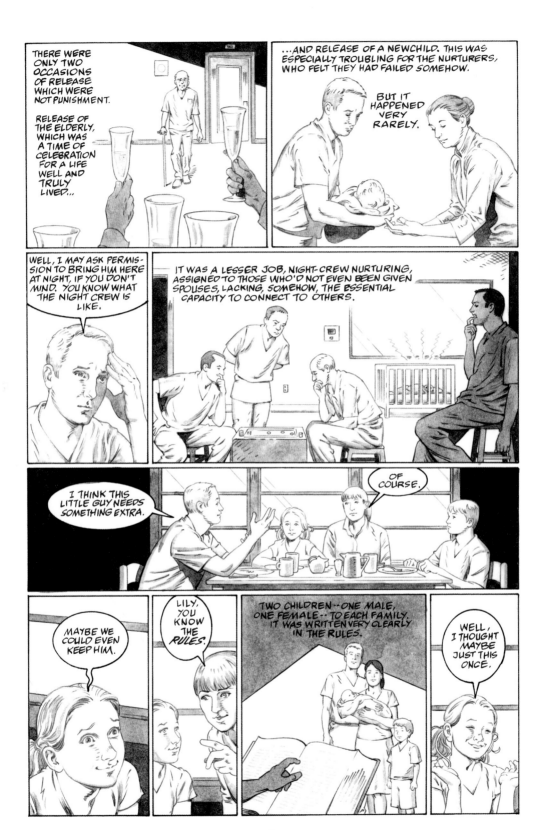

THERE WERE ONLY TWO OCCASIONS OF RELEASE WHICH WERE NOT PUNISHMENT.

RELEASE OF THE ELDERLY, WHICH WAS A TIME OF CELEBRATION FOR A LIFE WELL AND TRULY LIVED...

...AND RELEASE OF A NEWCHILD. THIS WAS ESPECIALLY TROUBLING FOR THE NURTURERS, WHO FELT THEY HAD FAILED SOMEHOW.

BUT IT HAPPENED VERY RARELY.

WELL, I MAY ASK PERMISSION TO BRING HIM HERE AT NIGHT, IF YOU DON'T MIND. YOU KNOW WHAT THE NIGHT CREW IS LIKE.

IT WAS A LESSER JOB, NIGHT-CREW NURTURING, ASSIGNED TO THOSE WHO'D NOT EVEN BEEN GIVEN SPOUSES, LACKING, SOMEHOW, THE ESSENTIAL CAPACITY TO CONNECT TO OTHERS.

I THINK THIS LITTLE GUY NEEDS SOMETHING EXTRA.

OF COURSE.

MAYBE WE COULD EVEN KEEP HIM.

LILY, YOU KNOW THE RULES.

TWO CHILDREN--ONE MALE, ONE FEMALE-- TO EACH FAMILY. IT WAS WRITTEN VERY CLEARLY IN THE RULES.

WELL, I THOUGHT MAYBE JUST THIS ONCE.

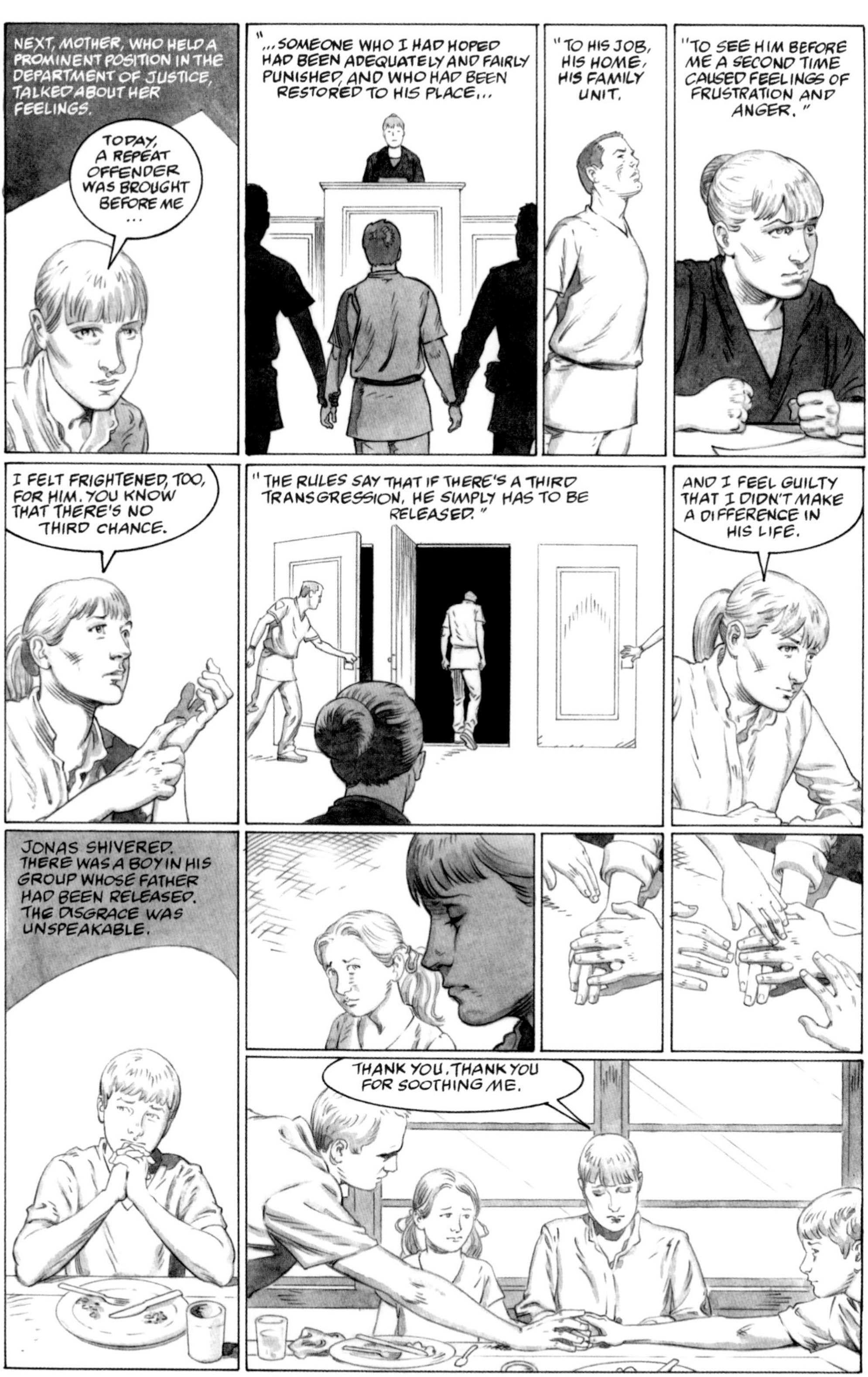
NEXT, MOTHER, WHO HELD A PROMINENT POSITION IN THE DEPARTMENT OF JUSTICE, TALKED ABOUT HER FEELINGS.
TODAY, A REPEAT OFFENDER WAS BROUGHT BEFORE ME ...
"...SOMEONE WHO I HAD HOPED HAD BEEN ADEQUATELY AND FAIRLY PUNISHED, AND WHO HAD BEEN RESTORED TO HIS PLACE...
"TO HIS JOB, HIS HOME, HIS FAMILY UNIT.
"TO SEE HIM BEFORE ME A SECOND TIME CAUSED FEELINGS OF FRUSTRATION AND ANGER."
I FELT FRIGHTENED, TOO, FOR HIM. YOU KNOW THAT THERE'S NO THIRD CHANCE.
"THE RULES SAY THAT IF THERE'S A THIRD TRANSGRESSION, HE SIMPLY HAS TO BE RELEASED."
AND I FEEL GUILTY THAT I DIDN'T MAKE A DIFFERENCE IN HIS LIFE.
JONAS SHIVERED. THERE WAS A BOY IN HIS GROUP WHOSE FATHER HAD BEEN RELEASED. THE DISGRACE WAS UNSPEAKABLE.
THANK YOU. THANK YOU FOR SOOTHING ME.

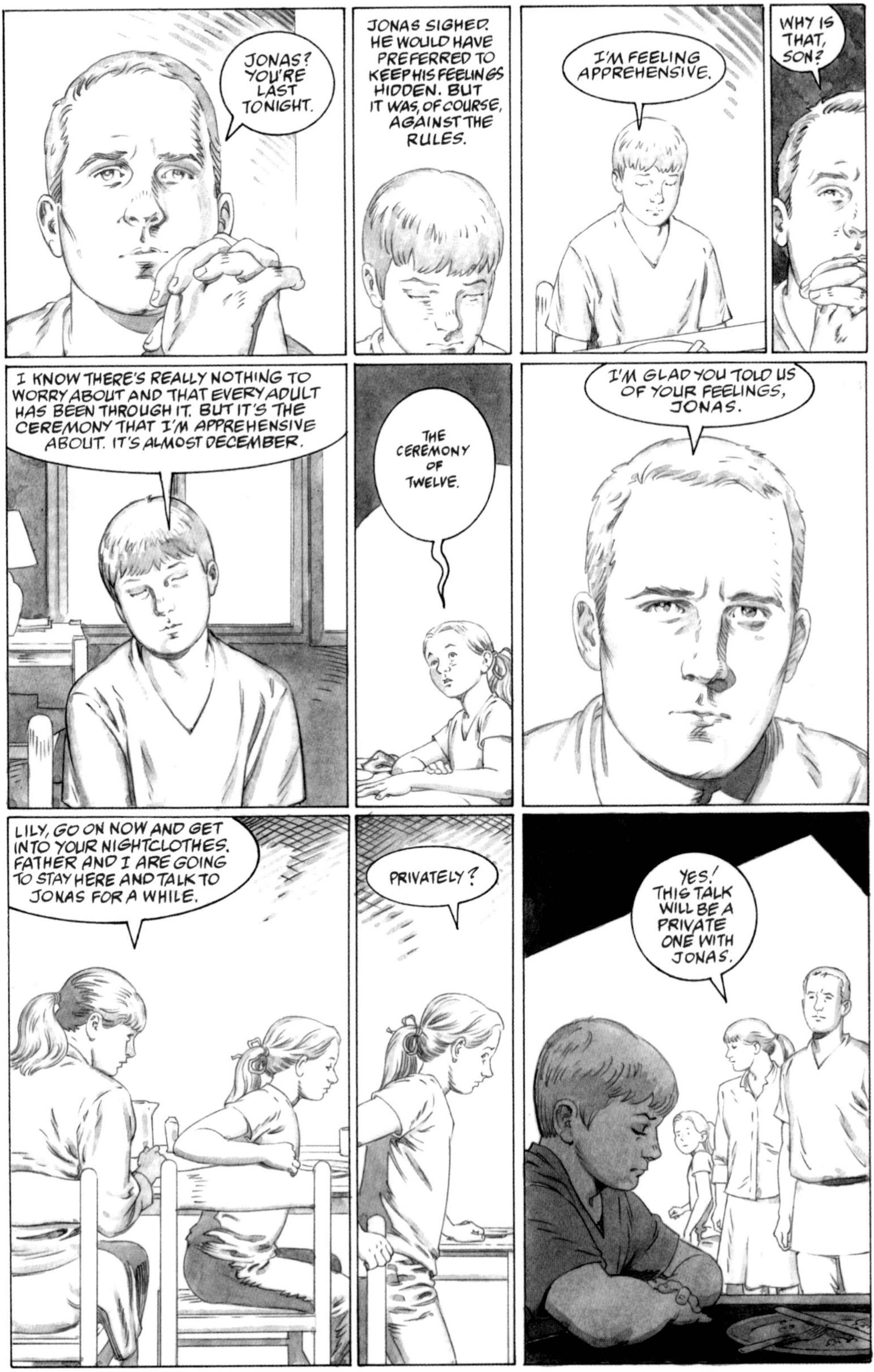
JONAS? YOU'RE LAST TONIGHT.
JONAS SIGHED. HE WOULD HAVE PREFERRED TO KEEP HIS FEELINGS HIDDEN. BUT IT WAS, OF COURSE, AGAINST THE RULES.
I'M FEELING APPREHENSIVE.
WHY IS THAT, SON?
I KNOW THERE'S REALLY NOTHING TO WORRY ABOUT AND THAT EVERY ADULT HAS BEEN THROUGH IT. BUT IT'S THE CEREMONY THAT I'M APPREHENSIVE ABOUT. IT'S ALMOST DECEMBER.
THE CEREMONY OF TWELVE.
I'M GLAD YOU TOLD US OF YOUR FEELINGS, JONAS.
LILY, GO ON NOW AND GET INTO YOUR NIGHTCLOTHES. FATHER AND I ARE GOING TO STAY HERE AND TALK TO JONAS FOR A WHILE.
PRIVATELY?
YES! THIS TALK WILL BE A PRIVATE ONE WITH JONAS.

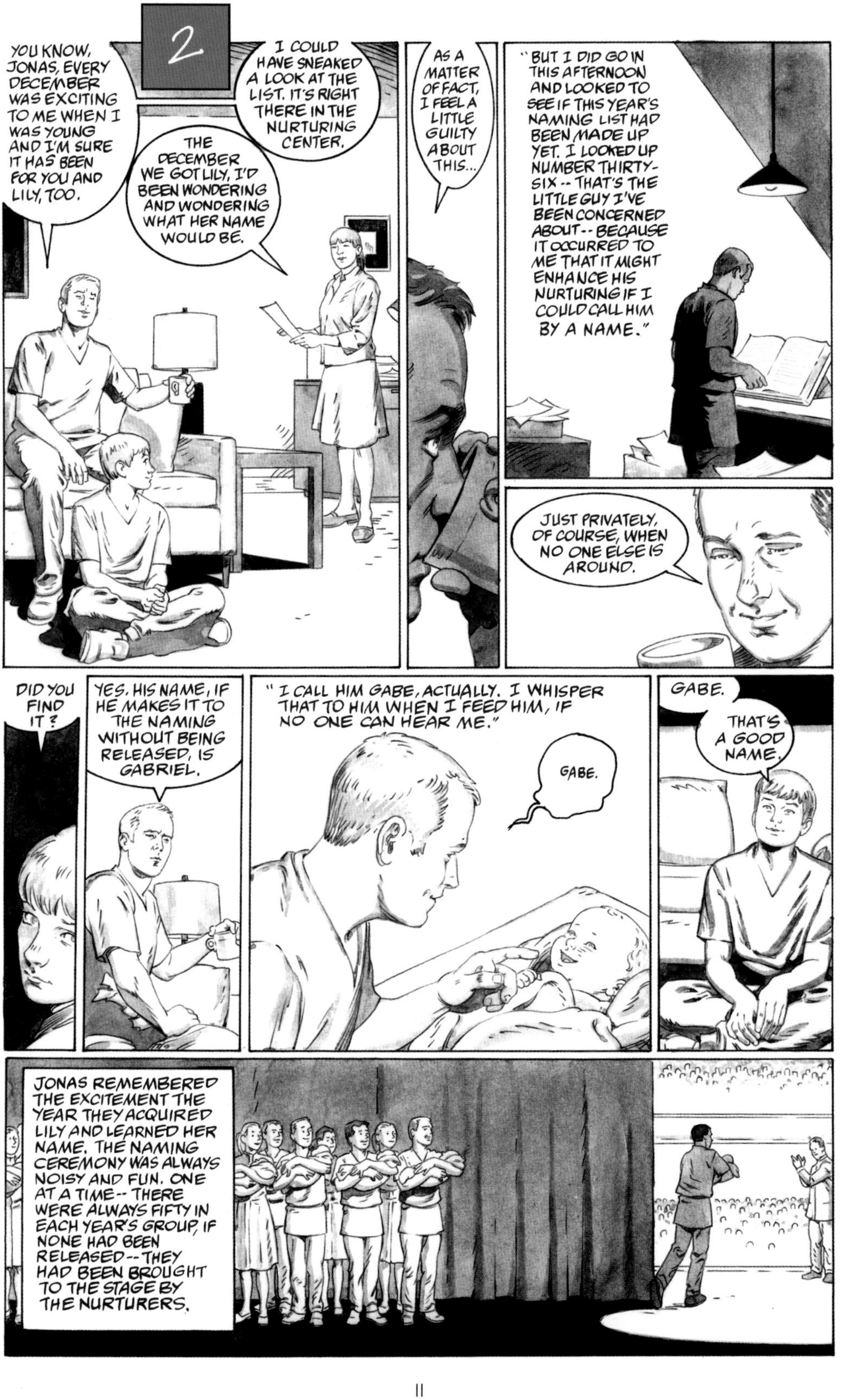
2
YOU KNOW, JONAS, EVERY DECEMBER WAS EXCITING TO ME WHEN I WAS YOUNG AND I'M SURE IT HAS BEEN FOR YOU AND LILY, TOO.
THE DECEMBER WE GOT LILY, I'D BEEN WONDERING AND WONDERING WHAT HER NAME WOULD BE.
I COULD HAVE SNEAKED A LOOK AT THE LIST. IT'S RIGHT THERE IN THE NURTURING CENTER.
AS A MATTER OF FACT, I FEEL A LITTLE GUILTY ABOUT THIS...
"BUT I DID GO IN THIS AFTERNOON AND LOOKED TO SEE IF THIS YEAR'S NAMING LIST HAD BEEN MADE UP YET. I LOOKED UP NUMBER THIRTY-SIX -- THAT'S THE LITTLE GUY I'VE BEEN CONCERNED ABOUT -- BECAUSE IT OCCURRED TO ME THAT IT MIGHT ENHANCE HIS NURTURING IF I COULD CALL HIM BY A NAME."
JUST PRIVATELY, OF COURSE, WHEN NO ONE ELSE IS AROUND.
DID YOU FIND IT?
YES. HIS NAME, IF HE MAKES IT TO THE NAMING WITHOUT BEING RELEASED, IS GABRIEL.
"I CALL HIM GABE, ACTUALLY. I WHISPER THAT TO HIM WHEN I FEED HIM, IF NO ONE CAN HEAR ME."
GABE.
GABE.
THAT'S A GOOD NAME.
JONAS REMEMBERED THE EXCITEMENT THE YEAR THEY ACQUIRED LILY AND LEARNED HER NAME. THE NAMING CEREMONY WAS ALWAYS NOISY AND FUN. ONE AT A TIME -- THERE WERE ALWAYS FIFTY IN EACH YEAR'S GROUP, IF NONE HAD BEEN RELEASED -- THEY HAD BEEN BROUGHT TO THE STAGE BY THE NURTURERS.

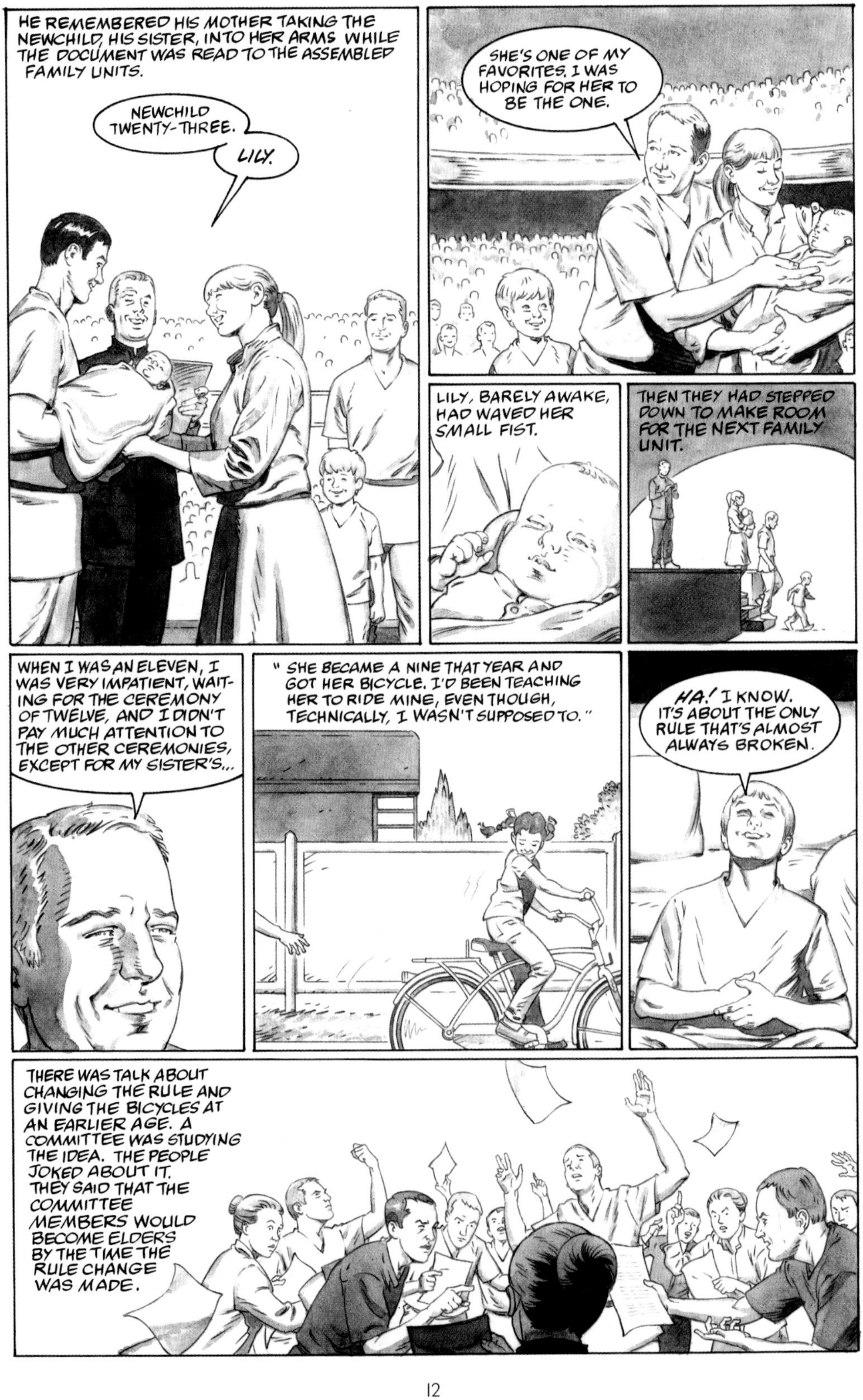
HE REMEMBERED HIS MOTHER TAKING THE NEWCHILD, HIS SISTER, INTO HER ARMS WHILE THE DOCUMENT WAS READ TO THE ASSEMBLED FAMILY UNITS.
NEWCHILD TWENTY-THREE.
LILY.
SHE'S ONE OF MY FAVORITES. I WAS HOPING FOR HER TO BE THE ONE.
LILY, BARELY AWAKE, HAD WAVED HER SMALL FIST.
THEN THEY HAD STEPPED DOWN TO MAKE ROOM FOR THE NEXT FAMILY UNIT.
WHEN I WAS AN ELEVEN, I WAS VERY IMPATIENT, WAITING FOR THE CEREMONY OF TWELVE, AND I DIDN'T PAY MUCH ATTENTION TO THE OTHER CEREMONIES, EXCEPT FOR MY SISTER'S...
" SHE BECAME A NINE THAT YEAR AND GOT HER BICYCLE. I'D BEEN TEACHING HER TO RIDE MINE, EVEN THOUGH, TECHNICALLY, I WASN'T SUPPOSED TO."
HA! I KNOW. IT'S ABOUT THE ONLY RULE THAT'S ALMOST ALWAYS BROKEN.
THERE WAS TALK ABOUT CHANGING THE RULE AND GIVING THE BICYCLES AT AN EARLIER AGE. A COMMITTEE WAS STUDYING THE IDEA. THE PEOPLE JOKED ABOUT IT. THEY SAID THAT THE COMMITTEE MEMBERS WOULD BECOME ELDERS BY THE TIME THE RULE CHANGE WAS MADE.

AND FINALLY IT WAS MY TURN. THE CEREMONY OF TWELVE.

"I REMEMBER HOW PROUD MY PARENTS LOOKED. BUT TO BE HONEST, JONAS, FOR ME THERE WAS NOT THE ELEMENT OF SUSPENSE THAT THERE IS WITH YOUR CEREMONY. BECAUSE I WAS ALREADY FAIRLY CERTAIN OF WHAT MY ASSIGNMENT WAS TO BE."

HOW COULD YOU HAVE KNOWN?

"WELL, IT WAS CLEAR TO ME WHAT MY APTITUDE WAS. I SPENT ALMOST ALL OF MY VOLUNTEER HOURS HELPING IN THE NURTURING CENTER. OF COURSE, THE ELDERS OBSERVED THAT."

SO I WAS PLEASED, BUT NOT AT ALL SURPRISED, WHEN MY ASSIGNMENT WAS ANNOUNCED AS NURTURER.

WERE ANY OF THE ELEVENS DISAPPOINTED YOUR YEAR?

NO, I DON'T THINK SO. THE ELDERS ARE SO CAREFUL IN THEIR SELECTIONS.

I THINK IT'S PROBABLY THE MOST IMPORTANT JOB IN OUR COMMUNITY.

THERE ARE VERY RARELY DISAPPOINT- MENTS, JONAS.

AND IF THERE ARE, YOU KNOW THERE'S AN APPEALS COURT.

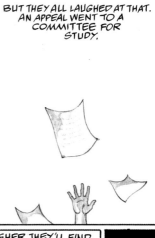

BUT THEY ALL LAUGHED AT THAT. AN APPEAL WENT TO A COMMITTEE FOR STUDY.

I WORRY A LITTLE ABOUT ASHER'S ASSIGNMENT. HE'S SUCH FUN BUT HE MAKES A GAME OF EVERYTHING.

THE ELDERS KNOW ASHER. THEY'LL FIND THE RIGHT ASSIGNMENT FOR HIM. BUT, JONAS, LET ME WARN YOU ABOUT SOMETHING THAT MAY NOT HAVE OCCURRED TO YOU.

WHAT'S THAT?

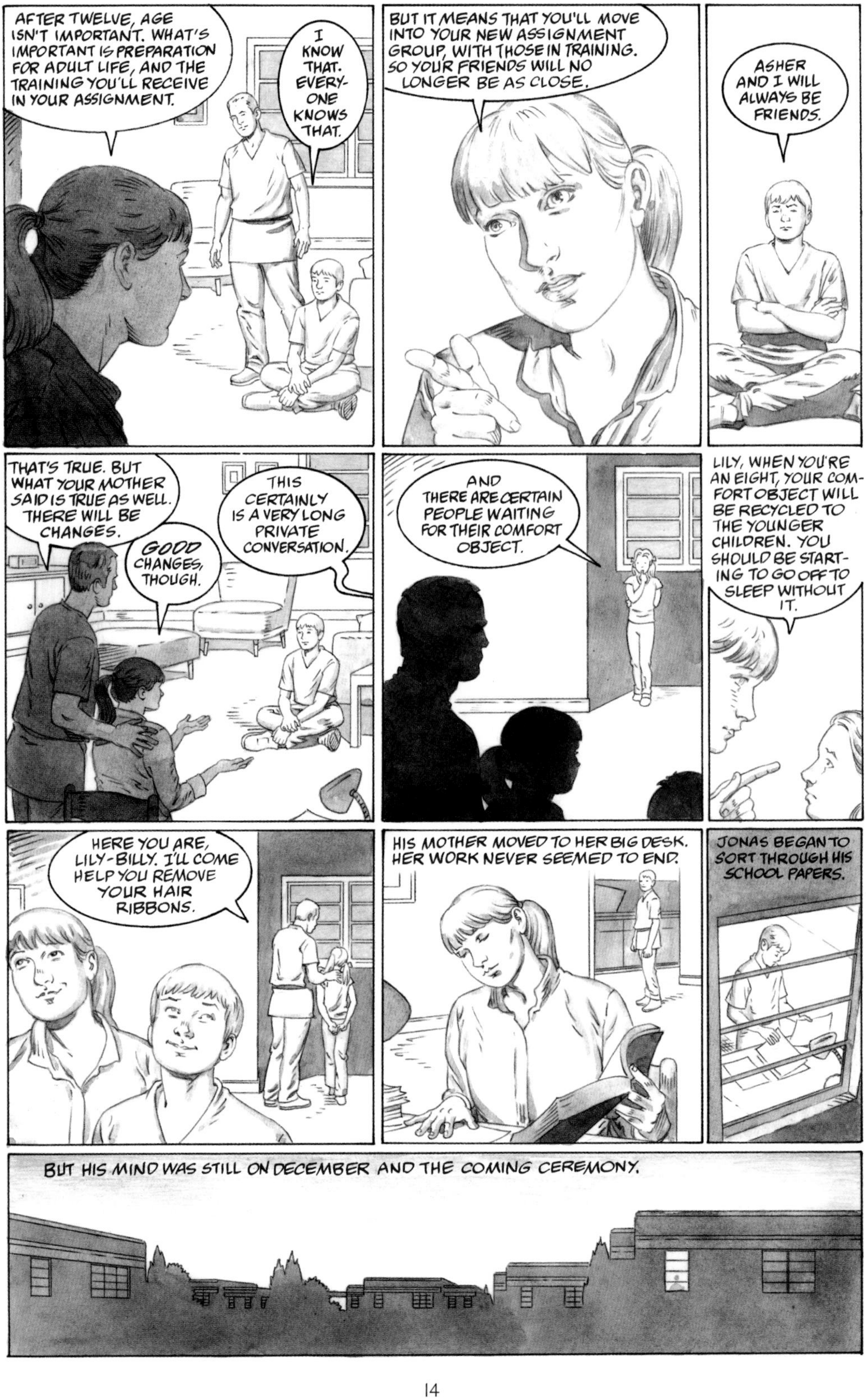
AFTER TWELVE, AGE ISN'T IMPORTANT. WHAT'S IMPORTANT IS PREPARATION FOR ADULT LIFE, AND THE TRAINING YOU'LL RECEIVE IN YOUR ASSIGNMENT.
I KNOW THAT. EVERY-ONE KNOWS THAT.
BUT IT MEANS THAT YOU'LL MOVE INTO YOUR NEW ASSIGNMENT GROUP, WITH THOSE IN TRAINING. SO YOUR FRIENDS WILL NO LONGER BE AS CLOSE.
ASHER AND I WILL ALWAYS BE FRIENDS.
THAT'S TRUE. BUT WHAT YOUR MOTHER SAID IS TRUE AS WELL. THERE WILL BE CHANGES.
GOOD CHANGES, THOUGH.
THIS CERTAINLY IS A VERY LONG PRIVATE CONVERSATION.
AND THERE ARE CERTAIN PEOPLE WAITING FOR THEIR COMFORT OBJECT.
LILY, WHEN YOU'RE AN EIGHT, YOUR COM-FORT OBJECT WILL BE RECYCLED TO THE YOUNGER CHILDREN. YOU SHOULD BE START-ING TO GO OFF TO SLEEP WITHOUT IT.
HERE YOU ARE, LILY-BILLY. I'LL COME HELP YOU REMOVE YOUR HAIR RIBBONS.
HIS MOTHER MOVED TO HER BIG DESK. HER WORK NEVER SEEMED TO END.
JONAS BEGAN TO SORT THROUGH HIS SCHOOL PAPERS.
BUT HIS MIND WAS STILL ON DECEMBER AND THE COMING CEREMONY.

OH, LOOK!

LOOK HOW TINY HE IS!

ISN'T HE CUTE?

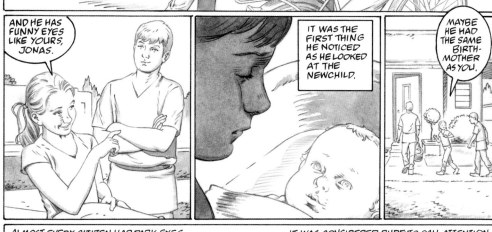

AND HE HAS FUNNY EYES LIKE YOURS, JONAS.

IT WAS THE FIRST THING HE NOTICED AS HE LOOKED AT THE NEWCHILD.

MAYBE HE HAD THE SAME BIRTH-MOTHER AS YOU.

ALMOST EVERY CITIZEN HAD DARK EYES, BUT NO ONE MENTIONED THE EXCEPTIONS.

IT WAS CONSIDERED RUDE TO CALL ATTENTION TO THINGS THAT WERE DIFFERENT ABOUT INDIVIDUALS.

NOW, SEEING THE NEWCHILD, HE WAS REMINDED THAT THE LIGHT EYES GAVE THE ONE WHO HAD THEM A CERTAIN LOOK...

...DEPTH...

...LIKE LOOKING INTO THE CLEAR WATER OF A RIVER.

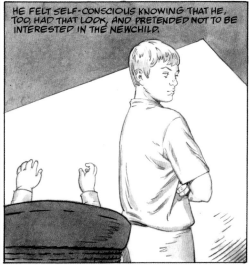

HE FELT SELF-CONSCIOUS KNOWING THAT HE, TOO, HAD THAT LOOK, AND PRETENDED NOT TO BE INTERESTED IN THE NEWCHILD.

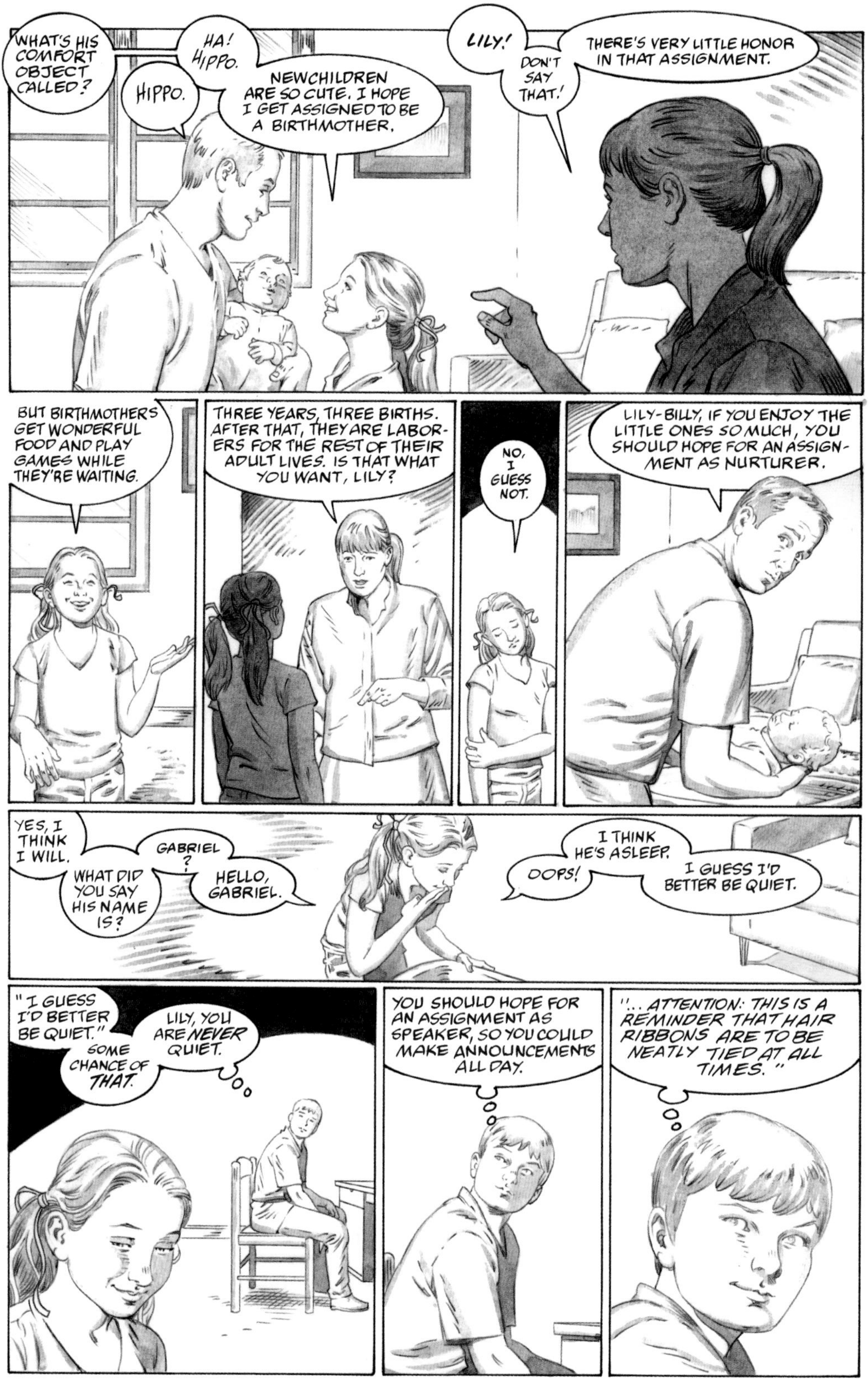
WHAT'S HIS COMFORT OBJECT CALLED?
HIPPO.
HA! HIPPO.
NEWCHILDREN ARE SO CUTE. I HOPE I GET ASSIGNED TO BE A BIRTHMOTHER.
LILY!
DON'T SAY THAT!
THERE'S VERY LITTLE HONOR IN THAT ASSIGNMENT.
BUT BIRTHMOTHERS GET WONDERFUL FOOD AND PLAY GAMES WHILE THEY'RE WAITING.
THREE YEARS, THREE BIRTHS. AFTER THAT, THEY ARE LABORERS FOR THE REST OF THEIR ADULT LIVES. IS THAT WHAT YOU WANT, LILY?
NO, I GUESS NOT.
LILY-BILLY, IF YOU ENJOY THE LITTLE ONES SO MUCH, YOU SHOULD HOPE FOR AN ASSIGNMENT AS NURTURER.
YES, I THINK I WILL.
WHAT DID YOU SAY HIS NAME IS?
GABRIEL?
HELLO, GABRIEL.
I THINK HE'S ASLEEP.
OOPS!
I GUESS I'D BETTER BE QUIET.
"I GUESS I'D BETTER BE QUIET."
SOME CHANCE OF THAT.
LILY, YOU ARE NEVER QUIET.
YOU SHOULD HOPE FOR AN ASSIGNMENT AS SPEAKER, SO YOU COULD MAKE ANNOUNCEMENTS ALL DAY.
"... ATTENTION: THIS IS A REMINDER THAT HAIR RIBBONS ARE TO BE NEATLY TIED AT ALL TIMES."

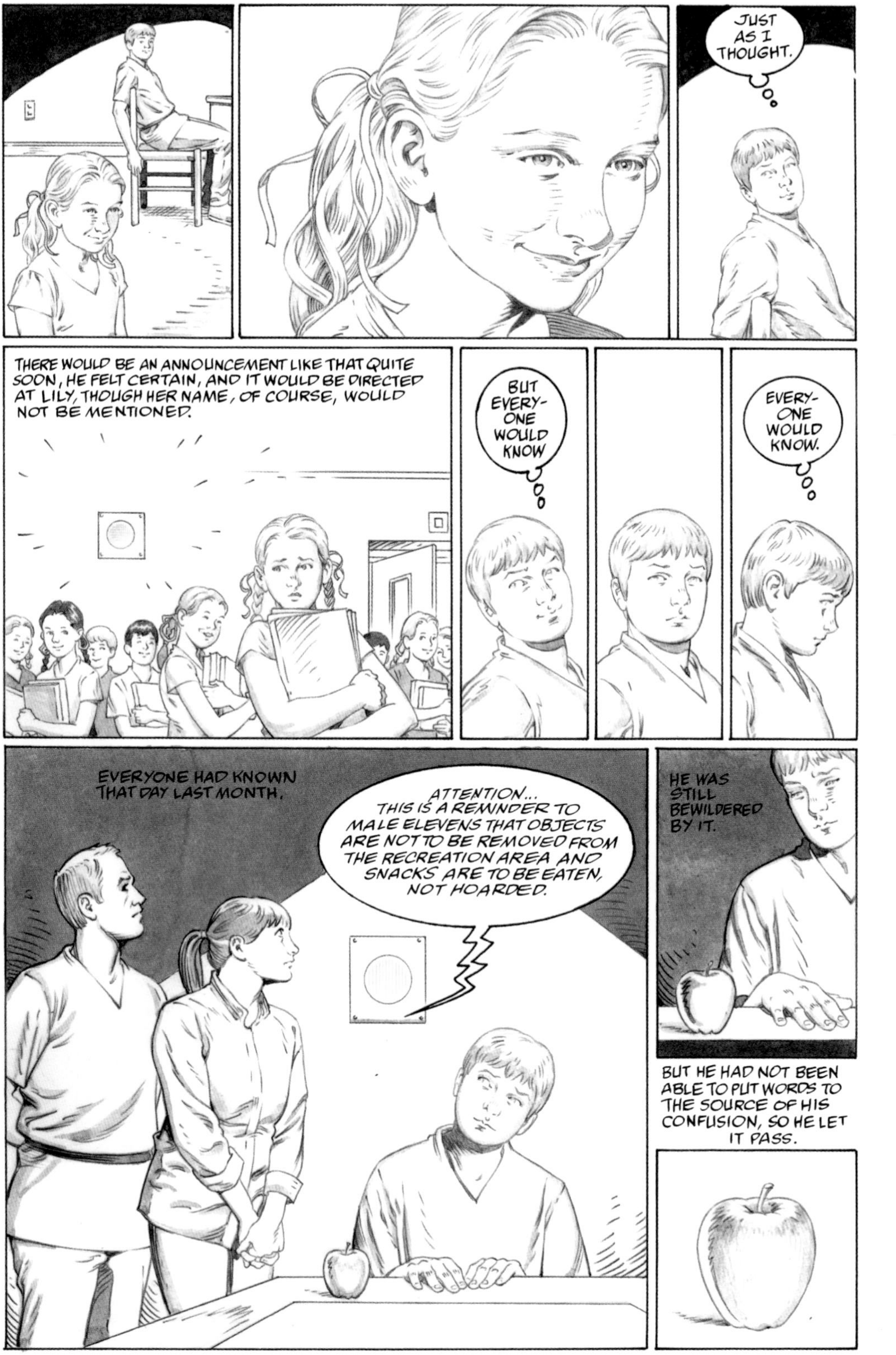
JUST AS I THOUGHT.
THERE WOULD BE AN ANNOUNCEMENT LIKE THAT QUITE SOON, HE FELT CERTAIN, AND IT WOULD BE DIRECTED AT LILY, THOUGH HER NAME, OF COURSE, WOULD NOT BE MENTIONED.
BUT EVERY-ONE WOULD KNOW
EVERY-ONE WOULD KNOW.
EVERYONE HAD KNOWN THAT DAY LAST MONTH.
ATTENTION... THIS IS A REMINDER TO MALE ELEVENS THAT OBJECTS ARE NOT TO BE REMOVED FROM THE RECREATION AREA AND SNACKS ARE TO BE EATEN, NOT HOARDED.
HE WAS STILL BEWILDERED BY IT.
BUT HE HAD NOT BEEN ABLE TO PUT WORDS TO THE SOURCE OF HIS CONFUSION, SO HE LET IT PASS.

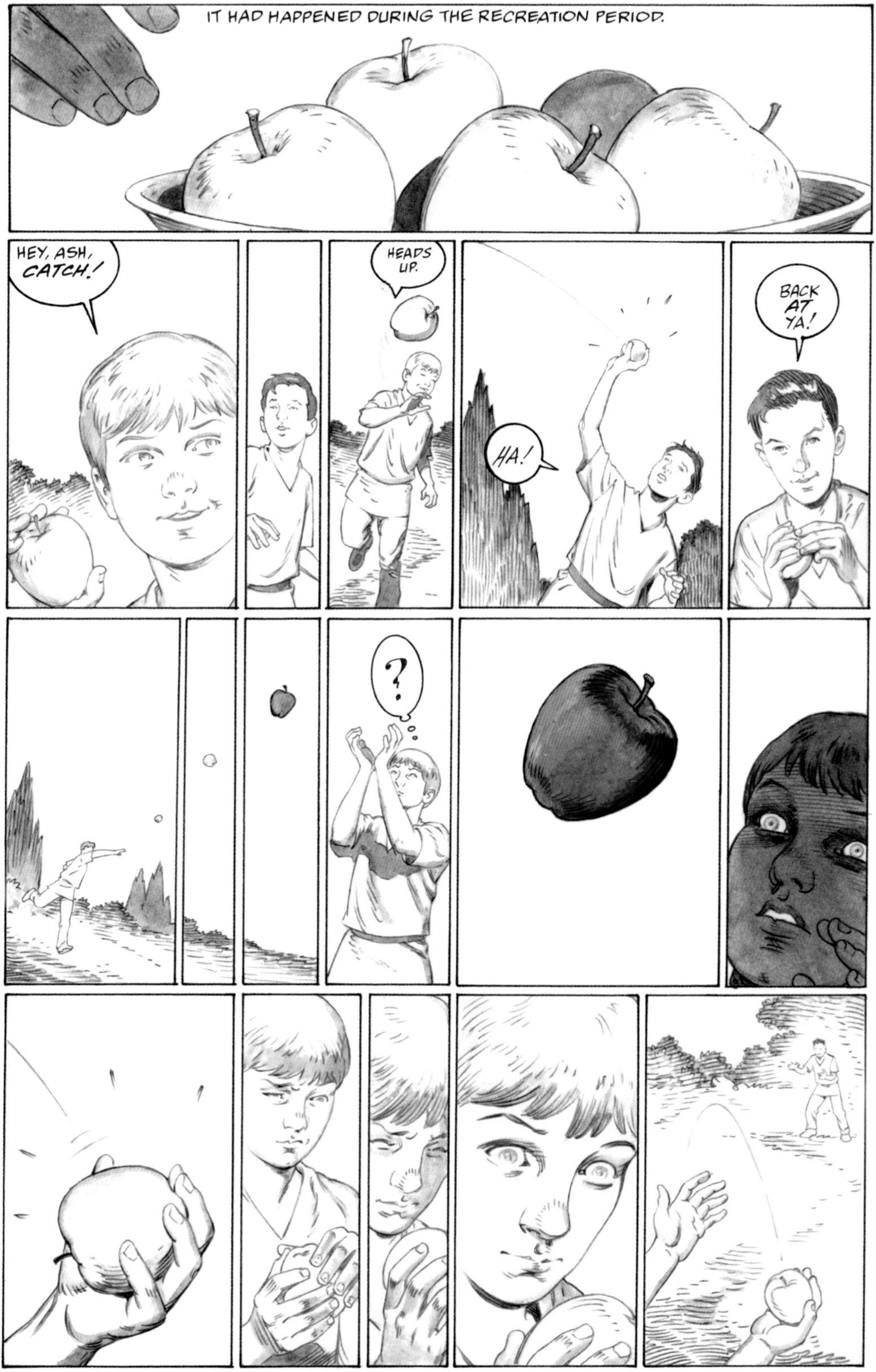
IT HAD HAPPENED DURING THE RECREATION PERIOD.
HEY, ASH, CATCH!
HEADS UP.
HA!
BACK AT YA!
?

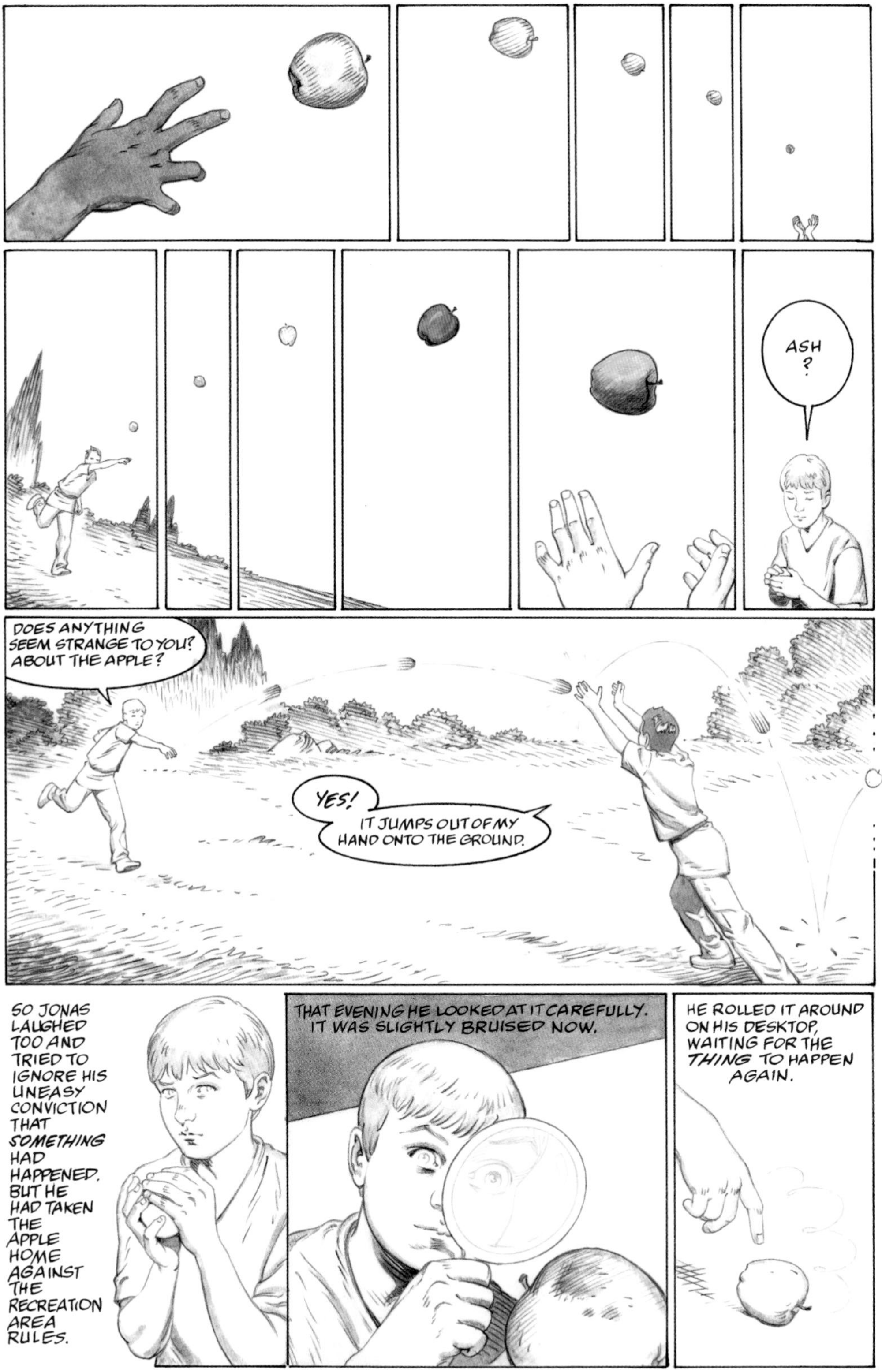
ASH ?
DOES ANYTHING SEEM STRANGE TO YOU? ABOUT THE APPLE?
YES!
IT JUMPS OUT OF MY HAND ONTO THE GROUND.
SO JONAS LAUGHED TOO AND TRIED TO IGNORE HIS UNEASY CONVICTION THAT SOMETHING HAD HAPPENED. BUT HE HAD TAKEN THE APPLE HOME AGAINST THE RECREATION AREA RULES.
THAT EVENING HE LOOKED AT IT CAREFULLY. IT WAS SLIGHTLY BRUISED NOW.
HE ROLLED IT AROUND ON HIS DESKTOP, WAITING FOR THE THING TO HAPPEN AGAIN.

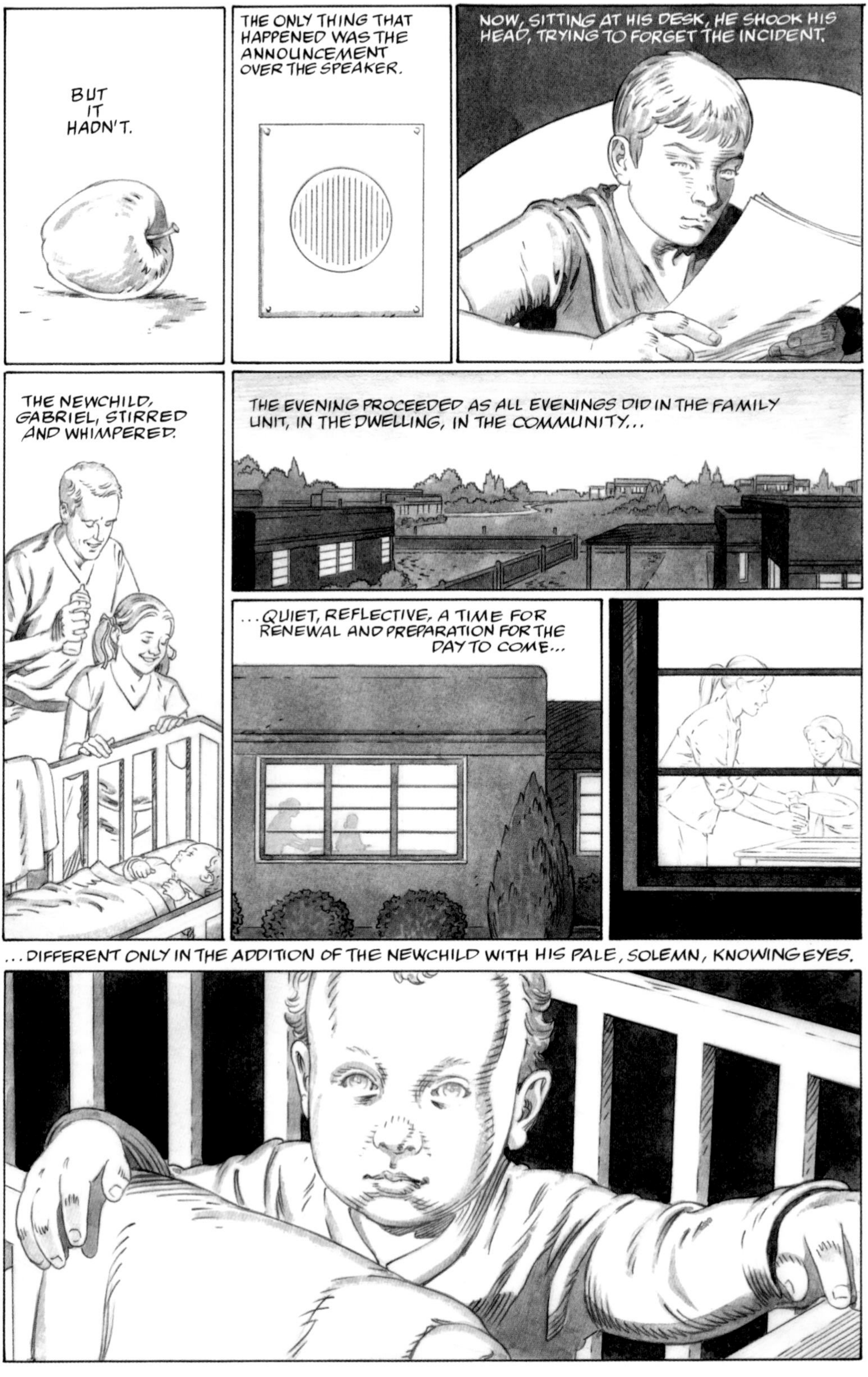
BUT IT HADN'T.
THE ONLY THING THAT HAPPENED WAS THE ANNOUNCEMENT OVER THE SPEAKER.
NOW, SITTING AT HIS DESK, HE SHOOK HIS HEAD, TRYING TO FORGET THE INCIDENT.
THE NEWCHILD, GABRIEL, STIRRED AND WHIMPERED.
THE EVENING PROCEEDED AS ALL EVENINGS DID IN THE FAMILY UNIT, IN THE DWELLING, IN THE COMMUNITY...
...QUIET, REFLECTIVE, A TIME FOR RENEWAL AND PREPARATION FOR THE DAY TO COME...
...DIFFERENT ONLY IN THE ADDITION OF THE NEWCHILD WITH HIS PALE, SOLEMN, KNOWING EYES.

JONAS RODE AT A
LEISURELY PACE, GLANCING
AT THE BIKE PORTS
BESIDE THE BUILDINGS
TO SEE IF HE COULD SPOT
ASHER'S. HE DIDN'T OFTEN
DO HIS VOLUNTEER HOURS
WITH HIS FRIEND BECAUSE
ASHER FREQUENTLY
FOOLED AROUND AND
MADE SERIOUS WORK A
LITTLE DIFFICULT, BUT
NOW, WITH TWELVE
COMING SO SOON AND
THE VOLUNTEER HOURS
ENDING, IT DIDN'T SEEM
TO MATTER.

THE FREEDOM TO CHOOSE WHERE TO SPEND THOSE HOURS HAD ALWAYS SEEMED A WONDERFUL LUXURY
TO JONAS; OTHER HOURS OF THE DAY WERE SO CAREFULLY REGULATED.

A MALE ELEVEN
NAMED BENJAMIN HAD
DONE HIS ENTIRE
FOUR YEARS IN THE
REHABILITATION
CENTER, WORKING
WITH CITIZENS
WHO HAD BEEN
INJURED.

JONAS WAS
IMPRESSED,
BUT NEVER
MENTIONED
IT, AS SUCH A
CONVERSATION
WOULD BE
AWKWARD.
THERE WAS
NEVER A
COMFORTABLE
WAY TO
DISCUSS ONE'S
SUCCESS
WITHOUT
BREAKING
THE RULE
AGAINST
BRAGGING.
IT WAS A
MINOR RULE,
PUNISHABLE
ONLY BY
GENTLE
CHASTISEMENT...

HE RODE PAST
THE COMMUNITY
STRUCTURES,
HOPING TO SPOT
ASHER'S BICYCLE.

...BUT
STILL.

HE PASSED THE
CHILDCARE CENTER...

... AND RODE THROUGH THE CENTRAL PLAZA, STILL SEARCHING.

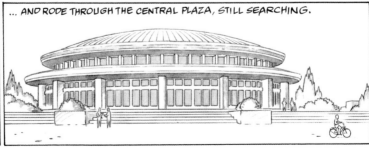

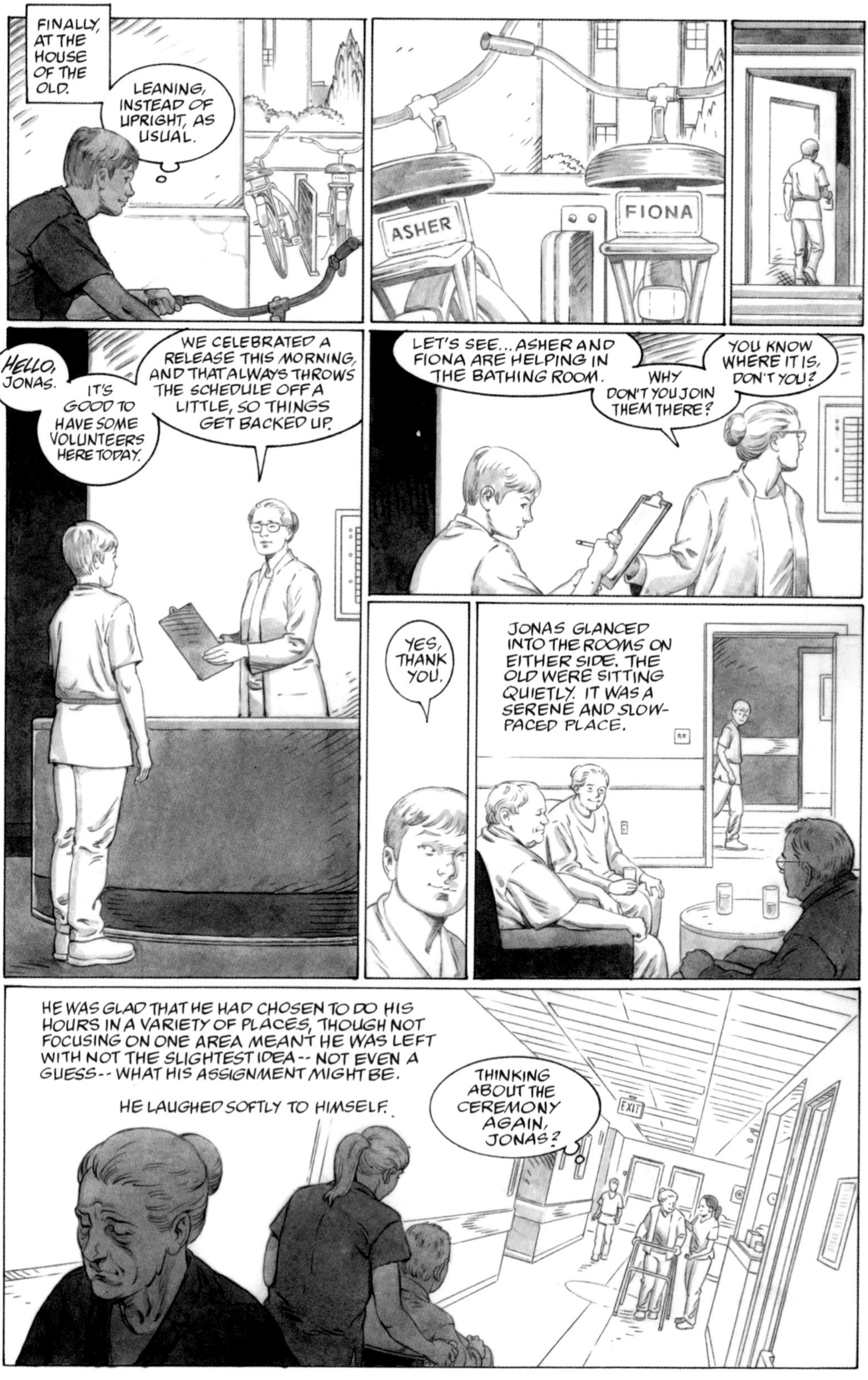
FINALLY, AT THE HOUSE OF THE OLD.
LEANING, INSTEAD OF UPRIGHT, AS USUAL.
ASHER
FIONA
HELLO, JONAS.
IT'S GOOD TO HAVE SOME VOLUNTEERS HERE TODAY.
WE CELEBRATED A RELEASE THIS MORNING, AND THAT ALWAYS THROWS THE SCHEDULE OFF A LITTLE, SO THINGS GET BACKED UP.
LET'S SEE... ASHER AND FIONA ARE HELPING IN THE BATHING ROOM.
WHY DON'T YOU JOIN THEM THERE?
YOU KNOW WHERE IT IS, DON'T YOU?
YES, THANK YOU.
JONAS GLANCED INTO THE ROOMS ON EITHER SIDE. THE OLD WERE SITTING QUIETLY. IT WAS A SERENE AND SLOW-PACED PLACE.
HE WAS GLAD THAT HE HAD CHOSEN TO DO HIS HOURS IN A VARIETY OF PLACES, THOUGH NOT FOCUSING ON ONE AREA MEANT HE WAS LEFT WITH NOT THE SLIGHTEST IDEA -- NOT EVEN A GUESS -- WHAT HIS ASSIGNMENT MIGHT BE.
HE LAUGHED SOFTLY TO HIMSELF.
THINKING ABOUT THE CEREMONY AGAIN, JONAS?
EXIT

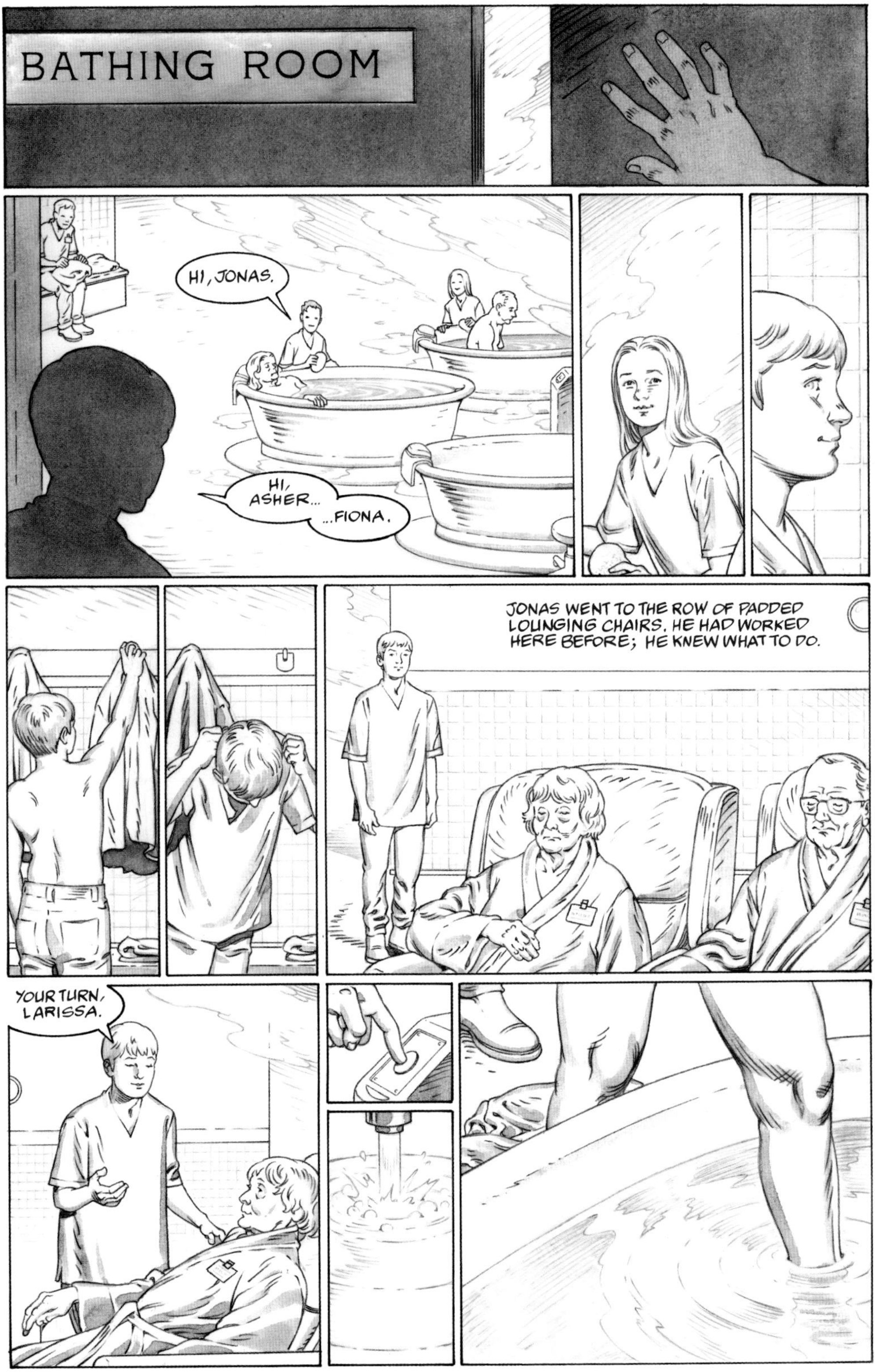
BATHING ROOM
HI, JONAS.
HI, ASHER... ...FIONA.
JONAS WENT TO THE ROW OF PADDED LOUNGING CHAIRS. HE HAD WORKED HERE BEFORE; HE KNEW WHAT TO DO.
YOUR TURN, LARISSA.

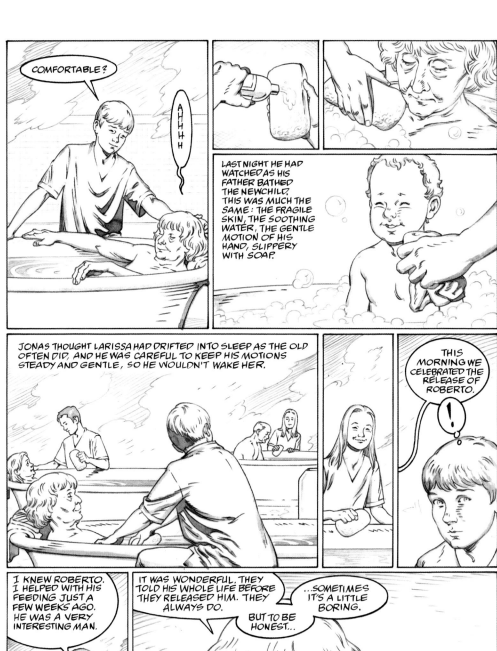

COMFORTABLE?

AHHH

LAST NIGHT HE HAD WATCHED AS HIS FATHER BATHED THE NEWCHILD. THIS WAS MUCH THE SAME: THE FRAGILE SKIN, THE SOOTHING WATER, THE GENTLE MOTION OF HIS HAND, SLIPPERY WITH SOAP.

JONAS THOUGHT LARISSA HAD DRIFTED INTO SLEEP AS THE OLD OFTEN DID, AND HE WAS CAREFUL TO KEEP HIS MOTIONS STEADY AND GENTLE, SO HE WOULDN'T WAKE HER.

THIS MORNING WE CELEBRATED THE RELEASE OF ROBERTO.

!

I KNEW ROBERTO. I HELPED WITH HIS FEEDING JUST A FEW WEEKS AGO. HE WAS A VERY INTERESTING MAN.

IT WAS WONDERFUL, THEY TOLD HIS WHOLE LIFE BEFORE THEY RELEASED HIM. THEY ALWAYS DO.

BUT TO BE HONEST...

...SOMETIMES IT'S A LITTLE BORING.

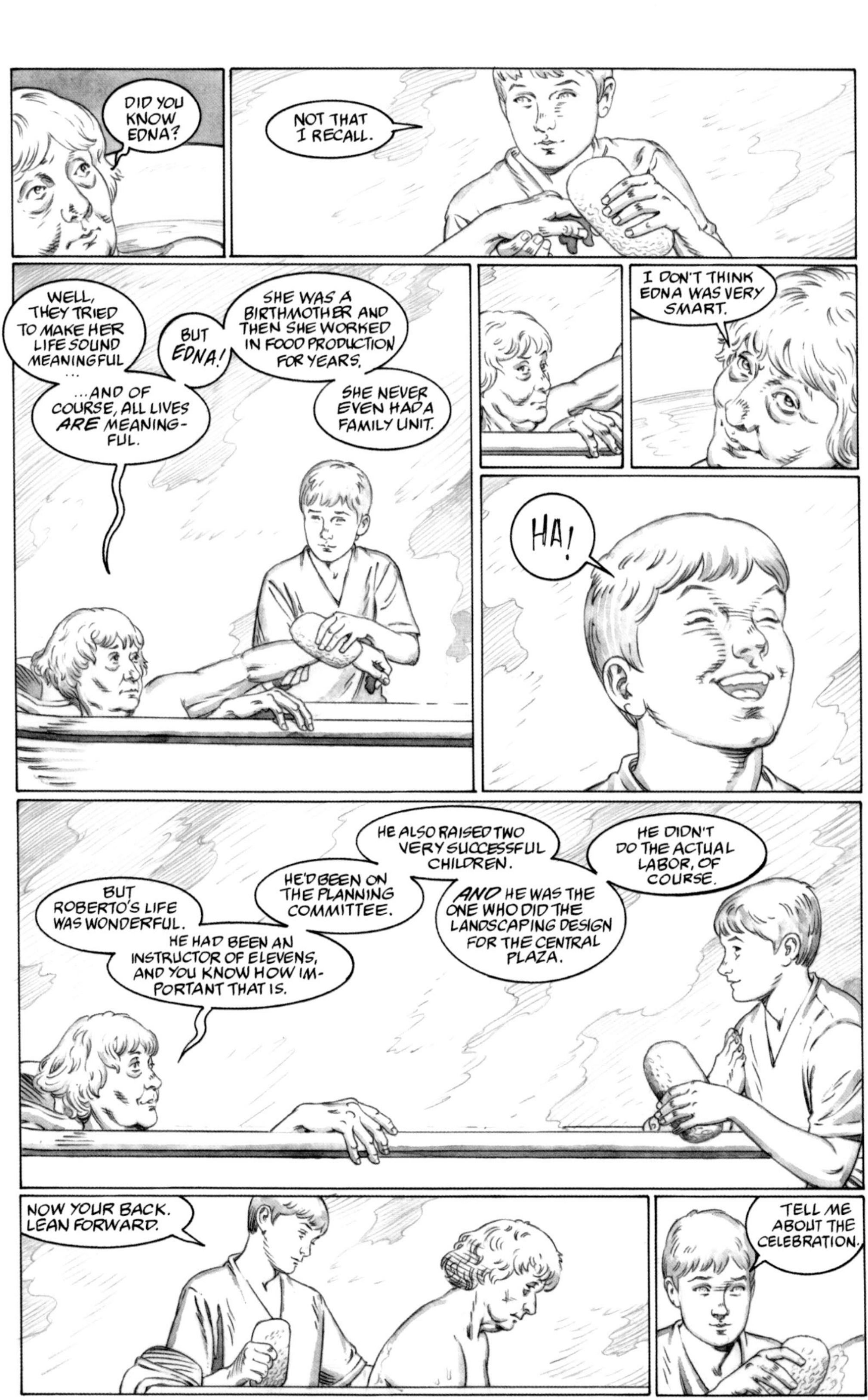
DID YOU KNOW EDNA?
NOT THAT I RECALL.
WELL, THEY TRIED TO MAKE HER LIFE SOUND MEANINGFUL . . .
. . .AND OF COURSE, ALL LIVES *ARE* MEANING-FUL.
BUT *EDNA!*
SHE WAS A BIRTHMOTHER AND THEN SHE WORKED IN FOOD PRODUCTION FOR YEARS.
SHE NEVER EVEN HAD A FAMILY UNIT.
I DON'T THINK EDNA WAS VERY SMART.
HA!
BUT ROBERTO'S LIFE WAS WONDERFUL.
HE HAD BEEN AN INSTRUCTOR OF ELEVENS, AND YOU KNOW HOW IM-PORTANT THAT IS.
HE'D BEEN ON THE PLANNING COMMITTEE.
HE ALSO RAISED TWO VERY SUCCESSFUL CHILDREN.
AND HE WAS THE ONE WHO DID THE LANDSCAPING DESIGN FOR THE CENTRAL PLAZA.
HE DIDN'T DO THE ACTUAL LABOR, OF COURSE.
NOW YOUR BACK. LEAN FORWARD.
TELL ME ABOUT THE CELEBRATION.

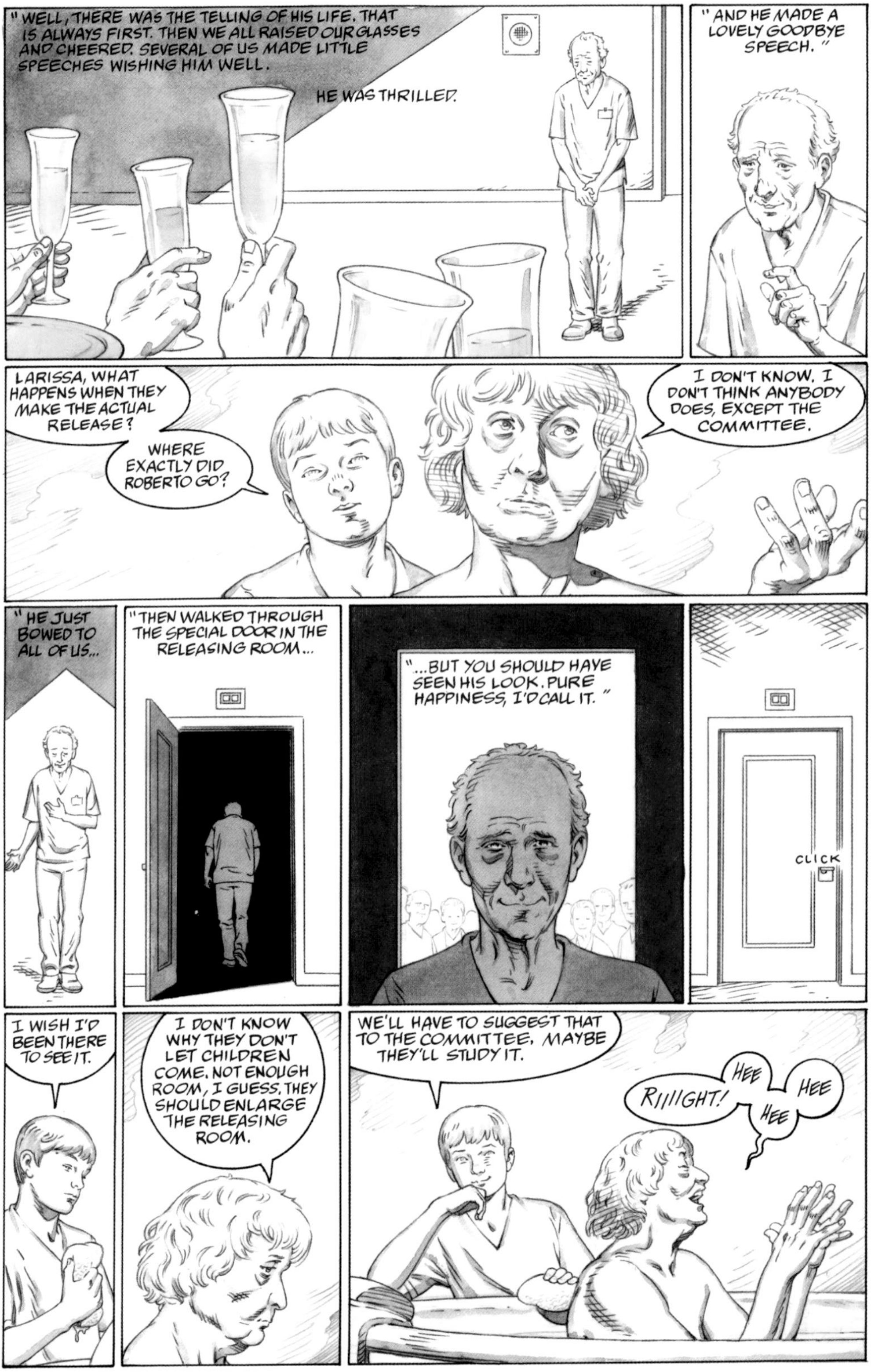
"WELL, THERE WAS THE TELLING OF HIS LIFE. THAT IS ALWAYS FIRST. THEN WE ALL RAISED OUR GLASSES AND CHEERED. SEVERAL OF US MADE LITTLE SPEECHES WISHING HIM WELL.
HE WAS THRILLED.
"AND HE MADE A LOVELY GOODBYE SPEECH."
LARISSA, WHAT HAPPENS WHEN THEY MAKE THE ACTUAL RELEASE?
WHERE EXACTLY DID ROBERTO GO?
I DON'T KNOW. I DON'T THINK ANYBODY DOES, EXCEPT THE COMMITTEE.
"HE JUST BOWED TO ALL OF US...
"THEN WALKED THROUGH THE SPECIAL DOOR IN THE RELEASING ROOM...
"...BUT YOU SHOULD HAVE SEEN HIS LOOK. PURE HAPPINESS, I'D CALL IT."
CLICK
I WISH I'D BEEN THERE TO SEE IT.
I DON'T KNOW WHY THEY DON'T LET CHILDREN COME. NOT ENOUGH ROOM, I GUESS. THEY SHOULD ENLARGE THE RELEASING ROOM.
WE'LL HAVE TO SUGGEST THAT TO THE COMMITTEE. MAYBE THEY'LL STUDY IT.
RIIIGHT!
HEE
HEE
HEE

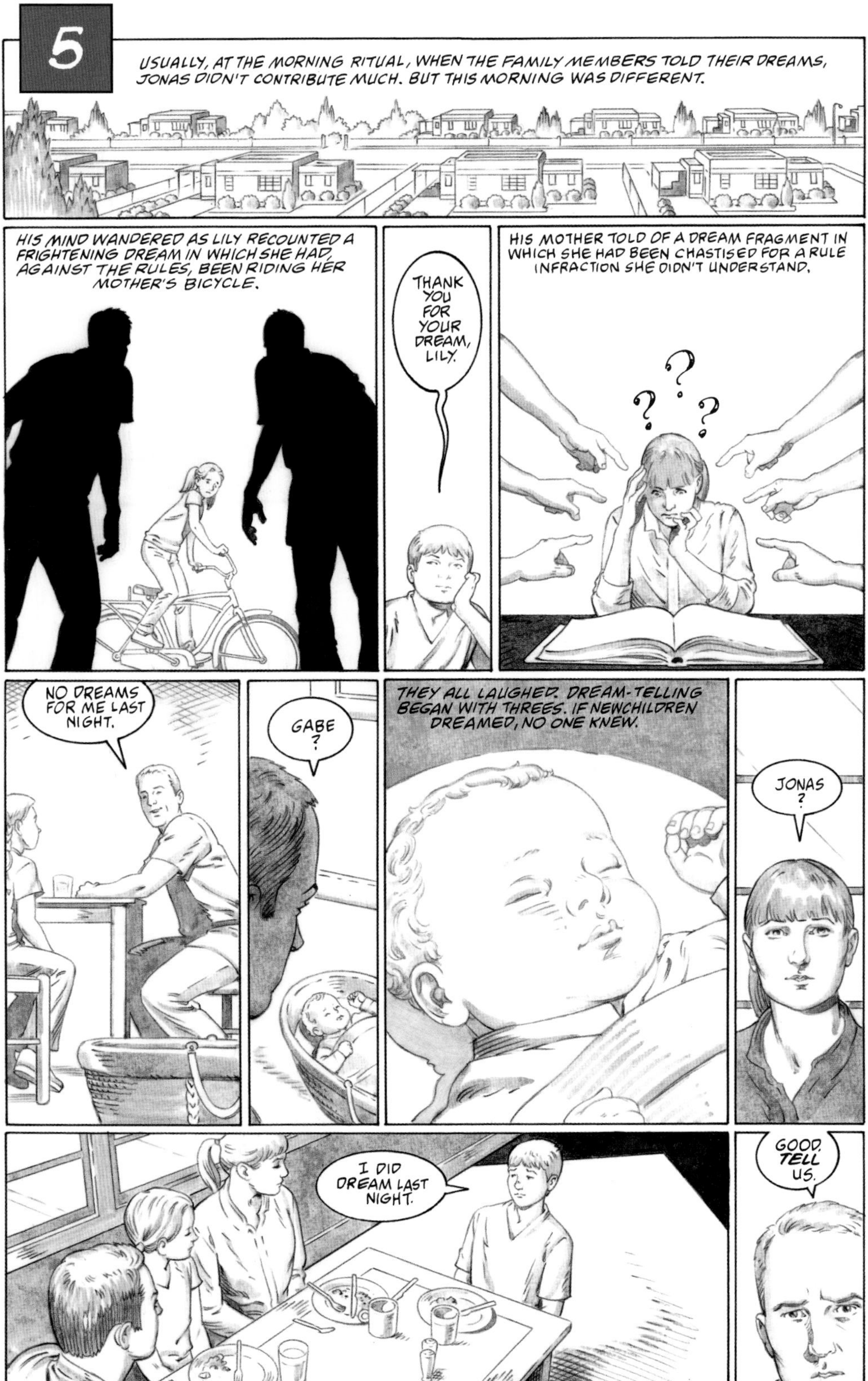
5
USUALLY, AT THE MORNING RITUAL, WHEN THE FAMILY MEMBERS TOLD THEIR DREAMS, JONAS DIDN'T CONTRIBUTE MUCH. BUT THIS MORNING WAS DIFFERENT.
HIS MIND WANDERED AS LILY RECOUNTED A FRIGHTENING DREAM IN WHICH SHE HAD, AGAINST THE RULES, BEEN RIDING HER MOTHER'S BICYCLE.
THANK YOU FOR YOUR DREAM, LILY.
HIS MOTHER TOLD OF A DREAM FRAGMENT IN WHICH SHE HAD BEEN CHASTISED FOR A RULE INFRACTION SHE DIDN'T UNDERSTAND.
NO DREAMS FOR ME LAST NIGHT.
GABE ?
THEY ALL LAUGHED. DREAM-TELLING BEGAN WITH THREES. IF NEWCHILDREN DREAMED, NO ONE KNEW.
JONAS ?
I DID DREAM LAST NIGHT.
GOOD. TELL US.

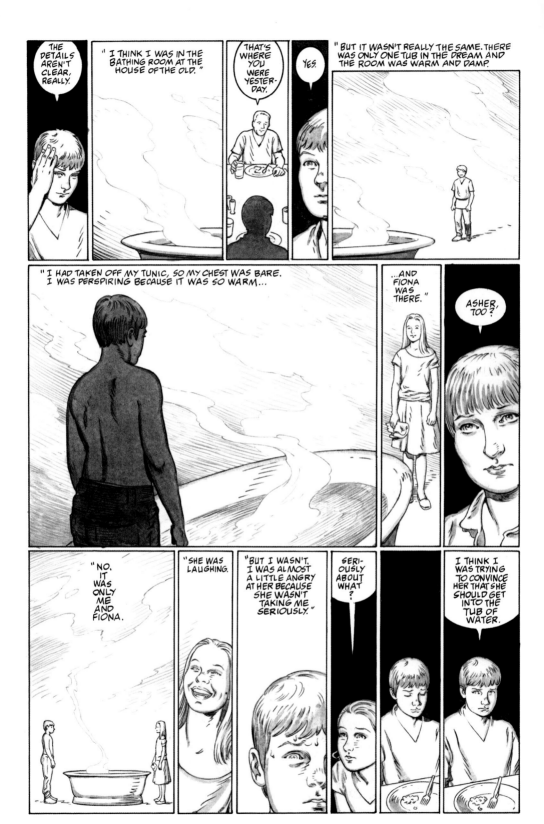

THE DETAILS AREN'T CLEAR, REALLY.

"I THINK I WAS IN THE BATHING ROOM AT THE HOUSE OF THE OLD."

THAT'S WHERE YOU WERE YESTERDAY.

YES.

"BUT IT WASN'T REALLY THE SAME. THERE WAS ONLY ONE TUB IN THE DREAM AND THE ROOM WAS WARM AND DAMP.

"I HAD TAKEN OFF MY TUNIC, SO MY CHEST WAS BARE. I WAS PERSPIRING BECAUSE IT WAS SO WARM...

...AND FIONA WAS THERE."

ASHER, TOO?

"NO. IT WAS ONLY ME AND FIONA.

"SHE WAS LAUGHING.

"BUT I WASN'T. I WAS ALMOST A LITTLE ANGRY AT HER BECAUSE SHE WASN'T TAKING ME SERIOUSLY."

SERI- OUSLY ABOUT WHAT?

I THINK I WAS TRYING TO CONVINCE HER THAT SHE SHOULD GET INTO THE TUB OF WATER.

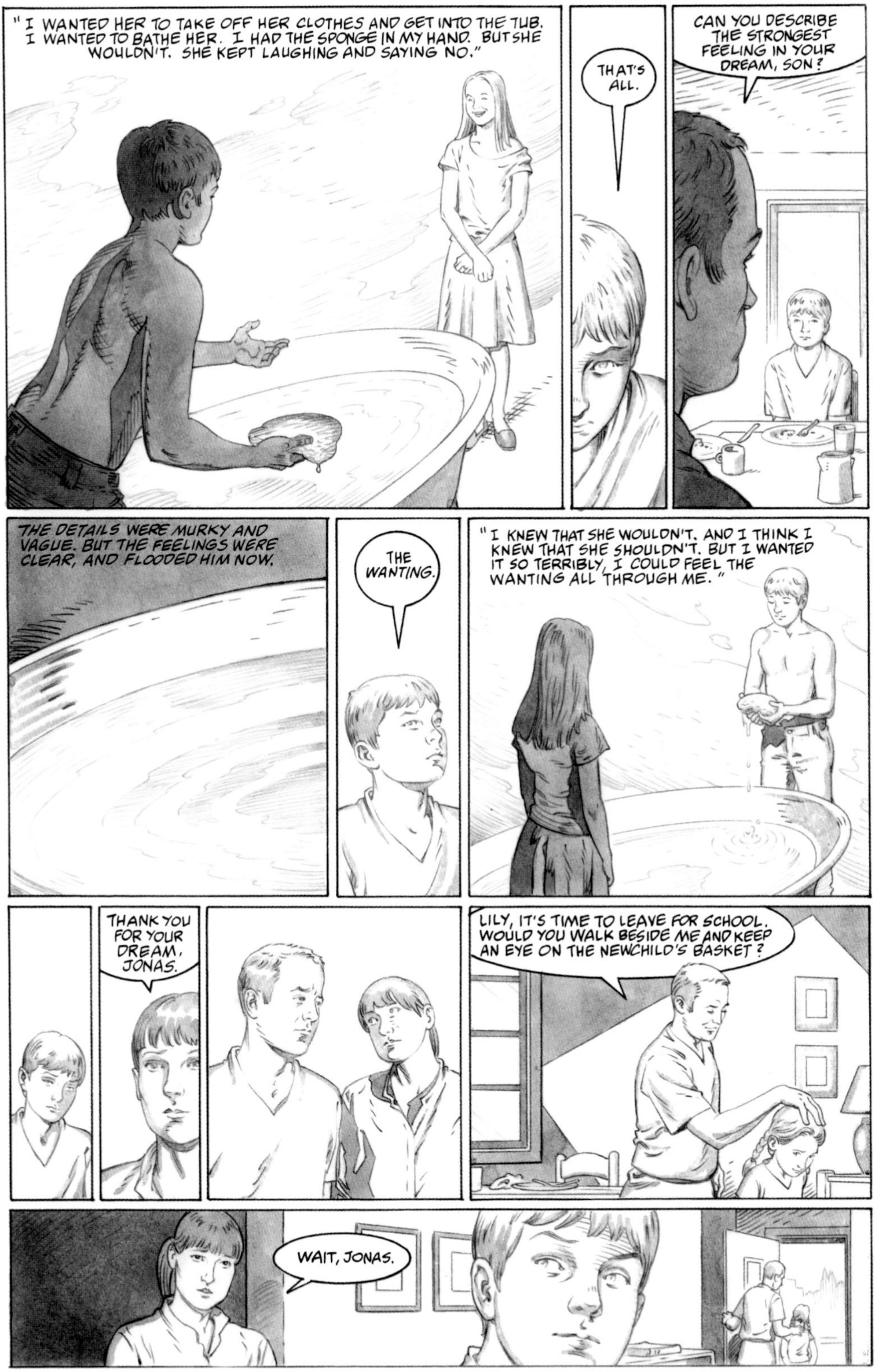
"I WANTED HER TO TAKE OFF HER CLOTHES AND GET INTO THE TUB. I WANTED TO BATHE HER. I HAD THE SPONGE IN MY HAND. BUT SHE WOULDN'T. SHE KEPT LAUGHING AND SAYING NO."
THAT'S ALL.
CAN YOU DESCRIBE THE STRONGEST FEELING IN YOUR DREAM, SON?
THE DETAILS WERE MURKY AND VAGUE. BUT THE FEELINGS WERE CLEAR, AND FLOODED HIM NOW.
THE WANTING.
"I KNEW THAT SHE WOULDN'T. AND I THINK I KNEW THAT SHE SHOULDN'T. BUT I WANTED IT SO TERRIBLY, I COULD FEEL THE WANTING ALL THROUGH ME."
THANK YOU FOR YOUR DREAM, JONAS.
LILY, IT'S TIME TO LEAVE FOR SCHOOL. WOULD YOU WALK BESIDE ME AND KEEP AN EYE ON THE NEWCHILD'S BASKET?
WAIT, JONAS.

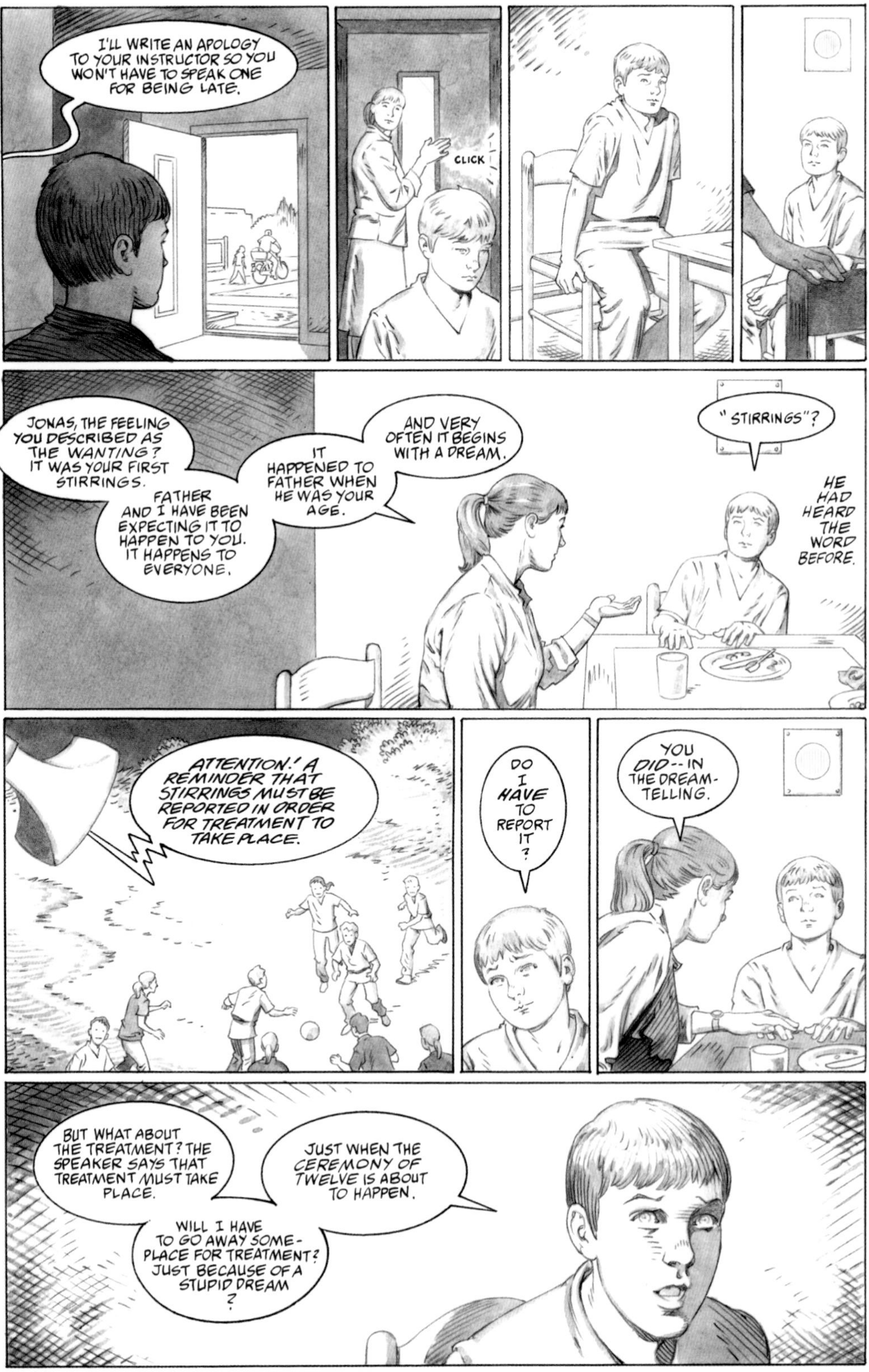
I'LL WRITE AN APOLOGY TO YOUR INSTRUCTOR SO YOU WON'T HAVE TO SPEAK ONE FOR BEING LATE.
CLICK
JONAS, THE FEELING YOU DESCRIBED AS THE WANTING? IT WAS YOUR FIRST STIRRINGS.
FATHER AND I HAVE BEEN EXPECTING IT TO HAPPEN TO YOU. IT HAPPENS TO EVERYONE.
IT HAPPENED TO FATHER WHEN HE WAS YOUR AGE.
AND VERY OFTEN IT BEGINS WITH A DREAM.
"STIRRINGS"?
HE HAD HEARD THE WORD BEFORE.
ATTENTION! A REMINDER THAT STIRRINGS MUST BE REPORTED IN ORDER FOR TREATMENT TO TAKE PLACE.
DO I HAVE TO REPORT IT?
YOU DID-- IN THE DREAM-TELLING.
BUT WHAT ABOUT THE TREATMENT? THE SPEAKER SAYS THAT TREATMENT MUST TAKE PLACE.
WILL I HAVE TO GO AWAY SOME-PLACE FOR TREATMENT? JUST BECAUSE OF A STUPID DREAM?
JUST WHEN THE CEREMONY OF TWELVE IS ABOUT TO HAPPEN.

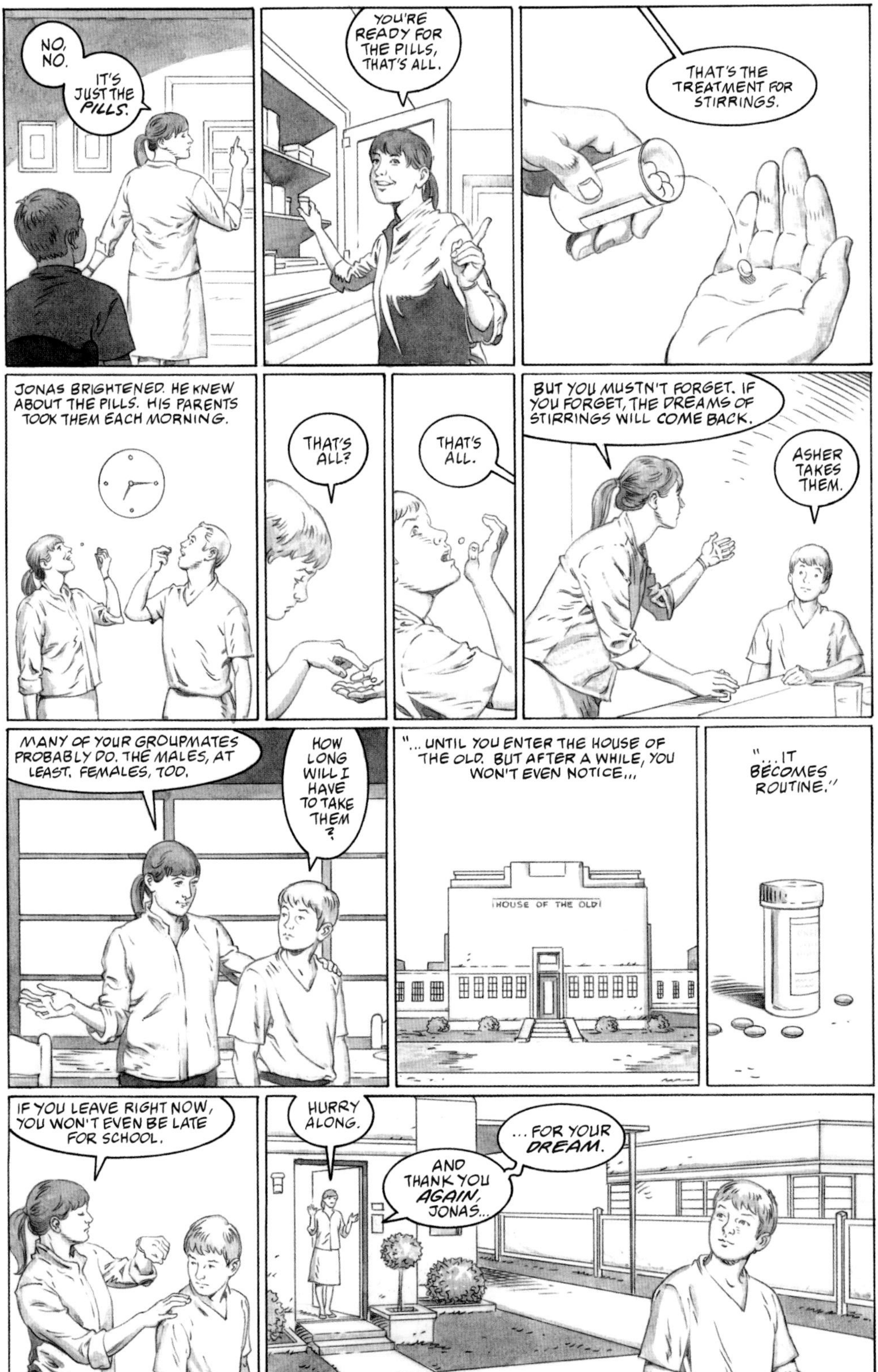
NO, NO.
IT'S JUST THE PILLS.
YOU'RE READY FOR THE PILLS, THAT'S ALL.
THAT'S THE TREATMENT FOR STIRRINGS.
JONAS BRIGHTENED. HE KNEW ABOUT THE PILLS. HIS PARENTS TOOK THEM EACH MORNING.
THAT'S ALL?
THAT'S ALL.
BUT YOU MUSTN'T FORGET. IF YOU FORGET, THE DREAMS OF STIRRINGS WILL COME BACK.
ASHER TAKES THEM.
MANY OF YOUR GROUPMATES PROBABLY DO. THE MALES, AT LEAST. FEMALES, TOO.
HOW LONG WILL I HAVE TO TAKE THEM?
"... UNTIL YOU ENTER THE HOUSE OF THE OLD. BUT AFTER A WHILE, YOU WON'T EVEN NOTICE...
HOUSE OF THE OLD
"... IT BECOMES ROUTINE."
IF YOU LEAVE RIGHT NOW, YOU WON'T EVEN BE LATE FOR SCHOOL.
HURRY ALONG.
AND THANK YOU AGAIN, JONAS...
... FOR YOUR DREAM.

PEDALING RAPIDLY DOWN THE PATH, JONAS FELT ODDLY PROUD TO HAVE JOINED THOSE WHO TOOK THE PILLS.

FOR A MOMENT, THOUGH, HE REMEMBERED THE DREAM AGAIN. THE DREAM HAD FELT PLEASURABLE.

THOUGH THE FEELINGS WERE CONFUSED, HE THOUGHT THAT HE HAD LIKED THE FEELINGS HIS MOTHER HAD CALLED STIRRINGS.

HE REMEMBERED THINKING UPON WAKING...

THAT WAS NICE. I WANT THOSE FEELINGS AGAIN.

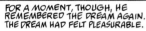

THEN, IN THE SAME WAY THAT HIS OWN DWELLING SLIPPED AWAY BEHIND HIM AS HE ROUNDED A CORNER ON HIS BICYCLE, THE DREAM SLIPPED AWAY FROM HIS THOUGHTS.

VERY BRIEFLY, A LITTLE GUILTILY, HE TRIED TO GRASP IT BACK.

BUT THE FEELINGS HAD DISAPPEARED.

THE STIRRINGS HAD GONE.

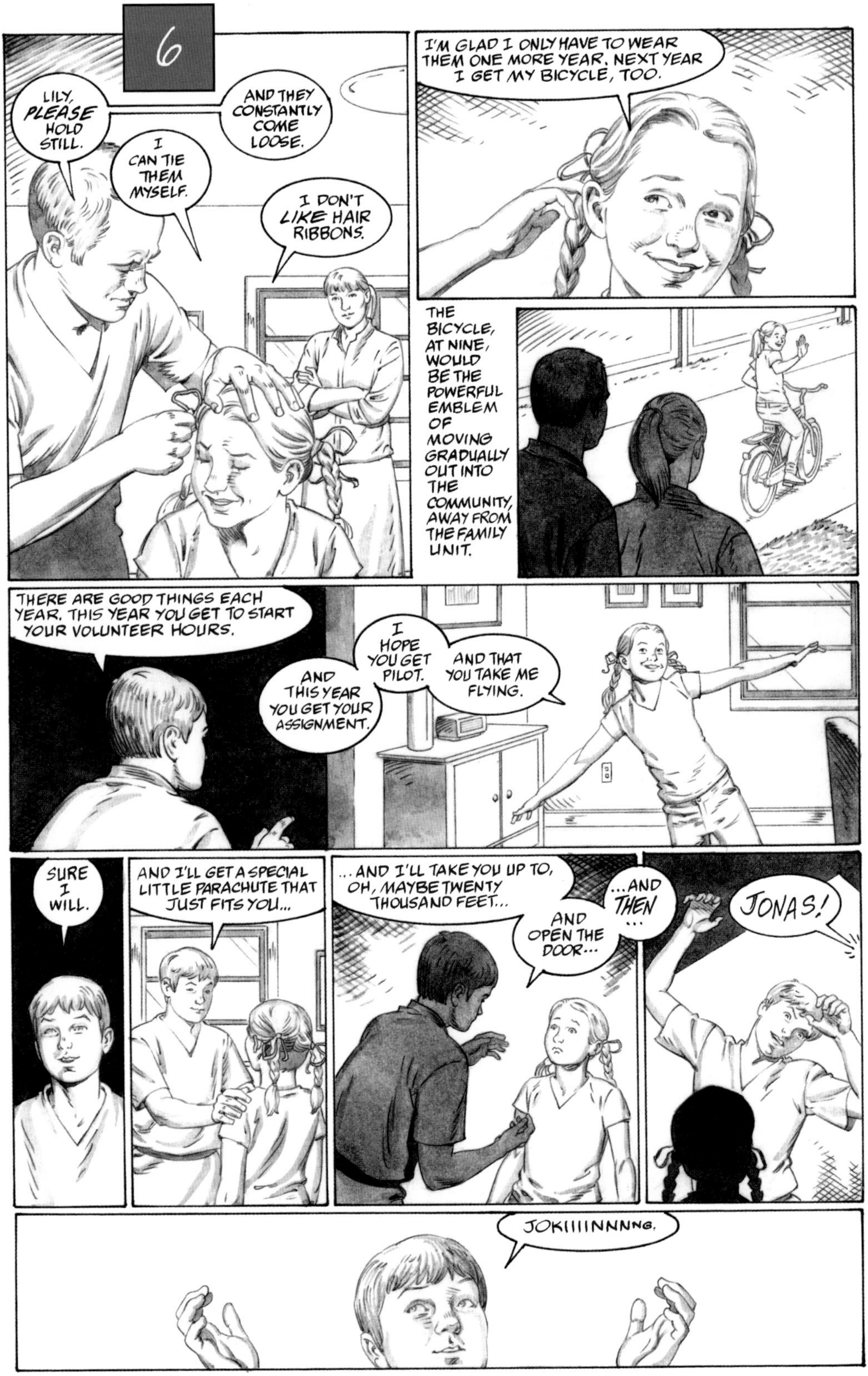
6
LILY, PLEASE HOLD STILL.
AND THEY CONSTANTLY COME LOOSE.
I CAN TIE THEM MYSELF.
I DON'T LIKE HAIR RIBBONS.
I'M GLAD I ONLY HAVE TO WEAR THEM ONE MORE YEAR. NEXT YEAR I GET MY BICYCLE, TOO.
THE BICYCLE, AT NINE, WOULD BE THE POWERFUL EMBLEM OF MOVING GRADUALLY OUT INTO THE COMMUNITY, AWAY FROM THE FAMILY UNIT.
THERE ARE GOOD THINGS EACH YEAR. THIS YEAR YOU GET TO START YOUR VOLUNTEER HOURS.
AND THIS YEAR YOU GET YOUR ASSIGNMENT.
I HOPE YOU GET PILOT.
AND THAT YOU TAKE ME FLYING.
SURE I WILL.
AND I'LL GET A SPECIAL LITTLE PARACHUTE THAT JUST FITS YOU...
...AND I'LL TAKE YOU UP TO, OH, MAYBE TWENTY THOUSAND FEET...
AND OPEN THE DOOR...
...AND THEN ...
JONAS!
JOKIIIINNNNG.

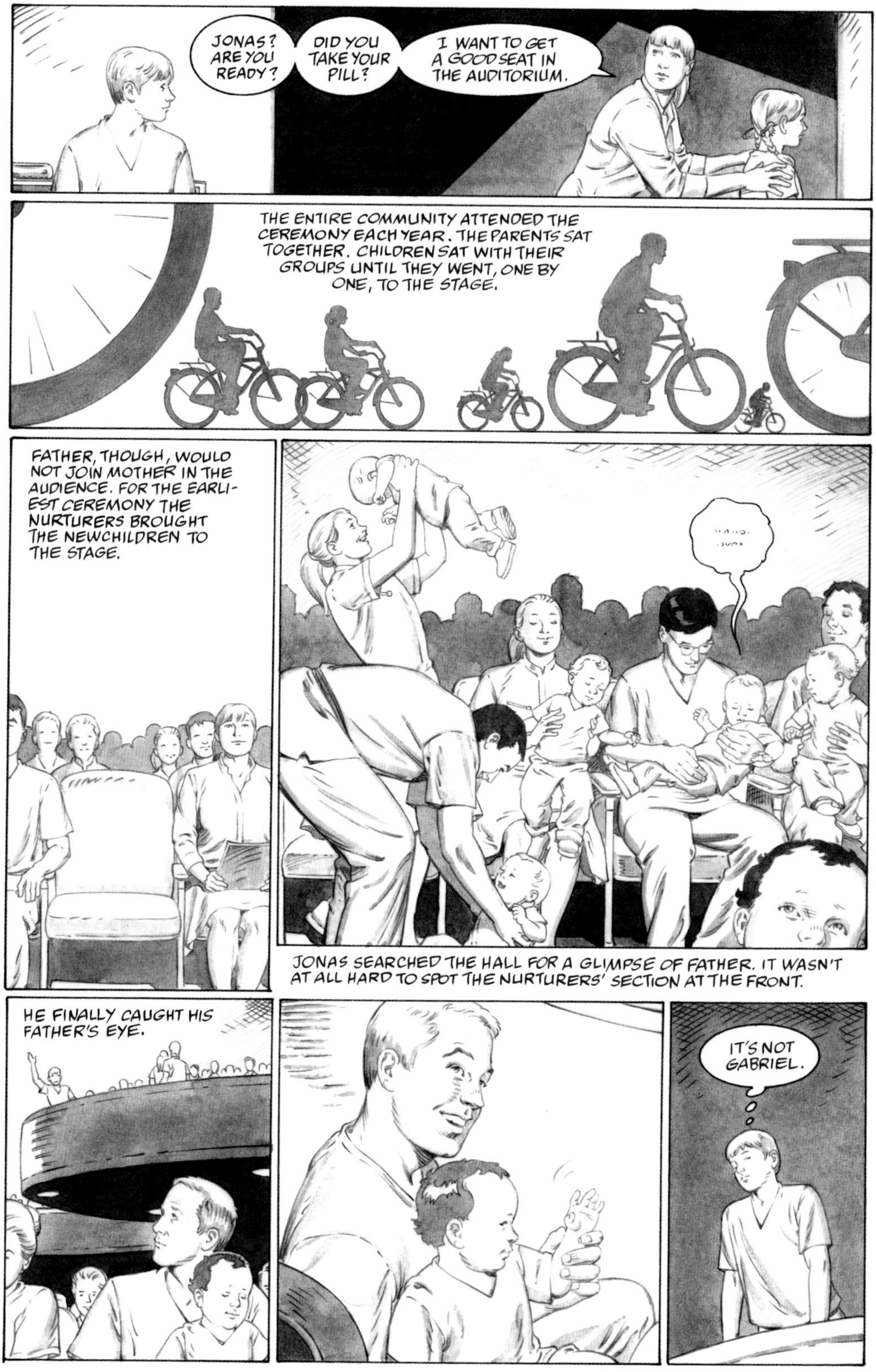

JONAS? ARE YOU READY?
DID YOU TAKE YOUR PILL?
I WANT TO GET A GOOD SEAT IN THE AUDITORIUM.
THE ENTIRE COMMUNITY ATTENDED THE CEREMONY EACH YEAR. THE PARENTS SAT TOGETHER. CHILDREN SAT WITH THEIR GROUPS UNTIL THEY WENT, ONE BY ONE, TO THE STAGE.
FATHER, THOUGH, WOULD NOT JOIN MOTHER IN THE AUDIENCE. FOR THE EARLIEST CEREMONY THE NURTURERS BROUGHT THE NEWCHILDREN TO THE STAGE.
JONAS SEARCHED THE HALL FOR A GLIMPSE OF FATHER. IT WASN'T AT ALL HARD TO SPOT THE NURTURERS' SECTION AT THE FRONT.
HE FINALLY CAUGHT HIS FATHER'S EYE.
IT'S NOT GABRIEL.

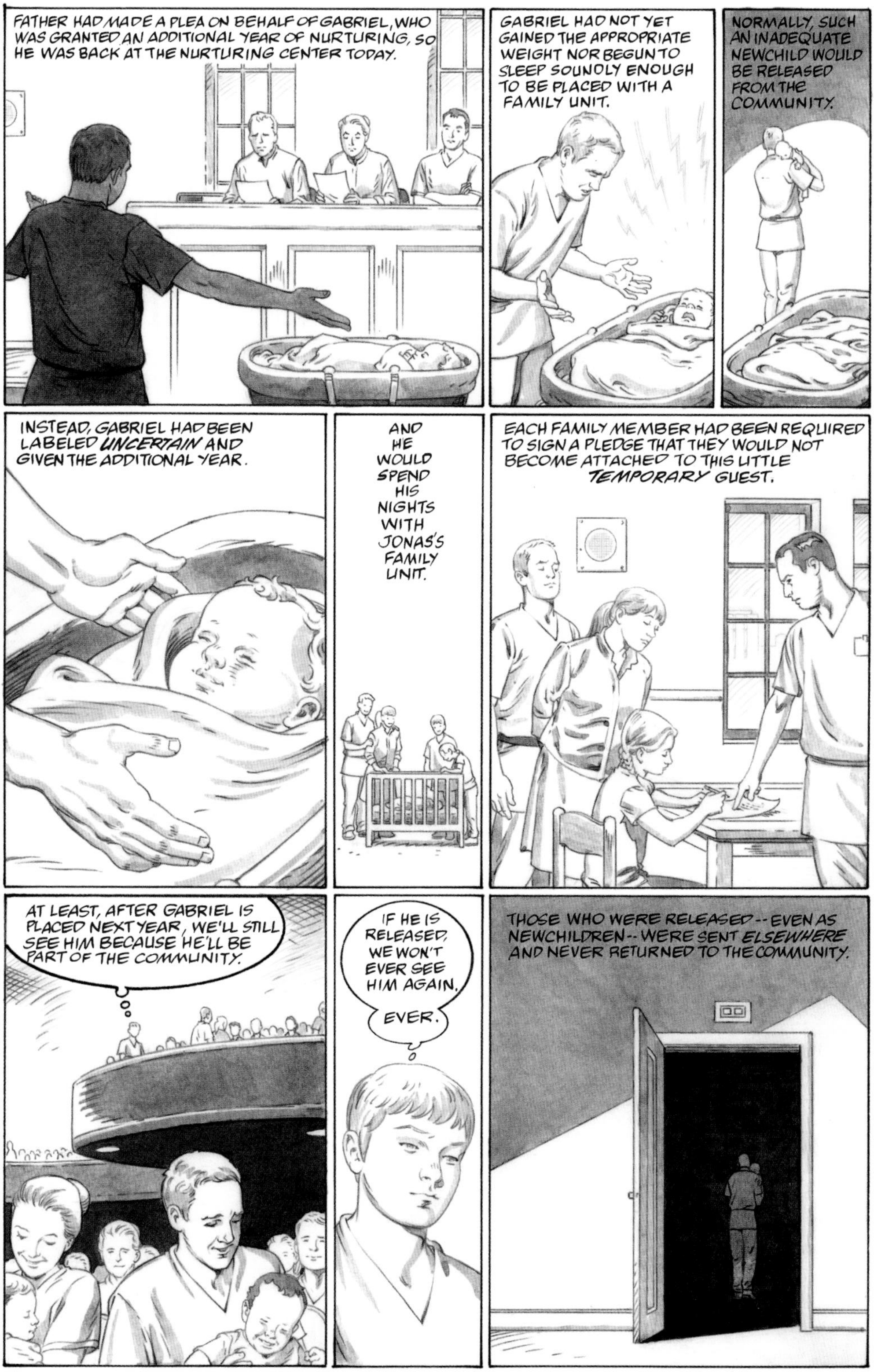
FATHER HAD MADE A PLEA ON BEHALF OF GABRIEL, WHO WAS GRANTED AN ADDITIONAL YEAR OF NURTURING, SO HE WAS BACK AT THE NURTURING CENTER TODAY.
GABRIEL HAD NOT YET GAINED THE APPROPRIATE WEIGHT NOR BEGUN TO SLEEP SOUNDLY ENOUGH TO BE PLACED WITH A FAMILY UNIT.
NORMALLY, SUCH AN INADEQUATE NEWCHILD WOULD BE RELEASED FROM THE COMMUNITY.
INSTEAD, GABRIEL HAD BEEN LABELED UNCERTAIN AND GIVEN THE ADDITIONAL YEAR.
AND HE WOULD SPEND HIS NIGHTS WITH JONAS'S FAMILY UNIT.
EACH FAMILY MEMBER HAD BEEN REQUIRED TO SIGN A PLEDGE THAT THEY WOULD NOT BECOME ATTACHED TO THIS LITTLE TEMPORARY GUEST.
AT LEAST, AFTER GABRIEL IS PLACED NEXT YEAR, WE'LL STILL SEE HIM BECAUSE HE'LL BE PART OF THE COMMUNITY.
IF HE IS RELEASED, WE WON'T EVER SEE HIM AGAIN.
EVER.
THOSE WHO WERE RELEASED -- EVEN AS NEWCHILDREN -- WERE SENT ELSEWHERE AND NEVER RETURNED TO THE COMMUNITY.

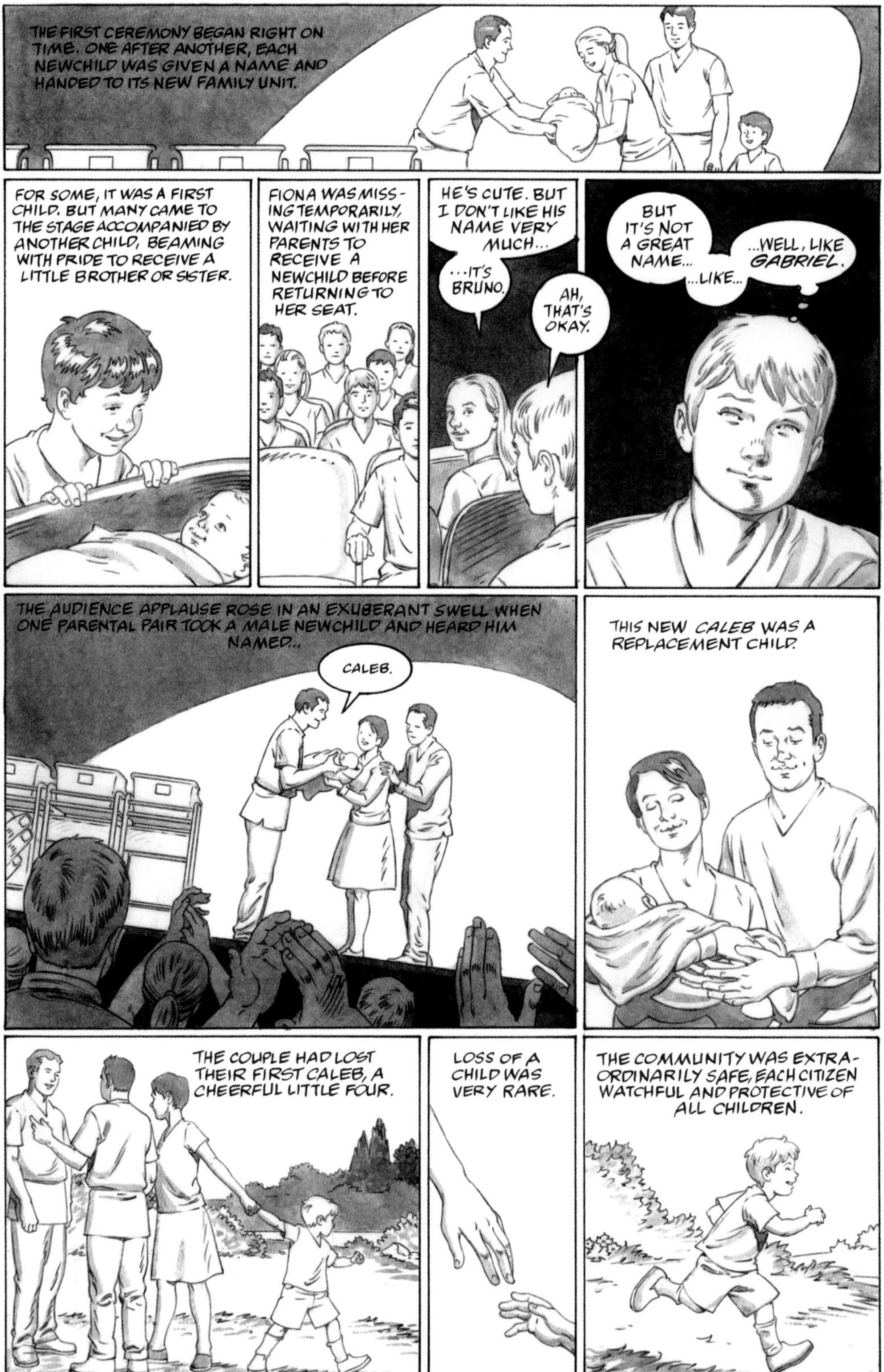
THE FIRST CEREMONY BEGAN RIGHT ON TIME. ONE AFTER ANOTHER, EACH NEWCHILD WAS GIVEN A NAME AND HANDED TO ITS NEW FAMILY UNIT.
FOR SOME, IT WAS A FIRST CHILD. BUT MANY CAME TO THE STAGE ACCOMPANIED BY ANOTHER CHILD, BEAMING WITH PRIDE TO RECEIVE A LITTLE BROTHER OR SISTER.
FIONA WAS MISSING TEMPORARILY, WAITING WITH HER PARENTS TO RECEIVE A NEWCHILD BEFORE RETURNING TO HER SEAT.
HE'S CUTE. BUT I DON'T LIKE HIS NAME VERY MUCH...
...IT'S BRUNO.
AH, THAT'S OKAY.
BUT IT'S NOT A GREAT NAME...
...LIKE...
...WELL, LIKE GABRIEL.
THE AUDIENCE APPLAUSE ROSE IN AN EXUBERANT SWELL WHEN ONE PARENTAL PAIR TOOK A MALE NEWCHILD AND HEARD HIM NAMED...
CALEB.
THIS NEW CALEB WAS A REPLACEMENT CHILD.
THE COUPLE HAD LOST THEIR FIRST CALEB, A CHEERFUL LITTLE FOUR.
LOSS OF A CHILD WAS VERY RARE.
THE COMMUNITY WAS EXTRAORDINARILY SAFE, EACH CITIZEN WATCHFUL AND PROTECTIVE OF ALL CHILDREN.

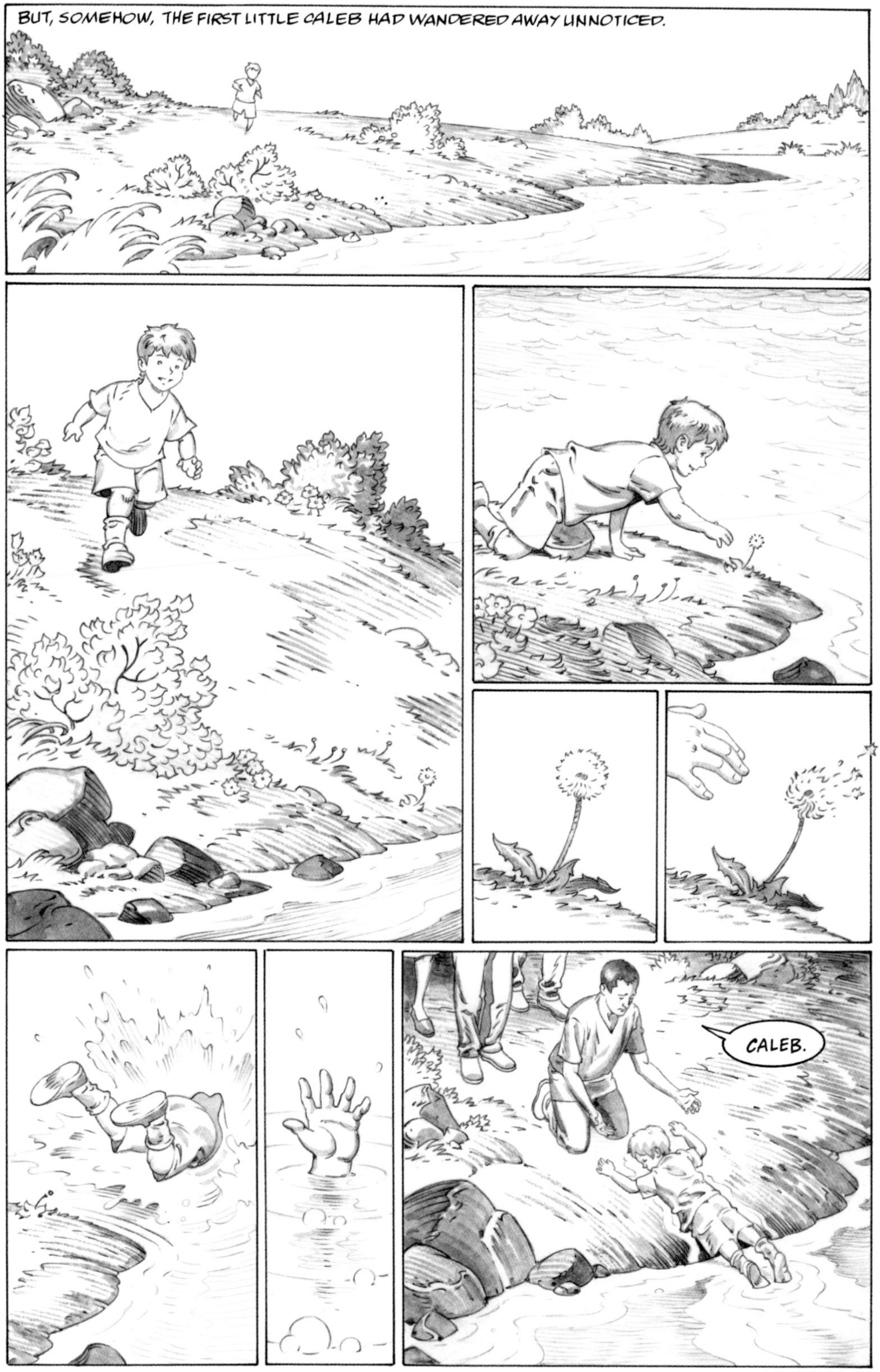
BUT, SOMEHOW, THE FIRST LITTLE CALEB HAD WANDERED AWAY UNNOTICED.
CALEB.

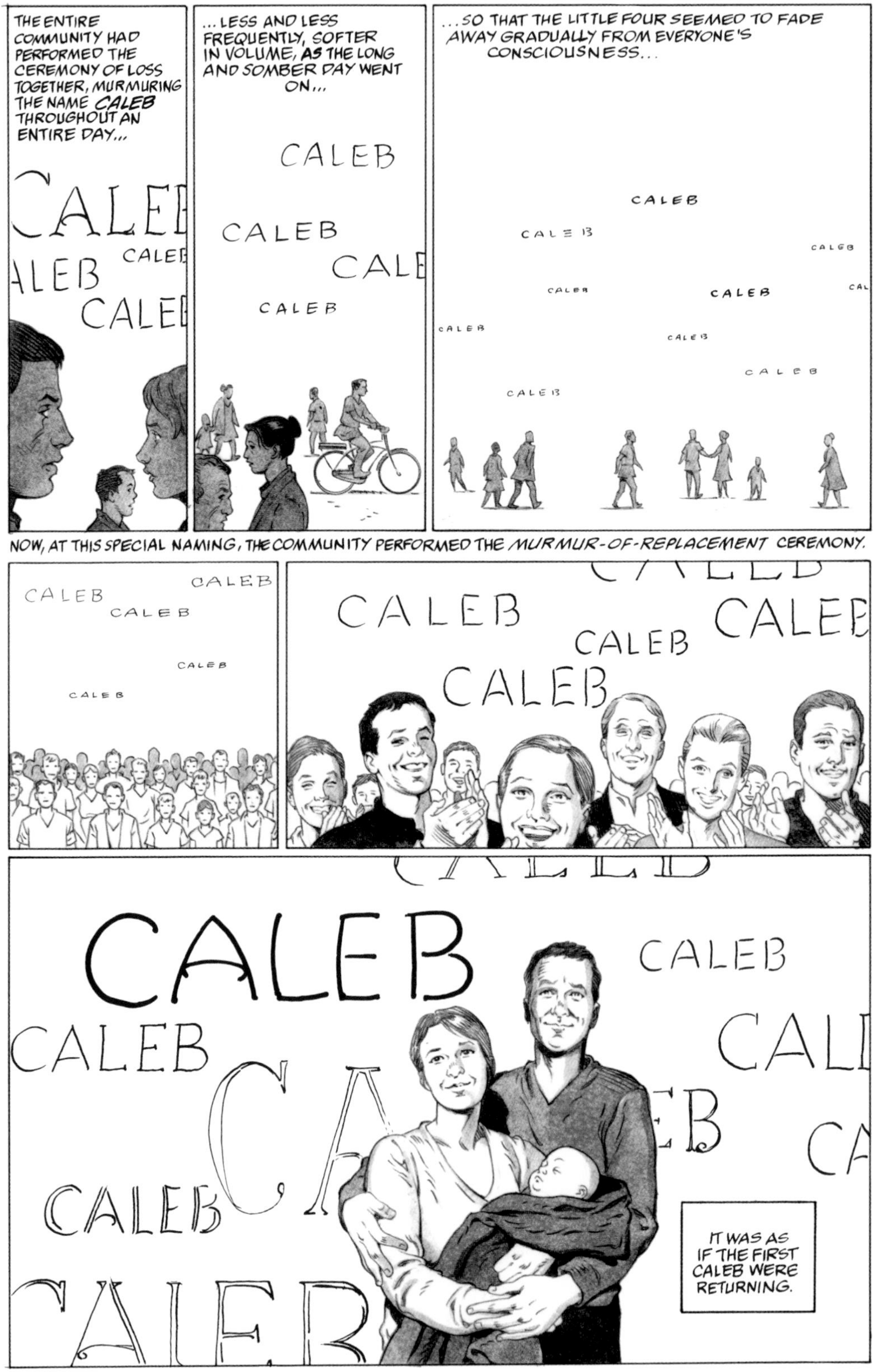
THE ENTIRE COMMUNITY HAD PERFORMED THE CEREMONY OF LOSS TOGETHER, MURMURING THE NAME CALEB THROUGHOUT AN ENTIRE DAY...
...LESS AND LESS FREQUENTLY, SOFTER IN VOLUME, AS THE LONG AND SOMBER DAY WENT ON...
...SO THAT THE LITTLE FOUR SEEMED TO FADE AWAY GRADUALLY FROM EVERYONE'S CONSCIOUSNESS...
NOW, AT THIS SPECIAL NAMING, THE COMMUNITY PERFORMED THE MURMUR-OF-REPLACEMENT CEREMONY.
IT WAS AS IF THE FIRST CALEB WERE RETURNING.

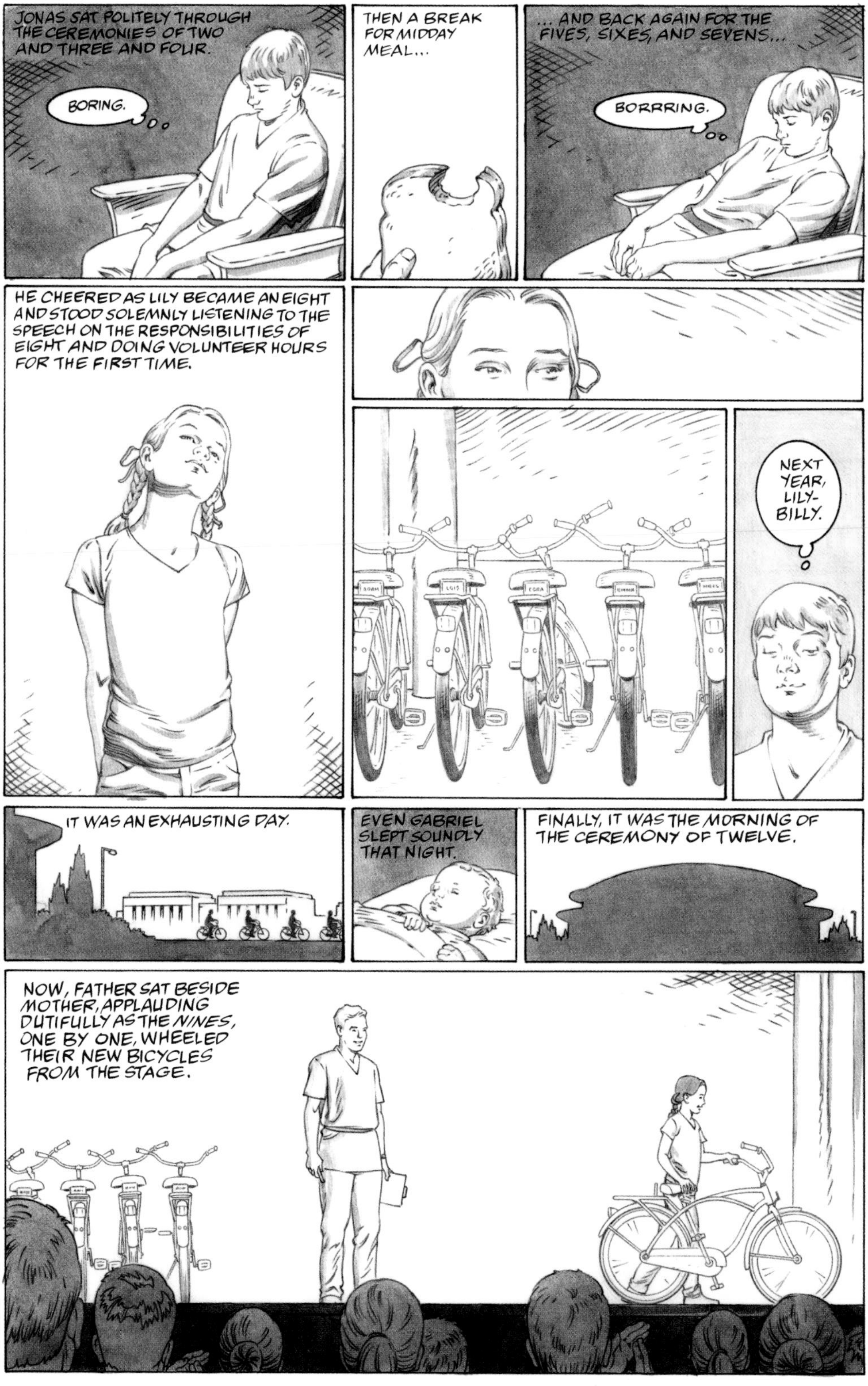
JONAS SAT POLITELY THROUGH THE CEREMONIES OF TWO AND THREE AND FOUR.
BORING.
THEN A BREAK FOR MIDDAY MEAL...
... AND BACK AGAIN FOR THE FIVES, SIXES, AND SEVENS...
BORRRING.
HE CHEERED AS LILY BECAME AN EIGHT AND STOOD SOLEMNLY LISTENING TO THE SPEECH ON THE RESPONSIBILITIES OF EIGHT AND DOING VOLUNTEER HOURS FOR THE FIRST TIME.
NEXT YEAR, LILY-BILLY.
IT WAS AN EXHAUSTING DAY.
EVEN GABRIEL SLEPT SOUNDLY THAT NIGHT.
FINALLY, IT WAS THE MORNING OF THE CEREMONY OF TWELVE.
NOW, FATHER SAT BESIDE MOTHER, APPLAUDING DUTIFULLY AS THE *NINES*, ONE BY ONE, WHEELED THEIR NEW BICYCLES FROM THE STAGE.

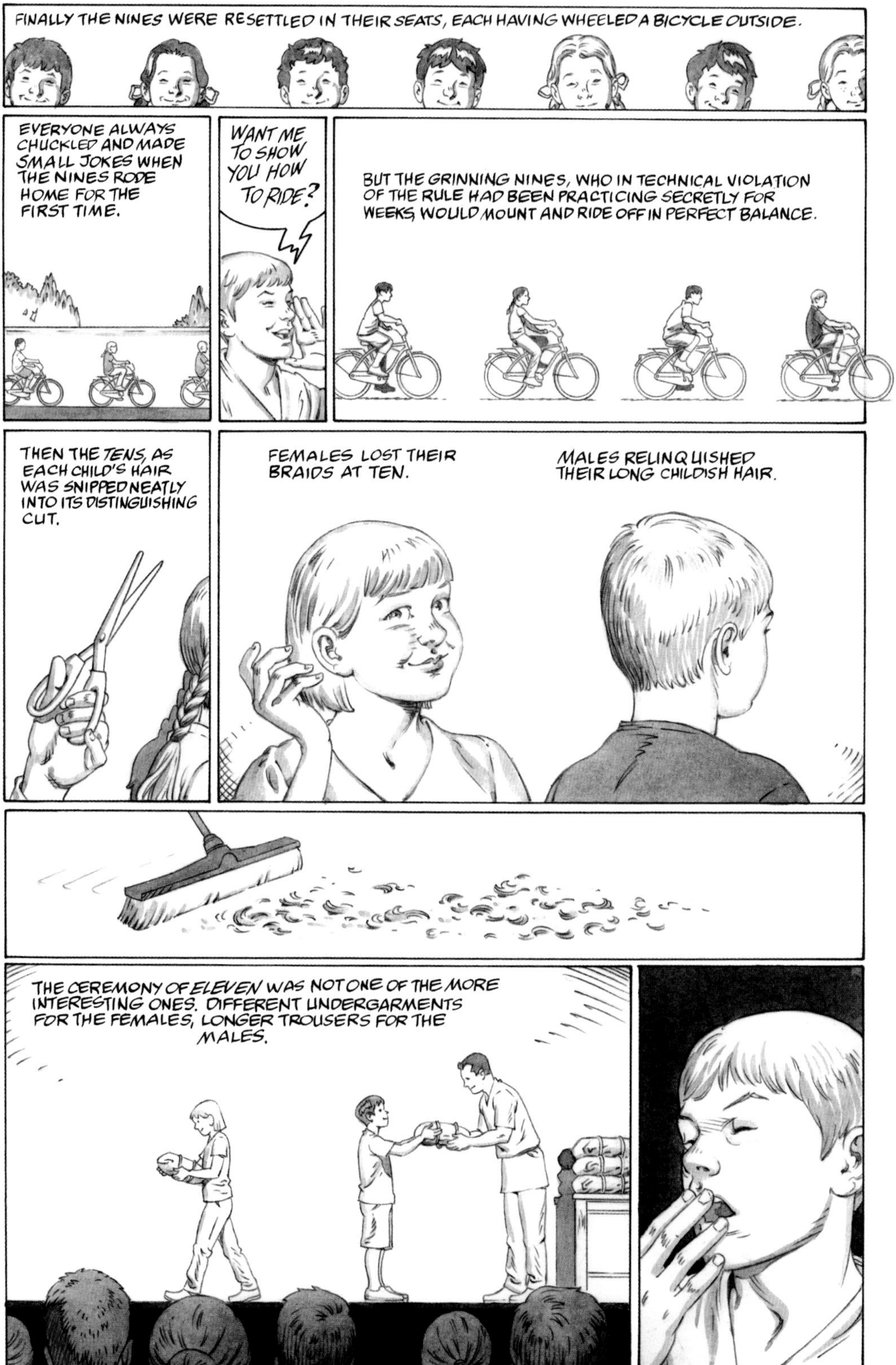
FINALLY THE NINES WERE RESETTLED IN THEIR SEATS, EACH HAVING WHEELED A BICYCLE OUTSIDE.
EVERYONE ALWAYS CHUCKLED AND MADE SMALL JOKES WHEN THE NINES RODE HOME FOR THE FIRST TIME.
WANT ME TO SHOW YOU HOW TO RIDE?
BUT THE GRINNING NINES, WHO IN TECHNICAL VIOLATION OF THE RULE HAD BEEN PRACTICING SECRETLY FOR WEEKS, WOULD MOUNT AND RIDE OFF IN PERFECT BALANCE.
THEN THE TENS, AS EACH CHILD'S HAIR WAS SNIPPED NEATLY INTO ITS DISTINGUISHING CUT.
FEMALES LOST THEIR BRAIDS AT TEN.
MALES RELINQUISHED THEIR LONG CHILDISH HAIR.
THE CEREMONY OF ELEVEN WAS NOT ONE OF THE MORE INTERESTING ONES. DIFFERENT UNDERGARMENTS FOR THE FEMALES, LONGER TROUSERS FOR THE MALES.

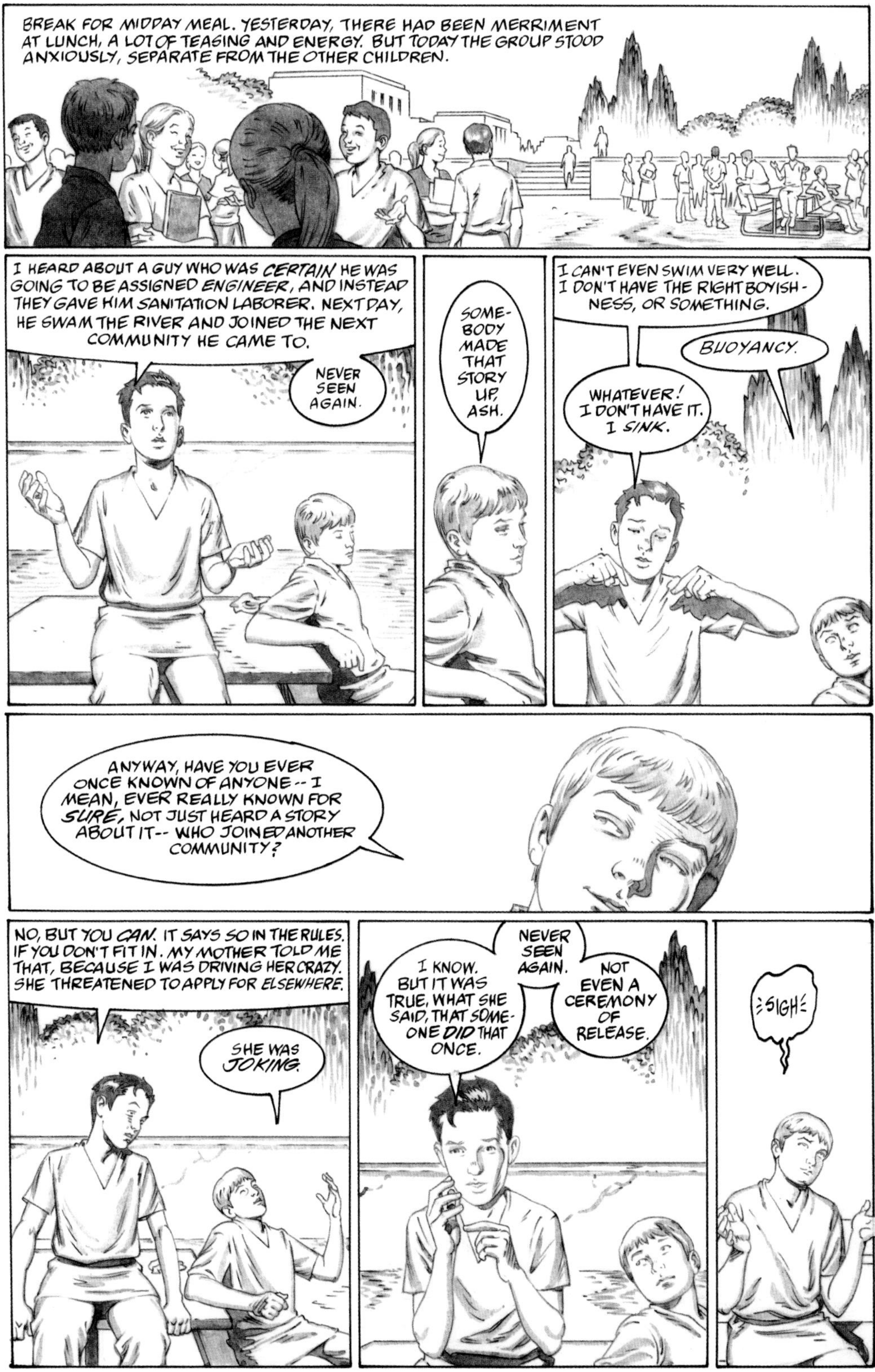
BREAK FOR MIDDAY MEAL. YESTERDAY, THERE HAD BEEN MERRIMENT AT LUNCH, A LOT OF TEASING AND ENERGY. BUT TODAY THE GROUP STOOD ANXIOUSLY, SEPARATE FROM THE OTHER CHILDREN.
I HEARD ABOUT A GUY WHO WAS CERTAIN HE WAS GOING TO BE ASSIGNED ENGINEER, AND INSTEAD THEY GAVE HIM SANITATION LABORER. NEXT DAY, HE SWAM THE RIVER AND JOINED THE NEXT COMMUNITY HE CAME TO.
NEVER SEEN AGAIN.
SOMEBODY MADE THAT STORY UP, ASH.
I CAN'T EVEN SWIM VERY WELL. I DON'T HAVE THE RIGHT BOYISHNESS, OR SOMETHING.
BUOYANCY.
WHATEVER! I DON'T HAVE IT. I SINK.
ANYWAY, HAVE YOU EVER ONCE KNOWN OF ANYONE -- I MEAN, EVER REALLY KNOWN FOR SURE, NOT JUST HEARD A STORY ABOUT IT-- WHO JOINED ANOTHER COMMUNITY?
NO, BUT YOU CAN. IT SAYS SO IN THE RULES. IF YOU DON'T FIT IN. MY MOTHER TOLD ME THAT, BECAUSE I WAS DRIVING HER CRAZY. SHE THREATENED TO APPLY FOR ELSEWHERE.
SHE WAS JOKING.
I KNOW. BUT IT WAS TRUE, WHAT SHE SAID, THAT SOMEONE DID THAT ONCE.
NEVER SEEN AGAIN.
NOT EVEN A CEREMONY OF RELEASE.
SIGH

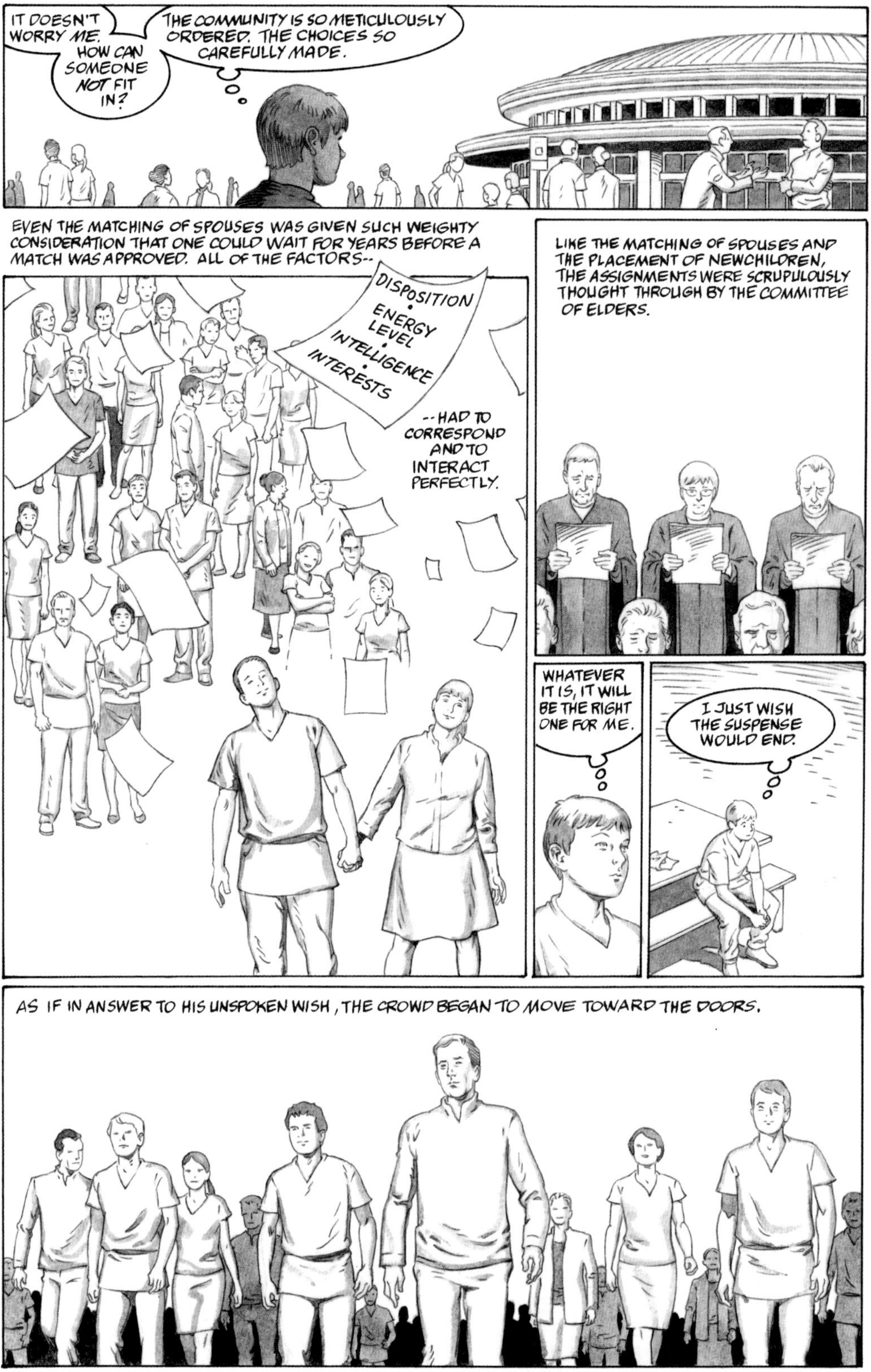
IT DOESN'T WORRY ME. HOW CAN SOMEONE NOT FIT IN?
THE COMMUNITY IS SO METICULOUSLY ORDERED. THE CHOICES SO CAREFULLY MADE.
EVEN THE MATCHING OF SPOUSES WAS GIVEN SUCH WEIGHTY CONSIDERATION THAT ONE COULD WAIT FOR YEARS BEFORE A MATCH WAS APPROVED. ALL OF THE FACTORS--
DISPOSITION • ENERGY LEVEL • INTELLIGENCE • INTERESTS
--HAD TO CORRESPOND AND TO INTERACT PERFECTLY.
LIKE THE MATCHING OF SPOUSES AND THE PLACEMENT OF NEWCHILDREN, THE ASSIGNMENTS WERE SCRUPULOUSLY THOUGHT THROUGH BY THE COMMITTEE OF ELDERS.
WHATEVER IT IS, IT WILL BE THE RIGHT ONE FOR ME.
I JUST WISH THE SUSPENSE WOULD END.
AS IF IN ANSWER TO HIS UNSPOKEN WISH, THE CROWD BEGAN TO MOVE TOWARD THE DOORS.

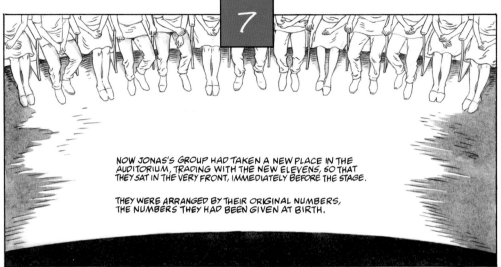

7

NOW JONAS'S GROUP HAD TAKEN A NEW PLACE IN THE AUDITORIUM, TRADING WITH THE NEW ELEVENS, SO THAT THEY SAT IN THE VERY FRONT, IMMEDIATELY BEFORE THE STAGE.

THEY WERE ARRANGED BY THEIR ORIGINAL NUMBERS, THE NUMBERS THEY HAD BEEN GIVEN AT BIRTH.

SOMETIMES THE PARENTS USED THE NUMBERS IN EXASPERATION AT A CHILD'S MISBEHAVIOR.

THAT'S *ENOUGH*, TWENTY-THREE.

JONAS WAS...

19 · 20 · 21 · 22

TECHNICALLY, JONAS'S FULL NUMBER WAS ELEVEN-NINETEEN, SINCE THERE WERE OTHER NINETEENS, OF COURSE, ONE IN EACH AGE GROUP. AND TODAY, NOW THAT THE NEW ELEVENS HAD BEEN ADVANCED THIS MORNING, THERE WERE *TWO* ELEVEN-NINETEENS.

19 · 19 · 19 · 19 · 19 · 19

AT THE MIDDAY BREAK, HE EXCHANGED SMILES WITH THE NEW ONE.

BUT THE DUPLICATION WAS ONLY FOR THESE FEW HOURS.

VERY SOON, HE WOULD BE A TWELVE, AN ADULT, LIKE HIS PARENTS, THOUGH A NEW ONE, AND UNTRAINED, STILL.

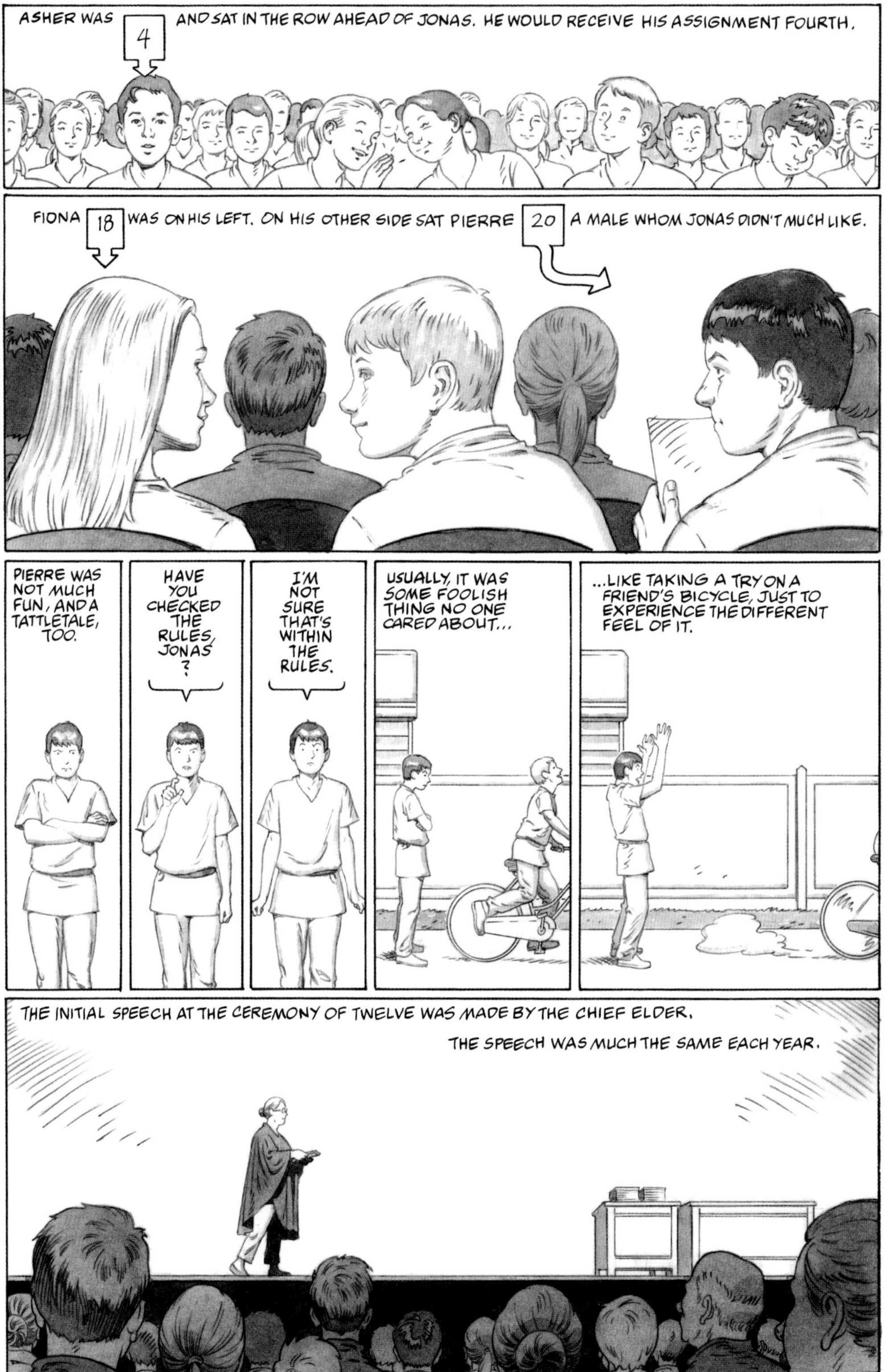
ASHER WAS 4 AND SAT IN THE ROW AHEAD OF JONAS. HE WOULD RECEIVE HIS ASSIGNMENT FOURTH.
FIONA 18 WAS ON HIS LEFT. ON HIS OTHER SIDE SAT PIERRE 20 A MALE WHOM JONAS DIDN'T MUCH LIKE.
PIERRE WAS NOT MUCH FUN, AND A TATTLETALE, TOO.
HAVE YOU CHECKED THE RULES, JONAS?
I'M NOT SURE THAT'S WITHIN THE RULES.
USUALLY, IT WAS SOME FOOLISH THING NO ONE CARED ABOUT...
...LIKE TAKING A TRY ON A FRIEND'S BICYCLE, JUST TO EXPERIENCE THE DIFFERENT FEEL OF IT.
THE INITIAL SPEECH AT THE CEREMONY OF TWELVE WAS MADE BY THE CHIEF ELDER.
THE SPEECH WAS MUCH THE SAME EACH YEAR.

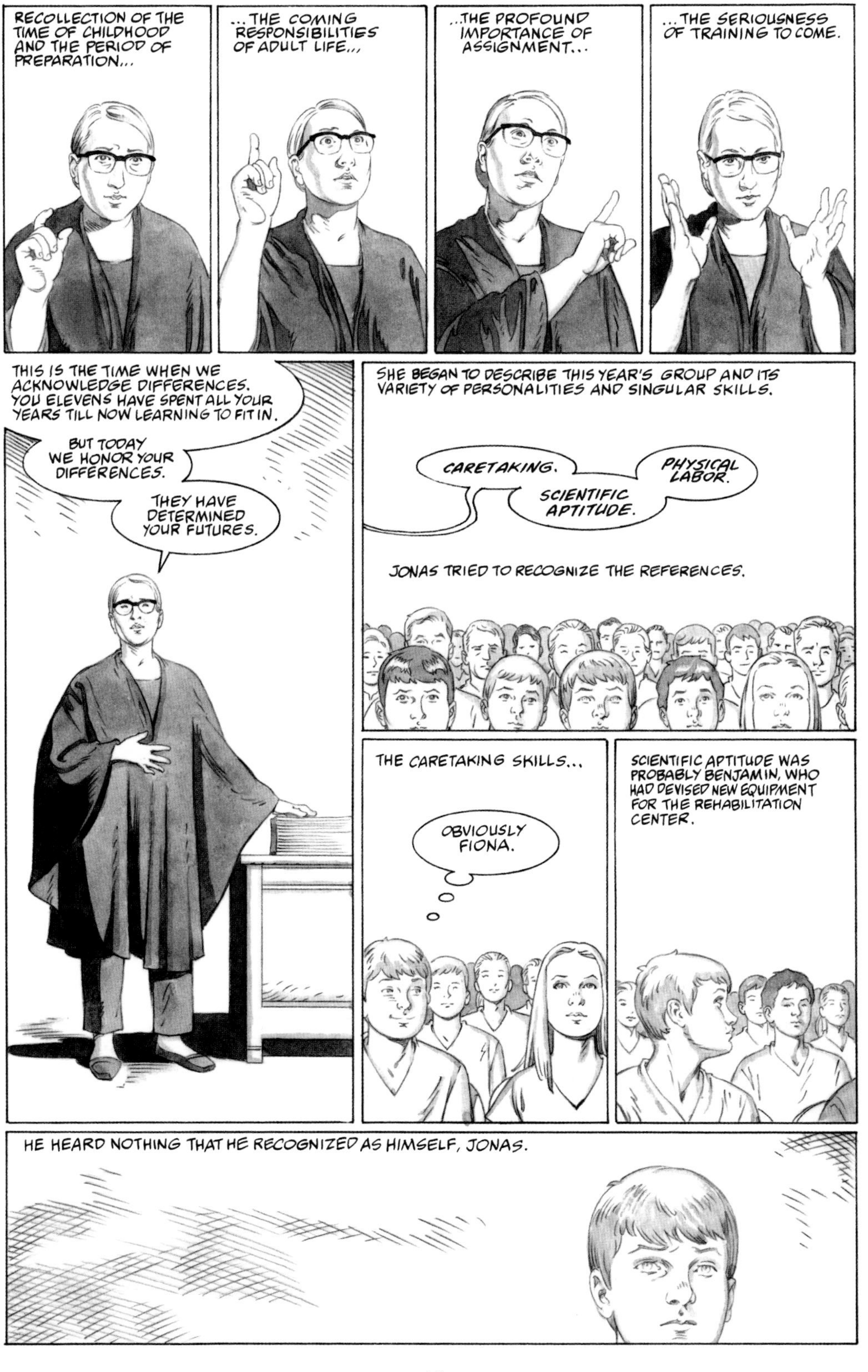
RECOLLECTION OF THE TIME OF CHILDHOOD AND THE PERIOD OF PREPARATION...
...THE COMING RESPONSIBILITIES OF ADULT LIFE...
...THE PROFOUND IMPORTANCE OF ASSIGNMENT...
...THE SERIOUSNESS OF TRAINING TO COME.
THIS IS THE TIME WHEN WE ACKNOWLEDGE DIFFERENCES. YOU ELEVENS HAVE SPENT ALL YOUR YEARS TILL NOW LEARNING TO FIT IN.
BUT TODAY WE HONOR YOUR DIFFERENCES.
THEY HAVE DETERMINED YOUR FUTURES.
SHE BEGAN TO DESCRIBE THIS YEAR'S GROUP AND ITS VARIETY OF PERSONALITIES AND SINGULAR SKILLS.
CARETAKING.
SCIENTIFIC APTITUDE.
PHYSICAL LABOR.
JONAS TRIED TO RECOGNIZE THE REFERENCES.
THE CARETAKING SKILLS...
OBVIOUSLY FIONA.
SCIENTIFIC APTITUDE WAS PROBABLY BENJAMIN, WHO HAD DEVISED NEW EQUIPMENT FOR THE REHABILITATION CENTER.
HE HEARD NOTHING THAT HE RECOGNIZED AS HIMSELF, JONAS.

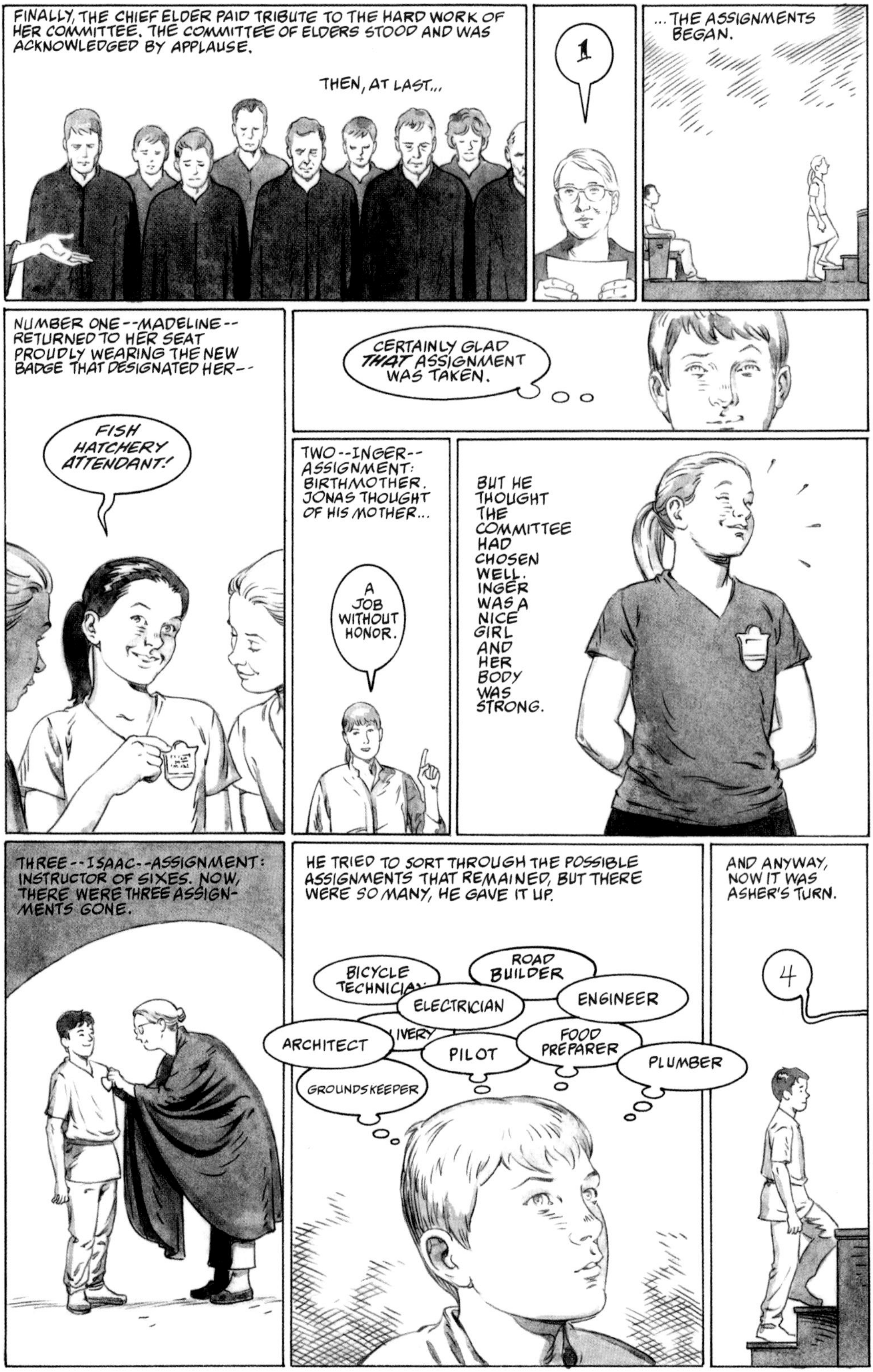
FINALLY, THE CHIEF ELDER PAID TRIBUTE TO THE HARD WORK OF HER COMMITTEE. THE COMMITTEE OF ELDERS STOOD AND WAS ACKNOWLEDGED BY APPLAUSE.
THEN, AT LAST...
1
...THE ASSIGNMENTS BEGAN.
NUMBER ONE--MADELINE--RETURNED TO HER SEAT PROUDLY WEARING THE NEW BADGE THAT DESIGNATED HER--
FISH HATCHERY ATTENDANT!
CERTAINLY GLAD *THAT* ASSIGNMENT WAS TAKEN.
TWO--INGER--ASSIGNMENT: BIRTHMOTHER. JONAS THOUGHT OF HIS MOTHER...
A JOB WITHOUT HONOR.
BUT HE THOUGHT THE COMMITTEE HAD CHOSEN WELL. INGER WAS A NICE GIRL AND HER BODY WAS STRONG.
THREE--ISAAC--ASSIGNMENT: INSTRUCTOR OF SIXES. NOW, THERE WERE THREE ASSIGNMENTS GONE.
HE TRIED TO SORT THROUGH THE POSSIBLE ASSIGNMENTS THAT REMAINED, BUT THERE WERE SO MANY, HE GAVE IT UP.
ROAD BUILDER
ELECTRICIAN
ENGINEER
ARCHITECT
PILOT
FOOD PREPARER
PLUMBER
GROUNDSKEEPER
AND ANYWAY, NOW IT WAS ASHER'S TURN.
4

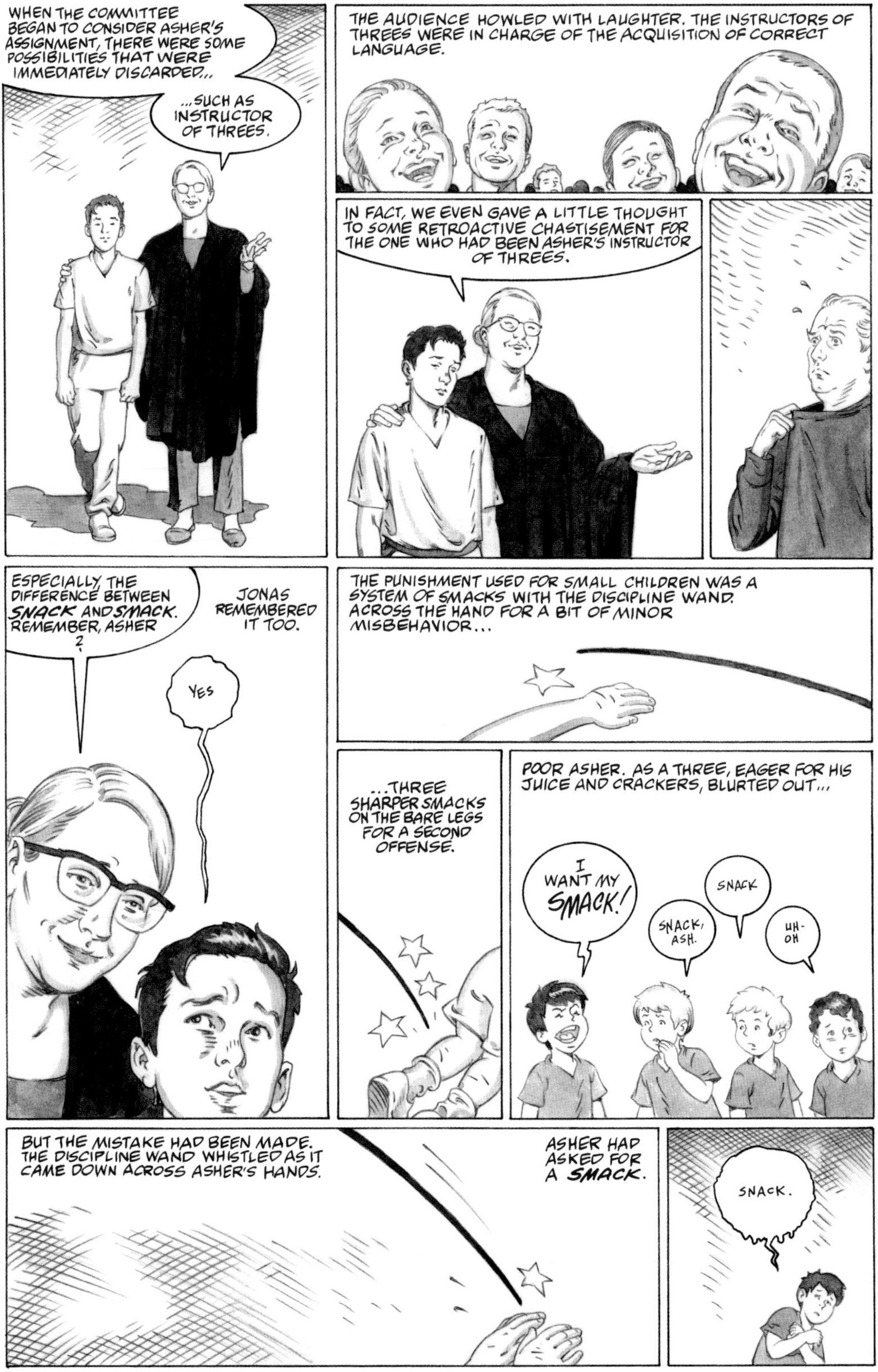
WHEN THE COMMITTEE BEGAN TO CONSIDER ASHER'S ASSIGNMENT, THERE WERE SOME POSSIBILITIES THAT WERE IMMEDIATELY DISCARDED...
...SUCH AS INSTRUCTOR OF THREES.
THE AUDIENCE HOWLED WITH LAUGHTER. THE INSTRUCTORS OF THREES WERE IN CHARGE OF THE ACQUISITION OF CORRECT LANGUAGE.
IN FACT, WE EVEN GAVE A LITTLE THOUGHT TO SOME RETROACTIVE CHASTISEMENT FOR THE ONE WHO HAD BEEN ASHER'S INSTRUCTOR OF THREES.
ESPECIALLY, THE DIFFERENCE BETWEEN SNACK AND SMACK. REMEMBER, ASHER?
JONAS REMEMBERED IT TOO.
YES
THE PUNISHMENT USED FOR SMALL CHILDREN WAS A SYSTEM OF SMACKS WITH THE DISCIPLINE WAND. ACROSS THE HAND FOR A BIT OF MINOR MISBEHAVIOR...
...THREE SHARPER SMACKS ON THE BARE LEGS FOR A SECOND OFFENSE.
POOR ASHER. AS A THREE, EAGER FOR HIS JUICE AND CRACKERS, BLURTED OUT...
I WANT MY SMACK!
SNACK, ASH.
SNACK
UH-OH
BUT THE MISTAKE HAD BEEN MADE. THE DISCIPLINE WAND WHISTLED AS IT CAME DOWN ACROSS ASHER'S HANDS.
ASHER HAD ASKED FOR A SMACK.
SNACK.

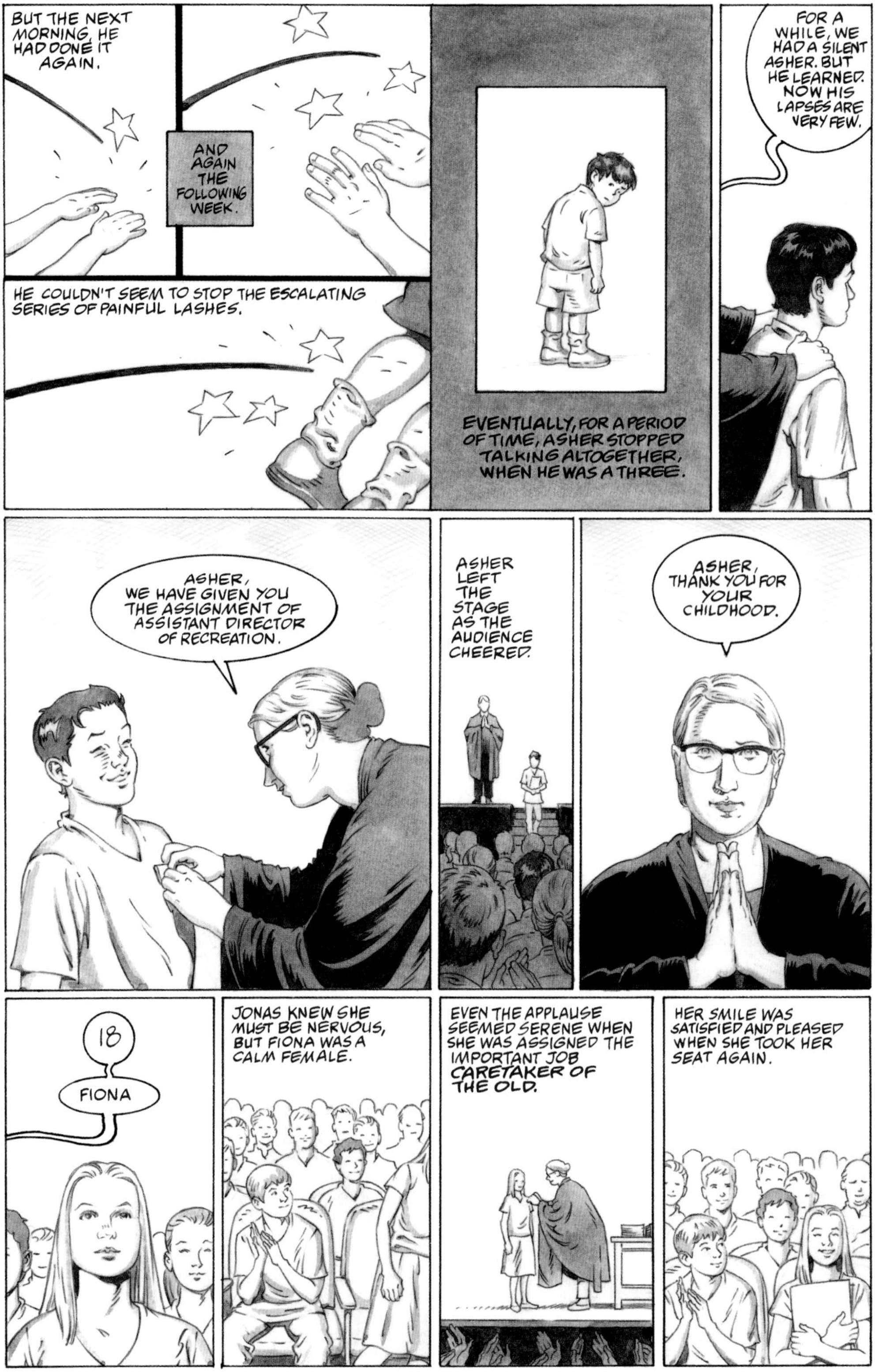

BUT THE NEXT MORNING, HE HAD DONE IT AGAIN.
AND AGAIN THE FOLLOWING WEEK.
HE COULDN'T SEEM TO STOP THE ESCALATING SERIES OF PAINFUL LASHES.
EVENTUALLY, FOR A PERIOD OF TIME, ASHER STOPPED TALKING ALTOGETHER, WHEN HE WAS A THREE.
FOR A WHILE, WE HAD A SILENT ASHER. BUT HE LEARNED. NOW HIS LAPSES ARE VERY FEW.
ASHER, WE HAVE GIVEN YOU THE ASSIGNMENT OF ASSISTANT DIRECTOR OF RECREATION.
ASHER LEFT THE STAGE AS THE AUDIENCE CHEERED.
ASHER, THANK YOU FOR YOUR CHILDHOOD.
18
FIONA
JONAS KNEW SHE MUST BE NERVOUS, BUT FIONA WAS A CALM FEMALE.
EVEN THE APPLAUSE SEEMED SERENE WHEN SHE WAS ASSIGNED THE IMPORTANT JOB CARETAKER OF THE OLD.
HER SMILE WAS SATISFIED AND PLEASED WHEN SHE TOOK HER SEAT AGAIN.

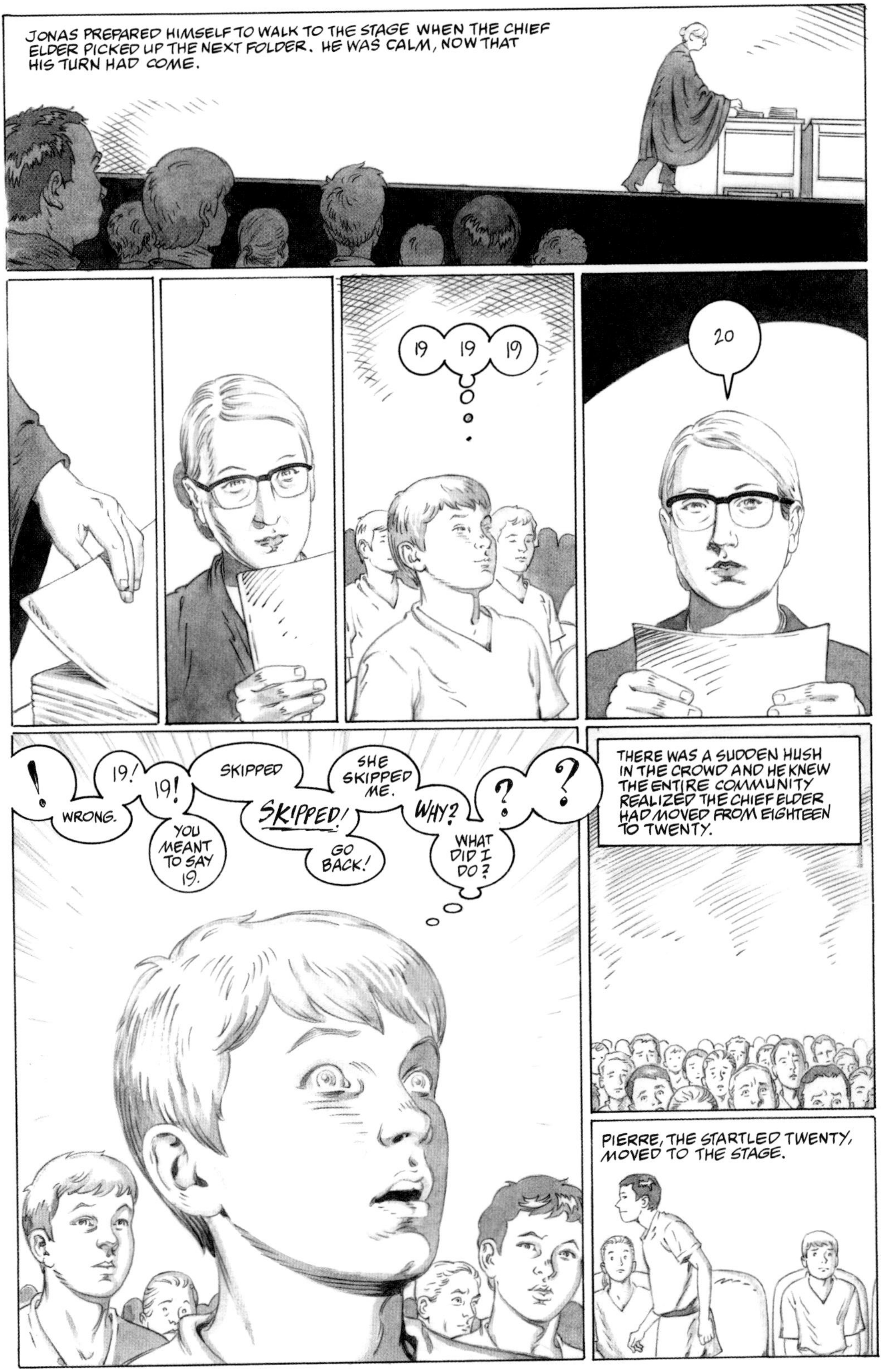

JONAS PREPARED HIMSELF TO WALK TO THE STAGE WHEN THE CHIEF ELDER PICKED UP THE NEXT FOLDER. HE WAS CALM, NOW THAT HIS TURN HAD COME.
19 19 19
20
!
WRONG.
19!
19!
YOU MEANT TO SAY 19.
SKIPPED
SKIPPED!
GO BACK!
SHE SKIPPED ME.
WHY?
WHAT DID I DO?
?
?
THERE WAS A SUDDEN HUSH IN THE CROWD AND HE KNEW THE ENTIRE COMMUNITY REALIZED THE CHIEF ELDER HAD MOVED FROM EIGHTEEN TO TWENTY.
PIERRE, THE STARTLED TWENTY, MOVED TO THE STAGE.

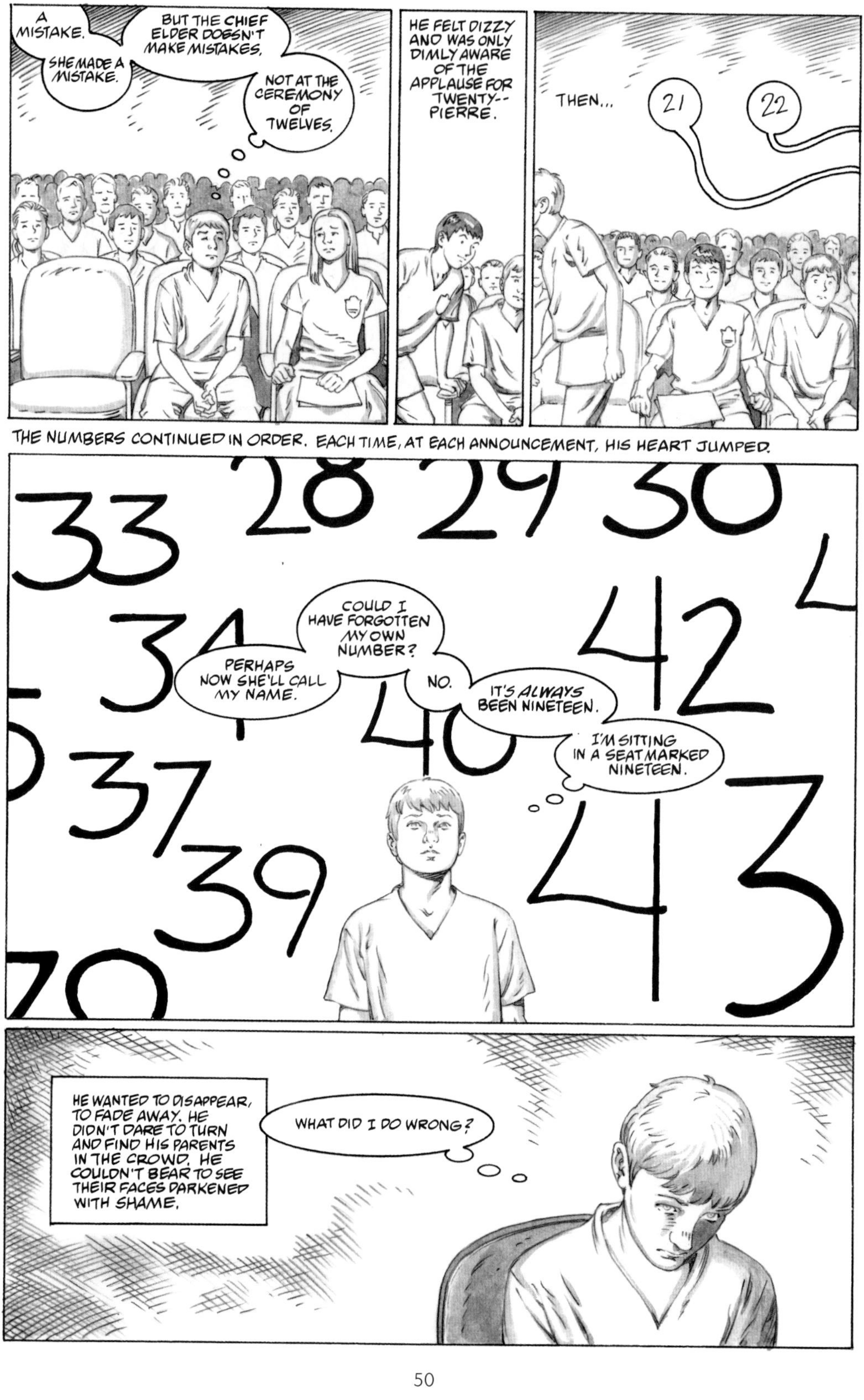
A MISTAKE.
SHE MADE A MISTAKE.
BUT THE CHIEF ELDER DOESN'T MAKE MISTAKES.
NOT AT THE CEREMONY OF TWELVES.
HE FELT DIZZY AND WAS ONLY DIMLY AWARE OF THE APPLAUSE FOR TWENTY-- PIERRE.
THEN...
21
22
THE NUMBERS CONTINUED IN ORDER. EACH TIME, AT EACH ANNOUNCEMENT, HIS HEART JUMPED.
PERHAPS NOW SHE'LL CALL MY NAME.
COULD I HAVE FORGOTTEN MY OWN NUMBER?
NO.
IT'S ALWAYS BEEN NINETEEN.
I'M SITTING IN A SEAT MARKED NINETEEN.
HE WANTED TO DISAPPEAR, TO FADE AWAY. HE DIDN'T DARE TO TURN AND FIND HIS PARENTS IN THE CROWD. HE COULDN'T BEAR TO SEE THEIR FACES DARKENED WITH SHAME.
WHAT DID I DO WRONG?

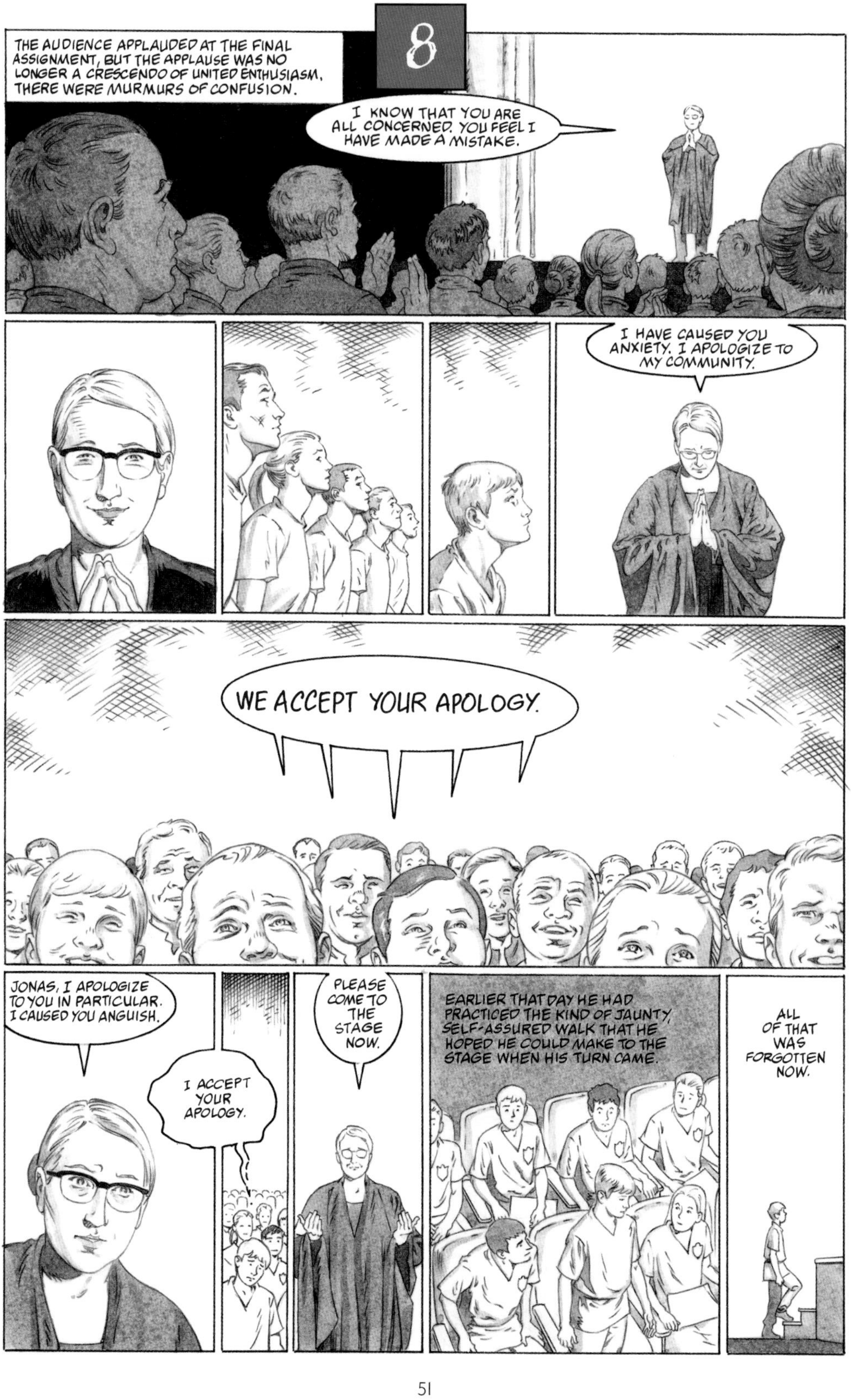
8
THE AUDIENCE APPLAUDED AT THE FINAL ASSIGNMENT, BUT THE APPLAUSE WAS NO LONGER A CRESCENDO OF UNITED ENTHUSIASM. THERE WERE MURMURS OF CONFUSION.
I KNOW THAT YOU ARE ALL CONCERNED. YOU FEEL I HAVE MADE A MISTAKE.
I HAVE CAUSED YOU ANXIETY. I APOLOGIZE TO MY COMMUNITY.
WE ACCEPT YOUR APOLOGY.
JONAS, I APOLOGIZE TO YOU IN PARTICULAR. I CAUSED YOU ANGUISH.
I ACCEPT YOUR APOLOGY.
PLEASE COME TO THE STAGE NOW.
EARLIER THAT DAY HE HAD PRACTICED THE KIND OF JAUNTY, SELF-ASSURED WALK THAT HE HOPED HE COULD MAKE TO THE STAGE WHEN HIS TURN CAME.
ALL OF THAT WAS FORGOTTEN NOW.

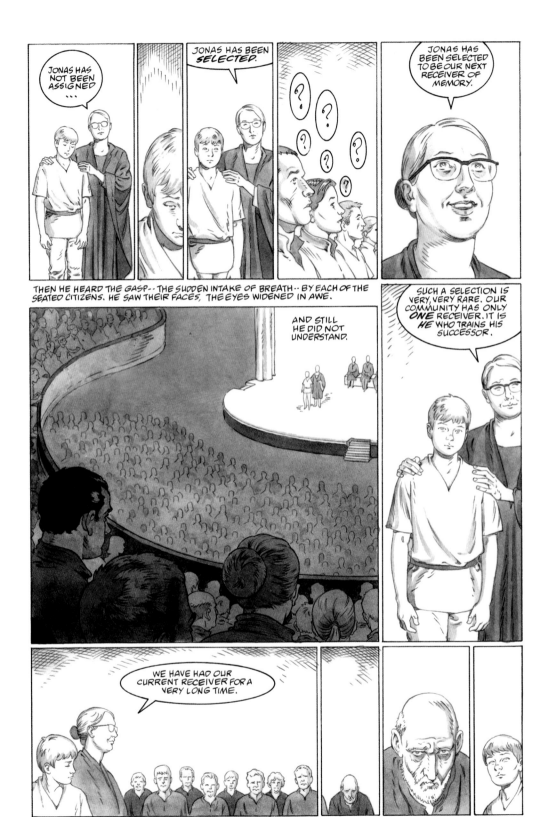

JONAS HAS NOT BEEN ASSIGNED...

JONAS HAS BEEN *SELECTED.*

JONAS HAS BEEN SELECTED TO BE OUR NEXT RECEIVER OF MEMORY.

THEN HE HEARD THE GASP-- THE SUDDEN INTAKE OF BREATH-- BY EACH OF THE SEATED CITIZENS. HE SAW THEIR FACES, THE EYES WIDENED IN AWE.

AND STILL HE DID NOT UNDERSTAND.

SUCH A SELECTION IS VERY, VERY RARE. OUR COMMUNITY HAS ONLY *ONE* RECEIVER. IT IS *HE* WHO TRAINS HIS SUCCESSOR.

WE HAVE HAD OUR CURRENT RECEIVER FOR A VERY LONG TIME.

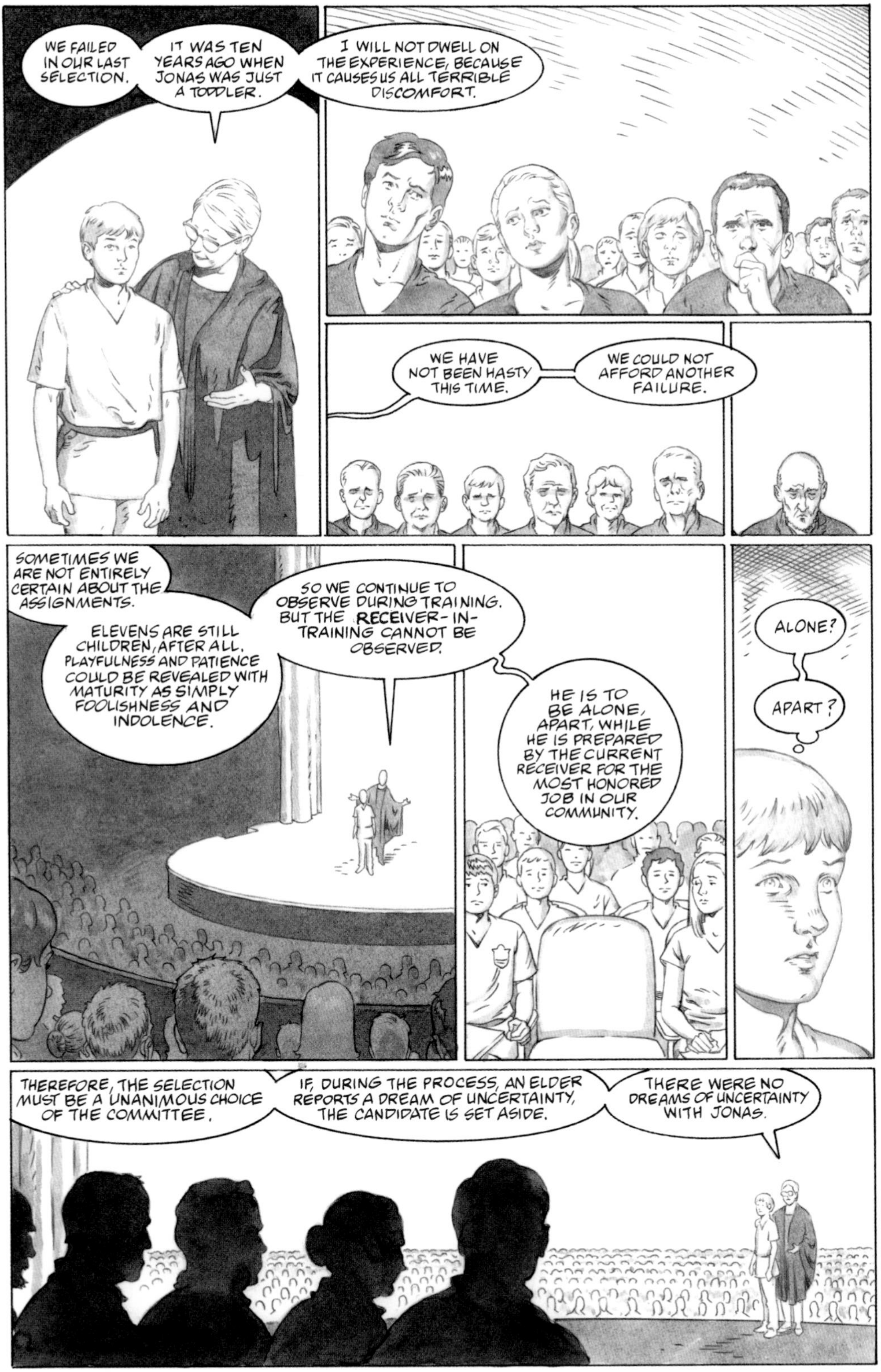
WE FAILED IN OUR LAST SELECTION.
IT WAS TEN YEARS AGO WHEN JONAS WAS JUST A TODDLER.
I WILL NOT DWELL ON THE EXPERIENCE, BECAUSE IT CAUSES US ALL TERRIBLE DISCOMFORT.
WE HAVE NOT BEEN HASTY THIS TIME.
WE COULD NOT AFFORD ANOTHER FAILURE.
SOMETIMES WE ARE NOT ENTIRELY CERTAIN ABOUT THE ASSIGNMENTS.
ELEVENS ARE STILL CHILDREN, AFTER ALL. PLAYFULNESS AND PATIENCE COULD BE REVEALED WITH MATURITY AS SIMPLY FOOLISHNESS AND INDOLENCE.
SO WE CONTINUE TO OBSERVE DURING TRAINING. BUT THE RECEIVER-IN-TRAINING CANNOT BE OBSERVED.
HE IS TO BE ALONE, APART, WHILE HE IS PREPARED BY THE CURRENT RECEIVER FOR THE MOST HONORED JOB IN OUR COMMUNITY.
ALONE?
APART?
THEREFORE, THE SELECTION MUST BE A UNANIMOUS CHOICE OF THE COMMITTEE.
IF, DURING THE PROCESS, AN ELDER REPORTS A DREAM OF UNCERTAINTY, THE CANDIDATE IS SET ASIDE.
THERE WERE NO DREAMS OF UNCERTAINTY WITH JONAS.

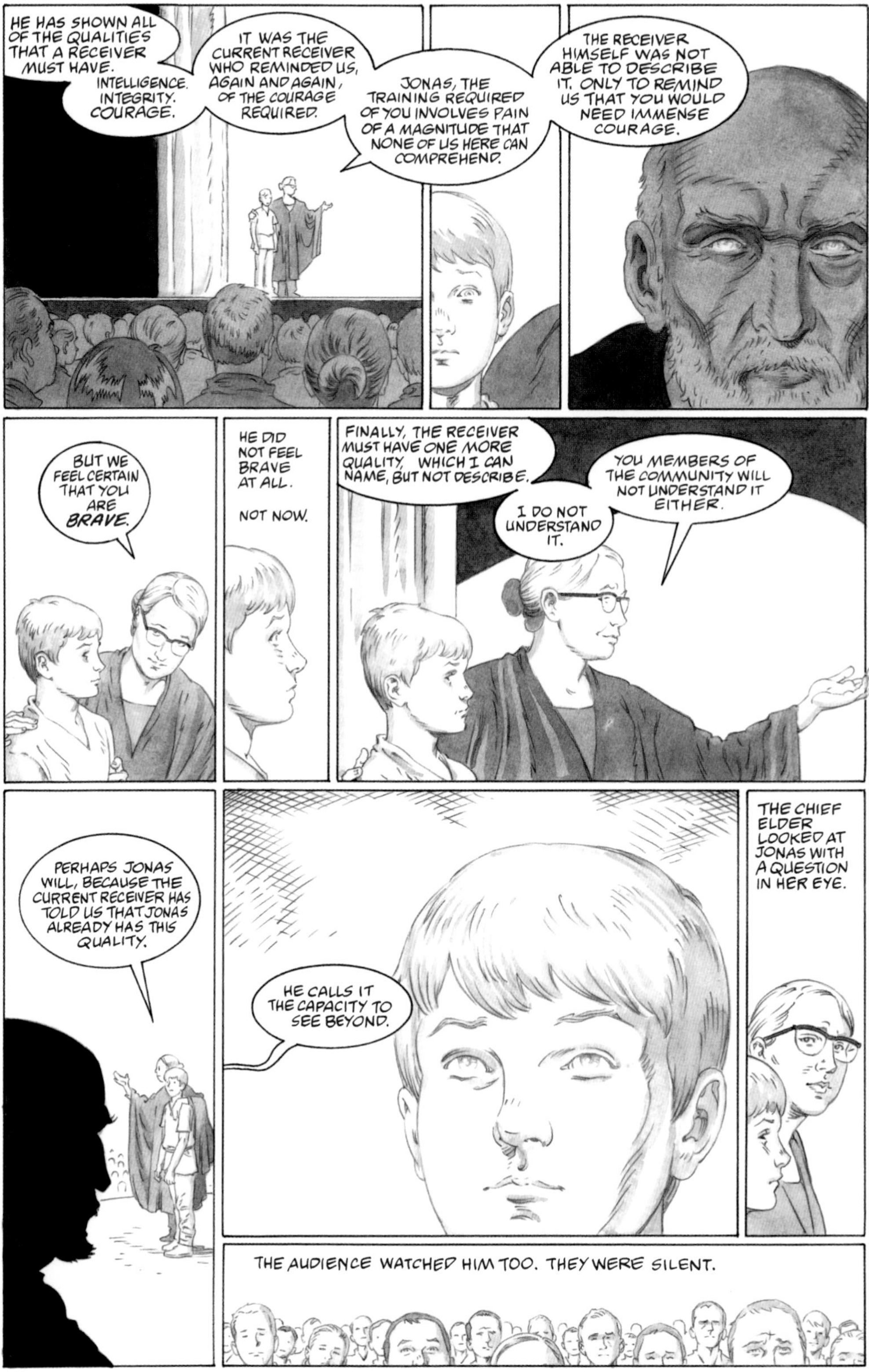
HE HAS SHOWN ALL OF THE QUALITIES THAT A RECEIVER MUST HAVE.
INTELLIGENCE. INTEGRITY. COURAGE.
IT WAS THE CURRENT RECEIVER WHO REMINDED US, AGAIN AND AGAIN, OF THE COURAGE REQUIRED.
JONAS, THE TRAINING REQUIRED OF YOU INVOLVES PAIN OF A MAGNITUDE THAT NONE OF US HERE CAN COMPREHEND.
THE RECEIVER HIMSELF WAS NOT ABLE TO DESCRIBE IT. ONLY TO REMIND US THAT YOU WOULD NEED IMMENSE COURAGE.
BUT WE FEEL CERTAIN THAT YOU ARE BRAVE.
HE DID NOT FEEL BRAVE AT ALL.
NOT NOW.
FINALLY, THE RECEIVER MUST HAVE ONE MORE QUALITY, WHICH I CAN NAME, BUT NOT DESCRIBE.
I DO NOT UNDERSTAND IT.
YOU MEMBERS OF THE COMMUNITY WILL NOT UNDERSTAND IT EITHER.
PERHAPS JONAS WILL, BECAUSE THE CURRENT RECEIVER HAS TOLD US THAT JONAS ALREADY HAS THIS QUALITY.
HE CALLS IT THE CAPACITY TO SEE BEYOND.
THE CHIEF ELDER LOOKED AT JONAS WITH A QUESTION IN HER EYE.
THE AUDIENCE WATCHED HIM TOO. THEY WERE SILENT.

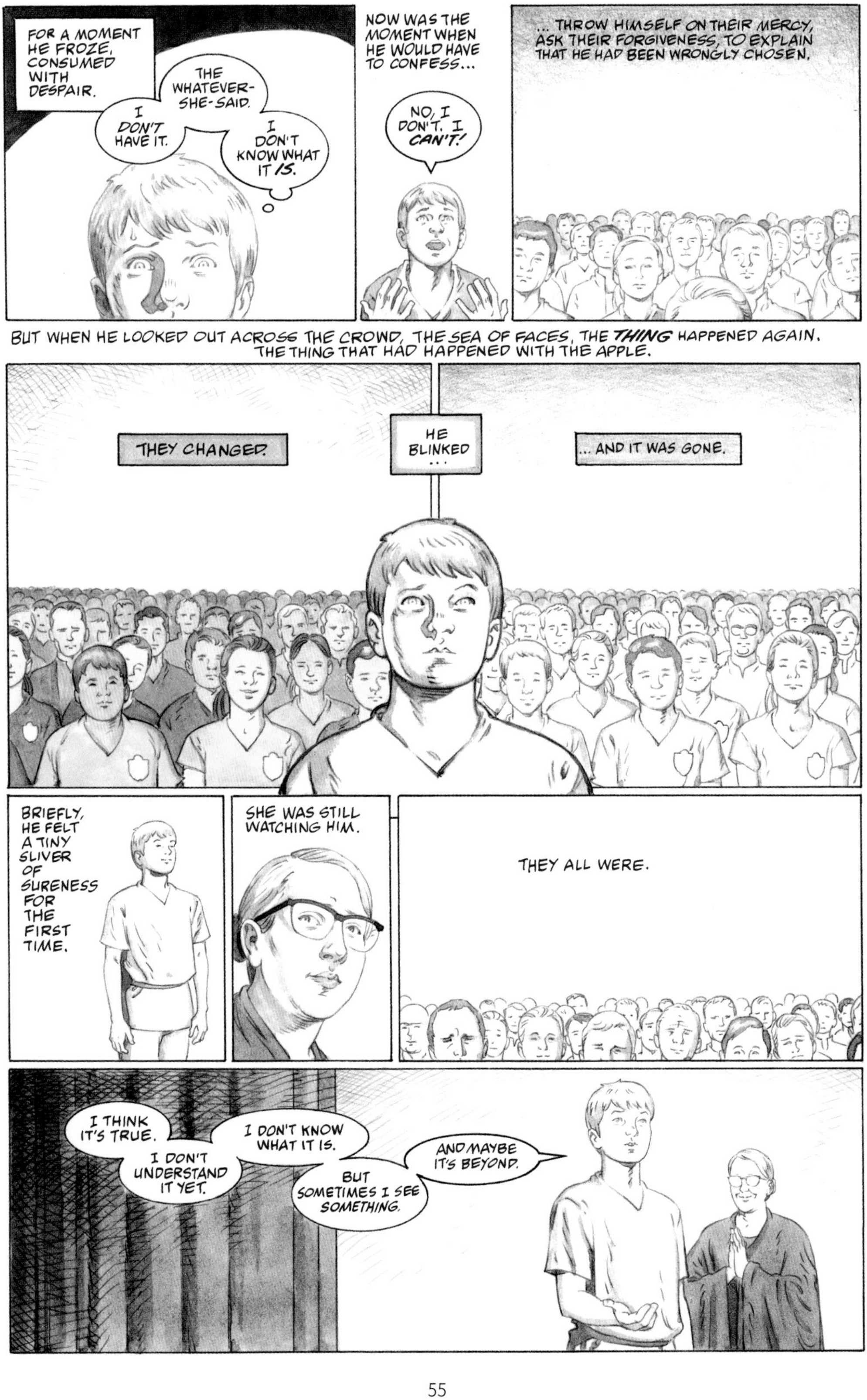

FOR A MOMENT HE FROZE, CONSUMED WITH DESPAIR.
THE WHATEVER-SHE-SAID.
I DON'T HAVE IT.
I DON'T KNOW WHAT IT IS.
NOW WAS THE MOMENT WHEN HE WOULD HAVE TO CONFESS...
NO, I DON'T. I CAN'T!
... THROW HIMSELF ON THEIR MERCY, ASK THEIR FORGIVENESS, TO EXPLAIN THAT HE HAD BEEN WRONGLY CHOSEN.
BUT WHEN HE LOOKED OUT ACROSS THE CROWD, THE SEA OF FACES, THE THING HAPPENED AGAIN. THE THING THAT HAD HAPPENED WITH THE APPLE.
THEY CHANGED.
HE BLINKED ...
... AND IT WAS GONE.
BRIEFLY, HE FELT A TINY SLIVER OF SURENESS FOR THE FIRST TIME.
SHE WAS STILL WATCHING HIM.
THEY ALL WERE.
I THINK IT'S TRUE.
I DON'T UNDERSTAND IT YET.
I DON'T KNOW WHAT IT IS.
BUT SOMETIMES I SEE SOMETHING.
AND MAYBE IT'S BEYOND.

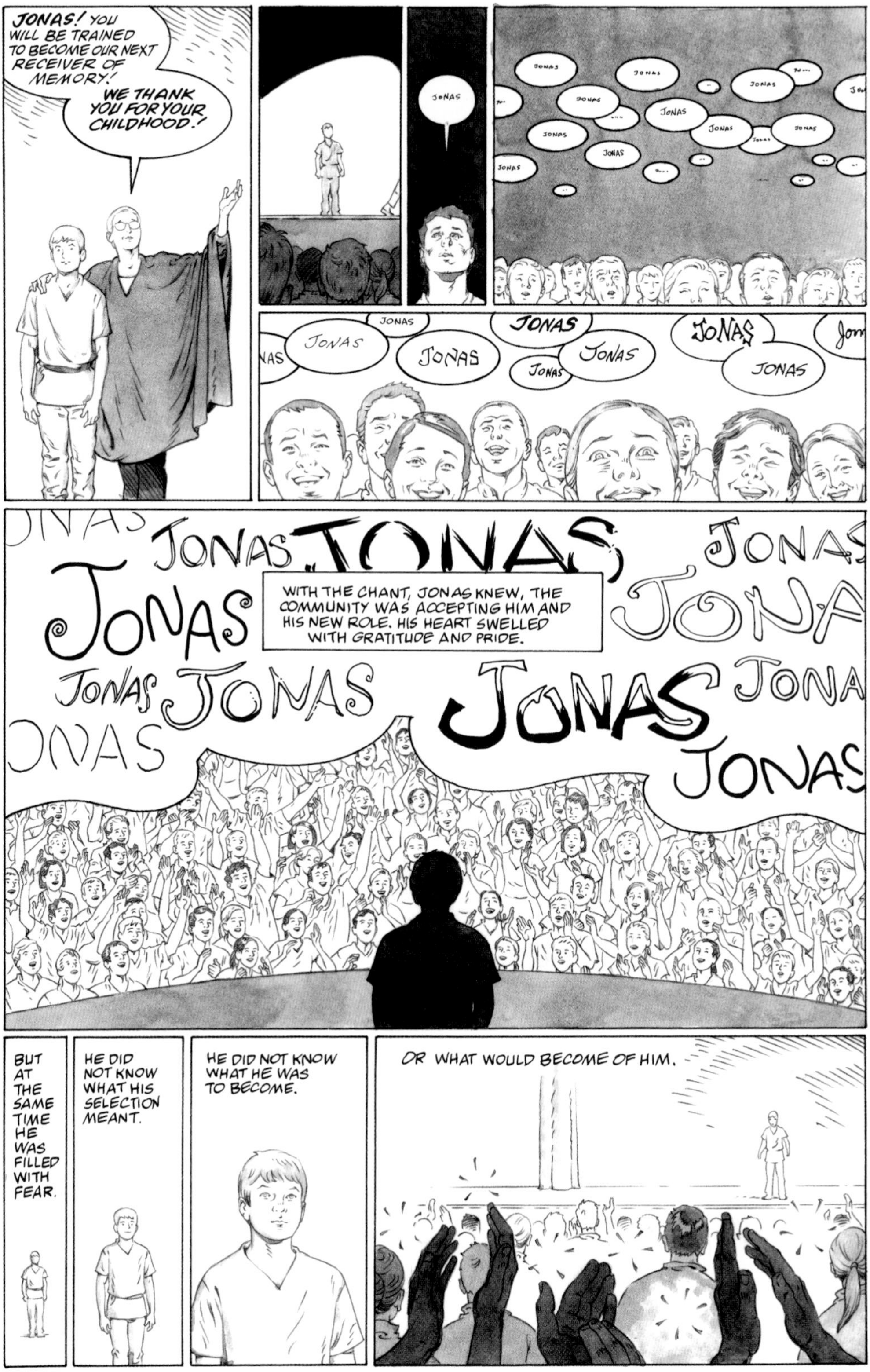
JONAS! YOU WILL BE TRAINED TO BECOME OUR NEXT RECEIVER OF MEMORY!
WE THANK YOU FOR YOUR CHILDHOOD!
JONAS
JONAS
JONAS
WITH THE CHANT, JONAS KNEW, THE COMMUNITY WAS ACCEPTING HIM AND HIS NEW ROLE. HIS HEART SWELLED WITH GRATITUDE AND PRIDE.
JONAS
BUT AT THE SAME TIME HE WAS FILLED WITH FEAR.
HE DID NOT KNOW WHAT HIS SELECTION MEANT.
HE DID NOT KNOW WHAT HE WAS TO BECOME.
OR WHAT WOULD BECOME OF HIM.

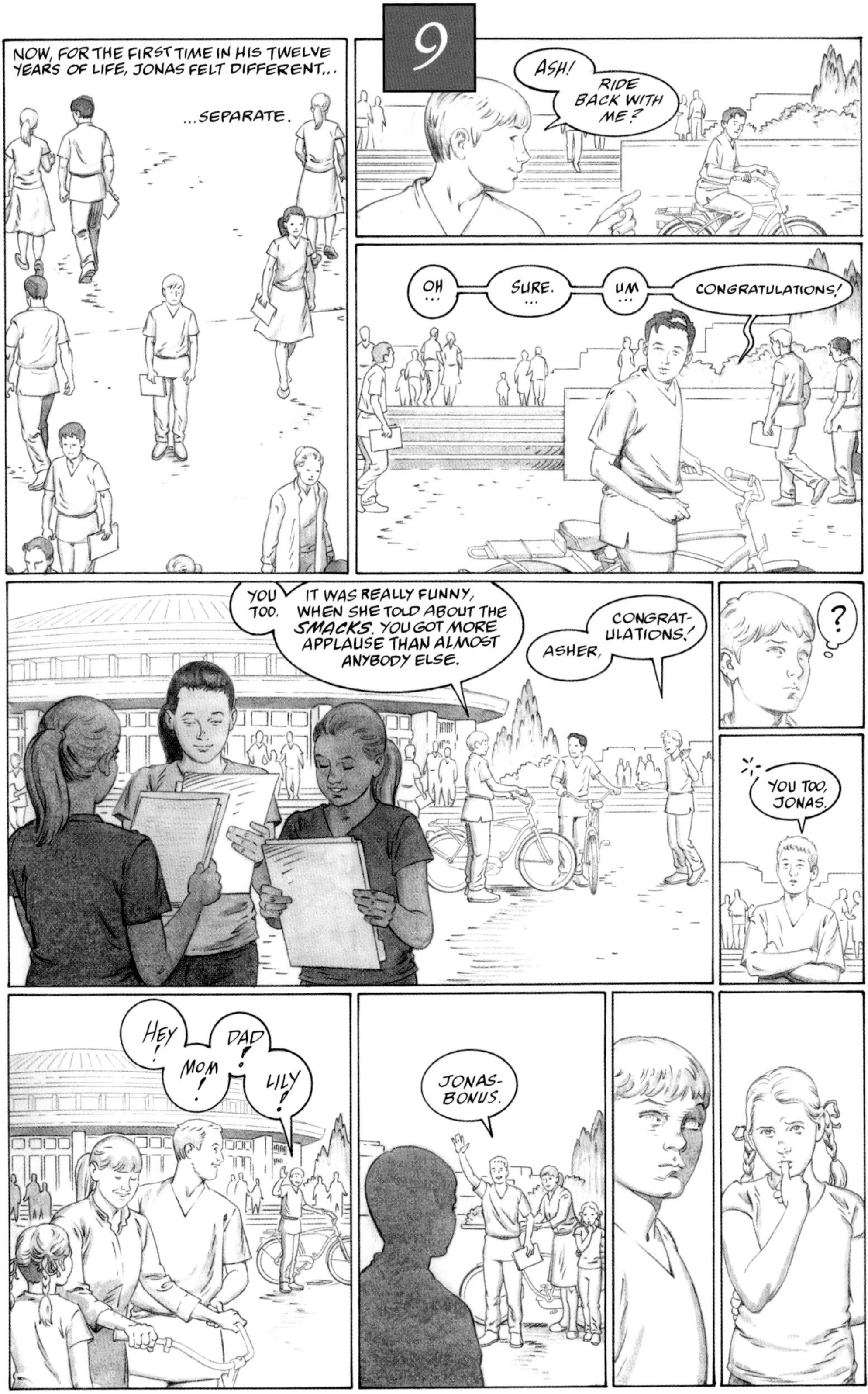
9
NOW, FOR THE FIRST TIME IN HIS TWELVE YEARS OF LIFE, JONAS FELT DIFFERENT...
...SEPARATE.
ASH!
RIDE BACK WITH ME?
OH...
SURE...
UM...
CONGRATULATIONS!
YOU TOO.
IT WAS REALLY FUNNY, WHEN SHE TOLD ABOUT THE SMACKS. YOU GOT MORE APPLAUSE THAN ALMOST ANYBODY ELSE.
ASHER,
CONGRATULATIONS!
?
YOU TOO, JONAS.
HEY!
MOM!
DAD!
LILY!
JONAS-BONUS.

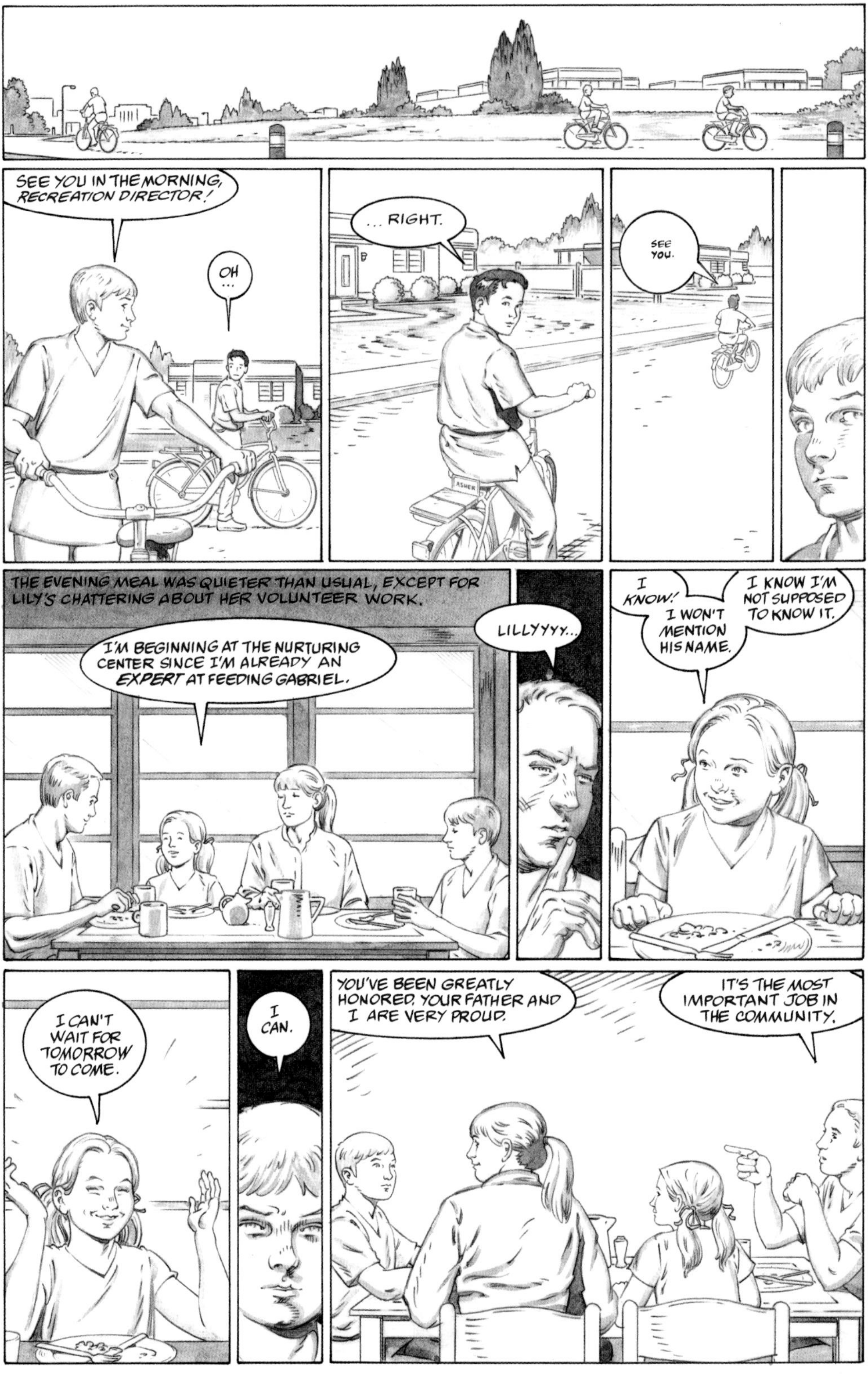
SEE YOU IN THE MORNING, RECREATION DIRECTOR!
OH ...
... RIGHT.
SEE YOU.
THE EVENING MEAL WAS QUIETER THAN USUAL, EXCEPT FOR LILY'S CHATTERING ABOUT HER VOLUNTEER WORK.
I'M BEGINNING AT THE NURTURING CENTER SINCE I'M ALREADY AN EXPERT AT FEEDING GABRIEL.
LILLYYYY...
I KNOW!
I WON'T MENTION HIS NAME.
I KNOW I'M NOT SUPPOSED TO KNOW IT.
I CAN'T WAIT FOR TOMORROW TO COME.
I CAN.
YOU'VE BEEN GREATLY HONORED. YOUR FATHER AND I ARE VERY PROUD.
IT'S THE MOST IMPORTANT JOB IN THE COMMUNITY.

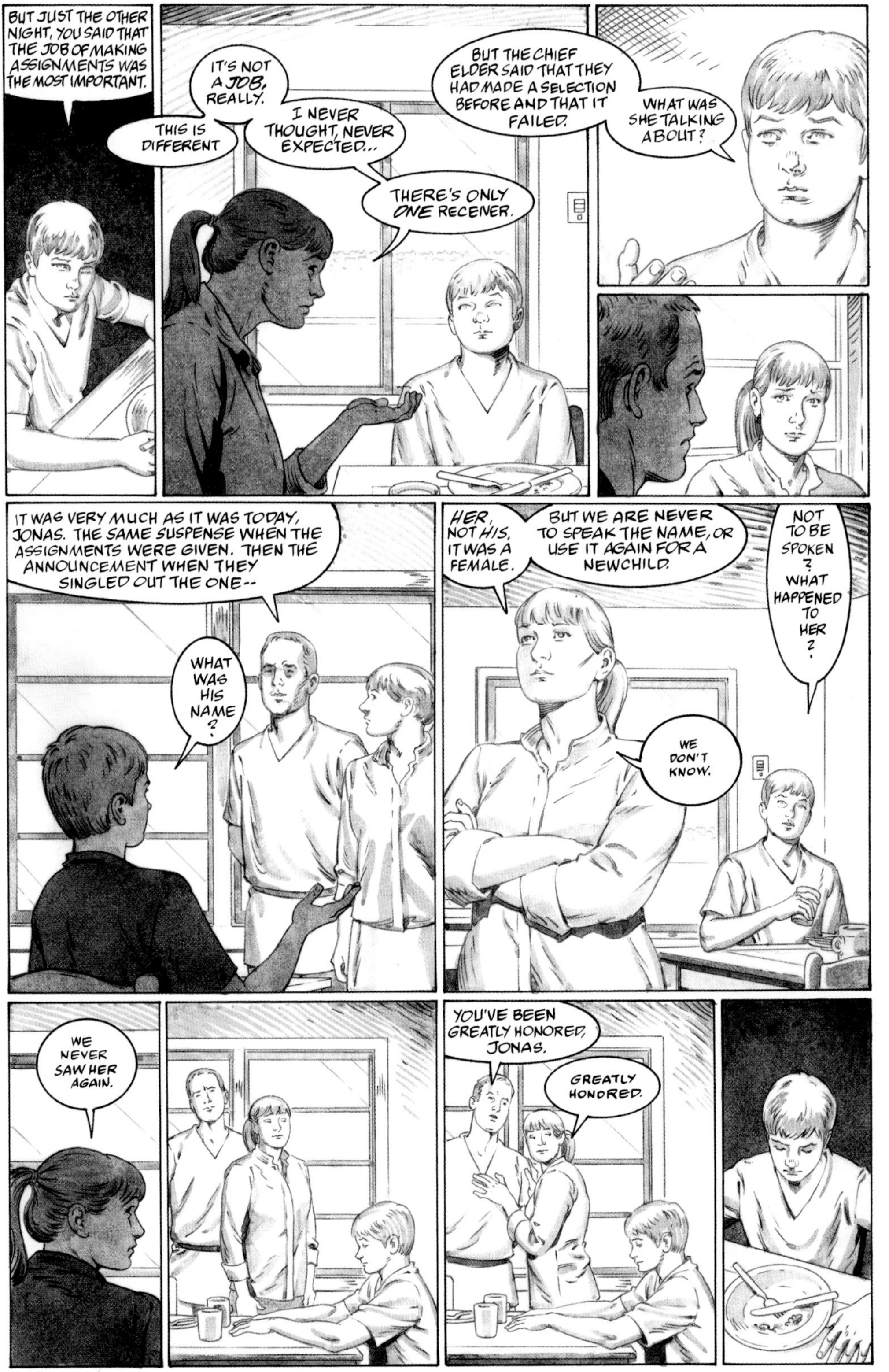
BUT JUST THE OTHER NIGHT, YOU SAID THAT THE JOB OF MAKING ASSIGNMENTS WAS THE MOST IMPORTANT.
IT'S NOT A JOB, REALLY.
THIS IS DIFFERENT
I NEVER THOUGHT, NEVER EXPECTED...
THERE'S ONLY ONE RECEIVER.
BUT THE CHIEF ELDER SAID THAT THEY HAD MADE A SELECTION BEFORE AND THAT IT FAILED.
WHAT WAS SHE TALKING ABOUT?
IT WAS VERY MUCH AS IT WAS TODAY, JONAS. THE SAME SUSPENSE WHEN THE ASSIGNMENTS WERE GIVEN. THEN THE ANNOUNCEMENT WHEN THEY SINGLED OUT THE ONE--
WHAT WAS HIS NAME?
HER, NOT HIS. IT WAS A FEMALE.
BUT WE ARE NEVER TO SPEAK THE NAME, OR USE IT AGAIN FOR A NEWCHILD.
NOT TO BE SPOKEN? WHAT HAPPENED TO HER?
WE DON'T KNOW.
WE NEVER SAW HER AGAIN.
YOU'VE BEEN GREATLY HONORED, JONAS.
GREATLY HONORED.

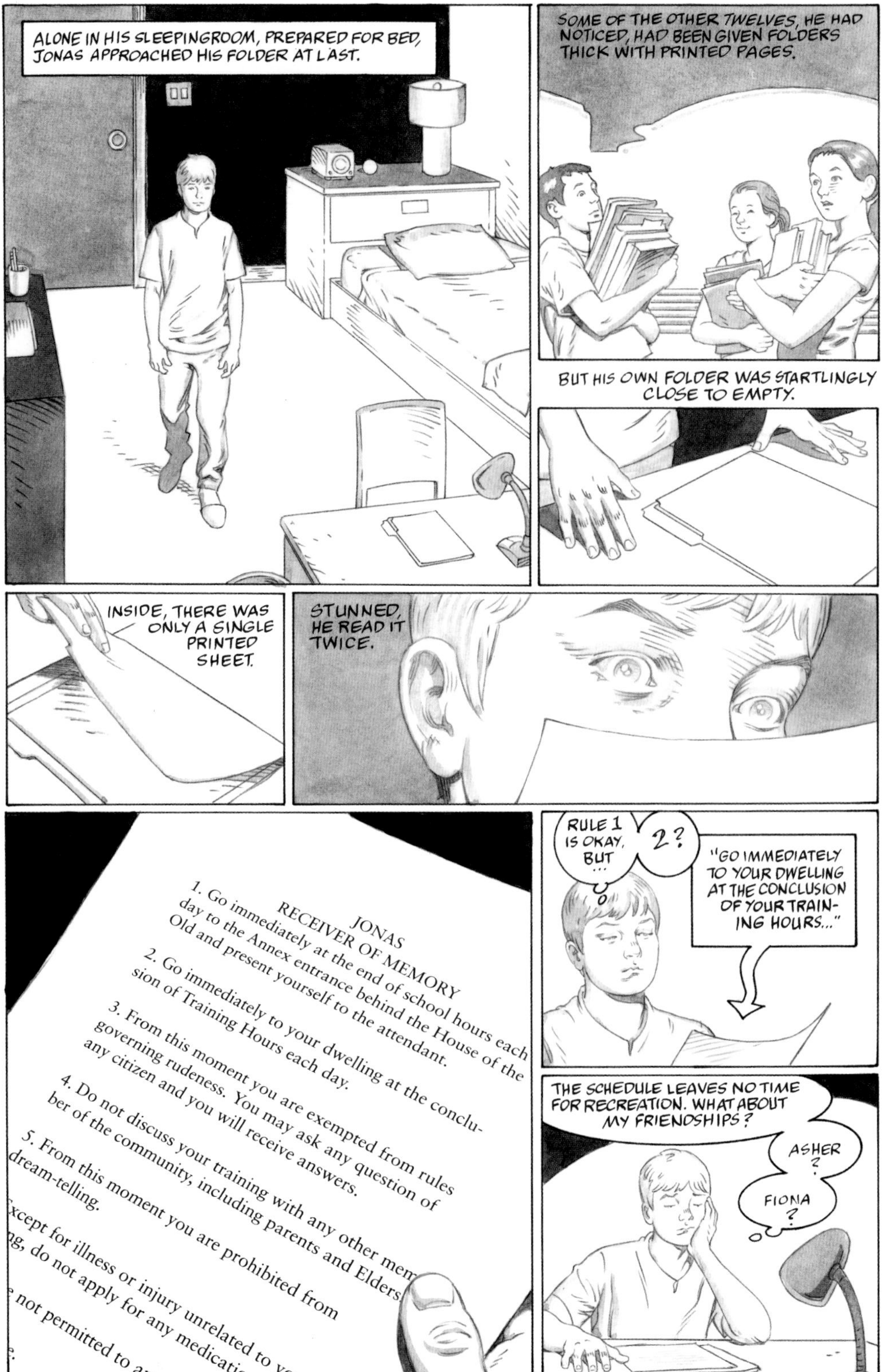
ALONE IN HIS SLEEPINGROOM, PREPARED FOR BED, JONAS APPROACHED HIS FOLDER AT LAST.
SOME OF THE OTHER TWELVES, HE HAD NOTICED, HAD BEEN GIVEN FOLDERS THICK WITH PRINTED PAGES.
BUT HIS OWN FOLDER WAS STARTLINGLY CLOSE TO EMPTY.
INSIDE, THERE WAS ONLY A SINGLE PRINTED SHEET.
STUNNED, HE READ IT TWICE.
JONAS
RECEIVER OF MEMORY
1. Go immediately at the end of school hours each day to the Annex entrance behind the House of the Old and present yourself to the attendant.
2. Go immediately to your dwelling at the conclusion of Training Hours each day.
3. From this moment you are exempted from rules governing rudeness. You may ask any question of any citizen and you will receive answers.
4. Do not discuss your training with any other mem ber of the community, including parents and Elders.
5. From this moment you are prohibited from dream-telling.
xcept for illness or injury unrelated to you g, do not apply for any medication
not permitted to app
RULE 1 IS OKAY, BUT ...
2?
"GO IMMEDIATELY TO YOUR DWELLING AT THE CONCLUSION OF YOUR TRAINING HOURS..."
THE SCHEDULE LEAVES NO TIME FOR RECREATION. WHAT ABOUT MY FRIENDSHIPS?
ASHER ?
FIONA ?

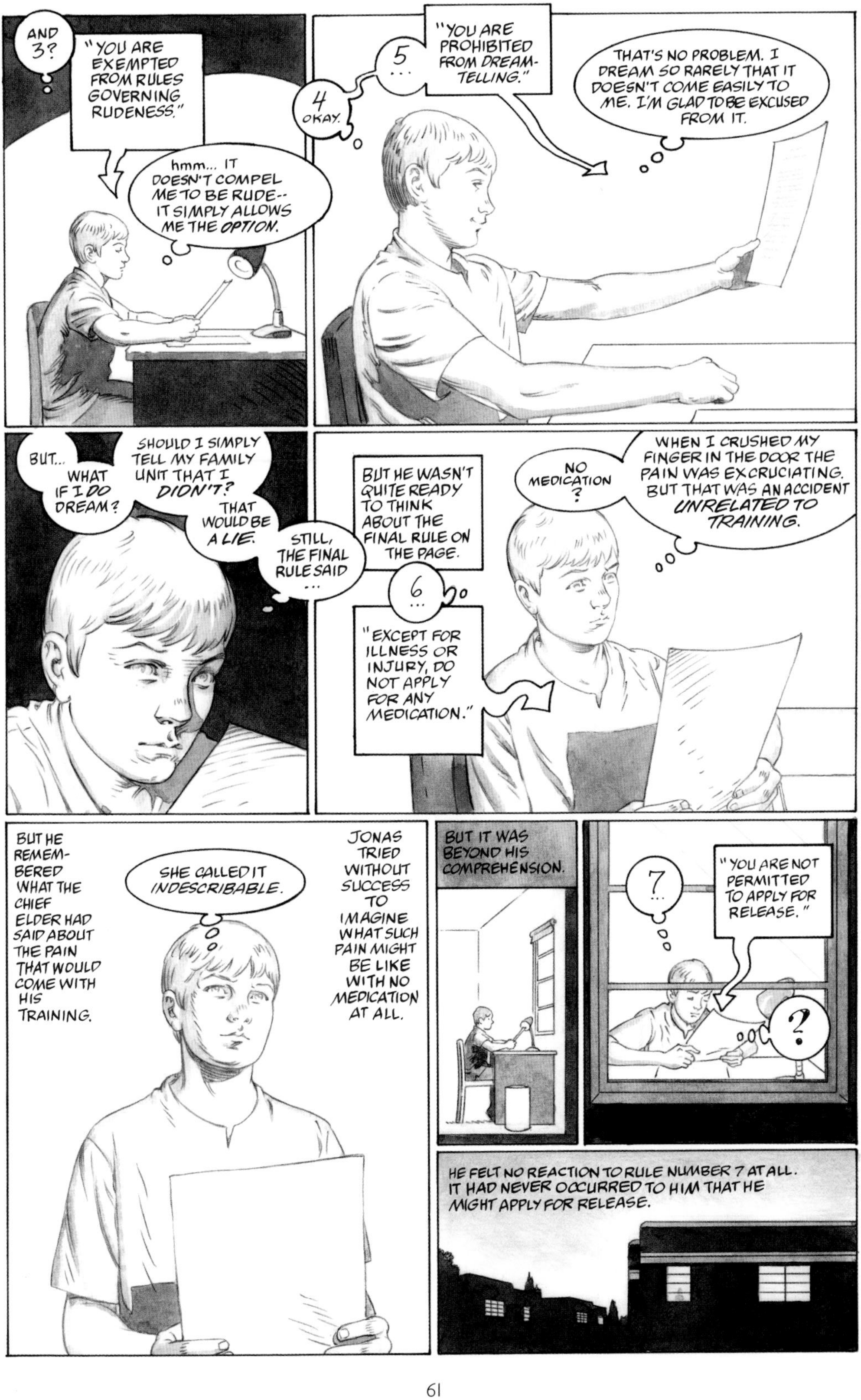
AND 3?
"YOU ARE EXEMPTED FROM RULES GOVERNING RUDENESS."
hmm... IT DOESN'T COMPEL ME TO BE RUDE-- IT SIMPLY ALLOWS ME THE OPTION.
4 OKAY.
5 ...
"YOU ARE PROHIBITED FROM DREAM-TELLING."
THAT'S NO PROBLEM. I DREAM SO RARELY THAT IT DOESN'T COME EASILY TO ME. I'M GLAD TO BE EXCUSED FROM IT.
BUT... WHAT IF I DO DREAM?
SHOULD I SIMPLY TELL MY FAMILY UNIT THAT I DIDN'T?
THAT WOULD BE A LIE.
STILL, THE FINAL RULE SAID ...
BUT HE WASN'T QUITE READY TO THINK ABOUT THE FINAL RULE ON THE PAGE.
6 ...
"EXCEPT FOR ILLNESS OR INJURY, DO NOT APPLY FOR ANY MEDICATION."
NO MEDICATION ?
WHEN I CRUSHED MY FINGER IN THE DOOR THE PAIN WAS EXCRUCIATING. BUT THAT WAS AN ACCIDENT UNRELATED TO TRAINING.
BUT HE REMEMBERED WHAT THE CHIEF ELDER HAD SAID ABOUT THE PAIN THAT WOULD COME WITH HIS TRAINING.
SHE CALLED IT INDESCRIBABLE.
JONAS TRIED WITHOUT SUCCESS TO IMAGINE WHAT SUCH PAIN MIGHT BE LIKE WITH NO MEDICATION AT ALL.
BUT IT WAS BEYOND HIS COMPREHENSION.
7 ...
"YOU ARE NOT PERMITTED TO APPLY FOR RELEASE."
?
HE FELT NO REACTION TO RULE NUMBER 7 AT ALL. IT HAD NEVER OCCURRED TO HIM THAT HE MIGHT APPLY FOR RELEASE.

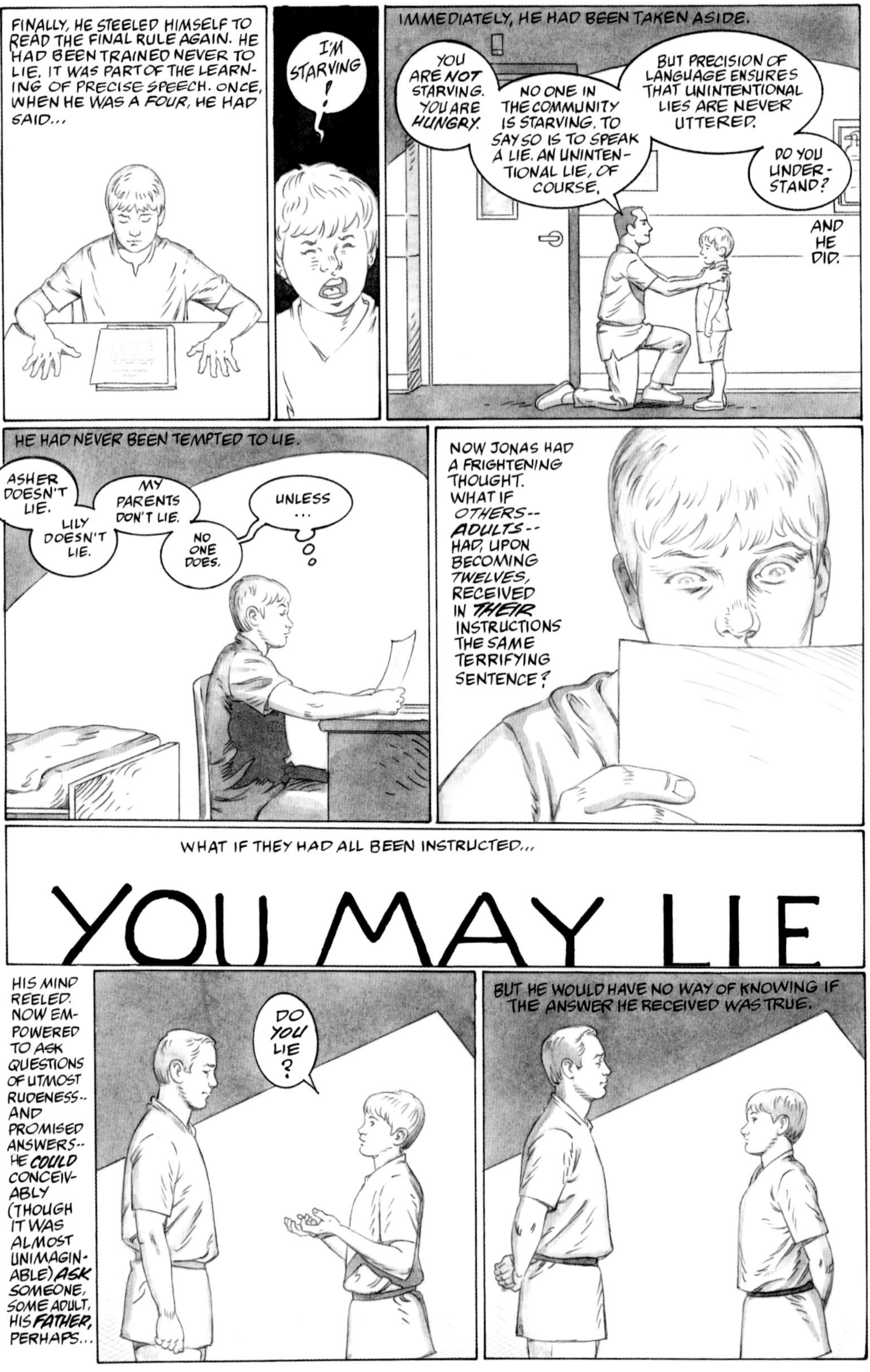
FINALLY, HE STEELED HIMSELF TO READ THE FINAL RULE AGAIN. HE HAD BEEN TRAINED NEVER TO LIE. IT WAS PART OF THE LEARNING OF PRECISE SPEECH. ONCE, WHEN HE WAS A FOUR, HE HAD SAID...
I'M STARVING!
IMMEDIATELY, HE HAD BEEN TAKEN ASIDE.
YOU ARE NOT STARVING. YOU ARE HUNGRY.
NO ONE IN THE COMMUNITY IS STARVING. TO SAY SO IS TO SPEAK A LIE. AN UNINTENTIONAL LIE, OF COURSE.
BUT PRECISION OF LANGUAGE ENSURES THAT UNINTENTIONAL LIES ARE NEVER UTTERED.
DO YOU UNDERSTAND?
AND HE DID.
HE HAD NEVER BEEN TEMPTED TO LIE.
ASHER DOESN'T LIE.
LILY DOESN'T LIE.
MY PARENTS DON'T LIE.
NO ONE DOES.
UNLESS ...
NOW JONAS HAD A FRIGHTENING THOUGHT. WHAT IF OTHERS-- ADULTS-- HAD, UPON BECOMING TWELVES, RECEIVED IN THEIR INSTRUCTIONS THE SAME TERRIFYING SENTENCE?
WHAT IF THEY HAD ALL BEEN INSTRUCTED...
YOU MAY LIE
HIS MIND REELED. NOW EMPOWERED TO ASK QUESTIONS OF UTMOST RUDENESS-- AND PROMISED ANSWERS-- HE COULD CONCEIVABLY (THOUGH IT WAS ALMOST UNIMAGINABLE) ASK SOMEONE, SOME ADULT, HIS FATHER, PERHAPS...
DO YOU LIE?
BUT HE WOULD HAVE NO WAY OF KNOWING IF THE ANSWER HE RECEIVED WAS TRUE.

10

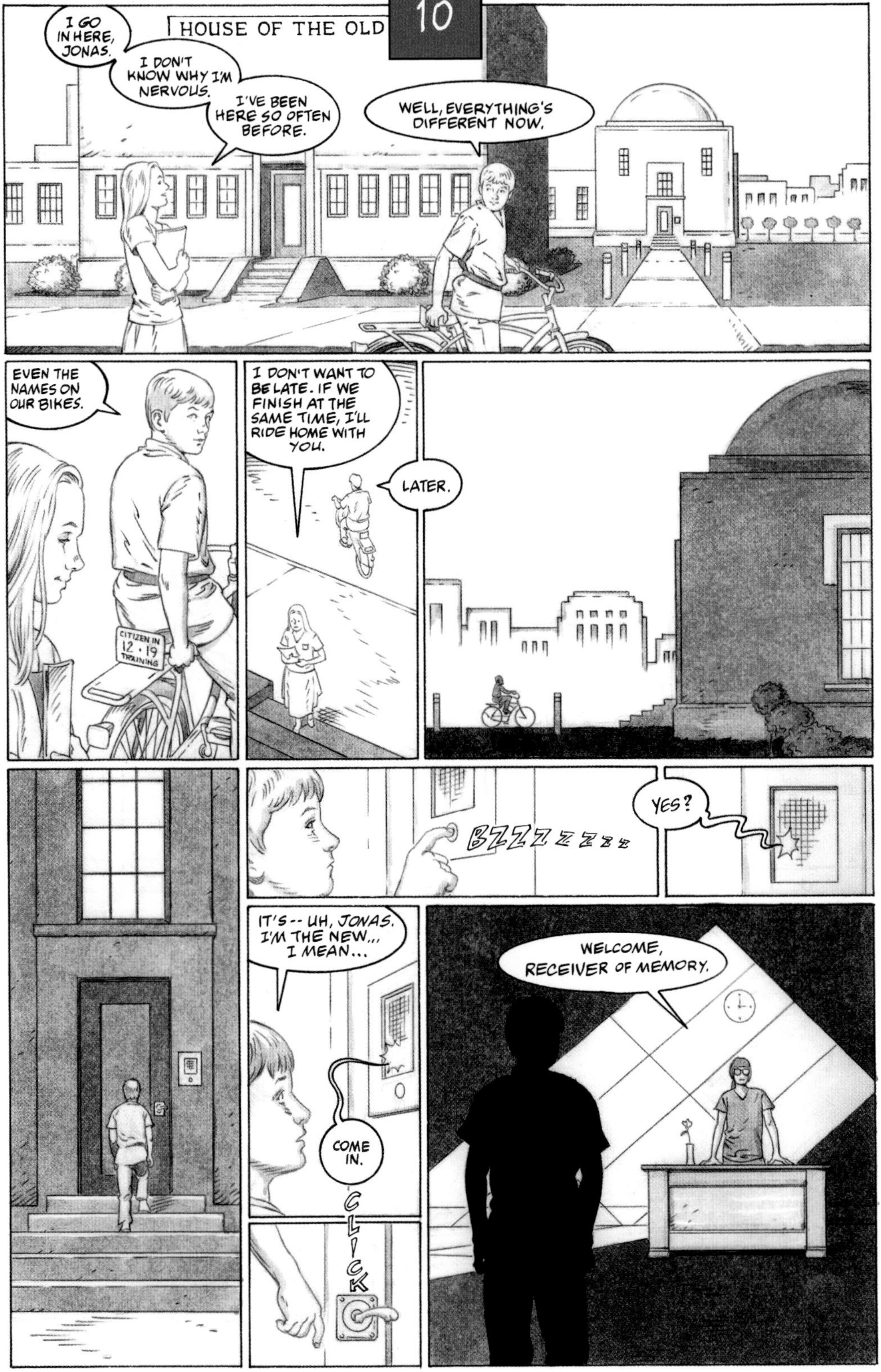
HOUSE OF THE OLD
I GO IN HERE, JONAS.
I DON'T KNOW WHY I'M NERVOUS.
I'VE BEEN HERE SO OFTEN BEFORE.
WELL, EVERYTHING'S DIFFERENT NOW.
EVEN THE NAMES ON OUR BIKES.
CITIZEN IN 12 · 19 TRAINING
I DON'T WANT TO BE LATE. IF WE FINISH AT THE SAME TIME, I'LL RIDE HOME WITH YOU.
LATER.
BZZZZZZZ
YES?
IT'S -- UH, JONAS. I'M THE NEW... I MEAN...
COME IN.
CLICK
WELCOME, RECEIVER OF MEMORY.

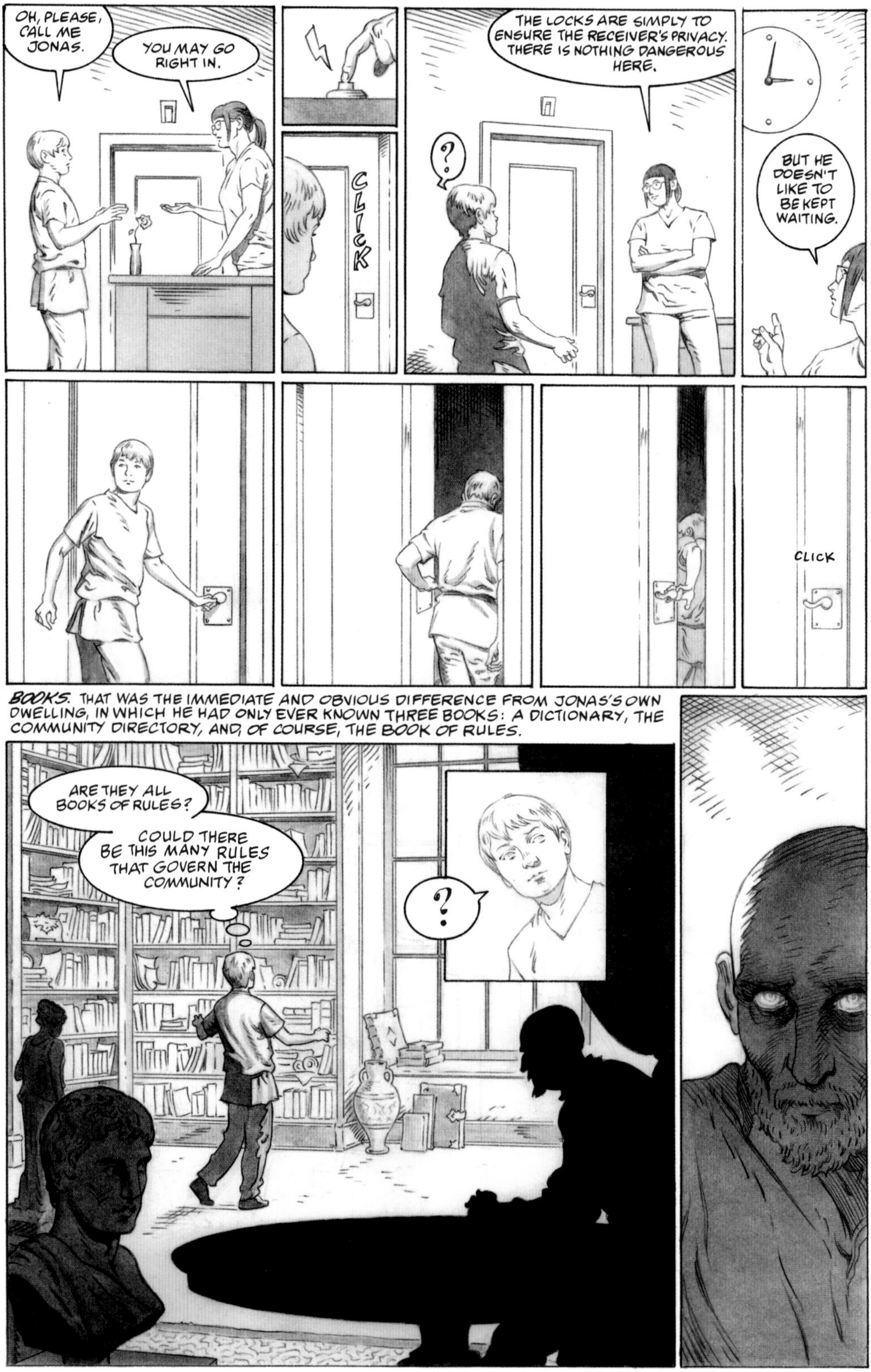
OH, PLEASE, CALL ME JONAS.
YOU MAY GO RIGHT IN.
CLICK
THE LOCKS ARE SIMPLY TO ENSURE THE RECEIVER'S PRIVACY. THERE IS NOTHING DANGEROUS HERE.
?
BUT HE DOESN'T LIKE TO BE KEPT WAITING.
CLICK
BOOKS. THAT WAS THE IMMEDIATE AND OBVIOUS DIFFERENCE FROM JONAS'S OWN DWELLING, IN WHICH HE HAD ONLY EVER KNOWN THREE BOOKS: A DICTIONARY, THE COMMUNITY DIRECTORY, AND, OF COURSE, THE BOOK OF RULES.
ARE THEY ALL BOOKS OF RULES?
COULD THERE BE THIS MANY RULES THAT GOVERN THE COMMUNITY?
?

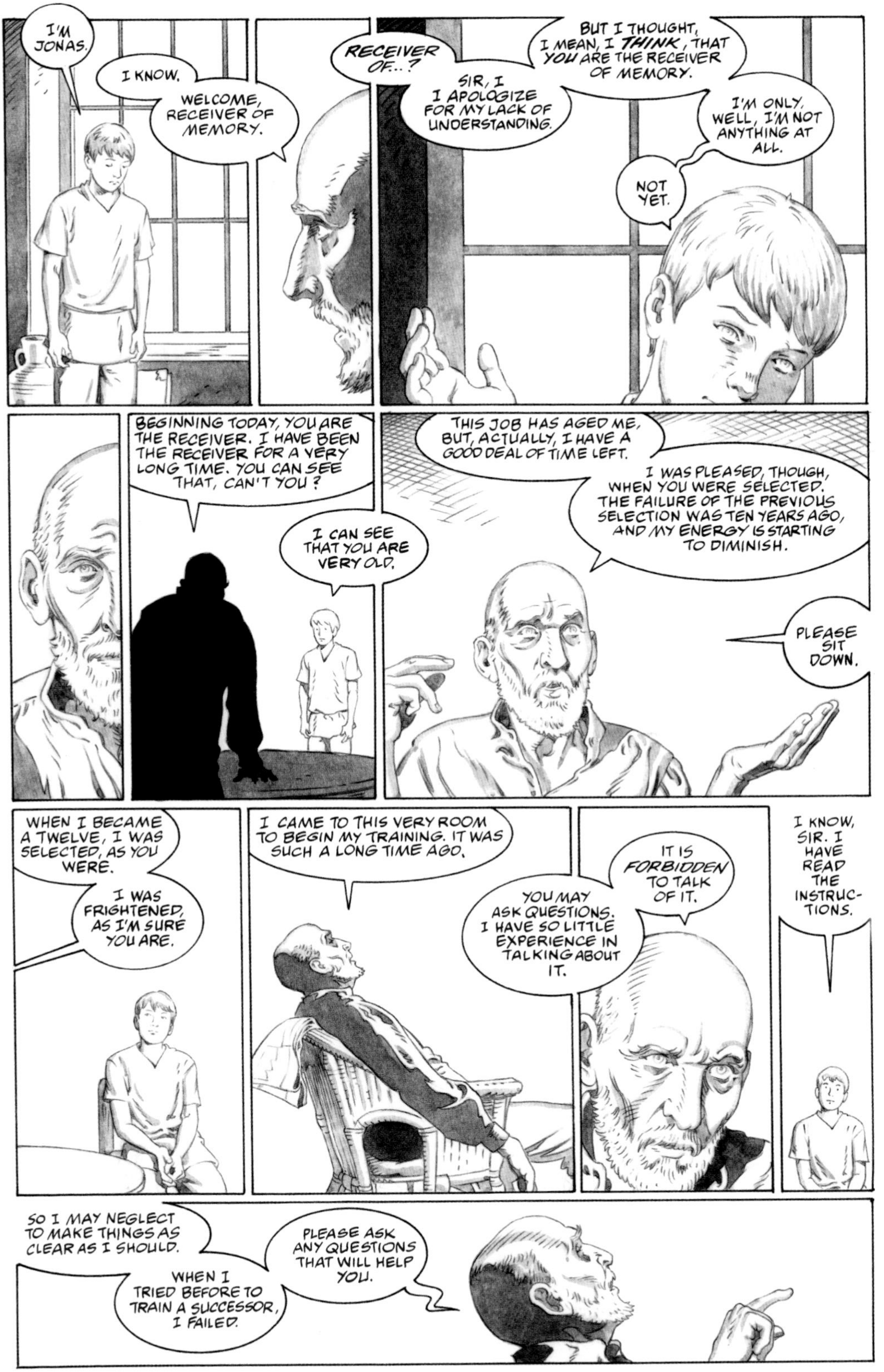
I'M JONAS.
I KNOW.
WELCOME, RECEIVER OF MEMORY.
RECEIVER OF...?
SIR, I I APOLOGIZE FOR MY LACK OF UNDERSTANDING.
BUT I THOUGHT, I MEAN, I THINK, THAT YOU ARE THE RECEIVER OF MEMORY.
I'M ONLY, WELL, I'M NOT ANYTHING AT ALL.
NOT YET.
BEGINNING TODAY, YOU ARE THE RECEIVER. I HAVE BEEN THE RECEIVER FOR A VERY LONG TIME. YOU CAN SEE THAT, CAN'T YOU?
I CAN SEE THAT YOU ARE VERY OLD.
THIS JOB HAS AGED ME, BUT, ACTUALLY, I HAVE A GOOD DEAL OF TIME LEFT.
I WAS PLEASED, THOUGH, WHEN YOU WERE SELECTED. THE FAILURE OF THE PREVIOUS SELECTION WAS TEN YEARS AGO, AND MY ENERGY IS STARTING TO DIMINISH.
PLEASE SIT DOWN.
WHEN I BECAME A TWELVE, I WAS SELECTED, AS YOU WERE.
I WAS FRIGHTENED, AS I'M SURE YOU ARE.
I CAME TO THIS VERY ROOM TO BEGIN MY TRAINING. IT WAS SUCH A LONG TIME AGO.
YOU MAY ASK QUESTIONS. I HAVE SO LITTLE EXPERIENCE IN TALKING ABOUT IT.
IT IS FORBIDDEN TO TALK OF IT.
I KNOW, SIR. I HAVE READ THE INSTRUC-TIONS.
SO I MAY NEGLECT TO MAKE THINGS AS CLEAR AS I SHOULD.
WHEN I TRIED BEFORE TO TRAIN A SUCCESSOR, I FAILED.
PLEASE ASK ANY QUESTIONS THAT WILL HELP YOU.

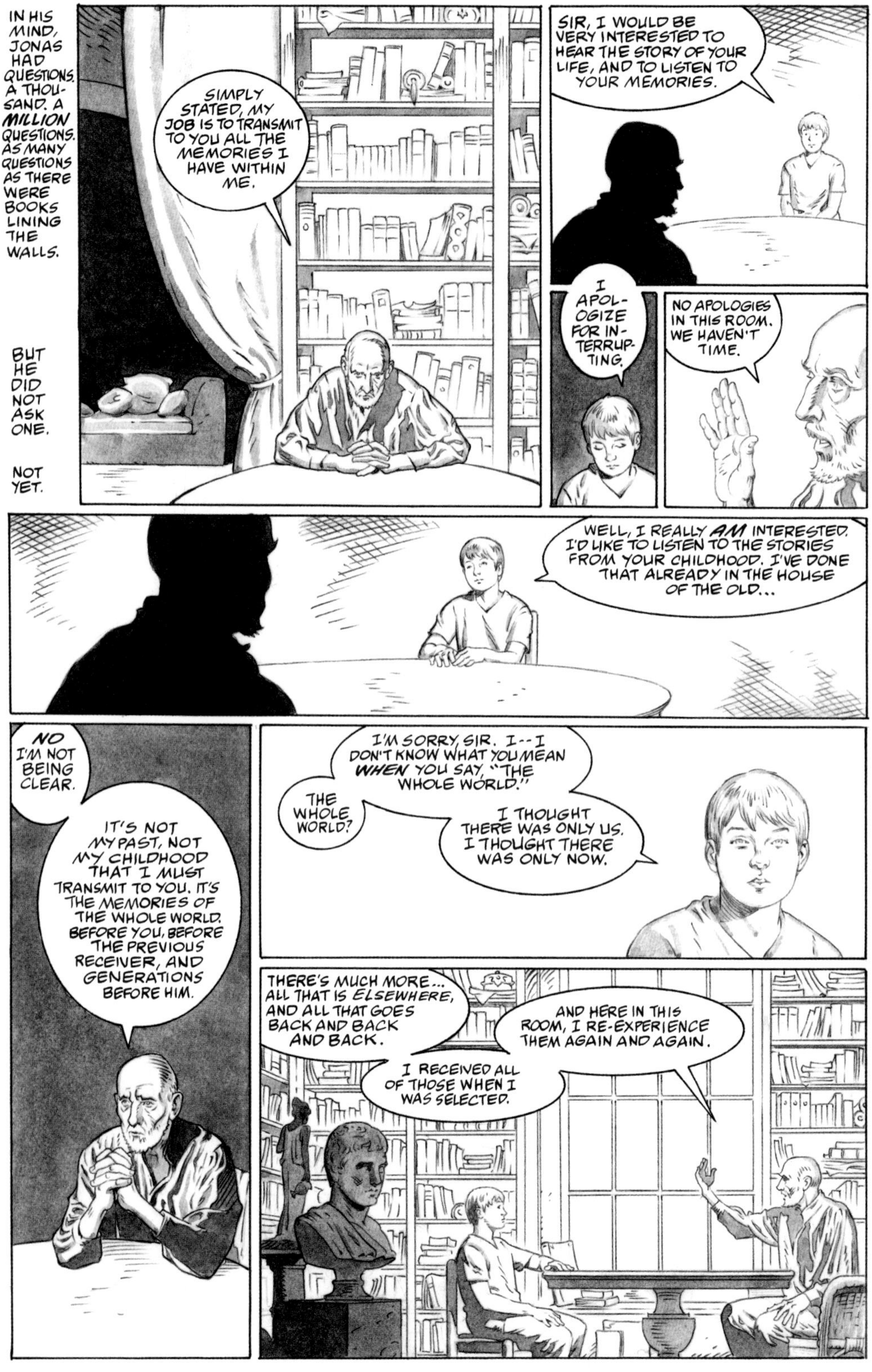
IN HIS MIND, JONAS HAD QUESTIONS. A THOUSAND. A MILLION QUESTIONS. AS MANY QUESTIONS AS THERE WERE BOOKS LINING THE WALLS.
SIMPLY STATED, MY JOB IS TO TRANSMIT TO YOU ALL THE MEMORIES I HAVE WITHIN ME.
BUT HE DID NOT ASK ONE.
NOT YET.
SIR, I WOULD BE VERY INTERESTED TO HEAR THE STORY OF YOUR LIFE, AND TO LISTEN TO YOUR MEMORIES.
I APOLOGIZE FOR INTERRUPTING.
NO APOLOGIES IN THIS ROOM. WE HAVEN'T TIME.
WELL, I REALLY AM INTERESTED. I'D LIKE TO LISTEN TO THE STORIES FROM YOUR CHILDHOOD. I'VE DONE THAT ALREADY IN THE HOUSE OF THE OLD...
NO I'M NOT BEING CLEAR.
IT'S NOT MY PAST, NOT MY CHILDHOOD THAT I MUST TRANSMIT TO YOU. IT'S THE MEMORIES OF THE WHOLE WORLD. BEFORE YOU, BEFORE THE PREVIOUS RECEIVER, AND GENERATIONS BEFORE HIM.
I'M SORRY, SIR. I--I DON'T KNOW WHAT YOU MEAN WHEN YOU SAY, "THE WHOLE WORLD."
THE WHOLE WORLD?
I THOUGHT THERE WAS ONLY US. I THOUGHT THERE WAS ONLY NOW.
THERE'S MUCH MORE... ALL THAT IS ELSEWHERE, AND ALL THAT GOES BACK AND BACK AND BACK.
I RECEIVED ALL OF THOSE WHEN I WAS SELECTED.
AND HERE IN THIS ROOM, I RE-EXPERIENCE THEM AGAIN AND AGAIN.

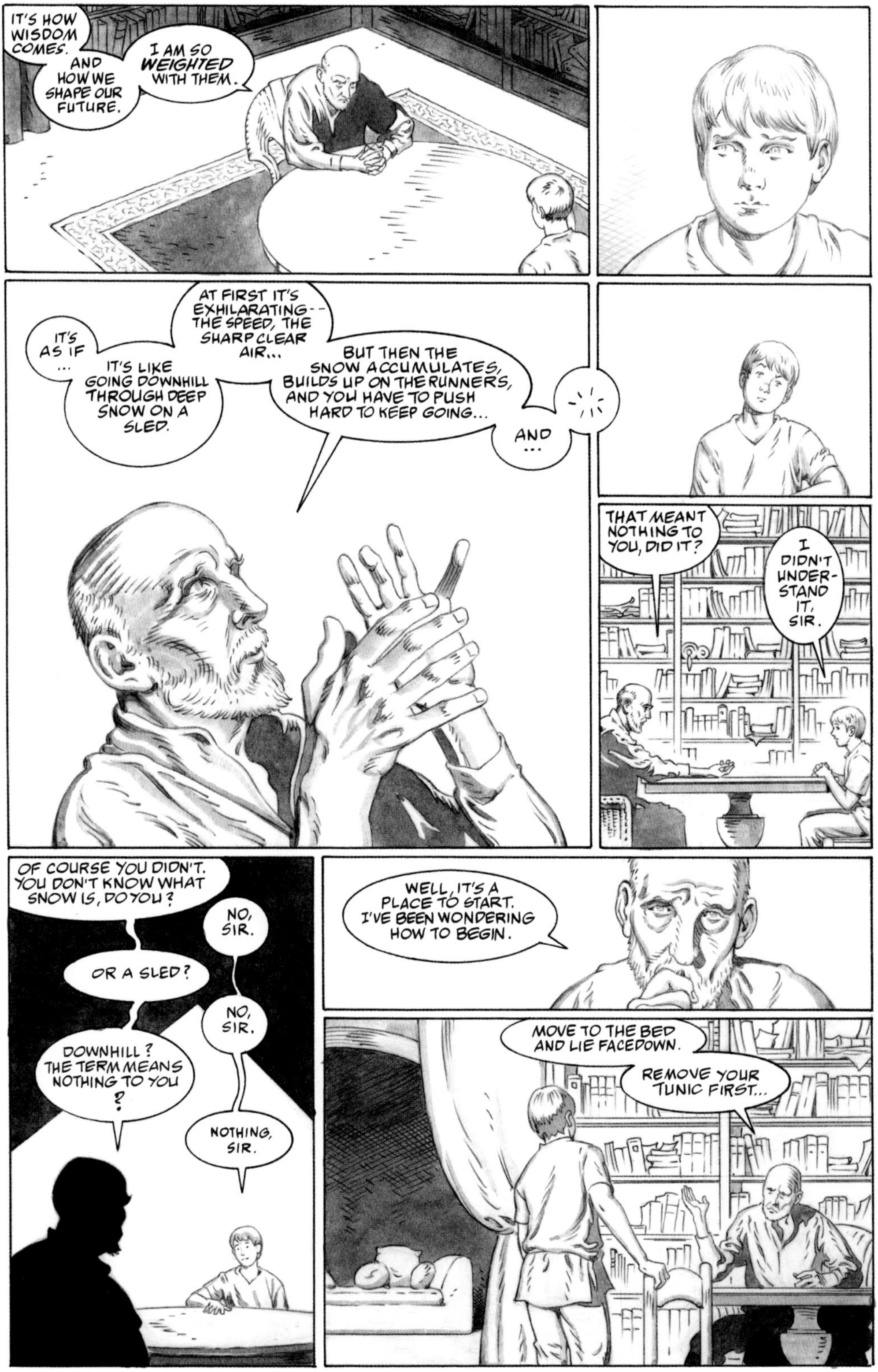
IT'S HOW WISDOM COMES.
AND HOW WE SHAPE OUR FUTURE.
I AM SO WEIGHTED WITH THEM.
IT'S AS IF ...
IT'S LIKE GOING DOWNHILL THROUGH DEEP SNOW ON A SLED.
AT FIRST IT'S EXHILARATING-- THE SPEED, THE SHARP CLEAR AIR...
BUT THEN THE SNOW ACCUMULATES, BUILDS UP ON THE RUNNERS, AND YOU HAVE TO PUSH HARD TO KEEP GOING...
AND ...
THAT MEANT NOTHING TO YOU, DID IT?
I DIDN'T UNDERSTAND IT, SIR.
OF COURSE YOU DIDN'T. YOU DON'T KNOW WHAT SNOW IS, DO YOU?
NO, SIR.
OR A SLED?
NO, SIR.
DOWNHILL? THE TERM MEANS NOTHING TO YOU ?
NOTHING, SIR.
WELL, IT'S A PLACE TO START. I'VE BEEN WONDERING HOW TO BEGIN.
MOVE TO THE BED AND LIE FACEDOWN.
REMOVE YOUR TUNIC FIRST...

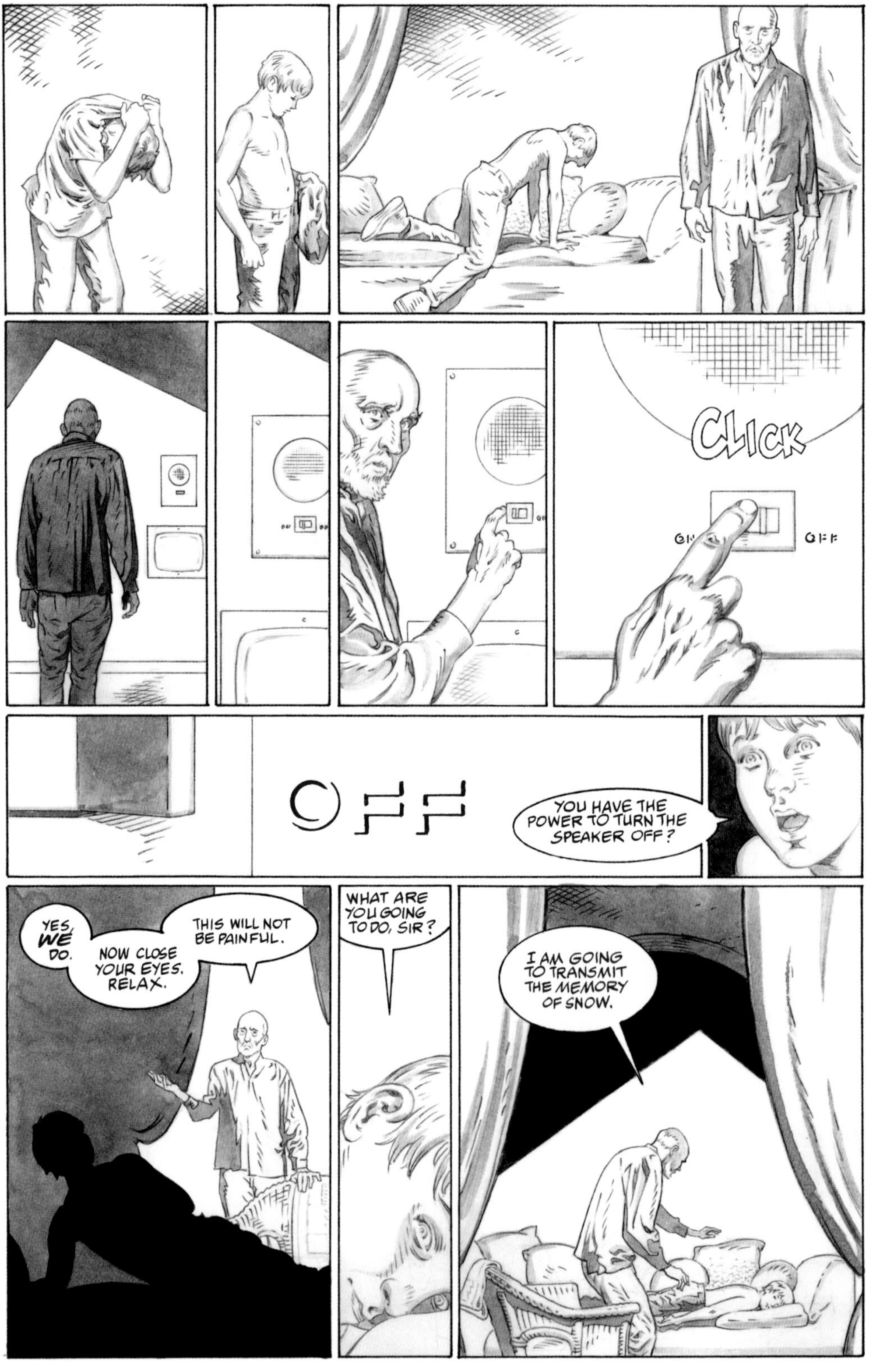
CLICK
ON
OFF
OFF
YOU HAVE THE POWER TO TURN THE SPEAKER OFF?
YES, WE DO.
NOW CLOSE YOUR EYES. RELAX.
THIS WILL NOT BE PAINFUL.
WHAT ARE YOU GOING TO DO, SIR?
I AM GOING TO TRANSMIT THE MEMORY OF SNOW.

11

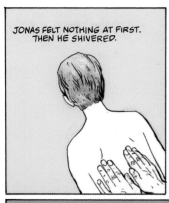

JONAS FELT NOTHING AT FIRST. THEN HE SHIVERED.

THE TOUCH OF THE OLD MAN'S HANDS FELT, SUDDENLY, COLD.

AT THE SAME INSTANT, BREATHING IN, HE FELT THE AIR CHANGE, AND HIS VERY BREATH WAS COLD.

TINY, COLD, FEATHERLIKE FEELINGS PEPPERED HIS BODY AND FACE. HE PUT OUT HIS TONGUE.

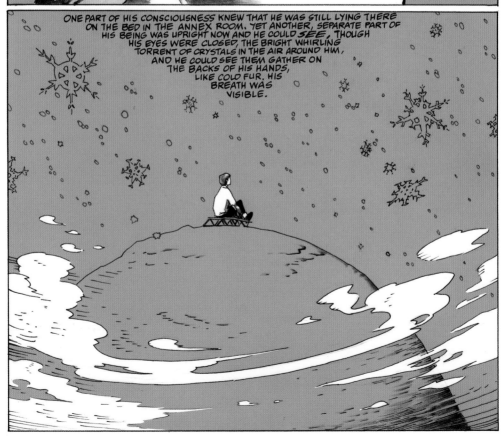

ONE PART OF HIS CONSCIOUSNESS KNEW THAT HE WAS STILL LYING THERE ON THE BED IN THE ANNEX ROOM. YET ANOTHER, SEPARATE PART OF HIS BEING WAS UPRIGHT NOW AND HE COULD *SEE*, THOUGH HIS EYES WERE CLOSED, THE BRIGHT WHIRLING TORRENT OF CRYSTALS IN THE AIR AROUND HIM, AND HE COULD SEE THEM GATHER ON THE BACKS OF HIS HANDS, LIKE COLD FUR. HIS BREATH WAS VISIBLE.

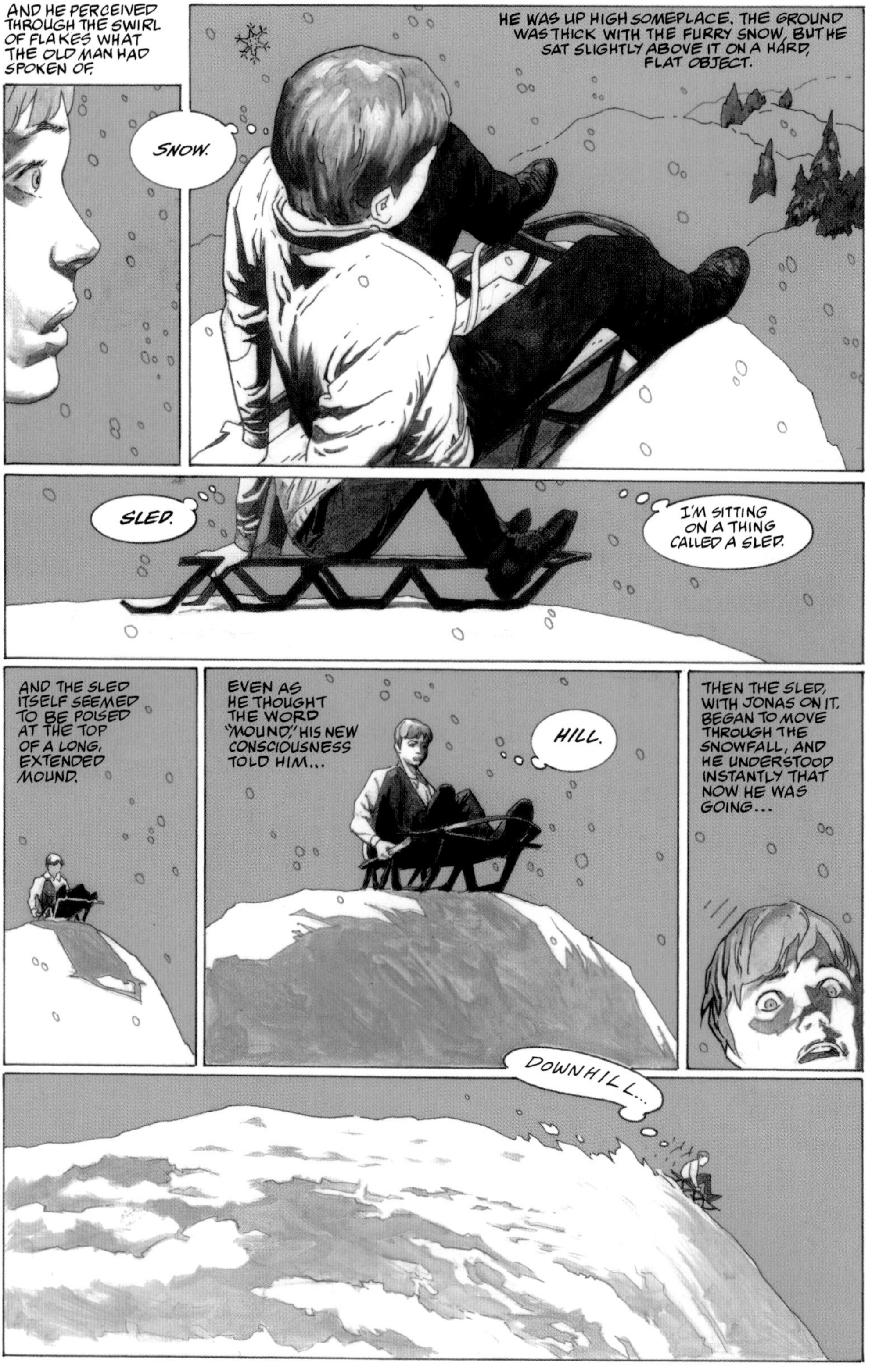
AND HE PERCEIVED THROUGH THE SWIRL OF FLAKES WHAT THE OLD MAN HAD SPOKEN OF.
HE WAS UP HIGH SOMEPLACE. THE GROUND WAS THICK WITH THE FURRY SNOW, BUT HE SAT SLIGHTLY ABOVE IT ON A HARD, FLAT OBJECT.
SNOW.
SLED.
I'M SITTING ON A THING CALLED A SLED.
AND THE SLED ITSELF SEEMED TO BE POISED AT THE TOP OF A LONG, EXTENDED MOUND.
EVEN AS HE THOUGHT THE WORD "MOUND," HIS NEW CONSCIOUSNESS TOLD HIM...
HILL.
THEN THE SLED, WITH JONAS ON IT, BEGAN TO MOVE THROUGH THE SNOWFALL, AND HE UNDERSTOOD INSTANTLY THAT NOW HE WAS GOING...
DOWNHILL...

A BREATHLESS GLEE OVERWHELMED HIM: THE SPEED, THE CLEAR COLD AIR, THE FEELING OF BALANCE AND EXCITEMENT AND PEACE.

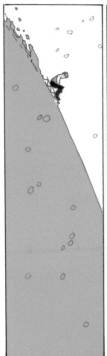 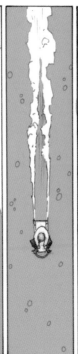 

THEN, AS THE ANGLE OF INCLINE LESSENED AS THE MOUND, THE *HILL*... FLATTENED, THE SLED'S FORWARD MOTION SLOWED.

THE OBSTRUCTION OF THE PILED SNOW WAS TOO MUCH FOR THE THIN RUNNERS OF THE SLED, AND HE CAME TO A S T O P.

A-HHH
A-HHH
A-HHH

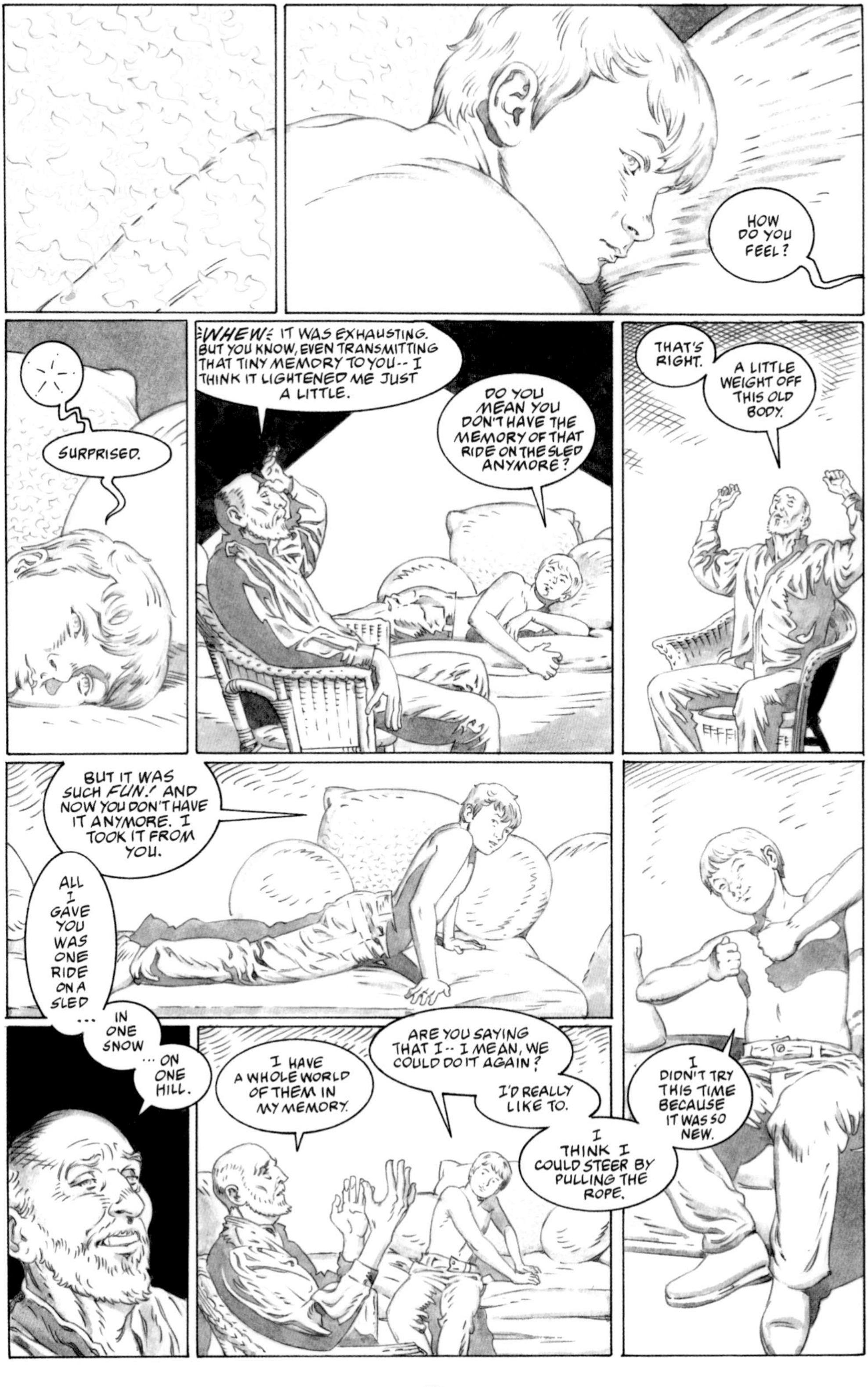
HOW DO YOU FEEL?
SURPRISED.
WHEW! IT WAS EXHAUSTING. BUT YOU KNOW, EVEN TRANSMITTING THAT TINY MEMORY TO YOU-- I THINK IT LIGHTENED ME JUST A LITTLE.
DO YOU MEAN YOU DON'T HAVE THE MEMORY OF THAT RIDE ON THE SLED ANYMORE?
THAT'S RIGHT.
A LITTLE WEIGHT OFF THIS OLD BODY.
BUT IT WAS SUCH FUN! AND NOW YOU DON'T HAVE IT ANYMORE. I TOOK IT FROM YOU.
ALL I GAVE YOU WAS ONE RIDE ON A SLED
... IN ONE SNOW
... ON ONE HILL.
I HAVE A WHOLE WORLD OF THEM IN MY MEMORY.
ARE YOU SAYING THAT I-- I MEAN, WE COULD DO IT AGAIN?
I'D REALLY LIKE TO.
I DIDN'T TRY THIS TIME BECAUSE IT WAS SO NEW.
I THINK I COULD STEER BY PULLING THE ROPE.

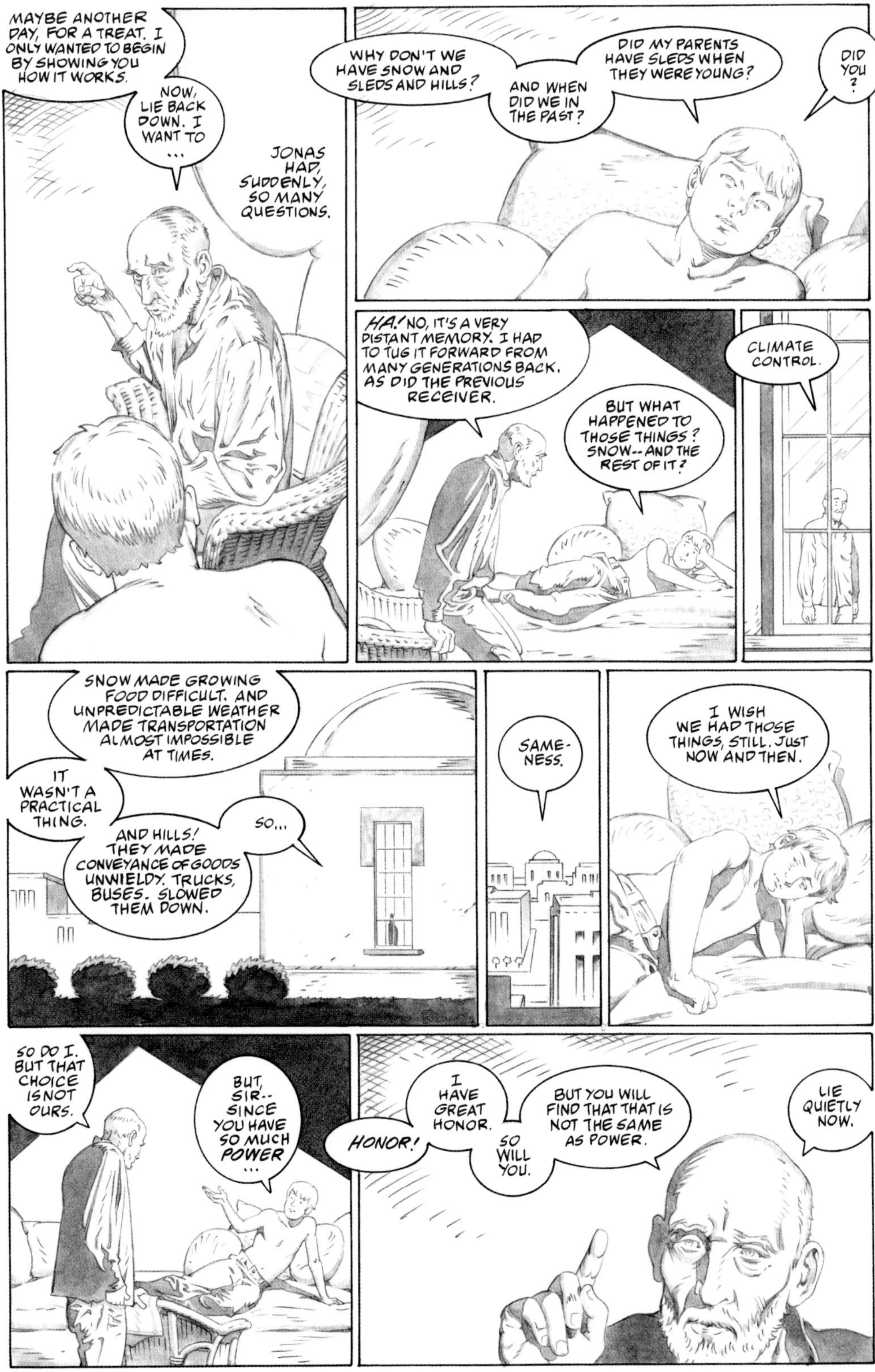
MAYBE ANOTHER DAY, FOR A TREAT. I ONLY WANTED TO BEGIN BY SHOWING YOU HOW IT WORKS.
NOW, LIE BACK DOWN. I WANT TO ...
JONAS HAD, SUDDENLY, SO MANY QUESTIONS.
WHY DON'T WE HAVE SNOW AND SLEDS AND HILLS?
AND WHEN DID WE IN THE PAST?
DID MY PARENTS HAVE SLEDS WHEN THEY WERE YOUNG?
DID YOU?
HA! NO, IT'S A VERY DISTANT MEMORY. I HAD TO TUG IT FORWARD FROM MANY GENERATIONS BACK. AS DID THE PREVIOUS RECEIVER.
BUT WHAT HAPPENED TO THOSE THINGS? SNOW-- AND THE REST OF IT?
CLIMATE CONTROL.
SNOW MADE GROWING FOOD DIFFICULT. AND UNPREDICTABLE WEATHER MADE TRANSPORTATION ALMOST IMPOSSIBLE AT TIMES.
IT WASN'T A PRACTICAL THING.
AND HILLS! THEY MADE CONVEYANCE OF GOODS UNWIELDY. TRUCKS, BUSES. SLOWED THEM DOWN.
SO...
SAME-NESS.
I WISH WE HAD THOSE THINGS, STILL. JUST NOW AND THEN.
SO DO I. BUT THAT CHOICE IS NOT OURS.
BUT, SIR-- SINCE YOU HAVE SO MUCH POWER ...
HONOR!
I HAVE GREAT HONOR.
SO WILL YOU.
BUT YOU WILL FIND THAT THAT IS NOT THE SAME AS POWER.
LIE QUIETLY NOW.

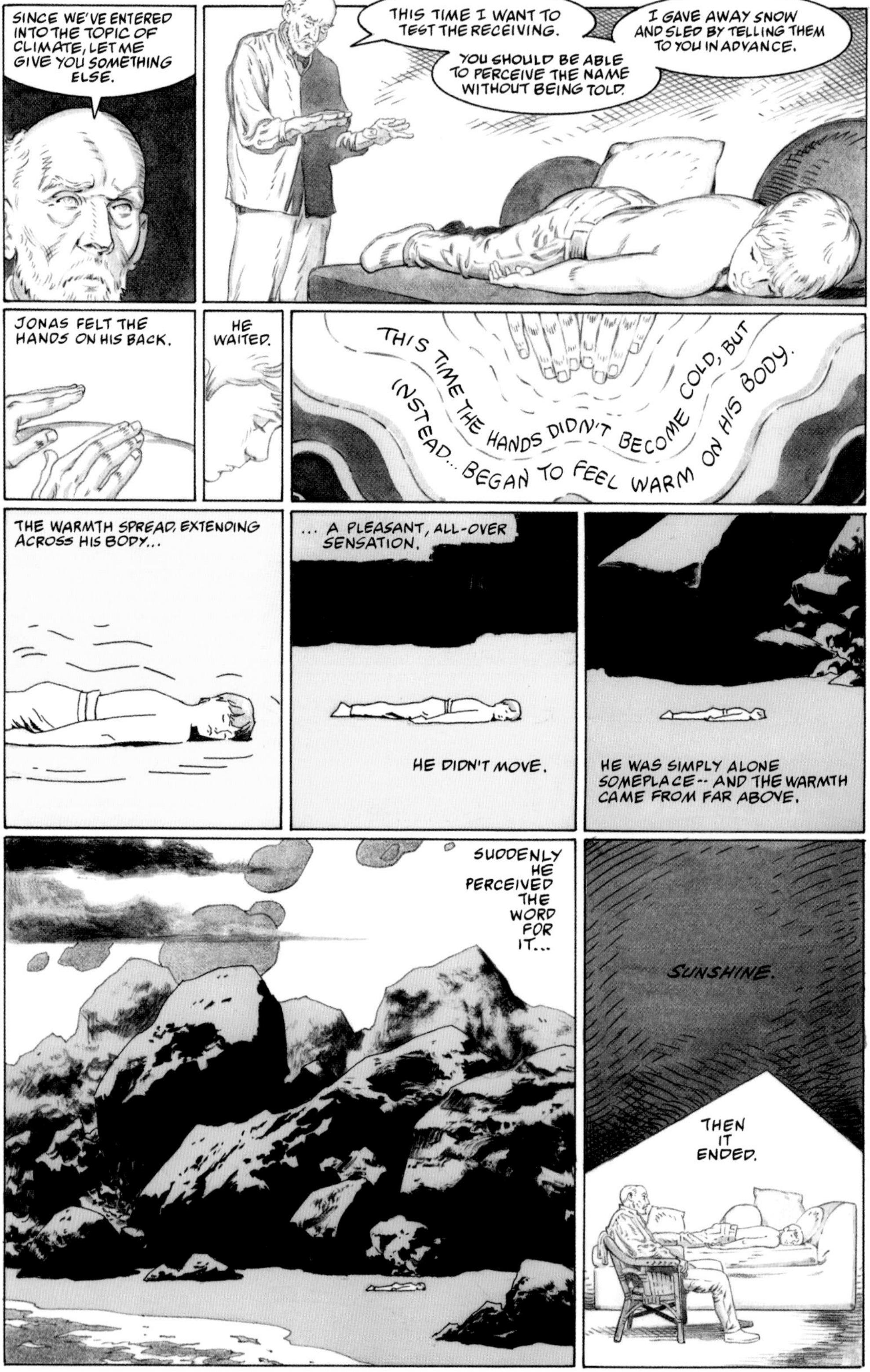

SINCE WE'VE ENTERED INTO THE TOPIC OF CLIMATE, LET ME GIVE YOU SOMETHING ELSE.
THIS TIME I WANT TO TEST THE RECEIVING.
YOU SHOULD BE ABLE TO PERCEIVE THE NAME WITHOUT BEING TOLD.
I GAVE AWAY SNOW AND SLED BY TELLING THEM TO YOU IN ADVANCE.
JONAS FELT THE HANDS ON HIS BACK.
HE WAITED.
THIS TIME THE HANDS DIDN'T BECOME COLD, BUT INSTEAD... BEGAN TO FEEL WARM ON HIS BODY.
THE WARMTH SPREAD, EXTENDING ACROSS HIS BODY...
... A PLEASANT, ALL-OVER SENSATION.
HE DIDN'T MOVE.
HE WAS SIMPLY ALONE SOMEPLACE-- AND THE WARMTH CAME FROM FAR ABOVE.
SUDDENLY HE PERCEIVED THE WORD FOR IT...
SUNSHINE.
THEN IT ENDED.

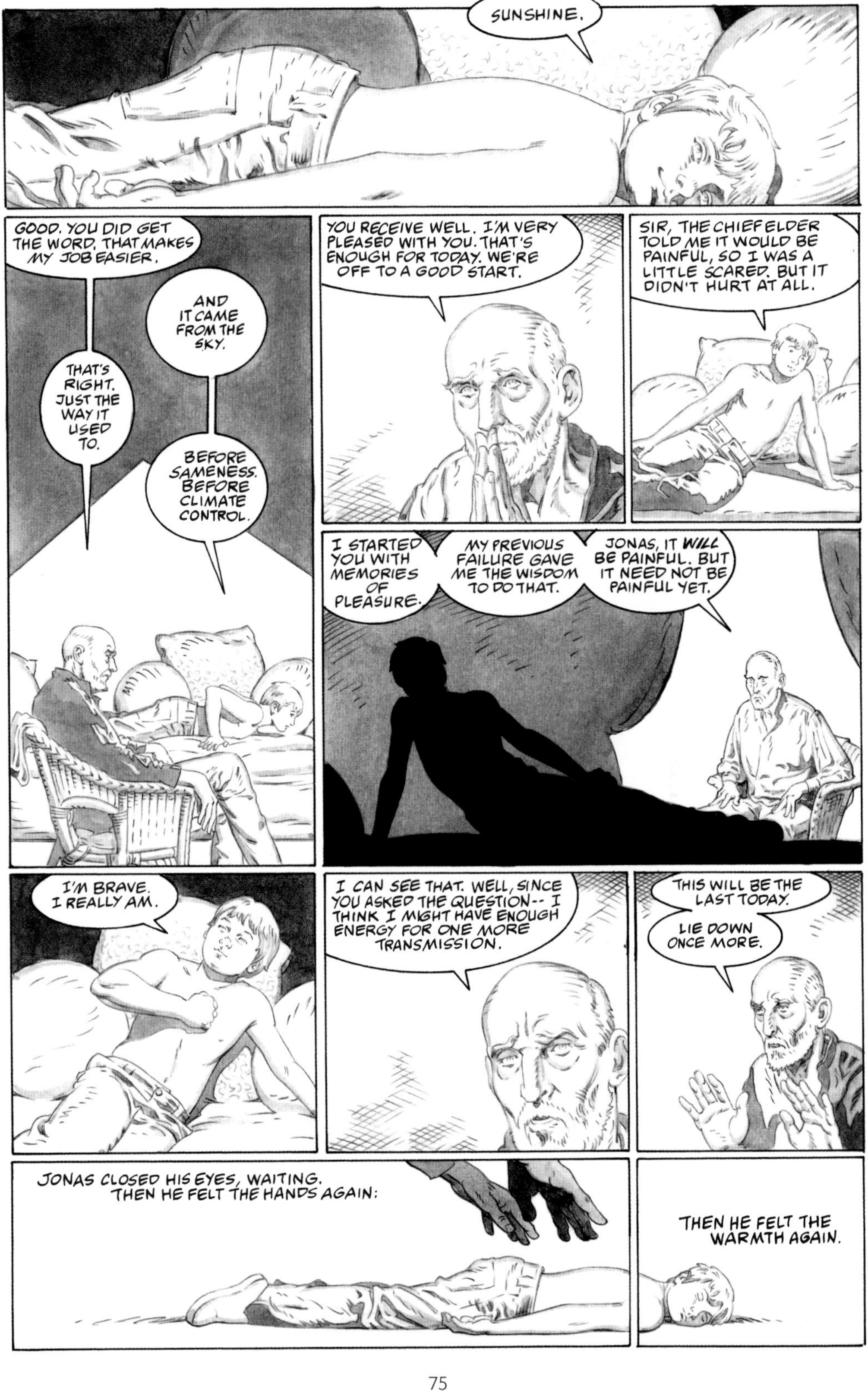
SUNSHINE.
GOOD. YOU DID GET THE WORD. THAT MAKES MY JOB EASIER.
AND IT CAME FROM THE SKY.
THAT'S RIGHT. JUST THE WAY IT USED TO.
BEFORE SAMENESS. BEFORE CLIMATE CONTROL.
YOU RECEIVE WELL. I'M VERY PLEASED WITH YOU. THAT'S ENOUGH FOR TODAY. WE'RE OFF TO A GOOD START.
SIR, THE CHIEF ELDER TOLD ME IT WOULD BE PAINFUL, SO I WAS A LITTLE SCARED. BUT IT DIDN'T HURT AT ALL.
I STARTED YOU WITH MEMORIES OF PLEASURE.
MY PREVIOUS FAILURE GAVE ME THE WISDOM TO DO THAT.
JONAS, IT **WILL** BE PAINFUL. BUT IT NEED NOT BE PAINFUL YET.
I'M BRAVE. I REALLY AM.
I CAN SEE THAT. WELL, SINCE YOU ASKED THE QUESTION-- I THINK I MIGHT HAVE ENOUGH ENERGY FOR ONE MORE TRANSMISSION.
THIS WILL BE THE LAST TODAY.
LIE DOWN ONCE MORE.
JONAS CLOSED HIS EYES, WAITING. THEN HE FELT THE HANDS AGAIN:
THEN HE FELT THE WARMTH AGAIN.

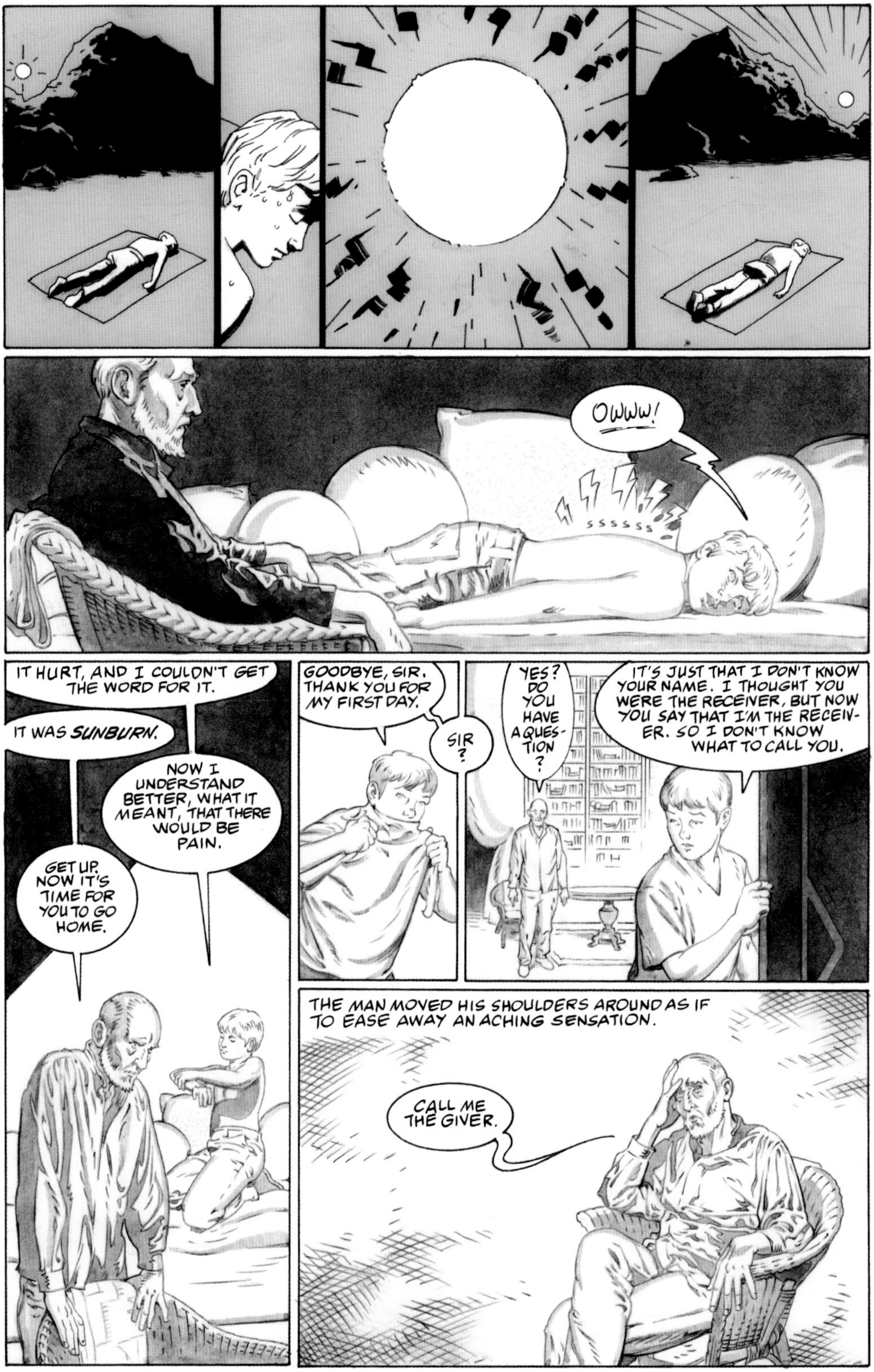
OWWW!
SSSSSS
IT HURT, AND I COULDN'T GET THE WORD FOR IT.
IT WAS SUNBURN.
NOW I UNDERSTAND BETTER, WHAT IT MEANT, THAT THERE WOULD BE PAIN.
GET UP. NOW IT'S TIME FOR YOU TO GO HOME.
GOODBYE, SIR. THANK YOU FOR MY FIRST DAY.
SIR?
YES? DO YOU HAVE A QUESTION?
IT'S JUST THAT I DON'T KNOW YOUR NAME. I THOUGHT YOU WERE THE RECEIVER, BUT NOW YOU SAY THAT I'M THE RECEIVER. SO I DON'T KNOW WHAT TO CALL YOU.
THE MAN MOVED HIS SHOULDERS AROUND AS IF TO EASE AWAY AN ACHING SENSATION.
CALL ME THE GIVER.

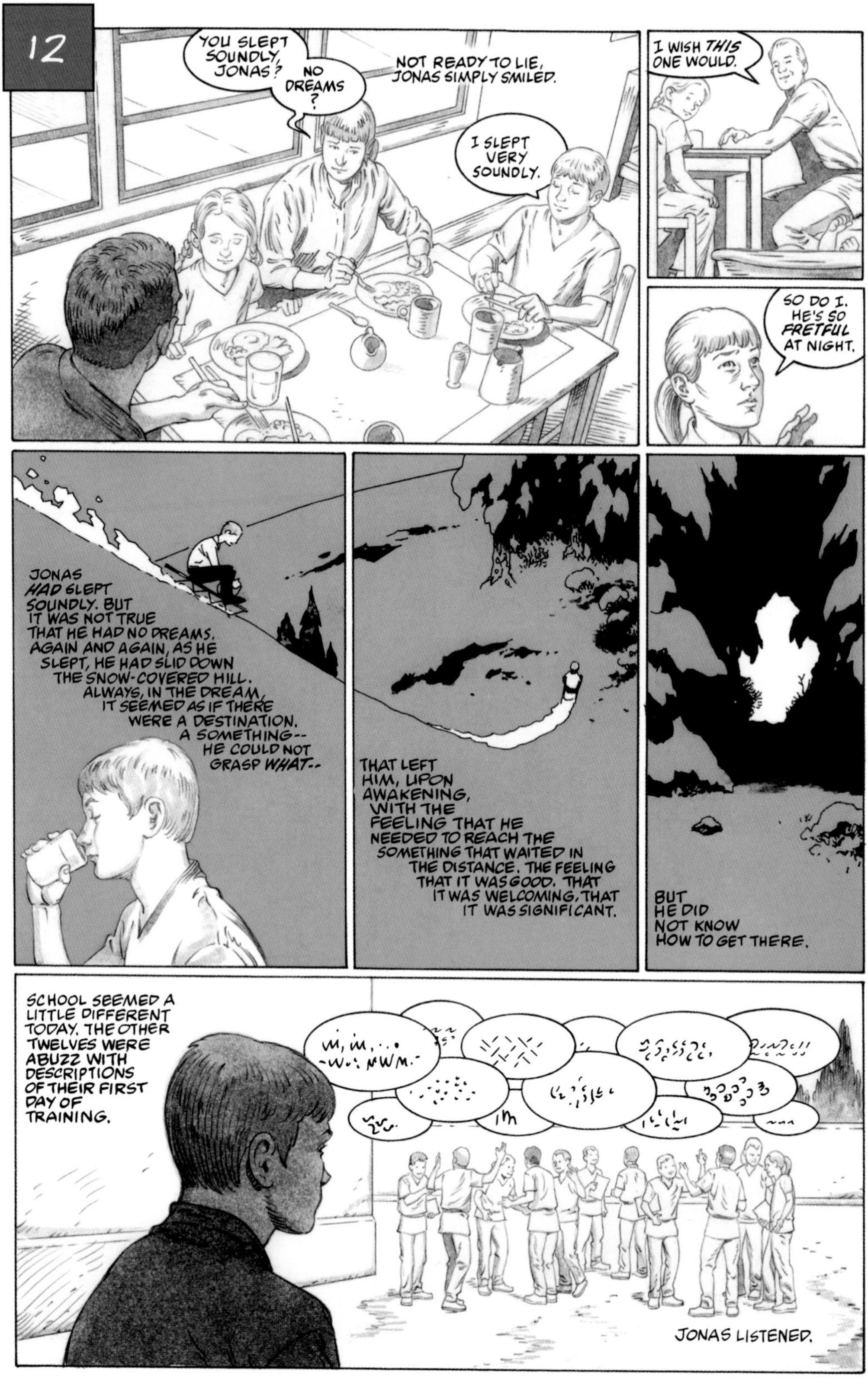
12
YOU SLEPT SOUNDLY, JONAS?
NO DREAMS?
NOT READY TO LIE, JONAS SIMPLY SMILED.
I SLEPT VERY SOUNDLY.
I WISH THIS ONE WOULD.
SO DO I. HE'S SO FRETFUL AT NIGHT.
JONAS HAD SLEPT SOUNDLY. BUT IT WAS NOT TRUE THAT HE HAD NO DREAMS. AGAIN AND AGAIN, AS HE SLEPT, HE HAD SLID DOWN THE SNOW-COVERED HILL. ALWAYS, IN THE DREAM, IT SEEMED AS IF THERE WERE A DESTINATION. A SOMETHING-- HE COULD NOT GRASP WHAT--
THAT LEFT HIM, UPON AWAKENING, WITH THE FEELING THAT HE NEEDED TO REACH THE SOMETHING THAT WAITED IN THE DISTANCE. THE FEELING THAT IT WAS GOOD. THAT IT WAS WELCOMING. THAT IT WAS SIGNIFICANT.
BUT HE DID NOT KNOW HOW TO GET THERE.
SCHOOL SEEMED A LITTLE DIFFERENT TODAY. THE OTHER TWELVES WERE ABUZZ WITH DESCRIPTIONS OF THEIR FIRST DAY OF TRAINING.
JONAS LISTENED.

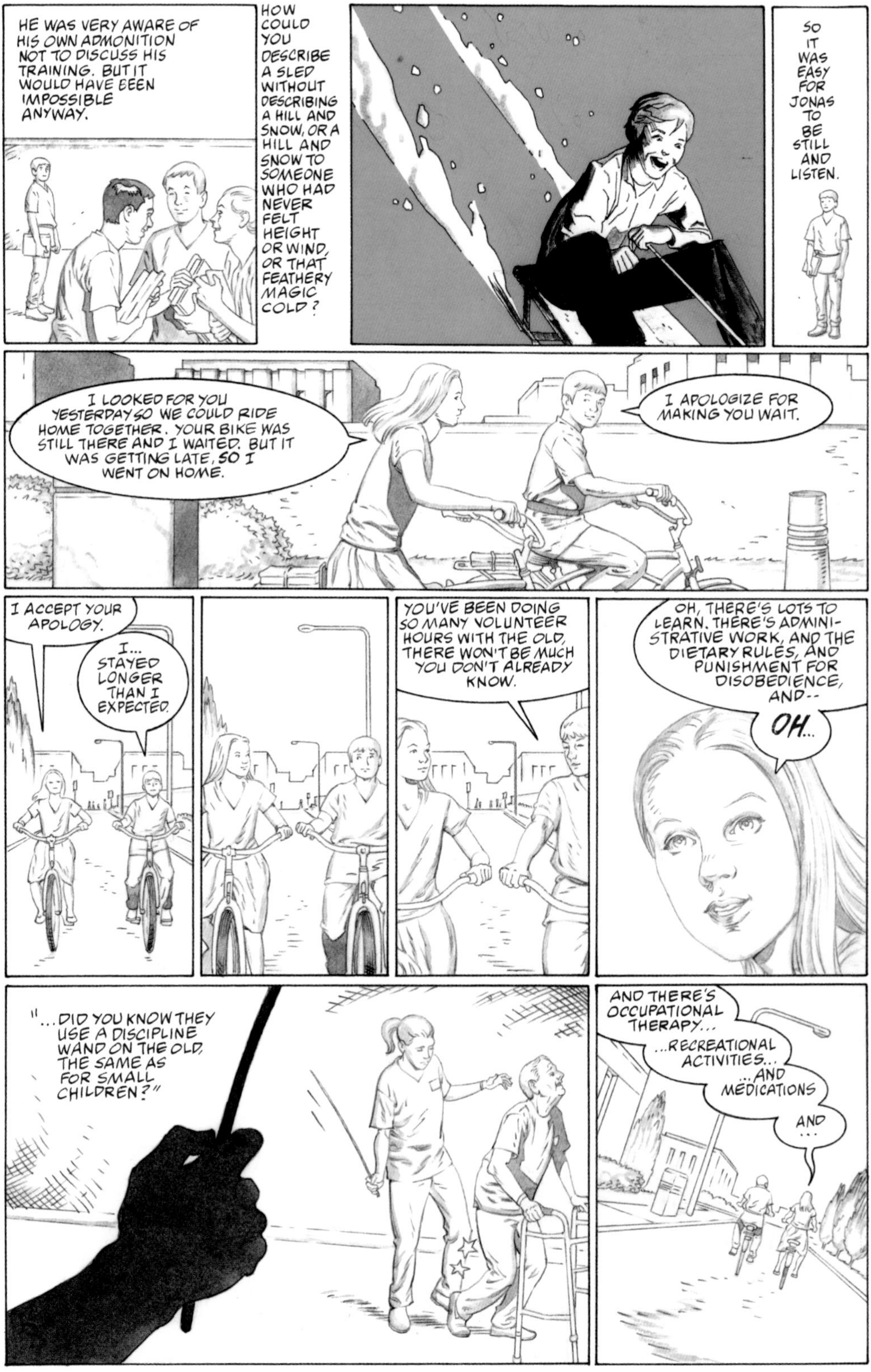
HE WAS VERY AWARE OF HIS OWN ADMONITION NOT TO DISCUSS HIS TRAINING. BUT IT WOULD HAVE BEEN IMPOSSIBLE ANYWAY.
HOW COULD YOU DESCRIBE A SLED WITHOUT DESCRIBING A HILL AND SNOW, OR A HILL AND SNOW TO SOMEONE WHO HAD NEVER FELT HEIGHT OR WIND, OR THAT FEATHERY MAGIC COLD?
SO IT WAS EASY FOR JONAS TO BE STILL AND LISTEN.
I LOOKED FOR YOU YESTERDAY SO WE COULD RIDE HOME TOGETHER. YOUR BIKE WAS STILL THERE AND I WAITED. BUT IT WAS GETTING LATE, SO I WENT ON HOME.
I APOLOGIZE FOR MAKING YOU WAIT.
I ACCEPT YOUR APOLOGY.
I... STAYED LONGER THAN I EXPECTED.
YOU'VE BEEN DOING SO MANY VOLUNTEER HOURS WITH THE OLD, THERE WON'T BE MUCH YOU DON'T ALREADY KNOW.
OH, THERE'S LOTS TO LEARN. THERE'S ADMINI-STRATIVE WORK, AND THE DIETARY RULES, AND PUNISHMENT FOR DISOBEDIENCE, AND--
OH...
"...DID YOU KNOW THEY USE A DISCIPLINE WAND ON THE OLD, THE SAME AS FOR SMALL CHILDREN?"
AND THERE'S OCCUPATIONAL THERAPY...
...RECREATIONAL ACTIVITIES...
...AND MEDICATIONS
AND ...

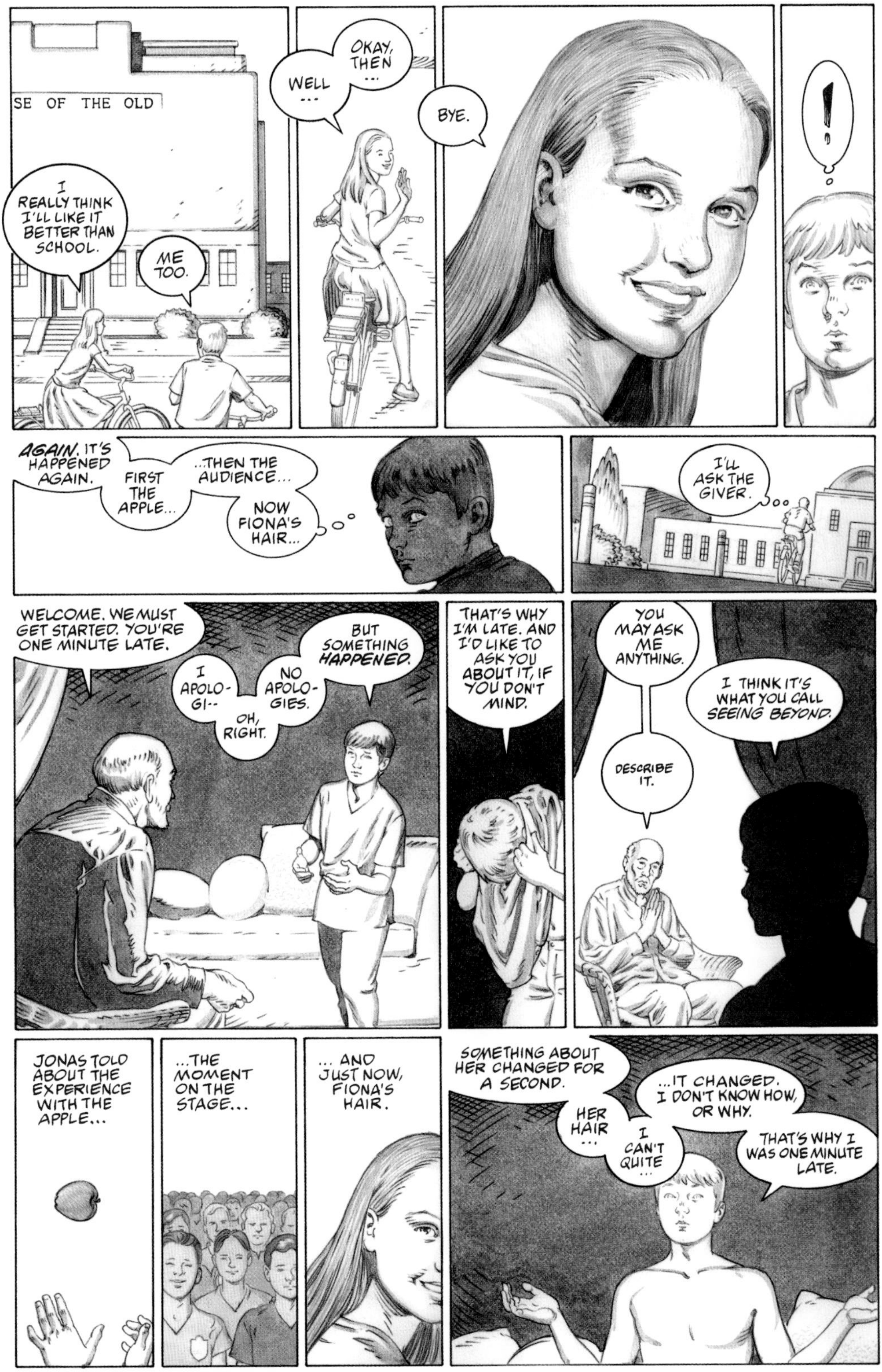

SE OF THE OLD
I REALLY THINK I'LL LIKE IT BETTER THAN SCHOOL.
ME TOO.
WELL ...
OKAY, THEN ...
BYE.
!
AGAIN. IT'S HAPPENED AGAIN.
FIRST THE APPLE...
...THEN THE AUDIENCE...
NOW FIONA'S HAIR...
I'LL ASK THE GIVER.
WELCOME. WE MUST GET STARTED. YOU'RE ONE MINUTE LATE.
I APOLOGI--
NO APOLOGIES.
OH, RIGHT.
BUT SOMETHING HAPPENED.
THAT'S WHY I'M LATE. AND I'D LIKE TO ASK YOU ABOUT IT, IF YOU DON'T MIND.
YOU MAY ASK ME ANYTHING.
I THINK IT'S WHAT YOU CALL SEEING BEYOND.
DESCRIBE IT.
JONAS TOLD ABOUT THE EXPERIENCE WITH THE APPLE...
...THE MOMENT ON THE STAGE...
... AND JUST NOW, FIONA'S HAIR.
SOMETHING ABOUT HER CHANGED FOR A SECOND.
HER HAIR ...
I CAN'T QUITE ...
...IT CHANGED. I DON'T KNOW HOW, OR WHY.
THAT'S WHY I WAS ONE MINUTE LATE.

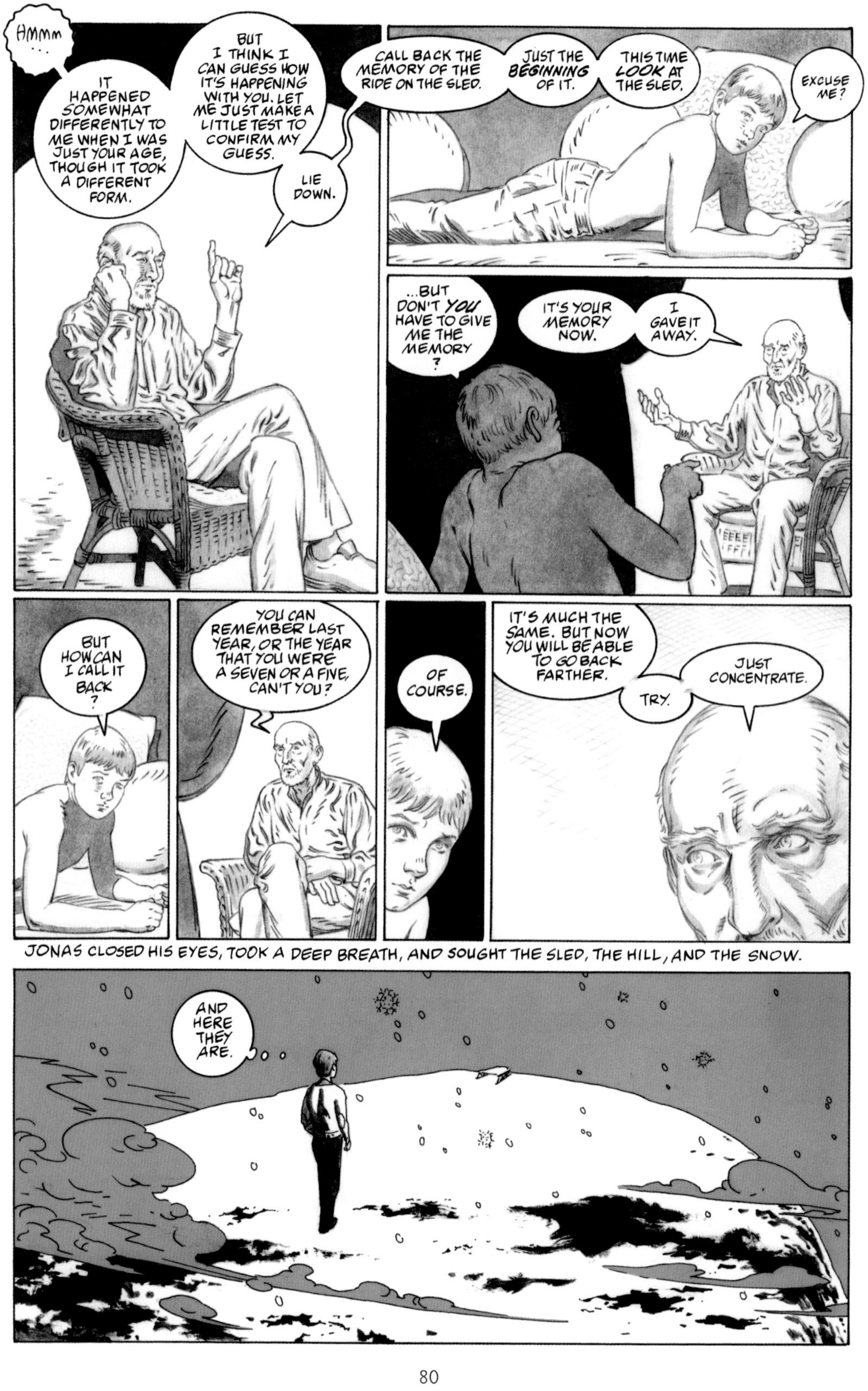
HMMM...
IT HAPPENED SOMEWHAT DIFFERENTLY TO ME WHEN I WAS JUST YOUR AGE, THOUGH IT TOOK A DIFFERENT FORM.
BUT I THINK I CAN GUESS HOW IT'S HAPPENING WITH YOU. LET ME JUST MAKE A LITTLE TEST TO CONFIRM MY GUESS.
LIE DOWN.
CALL BACK THE MEMORY OF THE RIDE ON THE SLED.
JUST THE *BEGINNING* OF IT.
THIS TIME *LOOK* AT THE SLED.
EXCUSE ME?
...BUT DON'T *YOU* HAVE TO GIVE ME THE MEMORY?
IT'S YOUR MEMORY NOW.
I GAVE IT AWAY.
BUT HOW CAN I CALL IT BACK?
YOU CAN REMEMBER LAST YEAR, OR THE YEAR THAT YOU WERE A SEVEN OR A FIVE, CAN'T YOU?
OF COURSE.
IT'S MUCH THE SAME. BUT NOW YOU WILL BE ABLE TO GO BACK FARTHER.
TRY.
JUST CONCENTRATE.
JONAS CLOSED HIS EYES, TOOK A DEEP BREATH, AND SOUGHT THE SLED, THE HILL, AND THE SNOW.
AND HERE THEY ARE.

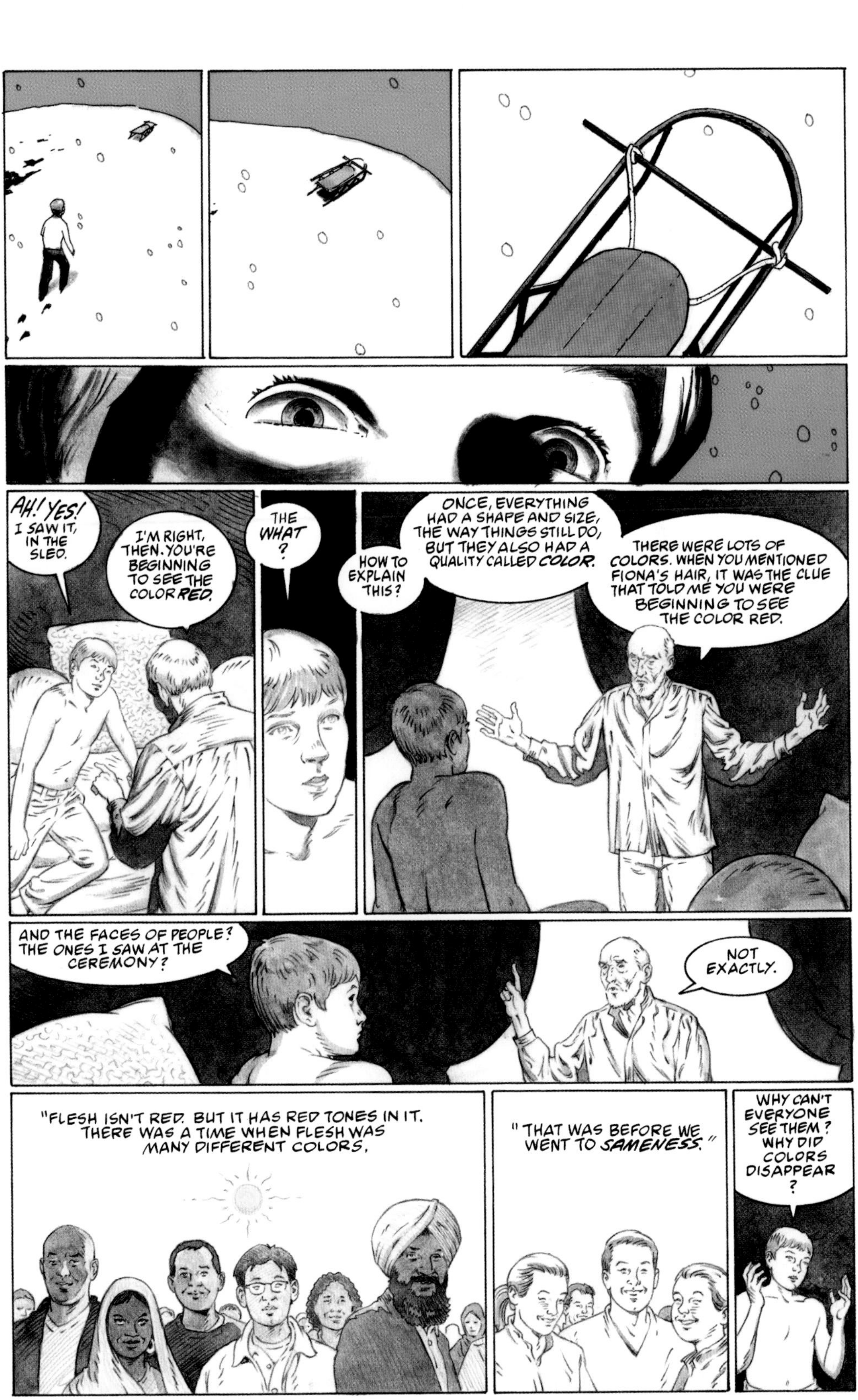
AH! YES! I SAW IT, IN THE SLED.
I'M RIGHT, THEN. YOU'RE BEGINNING TO SEE THE COLOR RED.
THE WHAT?
HOW TO EXPLAIN THIS?
ONCE, EVERYTHING HAD A SHAPE AND SIZE, THE WAY THINGS STILL DO, BUT THEY ALSO HAD A QUALITY CALLED COLOR.
THERE WERE LOTS OF COLORS. WHEN YOU MENTIONED FIONA'S HAIR, IT WAS THE CLUE THAT TOLD ME YOU WERE BEGINNING TO SEE THE COLOR RED.
AND THE FACES OF PEOPLE? THE ONES I SAW AT THE CEREMONY?
NOT EXACTLY.
"FLESH ISN'T RED. BUT IT HAS RED TONES IN IT. THERE WAS A TIME WHEN FLESH WAS MANY DIFFERENT COLORS,
"THAT WAS BEFORE WE WENT TO SAMENESS."
WHY CAN'T EVERYONE SEE THEM? WHY DID COLORS DISAPPEAR?

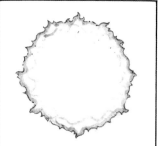

" OUR PEOPLE MADE THE CHOICE TO GO TO SAMENESS, BEFORE MY TIME. BACK, AND BACK, AND BACK.

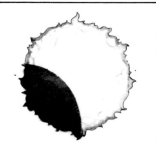

"WE RELINQUISHED COLOR WHEN WE RELINQUISHED SUNSHINE AND DID AWAY WITH DIFFERENCES.

"WE GAINED CONTROL OF MANY THINGS, BUT WE HAD TO LET GO OF OTHERS."

WE SHOULDN'T HAVE!

!

YOU'VE COME VERY QUICKLY TO THAT CONCLUSION. IT TOOK ME MANY YEARS. MAYBE YOUR WISDOM WILL COME MORE QUICKLY THAN MINE.

LIE BACK DOWN NOW. WE HAVE SO MUCH TO DO.

GIVER, HOW DID IT HAPPEN TO YOU WHEN YOU WERE BECOMING THE RECEIVER? YOU SAID THE SEEING BEYOND HAPPENED TO YOU, BUT NOT THE SAME WAY.

FOR ME, IT WAS HEARING BEYOND.

WHAT DID YOU HEAR?

MUSIC.

?

I BEGAN TO HEAR SOMETHING TRULY REMARKABLE, AND IT IS CALLED MUSIC. I'LL TELL YOU ABOUT IT ANOTHER DAY.

NOW WE MUST WORK. I'VE THOUGHT OF A WAY TO HELP YOU WITH THE CONCEPT OF COLOR.

I'M GOING TO GIVE YOU A MEMORY OF A RAINBOW.

82

13

DAYS WENT BY, AND WEEKS. JONAS LEARNED, THROUGH THE MEMORIES, THE NAMES OF COLORS, AND NOW HE BEGAN TO SEE THEM ALL, IN HIS ORDINARY LIFE.

BUT THEY DIDN'T LAST.

IT WILL BE A VERY LONG TIME BEFORE YOU HAVE THE COLORS TO KEEP.

BUT I *WANT* THEM. IT ISN'T FAIR THAT NOTHING HAS COLOR.

WELL... IF EVERYTHING'S THE SAME, THEN THERE AREN'T ANY CHOICES! I WANT TO WAKE UP IN THE MORNING AND *DECIDE* THINGS! A BLUE TUNIC, OR A RED ONE.

NOT FAIR? EXPLAIN WHAT YOU MEAN.

I KNOW IT'S NOT IMPORTANT WHAT YOU WEAR... BUT...

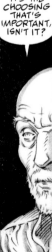

IT'S THE CHOOSING THAT'S IMPORTANT, ISN'T IT?

YES! MY LITTLE BROTHER-- NO, THAT'S NOT ACCURATE-- THIS *NEWCHILD* THAT MY FAMILY TAKES CARE OF... HIS NAME'S GABRIEL?

YES, I KNOW ABOUT GABRIEL.

"WELL, HE'S RIGHT AT THE AGE WHERE HE'S LEARNING SO MUCH. WHAT IF WE COULD HOLD UP THINGS THAT WERE BRIGHT RED, OR BRIGHT YELLOW, AND HE COULD *CHOOSE*... INSTEAD OF THE SAMENESS."

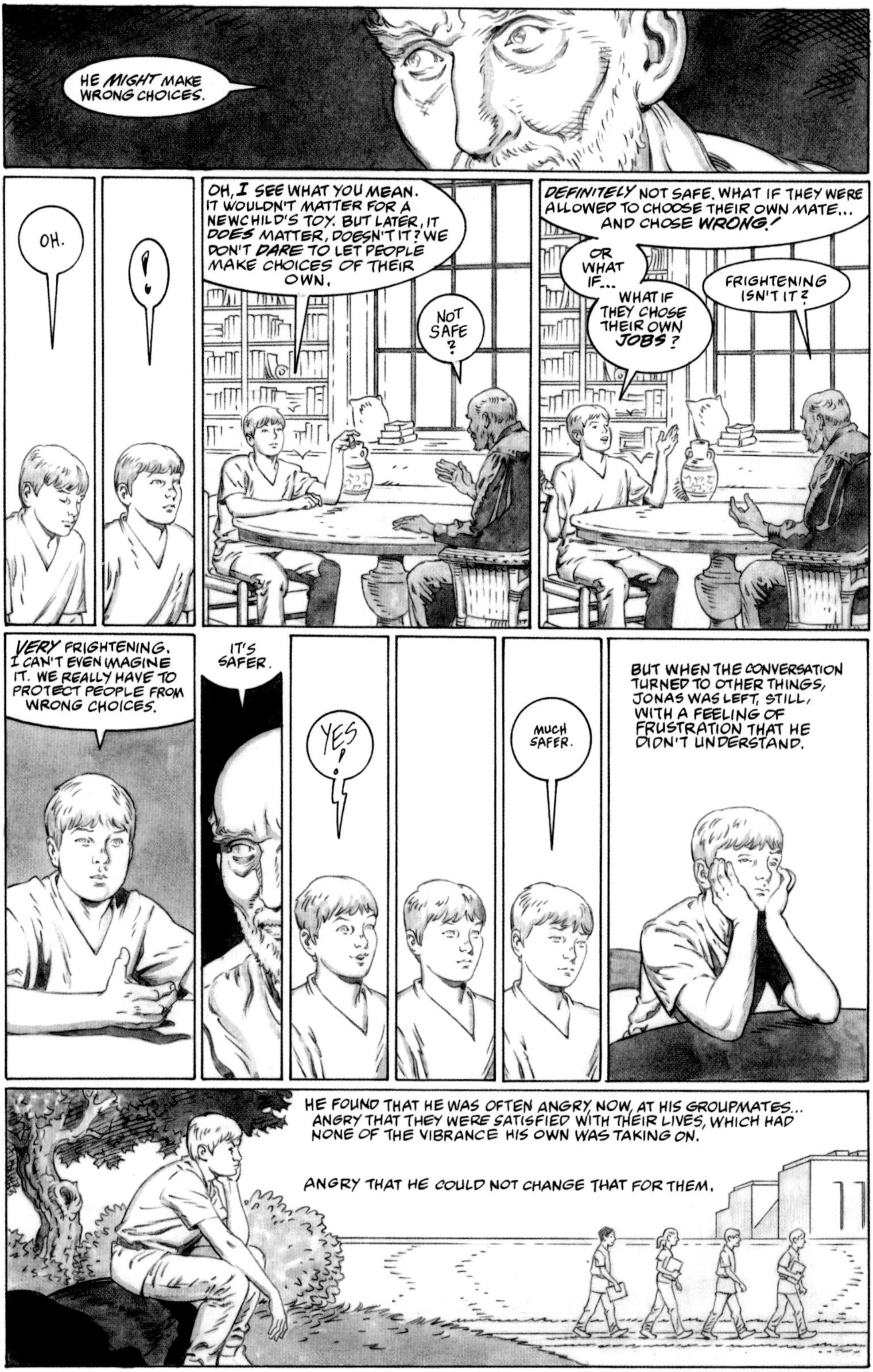
HE MIGHT MAKE WRONG CHOICES.
OH.
!
OH, I SEE WHAT YOU MEAN. IT WOULDN'T MATTER FOR A NEWCHILD'S TOY. BUT LATER, IT DOES MATTER, DOESN'T IT? WE DON'T DARE TO LET PEOPLE MAKE CHOICES OF THEIR OWN.
NOT SAFE?
DEFINITELY NOT SAFE. WHAT IF THEY WERE ALLOWED TO CHOOSE THEIR OWN MATE... AND CHOSE WRONG!
OR WHAT IF... WHAT IF THEY CHOSE THEIR OWN JOBS?
FRIGHTENING ISN'T IT?
VERY FRIGHTENING. I CAN'T EVEN IMAGINE IT. WE REALLY HAVE TO PROTECT PEOPLE FROM WRONG CHOICES.
IT'S SAFER.
YES!
MUCH SAFER.
BUT WHEN THE CONVERSATION TURNED TO OTHER THINGS, JONAS WAS LEFT, STILL, WITH A FEELING OF FRUSTRATION THAT HE DIDN'T UNDERSTAND.
HE FOUND THAT HE WAS OFTEN ANGRY, NOW, AT HIS GROUPMATES... ANGRY THAT THEY WERE SATISFIED WITH THEIR LIVES, WHICH HAD NONE OF THE VIBRANCE HIS OWN WAS TAKING ON.
ANGRY THAT HE COULD NOT CHANGE THAT FOR THEM.

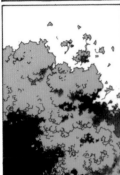

ONE EVENING HE CAME HOME WEIGHTED WITH NEW KNOWLEDGE. THE GIVER HAD CHOSEN A STARTLING AND DISTURBING NEW MEMORY.

HE HAD FOUND HIMSELF IN A HOT AND WINDSWEPT PLACE.

GUNS!

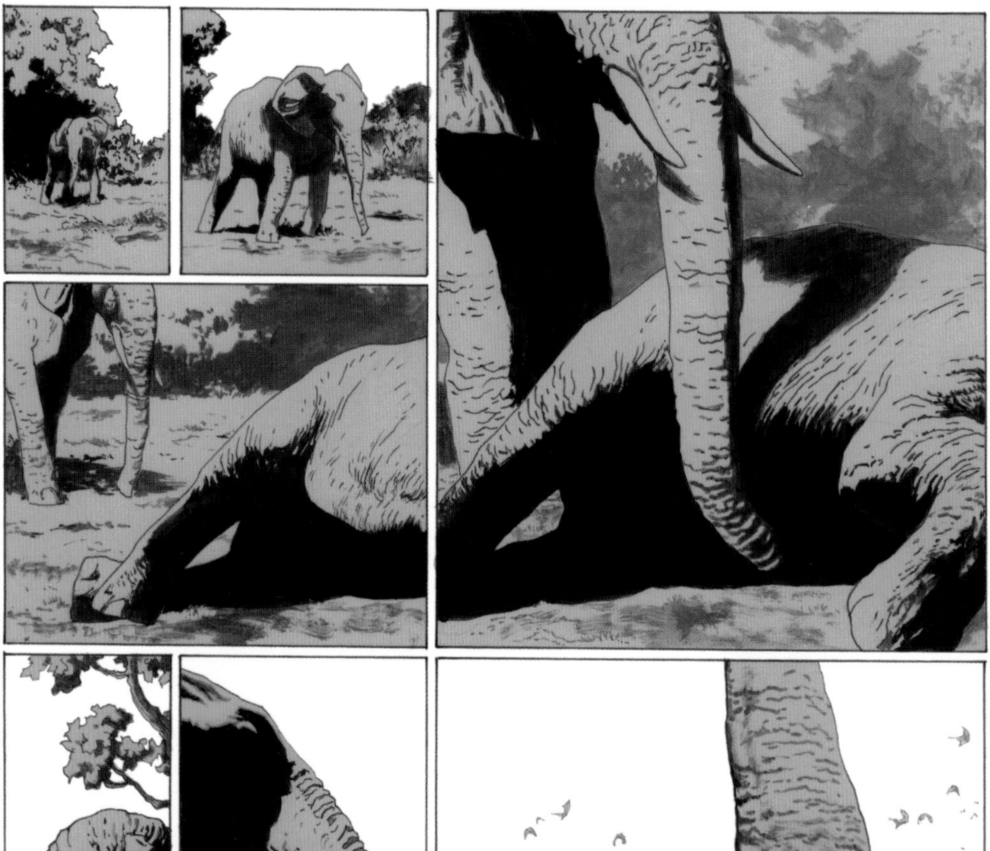

THE CREATURE'S SOUND OF RAGE AND GRIEF SEEMED NEVER TO END.
IT CONTINUED TO ROAR INTO HIS CONSCIOUSNESS AS HE PEDALED SLOWLY HOME.

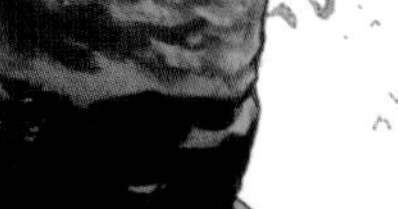

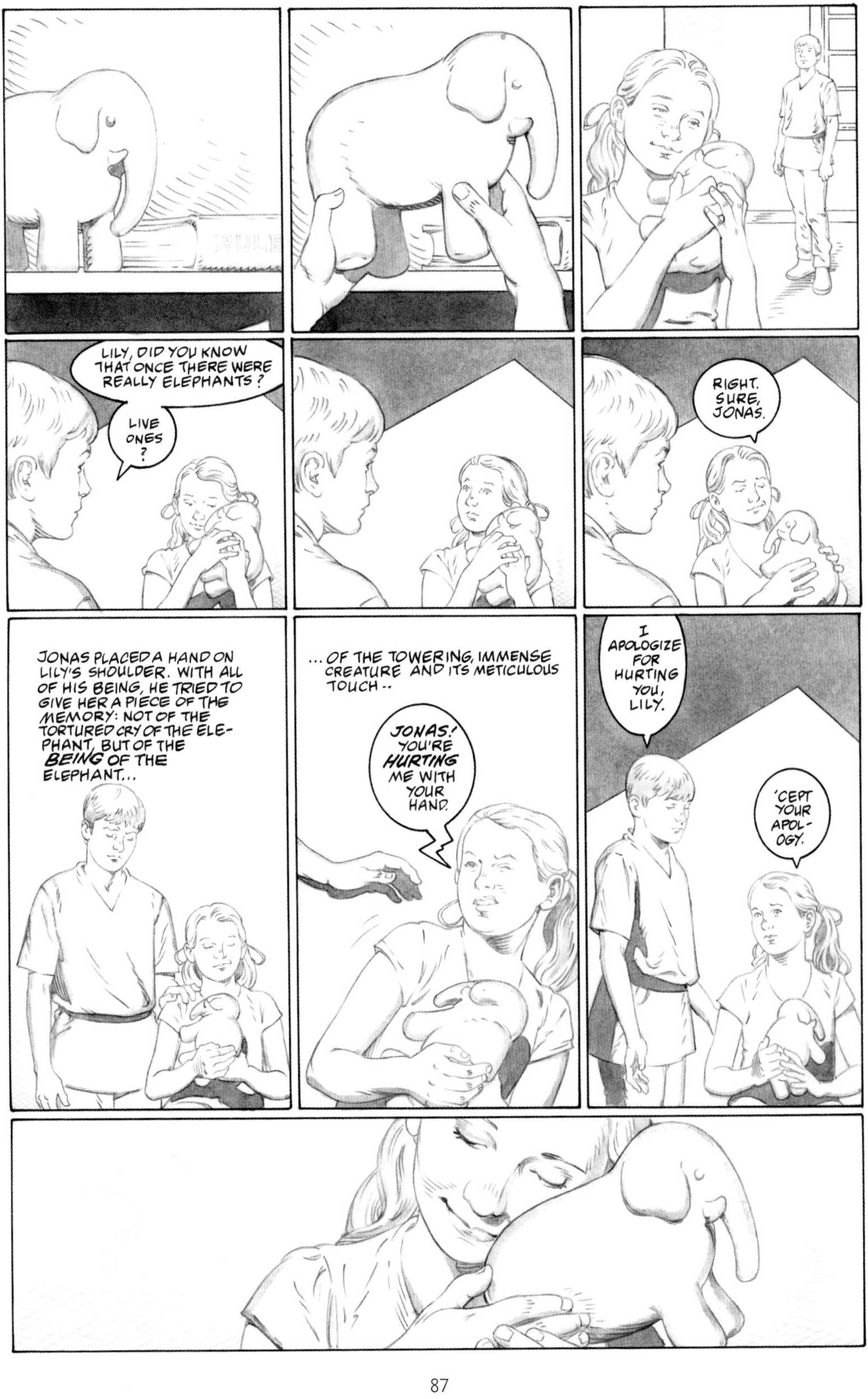
LILY, DID YOU KNOW THAT ONCE THERE WERE REALLY ELEPHANTS?
LIVE ONES?
RIGHT. SURE, JONAS.
JONAS PLACED A HAND ON LILY'S SHOULDER. WITH ALL OF HIS BEING, HE TRIED TO GIVE HER A PIECE OF THE MEMORY: NOT OF THE TORTURED CRY OF THE ELEPHANT, BUT OF THE BEING OF THE ELEPHANT...
...OF THE TOWERING, IMMENSE CREATURE AND ITS METICULOUS TOUCH--
JONAS! YOU'RE HURTING ME WITH YOUR HAND.
I APOLOGIZE FOR HURTING YOU, LILY.
'CEPT YOUR APOLOGY.

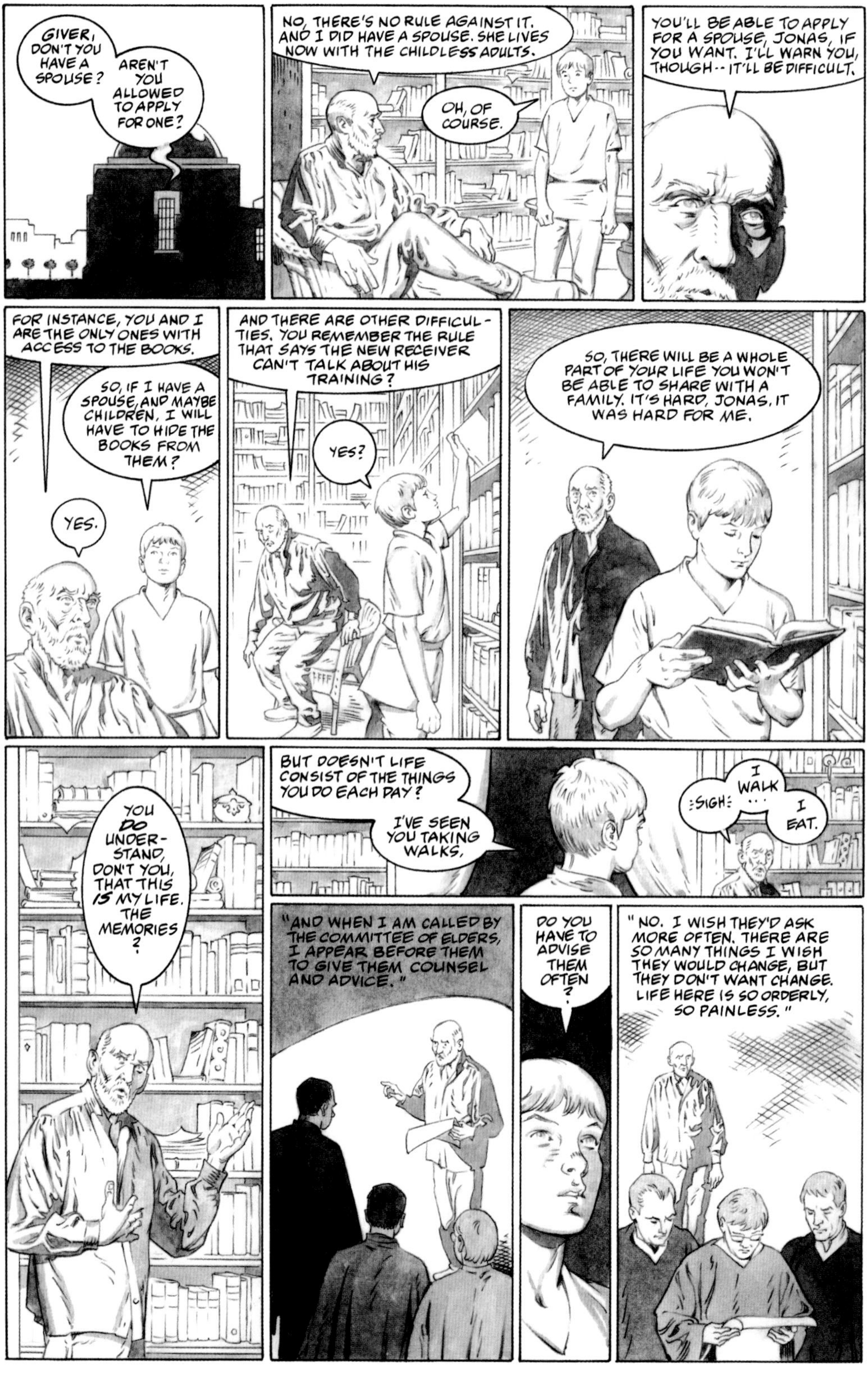
GIVER, DON'T YOU HAVE A SPOUSE?
AREN'T YOU ALLOWED TO APPLY FOR ONE?
NO, THERE'S NO RULE AGAINST IT. AND I DID HAVE A SPOUSE. SHE LIVES NOW WITH THE CHILDLESS ADULTS.
OH, OF COURSE.
YOU'LL BE ABLE TO APPLY FOR A SPOUSE, JONAS, IF YOU WANT. I'LL WARN YOU, THOUGH-- IT'LL BE DIFFICULT.
FOR INSTANCE, YOU AND I ARE THE ONLY ONES WITH ACCESS TO THE BOOKS.
SO, IF I HAVE A SPOUSE, AND MAYBE CHILDREN, I WILL HAVE TO HIDE THE BOOKS FROM THEM?
YES.
AND THERE ARE OTHER DIFFICUL-TIES. YOU REMEMBER THE RULE THAT SAYS THE NEW RECEIVER CAN'T TALK ABOUT HIS TRAINING?
YES?
SO, THERE WILL BE A WHOLE PART OF YOUR LIFE YOU WON'T BE ABLE TO SHARE WITH A FAMILY. IT'S HARD, JONAS. IT WAS HARD FOR ME.
YOU DO UNDER-STAND, DON'T YOU, THAT THIS IS MY LIFE. THE MEMORIES?
BUT DOESN'T LIFE CONSIST OF THE THINGS YOU DO EACH DAY?
I'VE SEEN YOU TAKING WALKS,
:SIGH:
I WALK . . . I EAT.
"AND WHEN I AM CALLED BY THE COMMITTEE OF ELDERS, I APPEAR BEFORE THEM TO GIVE THEM COUNSEL AND ADVICE."
DO YOU HAVE TO ADVISE THEM OFTEN?
"NO. I WISH THEY'D ASK MORE OFTEN. THERE ARE SO MANY THINGS I WISH THEY WOULD CHANGE, BUT THEY DON'T WANT CHANGE. LIFE HERE IS SO ORDERLY, SO PAINLESS."

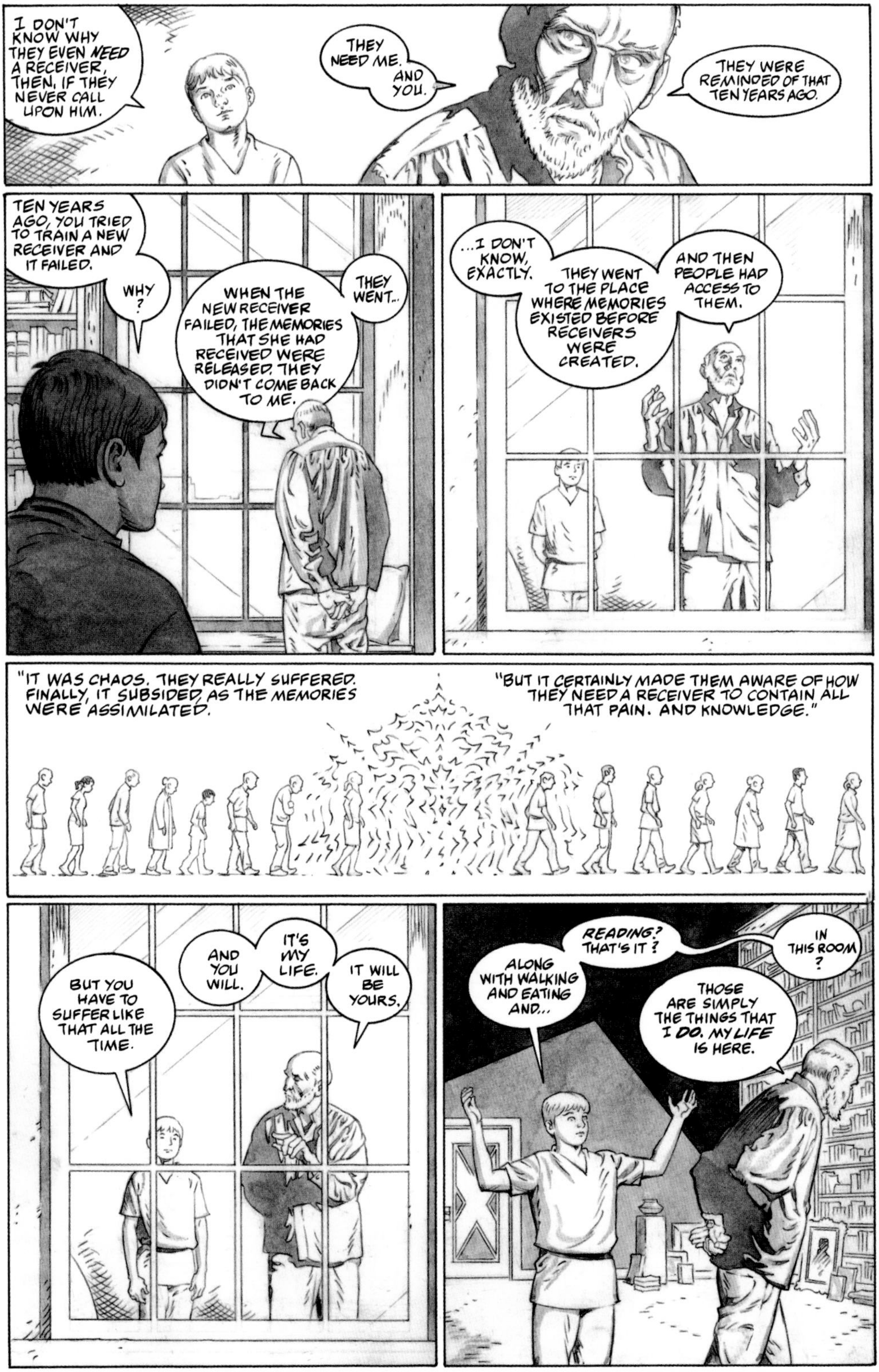
I DON'T KNOW WHY THEY EVEN *NEED* A RECEIVER, THEN, IF THEY NEVER CALL UPON HIM.
THEY NEED ME.
AND YOU.
THEY WERE REMINDED OF THAT TEN YEARS AGO.
TEN YEARS AGO, YOU TRIED TO TRAIN A NEW RECEIVER AND IT FAILED.
WHY?
WHEN THE NEW RECEIVER FAILED, THE MEMORIES THAT SHE HAD RECEIVED WERE RELEASED. THEY DIDN'T COME BACK TO ME.
THEY WENT...
...I DON'T KNOW, EXACTLY.
THEY WENT TO THE PLACE WHERE MEMORIES EXISTED BEFORE RECEIVERS WERE CREATED.
AND THEN PEOPLE HAD ACCESS TO THEM.
"IT WAS CHAOS. THEY REALLY SUFFERED. FINALLY, IT SUBSIDED AS THE MEMORIES WERE ASSIMILATED.
"BUT IT CERTAINLY MADE THEM AWARE OF HOW THEY NEED A RECEIVER TO CONTAIN ALL THAT PAIN. AND KNOWLEDGE."
BUT YOU HAVE TO SUFFER LIKE THAT ALL THE TIME.
AND YOU WILL.
IT'S MY LIFE.
IT WILL BE YOURS.
ALONG WITH WALKING AND EATING AND...
READING? THAT'S IT?
IN THIS ROOM?
THOSE ARE SIMPLY THE THINGS THAT I *DO*. MY *LIFE* IS HERE.

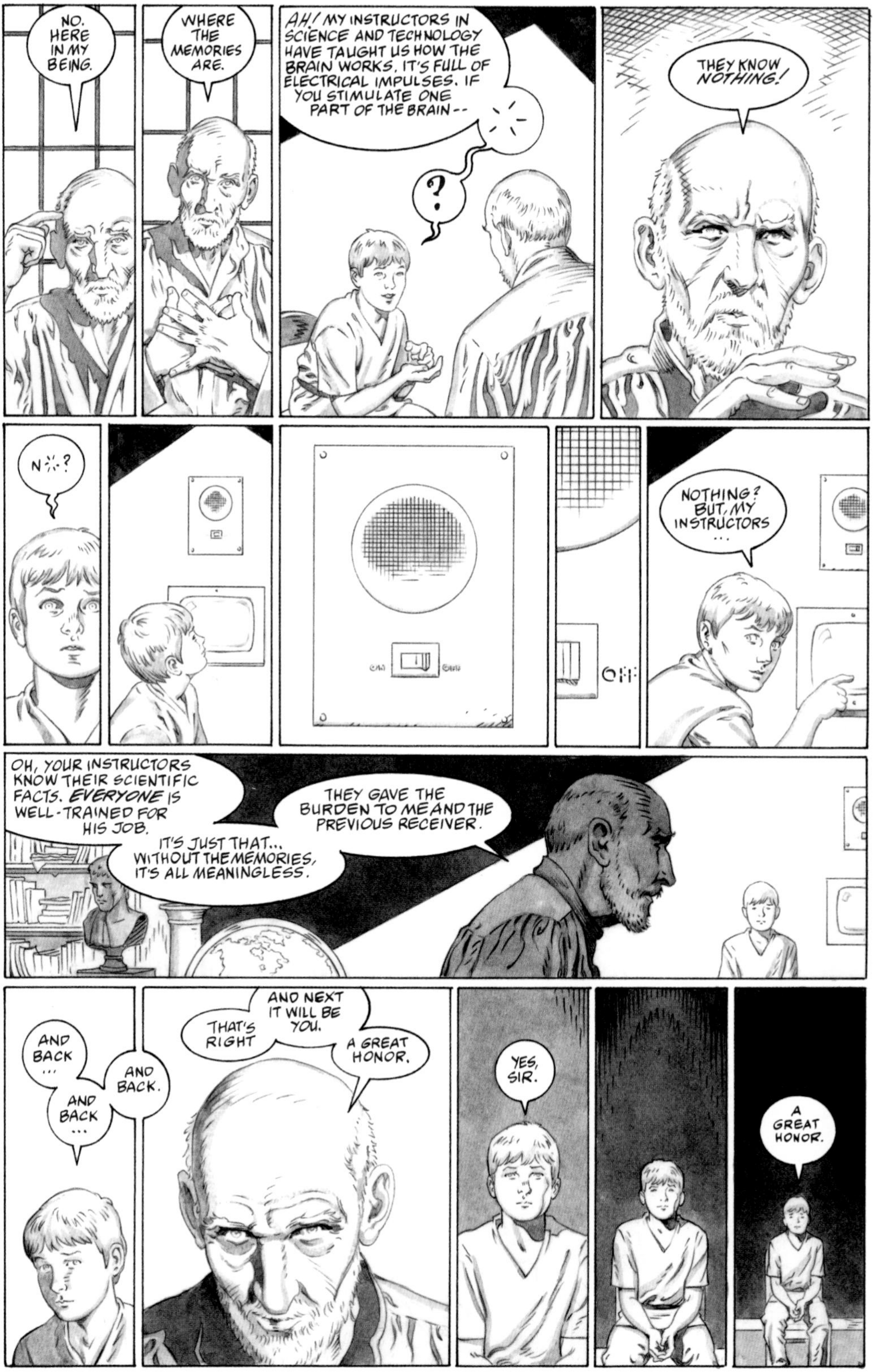
NO. HERE IN MY BEING.
WHERE THE MEMORIES ARE.
AH! MY INSTRUCTORS IN SCIENCE AND TECHNOLOGY HAVE TAUGHT US HOW THE BRAIN WORKS. IT'S FULL OF ELECTRICAL IMPULSES. IF YOU STIMULATE ONE PART OF THE BRAIN--
?
THEY KNOW NOTHING!
N...?
NOTHING? BUT, MY INSTRUCTORS ...
OFF
OH, YOUR INSTRUCTORS KNOW THEIR SCIENTIFIC FACTS. EVERYONE IS WELL-TRAINED FOR HIS JOB.
THEY GAVE THE BURDEN TO ME AND THE PREVIOUS RECEIVER.
IT'S JUST THAT... WITHOUT THE MEMORIES, IT'S ALL MEANINGLESS.
AND BACK ...
AND BACK ...
AND BACK.
THAT'S RIGHT
AND NEXT IT WILL BE YOU.
A GREAT HONOR.
YES, SIR.
A GREAT HONOR.

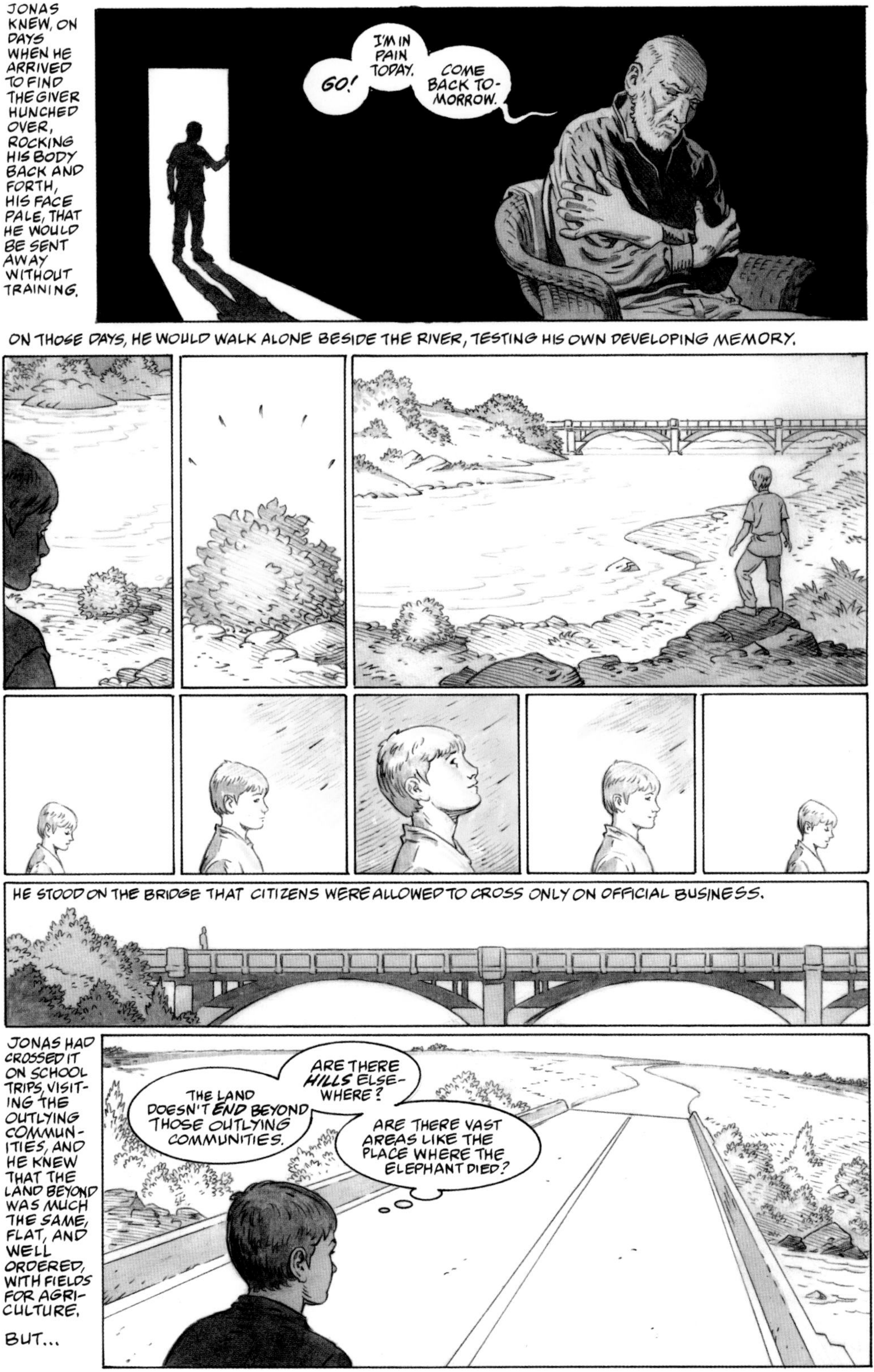
JONAS KNEW, ON DAYS WHEN HE ARRIVED TO FIND THE GIVER HUNCHED OVER, ROCKING HIS BODY BACK AND FORTH, HIS FACE PALE, THAT HE WOULD BE SENT AWAY WITHOUT TRAINING.
GO!
I'M IN PAIN TODAY.
COME BACK TO-MORROW.
ON THOSE DAYS, HE WOULD WALK ALONE BESIDE THE RIVER, TESTING HIS OWN DEVELOPING MEMORY.
HE STOOD ON THE BRIDGE THAT CITIZENS WERE ALLOWED TO CROSS ONLY ON OFFICIAL BUSINESS.
JONAS HAD CROSSED IT ON SCHOOL TRIPS, VISITING THE OUTLYING COMMUN-ITIES, AND HE KNEW THAT THE LAND BEYOND WAS MUCH THE SAME, FLAT, AND WELL ORDERED, WITH FIELDS FOR AGRI-CULTURE.
BUT...
THE LAND DOESN'T END BEYOND THOSE OUTLYING COMMUNITIES.
ARE THERE HILLS ELSE-WHERE?
ARE THERE VAST AREAS LIKE THE PLACE WHERE THE ELEPHANT DIED?

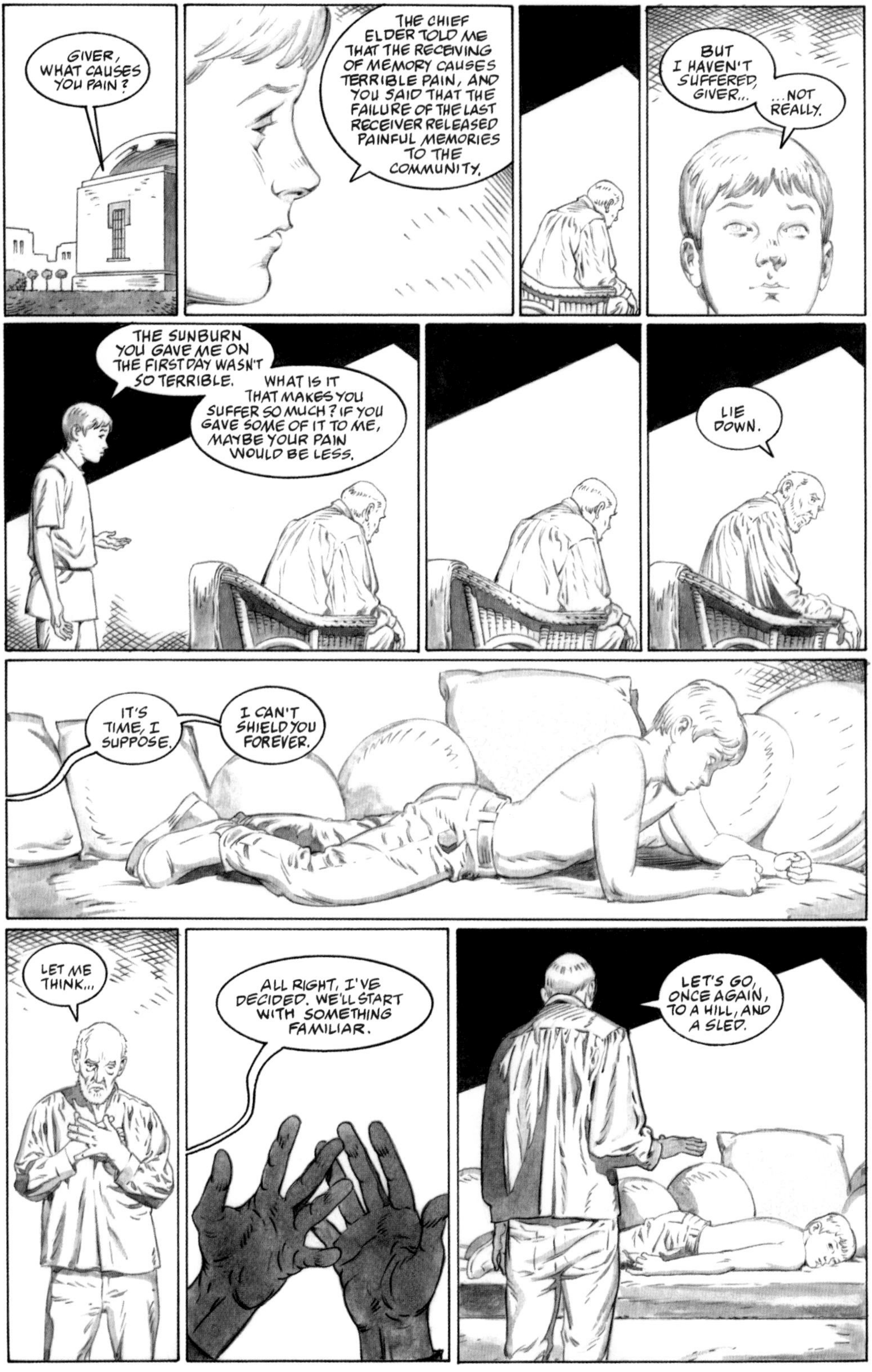
GIVER, WHAT CAUSES YOU PAIN?
THE CHIEF ELDER TOLD ME THAT THE RECEIVING OF MEMORY CAUSES TERRIBLE PAIN, AND YOU SAID THAT THE FAILURE OF THE LAST RECEIVER RELEASED PAINFUL MEMORIES TO THE COMMUNITY.
BUT I HAVEN'T SUFFERED, GIVER...
...NOT REALLY.
THE SUNBURN YOU GAVE ME ON THE FIRST DAY WASN'T SO TERRIBLE.
WHAT IS IT THAT MAKES YOU SUFFER SO MUCH? IF YOU GAVE SOME OF IT TO ME, MAYBE YOUR PAIN WOULD BE LESS.
LIE DOWN.
IT'S TIME, I SUPPOSE.
I CAN'T SHIELD YOU FOREVER.
LET ME THINK...
ALL RIGHT, I'VE DECIDED. WE'LL START WITH SOMETHING FAMILIAR.
LET'S GO, ONCE AGAIN, TO A HILL, AND A SLED.

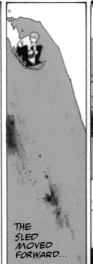

14

IT WAS MUCH THE SAME, THIS MEMORY, THOUGH THE HILL WAS STEEPER. IT WAS COLDER, ALSO, AND HE COULD SEE THAT THE SNOW WAS NOT THICK AND SOFT AS IT HAD BEEN BEFORE, BUT HARD, AND COATED WITH BLUISH ICE.

THE SLED MOVED FORWARD...

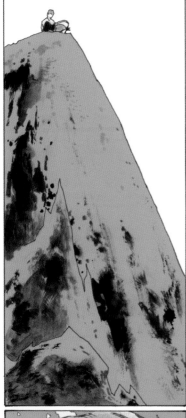

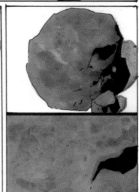

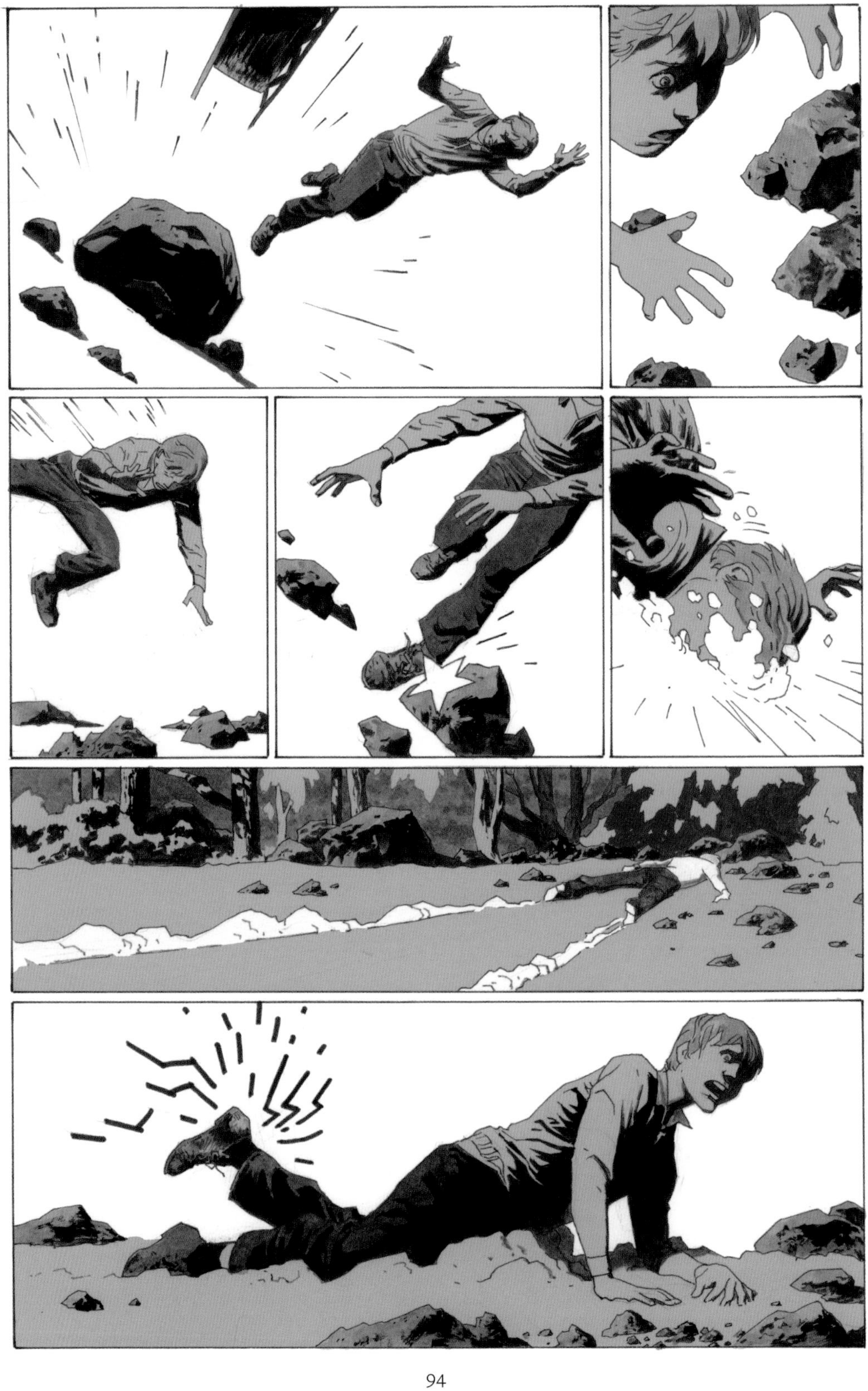

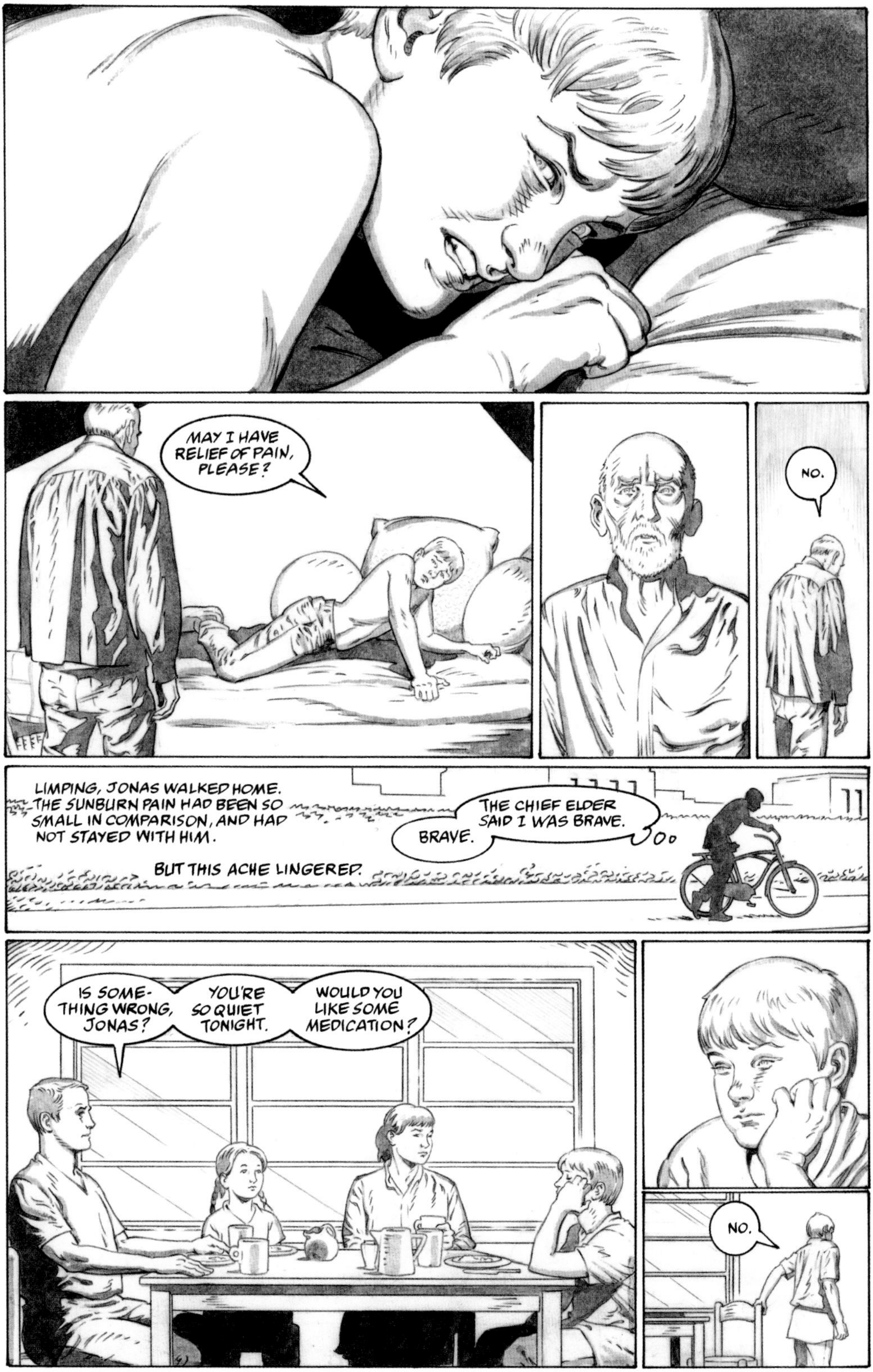
MAY I HAVE RELIEF OF PAIN, PLEASE?
NO.
LIMPING, JONAS WALKED HOME. THE SUNBURN PAIN HAD BEEN SO SMALL IN COMPARISON, AND HAD NOT STAYED WITH HIM.
BUT THIS ACHE LINGERED.
THE CHIEF ELDER SAID I WAS BRAVE.
BRAVE.
IS SOMETHING WRONG, JONAS?
YOU'RE SO QUIET TONIGHT.
WOULD YOU LIKE SOME MEDICATION?
NO.

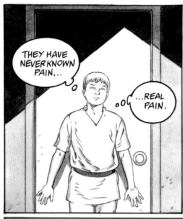

THEY HAVE NEVER KNOWN PAIN...

...REAL PAIN.

THE REALIZATION MADE HIM FEEL DESPERATELY LONELY, AND HE RUBBED HIS THROBBING LEG.

HE EVENTUALLY SLEPT. AGAIN AND AGAIN HE DREAMED OF THE ANGUISH AND THE ISOLATION ON THE FORSAKEN HILL.

THE DAILY TRAINING CONTINUED, AND NOW IT ALWAYS INCLUDED PAIN. THE AGONY OF THE FRACTURED LEG BEGAN TO SEEM NO MORE THAN A MILD DISCOMFORT AS THE GIVER LED JONAS FIRMLY, LITTLE BY LITTLE, INTO THE DEEP AND TERRIBLE SUFFERING OF THE PAST.

EACH TIME, IN HIS KINDNESS, THE GIVER ENDED THE AFTERNOON WITH A COLOR-FILLED MEMORY OF PLEASURE.

IT WAS NOT ENOUGH TO ASSUAGE THE PAIN THAT JONAS WAS BEGINNING TO KNOW.

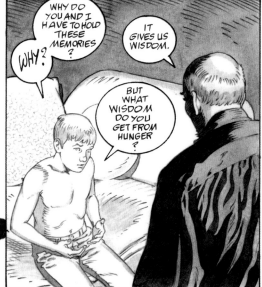

WHY DO YOU AND I HAVE TO HOLD THESE MEMORIES?

WHY?

IT GIVES US WISDOM.

BUT WHAT WISDOM DO YOU GET FROM HUNGER?

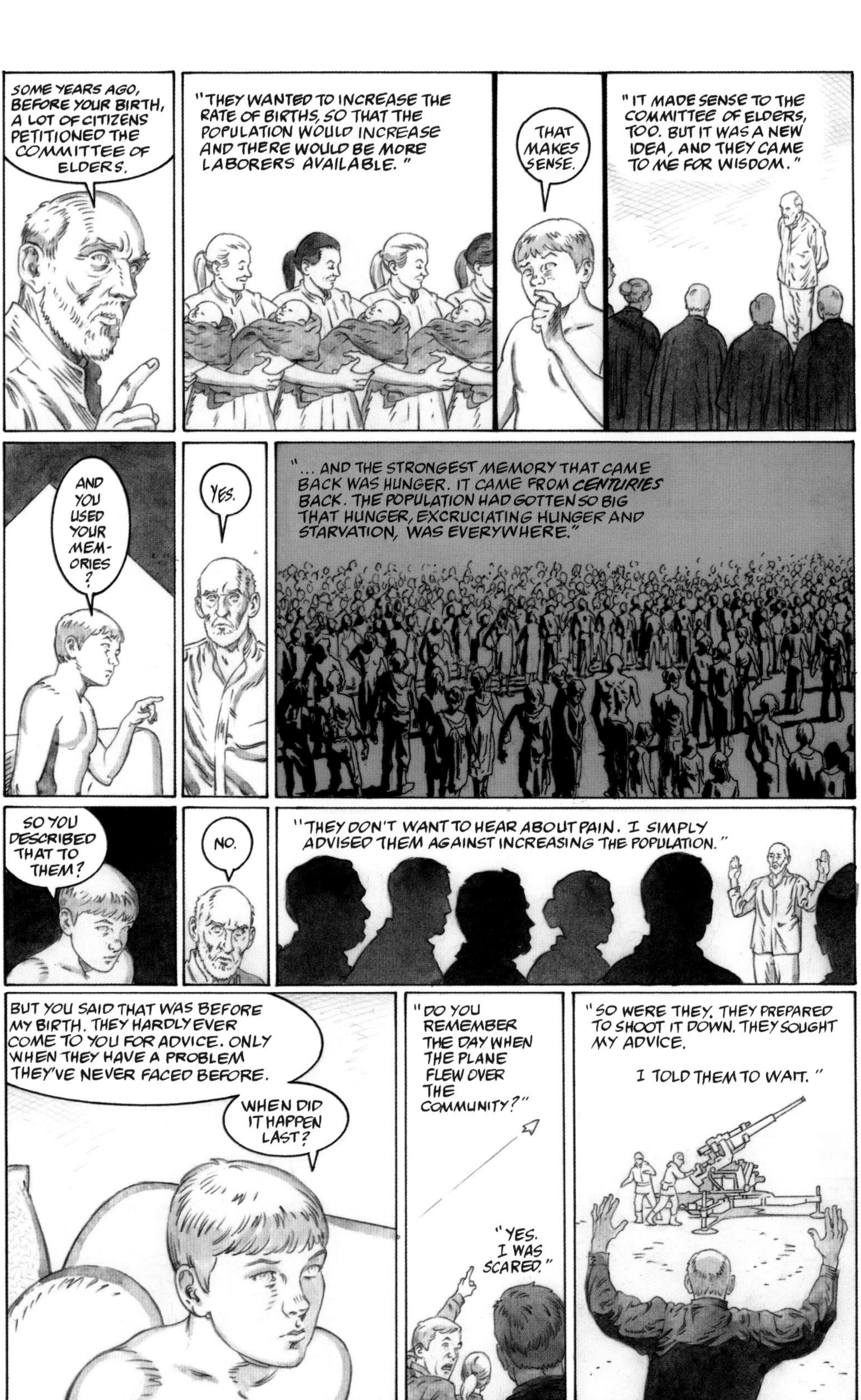
SOME YEARS AGO, BEFORE YOUR BIRTH, A LOT OF CITIZENS PETITIONED THE COMMITTEE OF ELDERS.
"THEY WANTED TO INCREASE THE RATE OF BIRTHS, SO THAT THE POPULATION WOULD INCREASE AND THERE WOULD BE MORE LABORERS AVAILABLE."
THAT MAKES SENSE.
"IT MADE SENSE TO THE COMMITTEE OF ELDERS, TOO. BUT IT WAS A NEW IDEA, AND THEY CAME TO ME FOR WISDOM."
AND YOU USED YOUR MEM-ORIES?
YES.
"... AND THE STRONGEST MEMORY THAT CAME BACK WAS HUNGER. IT CAME FROM CENTURIES BACK. THE POPULATION HAD GOTTEN SO BIG THAT HUNGER, EXCRUCIATING HUNGER AND STARVATION, WAS EVERYWHERE."
SO YOU DESCRIBED THAT TO THEM?
NO.
"THEY DON'T WANT TO HEAR ABOUT PAIN. I SIMPLY ADVISED THEM AGAINST INCREASING THE POPULATION."
BUT YOU SAID THAT WAS BEFORE MY BIRTH. THEY HARDLY EVER COME TO YOU FOR ADVICE. ONLY WHEN THEY HAVE A PROBLEM THEY'VE NEVER FACED BEFORE.
WHEN DID IT HAPPEN LAST?
"DO YOU REMEMBER THE DAY WHEN THE PLANE FLEW OVER THE COMMUNITY?"
"YES. I WAS SCARED."
"SO WERE THEY. THEY PREPARED TO SHOOT IT DOWN. THEY SOUGHT MY ADVICE.
I TOLD THEM TO WAIT."

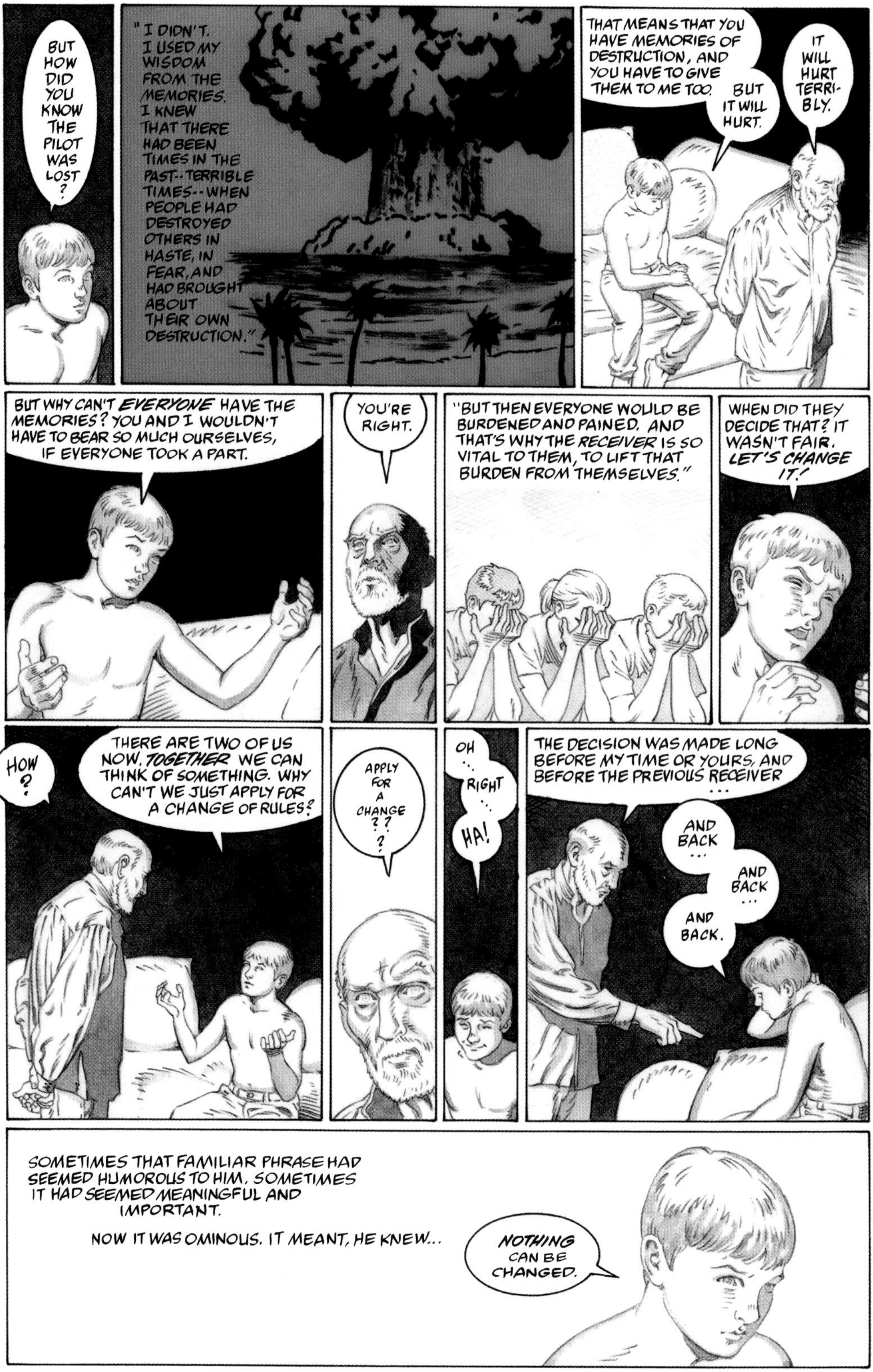
BUT HOW DID YOU KNOW THE PILOT WAS LOST?
"I DIDN'T. I USED MY WISDOM FROM THE MEMORIES. I KNEW THAT THERE HAD BEEN TIMES IN THE PAST--TERRIBLE TIMES--WHEN PEOPLE HAD DESTROYED OTHERS IN HASTE, IN FEAR, AND HAD BROUGHT ABOUT THEIR OWN DESTRUCTION."
THAT MEANS THAT YOU HAVE MEMORIES OF DESTRUCTION, AND YOU HAVE TO GIVE THEM TO ME TOO.
BUT IT WILL HURT.
IT WILL HURT TERRIBLY.
BUT WHY CAN'T EVERYONE HAVE THE MEMORIES? YOU AND I WOULDN'T HAVE TO BEAR SO MUCH OURSELVES, IF EVERYONE TOOK A PART.
YOU'RE RIGHT.
"BUT THEN EVERYONE WOULD BE BURDENED AND PAINED. AND THAT'S WHY THE RECEIVER IS SO VITAL TO THEM, TO LIFT THAT BURDEN FROM THEMSELVES."
WHEN DID THEY DECIDE THAT? IT WASN'T FAIR. LET'S CHANGE IT!
HOW?
THERE ARE TWO OF US NOW. TOGETHER WE CAN THINK OF SOMETHING. WHY CAN'T WE JUST APPLY FOR A CHANGE OF RULES?
APPLY FOR A CHANGE???
OH... RIGHT...
HA!
THE DECISION WAS MADE LONG BEFORE MY TIME OR YOURS, AND BEFORE THE PREVIOUS RECEIVER...
AND BACK...
AND BACK...
AND BACK.
SOMETIMES THAT FAMILIAR PHRASE HAD SEEMED HUMOROUS TO HIM, SOMETIMES IT HAD SEEMED MEANINGFUL AND IMPORTANT.
NOW IT WAS OMINOUS. IT MEANT, HE KNEW...
NOTHING CAN BE CHANGED.

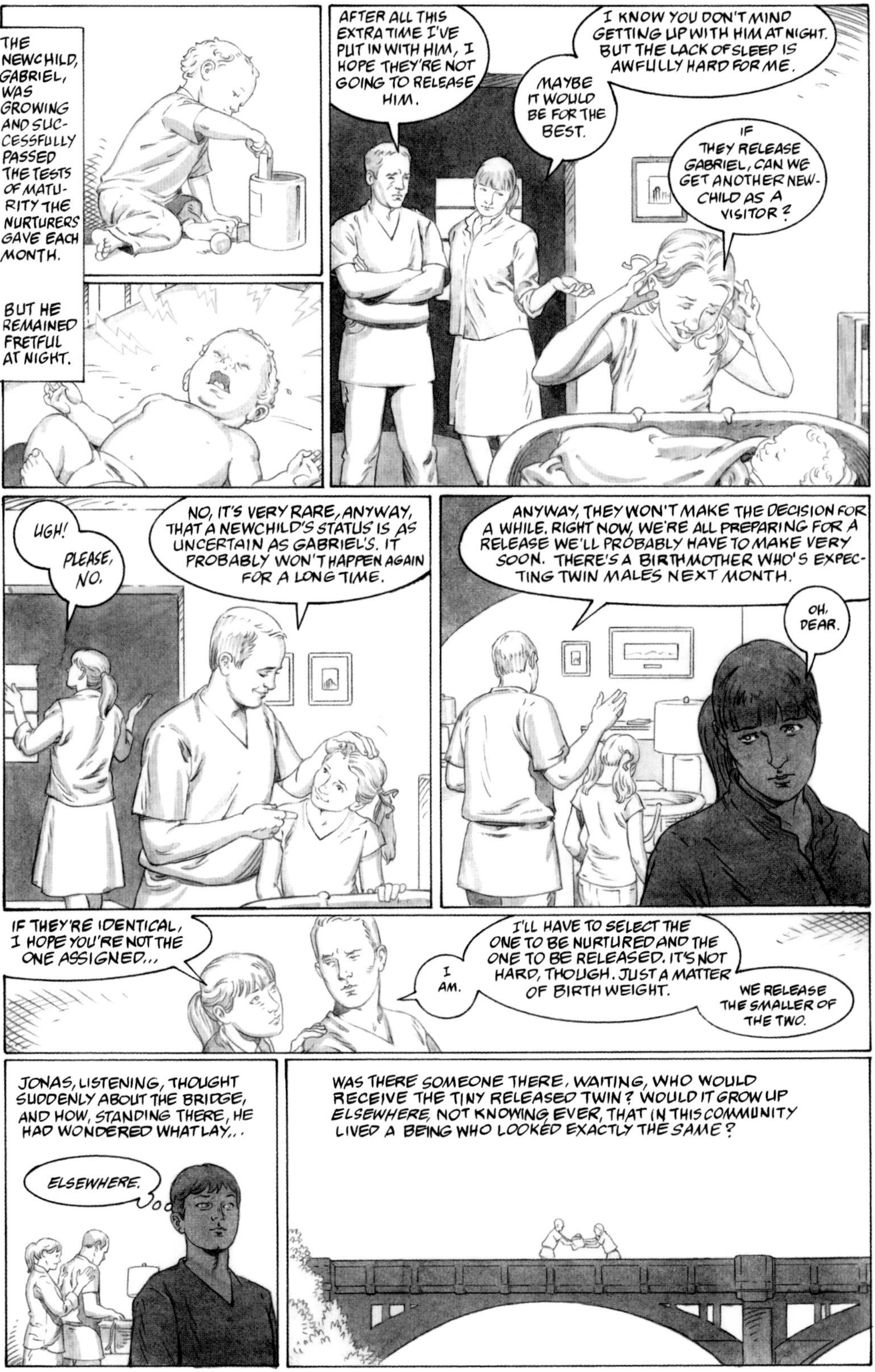
THE NEWCHILD, GABRIEL, WAS GROWING AND SUCCESSFULLY PASSED THE TESTS OF MATURITY THE NURTURERS GAVE EACH MONTH.
BUT HE REMAINED FRETFUL AT NIGHT.
AFTER ALL THIS EXTRA TIME I'VE PUT IN WITH HIM, I HOPE THEY'RE NOT GOING TO RELEASE HIM.
I KNOW YOU DON'T MIND GETTING UP WITH HIM AT NIGHT. BUT THE LACK OF SLEEP IS AWFULLY HARD FOR ME.
MAYBE IT WOULD BE FOR THE BEST.
IF THEY RELEASE GABRIEL, CAN WE GET ANOTHER NEWCHILD AS A VISITOR?
UGH! PLEASE, NO.
NO, IT'S VERY RARE, ANYWAY, THAT A NEWCHILD'S STATUS IS AS UNCERTAIN AS GABRIEL'S. IT PROBABLY WON'T HAPPEN AGAIN FOR A LONG TIME.
ANYWAY, THEY WON'T MAKE THE DECISION FOR A WHILE. RIGHT NOW, WE'RE ALL PREPARING FOR A RELEASE WE'LL PROBABLY HAVE TO MAKE VERY SOON. THERE'S A BIRTHMOTHER WHO'S EXPECTING TWIN MALES NEXT MONTH.
OH, DEAR.
IF THEY'RE IDENTICAL, I HOPE YOU'RE NOT THE ONE ASSIGNED...
I AM.
I'LL HAVE TO SELECT THE ONE TO BE NURTURED AND THE ONE TO BE RELEASED. IT'S NOT HARD, THOUGH. JUST A MATTER OF BIRTH WEIGHT.
WE RELEASE THE SMALLER OF THE TWO.
JONAS, LISTENING, THOUGHT SUDDENLY ABOUT THE BRIDGE, AND HOW, STANDING THERE, HE HAD WONDERED WHAT LAY...
ELSEWHERE.
WAS THERE SOMEONE THERE, WAITING, WHO WOULD RECEIVE THE TINY RELEASED TWIN? WOULD IT GROW UP ELSEWHERE, NOT KNOWING EVER, THAT IN THIS COMMUNITY LIVED A BEING WHO LOOKED EXACTLY THE SAME?

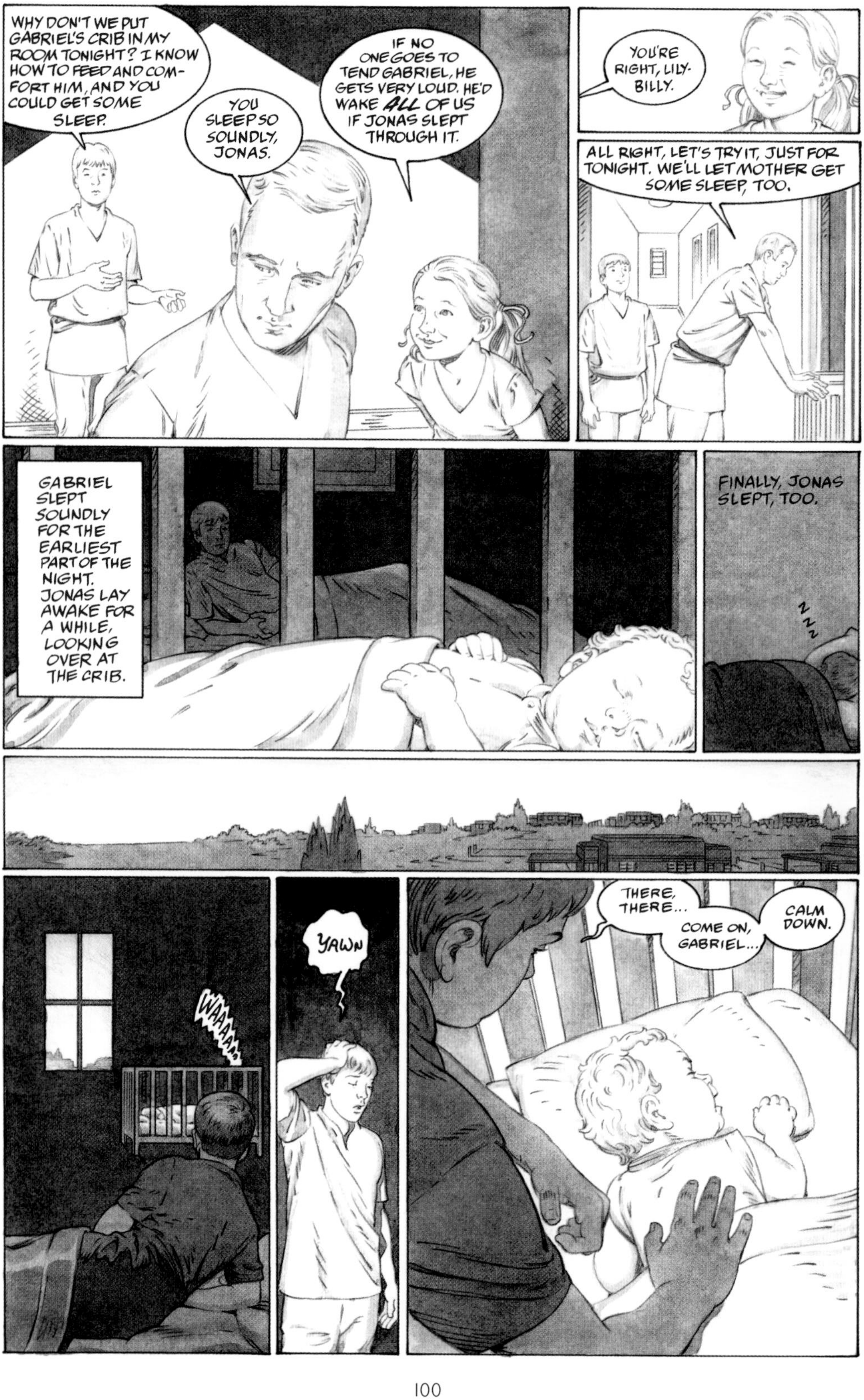
WHY DON'T WE PUT GABRIEL'S CRIB IN MY ROOM TONIGHT? I KNOW HOW TO FEED AND COMFORT HIM, AND YOU COULD GET SOME SLEEP.
YOU SLEEP SO SOUNDLY, JONAS.
IF NO ONE GOES TO TEND GABRIEL, HE GETS VERY LOUD. HE'D WAKE ALL OF US IF JONAS SLEPT THROUGH IT.
YOU'RE RIGHT, LILY-BILLY.
ALL RIGHT, LET'S TRY IT, JUST FOR TONIGHT. WE'LL LET MOTHER GET SOME SLEEP, TOO.
GABRIEL SLEPT SOUNDLY FOR THE EARLIEST PART OF THE NIGHT. JONAS LAY AWAKE FOR A WHILE, LOOKING OVER AT THE CRIB.
FINALLY, JONAS SLEPT, TOO.
Z Z Z
WAAAAAA
YAWN
THERE, THERE...
COME ON, GABRIEL...
CALM DOWN.

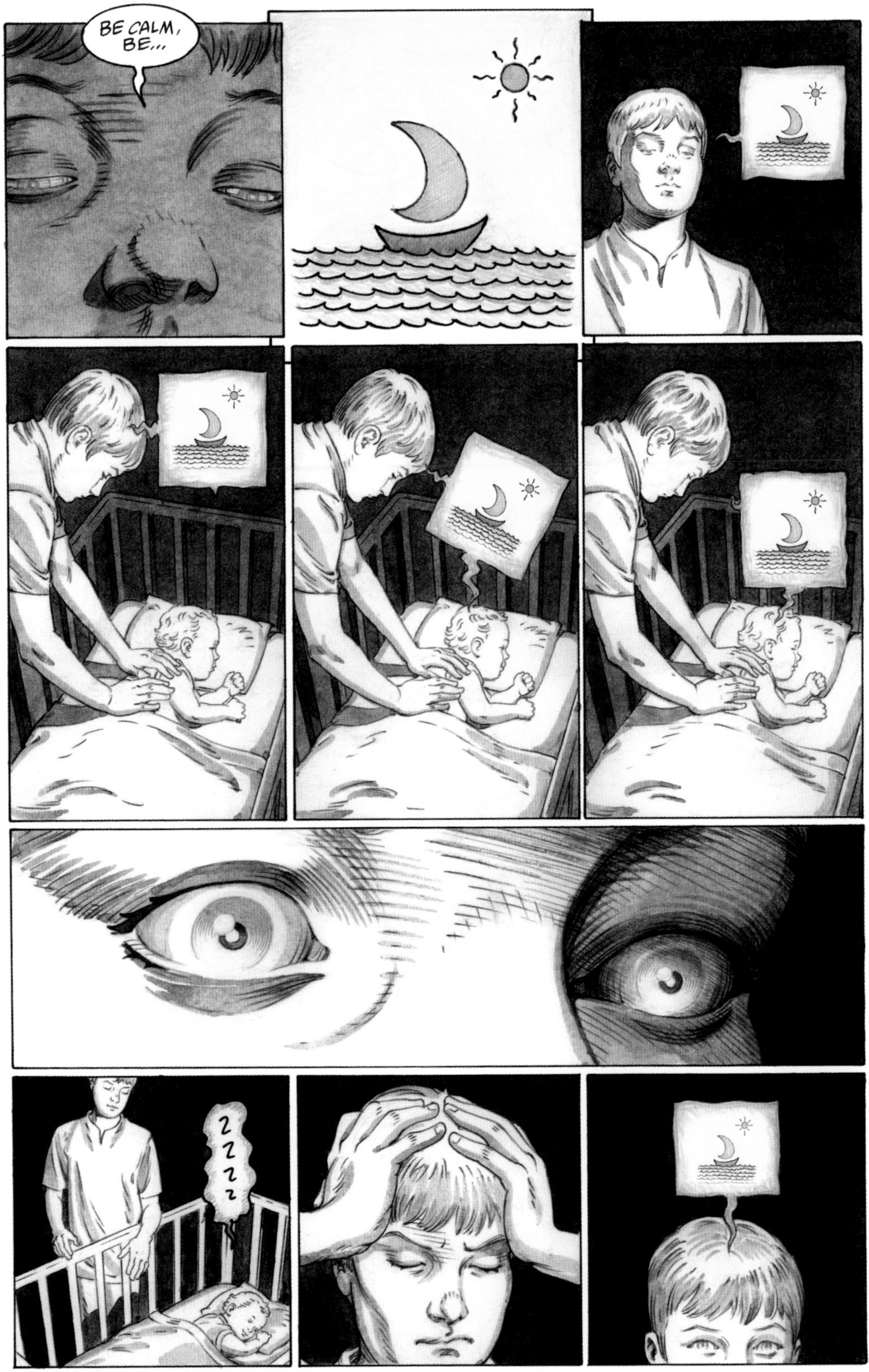
BE CALM,
BE...
ZZZZ

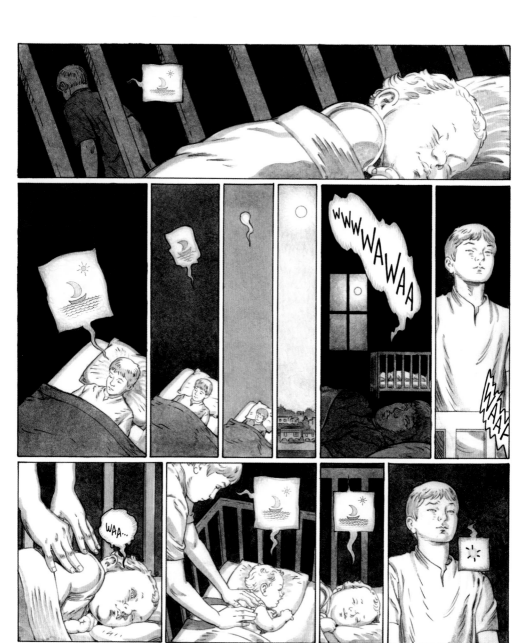

JONAS NO LONGER HAD ANY MORE THAN A WISP OF THE SAIL-BOAT MEMORY, AND HE FELT A SMALL LACK WHERE IT HAD BEEN.

SHOULD I CONFESS TO THE GIVER THAT I'VE GIVEN A MEMORY AWAY?

I'M NOT YET QUALIFIED TO BE A GIVER MYSELF.

AND GABRIEL HASN'T BEEN SELECTED TO BE A RECEIVER.

HE DECIDED NOT TO TELL.

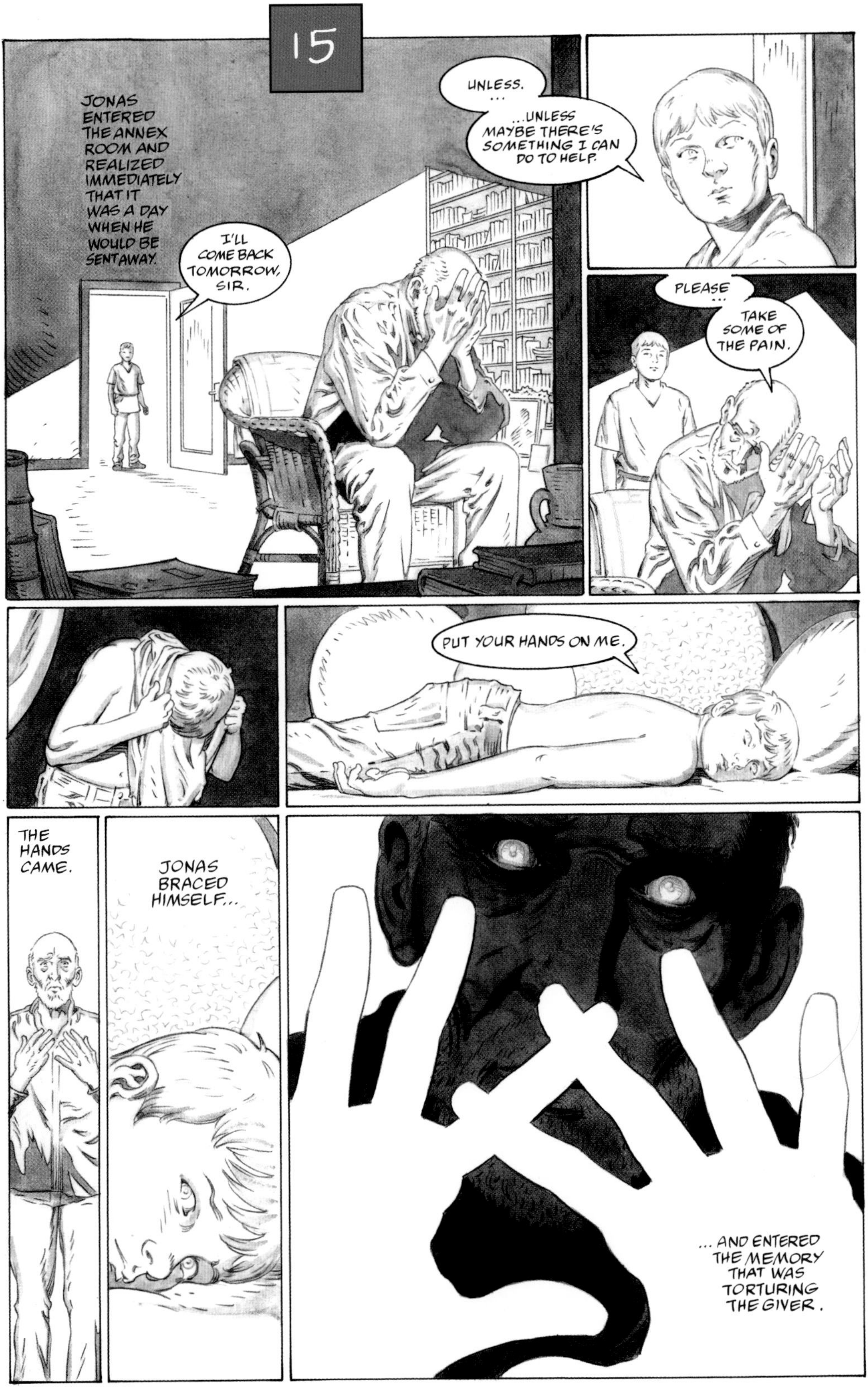
15
JONAS ENTERED THE ANNEX ROOM AND REALIZED IMMEDIATELY THAT IT WAS A DAY WHEN HE WOULD BE SENT AWAY.
I'LL COME BACK TOMORROW, SIR.
UNLESS. ...
...UNLESS MAYBE THERE'S SOMETHING I CAN DO TO HELP.
PLEASE ...
TAKE SOME OF THE PAIN.
PUT YOUR HANDS ON ME.
THE HANDS CAME.
JONAS BRACED HIMSELF...
...AND ENTERED THE MEMORY THAT WAS TORTURING THE GIVER.

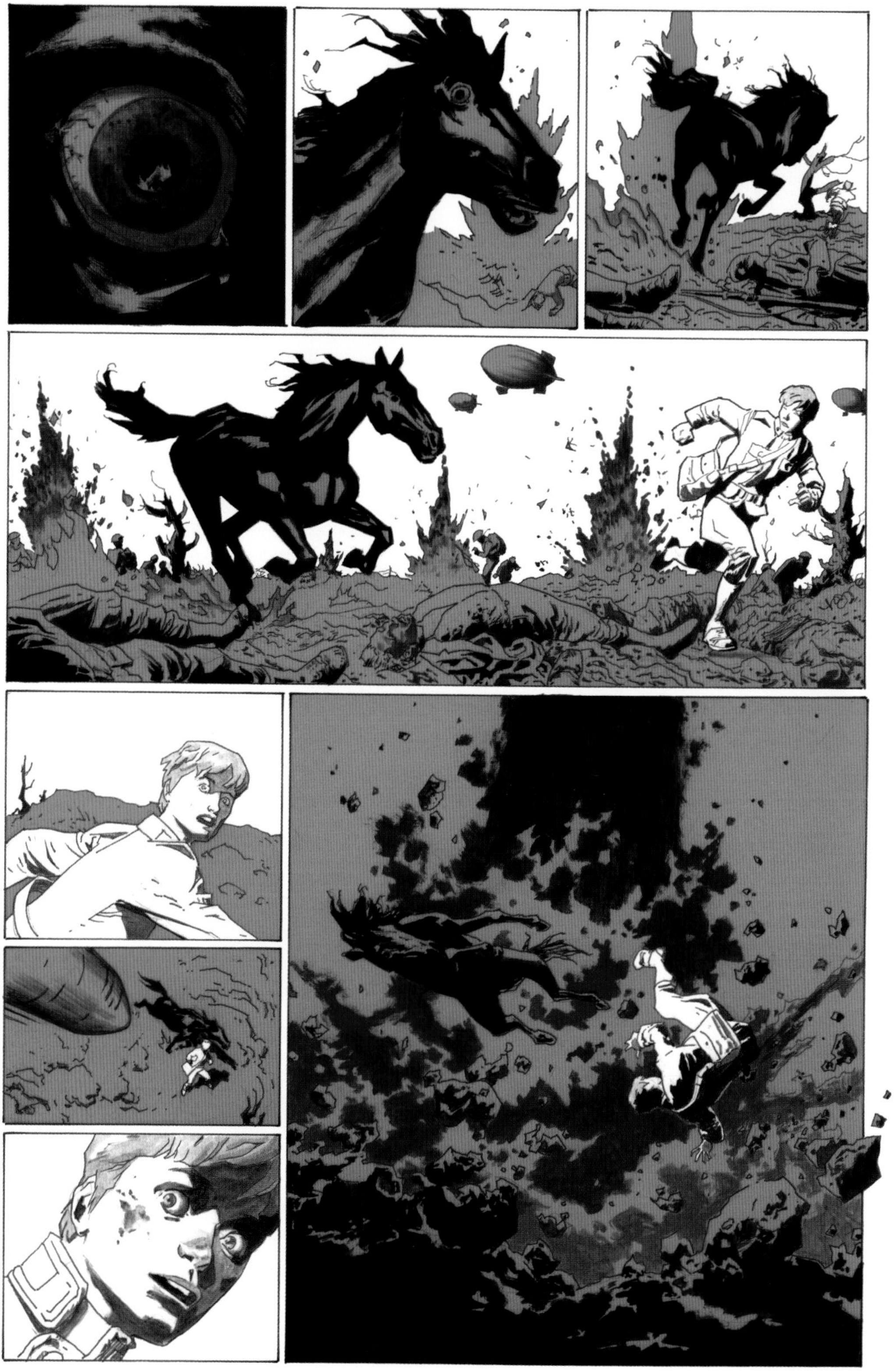

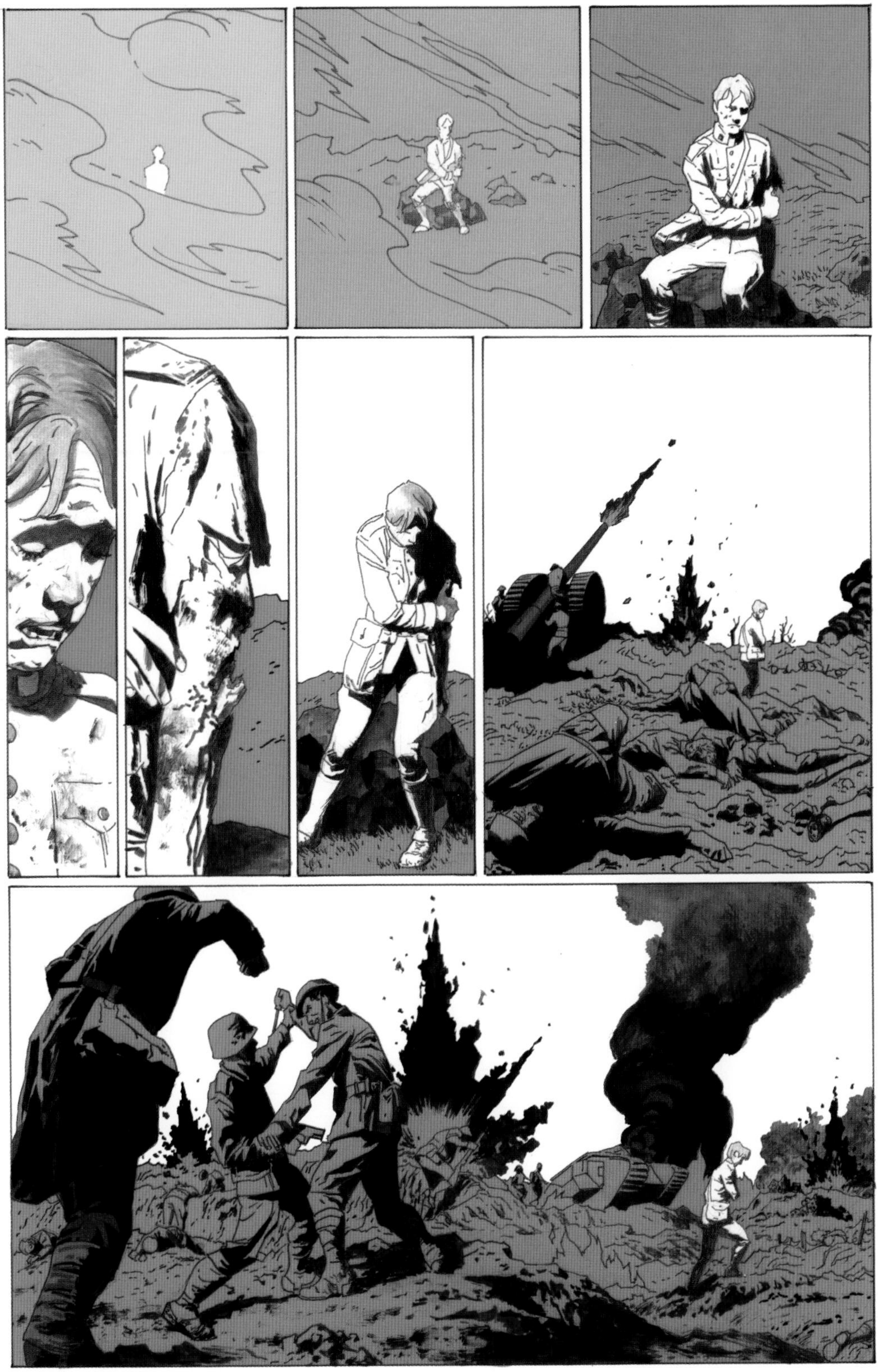

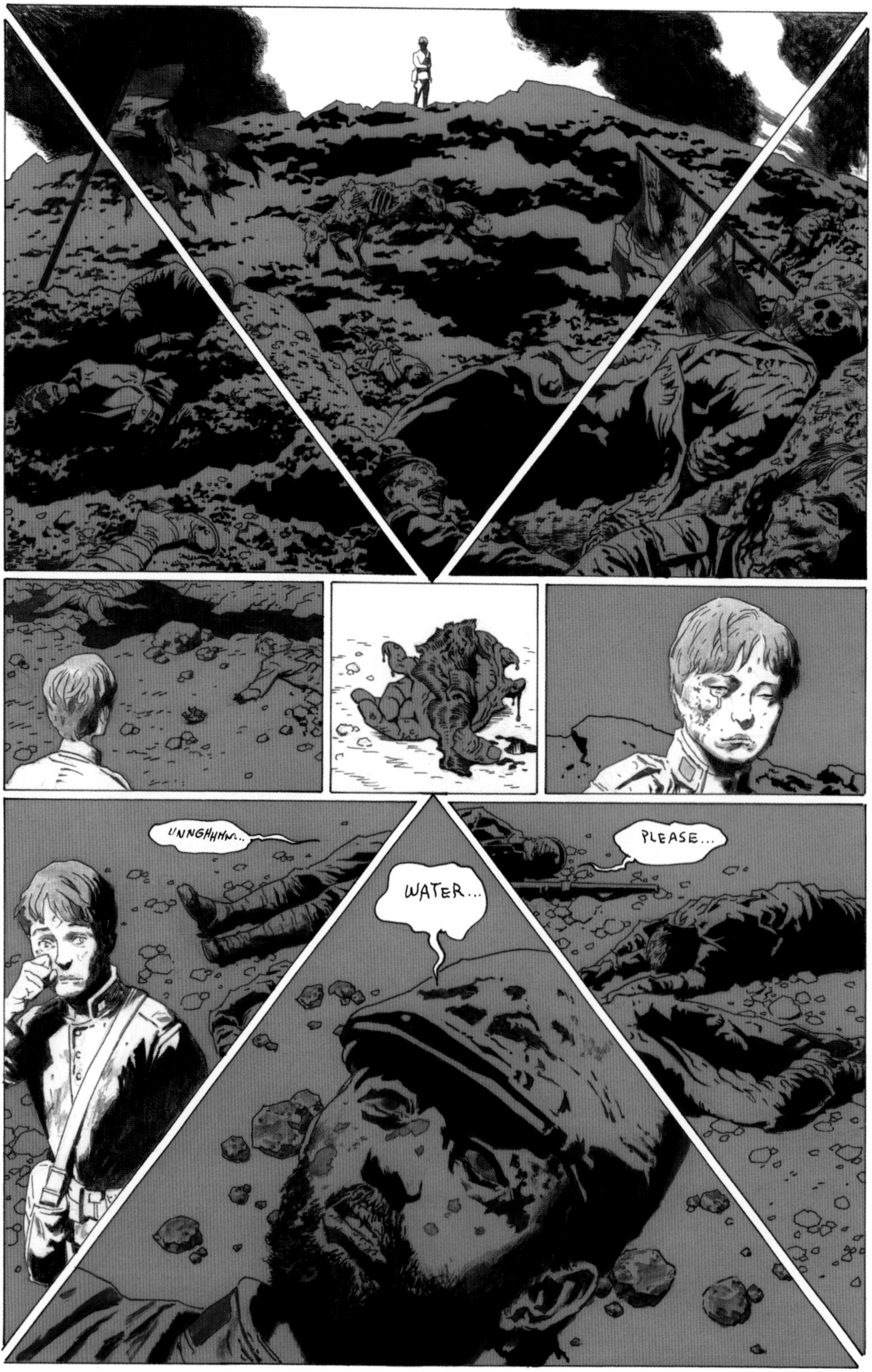
UNNGHHHN...
WATER...
PLEASE...

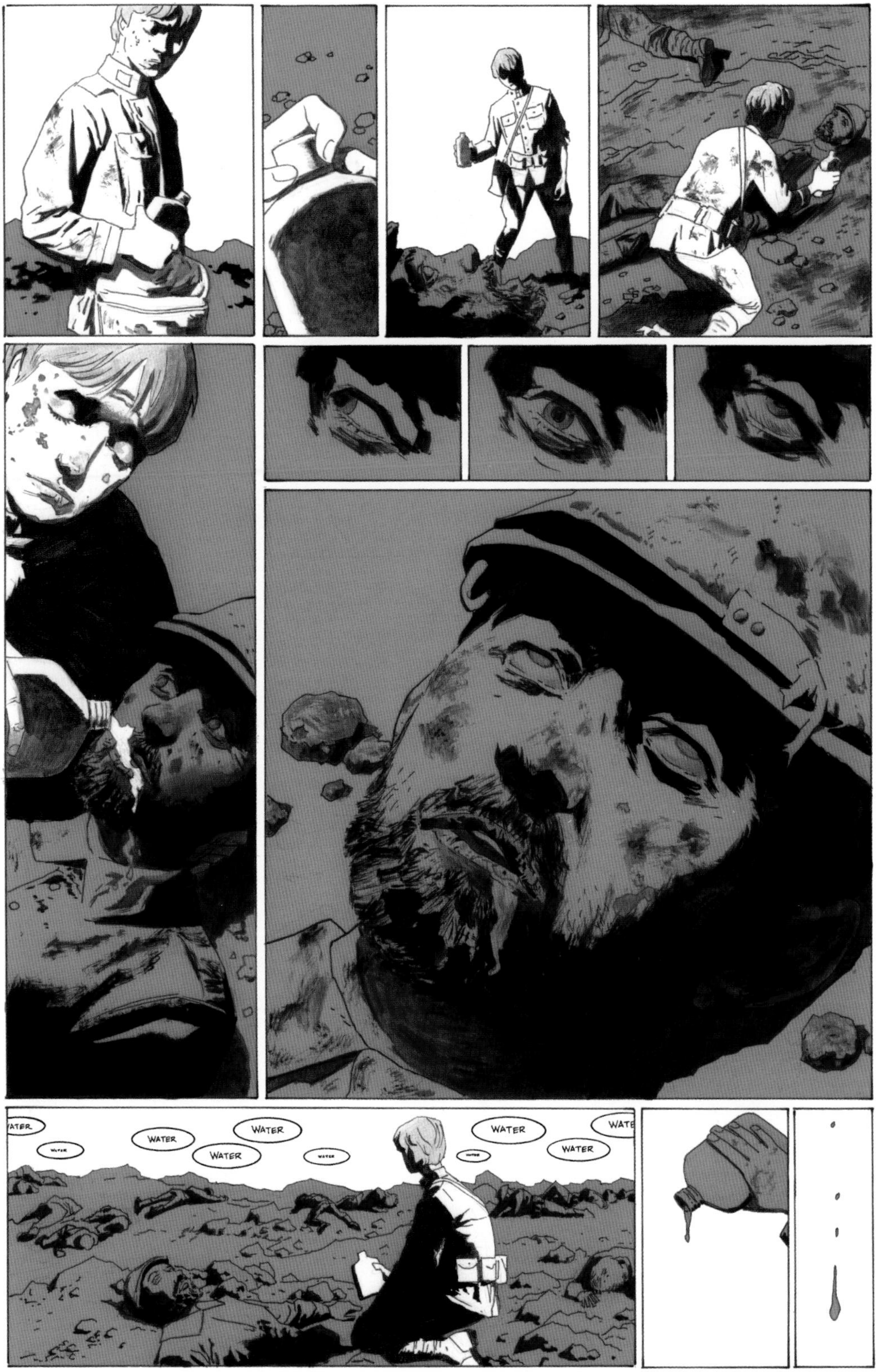
ATER
WATER
WATER
WATER
WATER
WATER
WATE

FROM THE DISTANCE JONAS COULD HEAR THE THUD OF CANNONS. OVERCOME BY PAIN, HE LAY THERE IN THE FEARSOME STENCH FOR HOURS, LISTENED TO THE MEN AND ANIMALS DIE, AND CAME TO LEARN WHAT WARFARE MEANT.

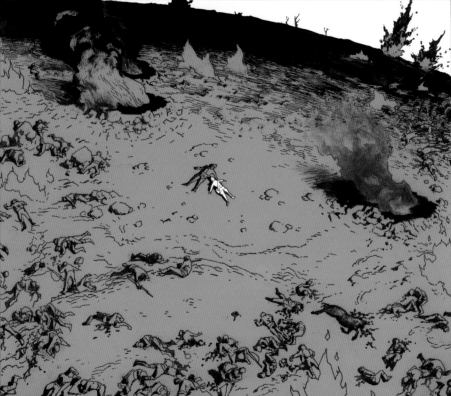

FORGIVE ME.

108

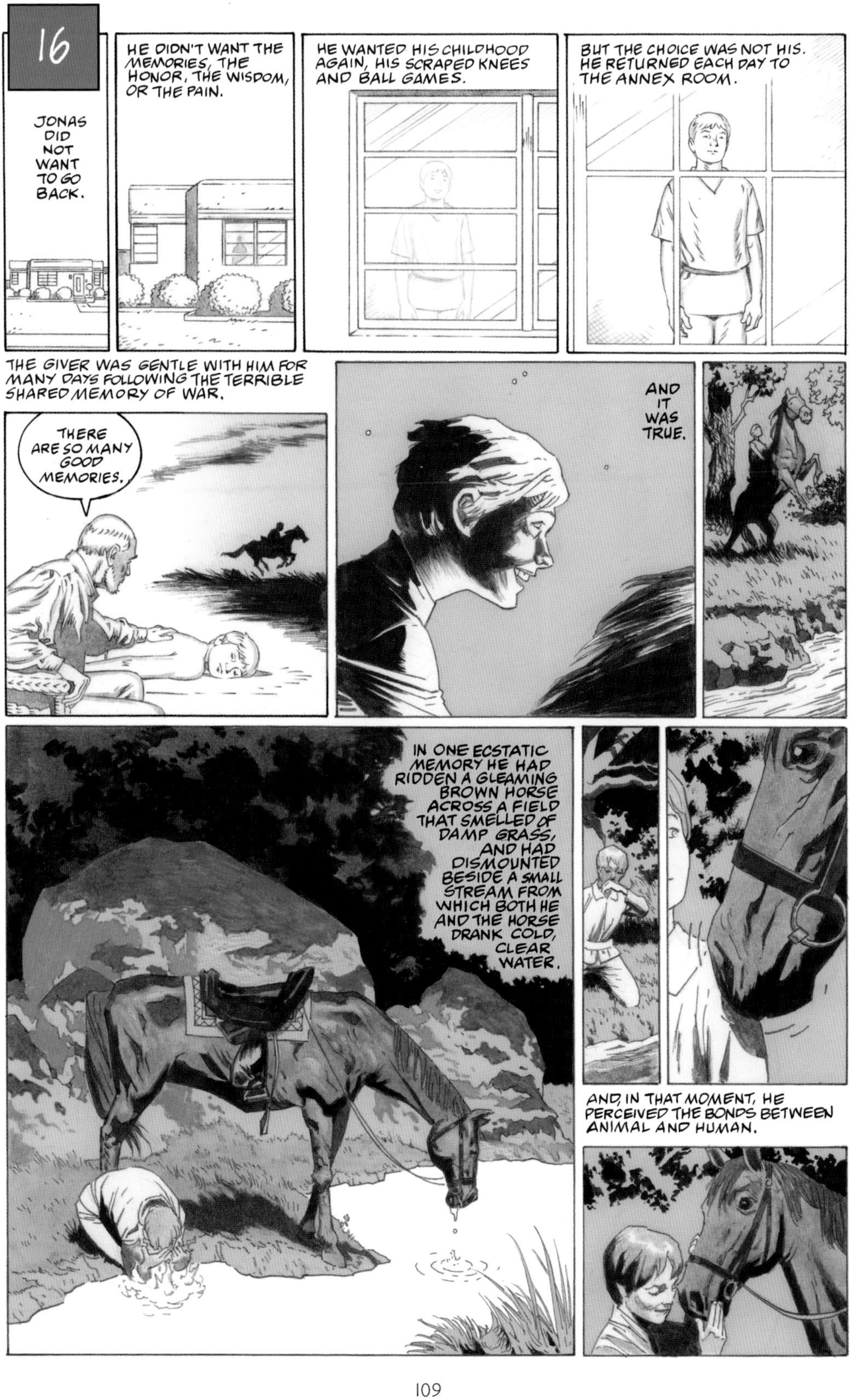
16
JONAS DID NOT WANT TO GO BACK.
HE DIDN'T WANT THE MEMORIES, THE HONOR, THE WISDOM, OR THE PAIN.
HE WANTED HIS CHILDHOOD AGAIN, HIS SCRAPED KNEES AND BALL GAMES.
BUT THE CHOICE WAS NOT HIS. HE RETURNED EACH DAY TO THE ANNEX ROOM.
THE GIVER WAS GENTLE WITH HIM FOR MANY DAYS FOLLOWING THE TERRIBLE SHARED MEMORY OF WAR.
THERE ARE SO MANY GOOD MEMORIES.
AND IT WAS TRUE.
IN ONE ECSTATIC MEMORY HE HAD RIDDEN A GLEAMING BROWN HORSE ACROSS A FIELD THAT SMELLED OF DAMP GRASS, AND HAD DISMOUNTED BESIDE A SMALL STREAM FROM WHICH BOTH HE AND THE HORSE DRANK COLD, CLEAR WATER.
AND, IN THAT MOMENT, HE PERCEIVED THE BONDS BETWEEN ANIMAL AND HUMAN.

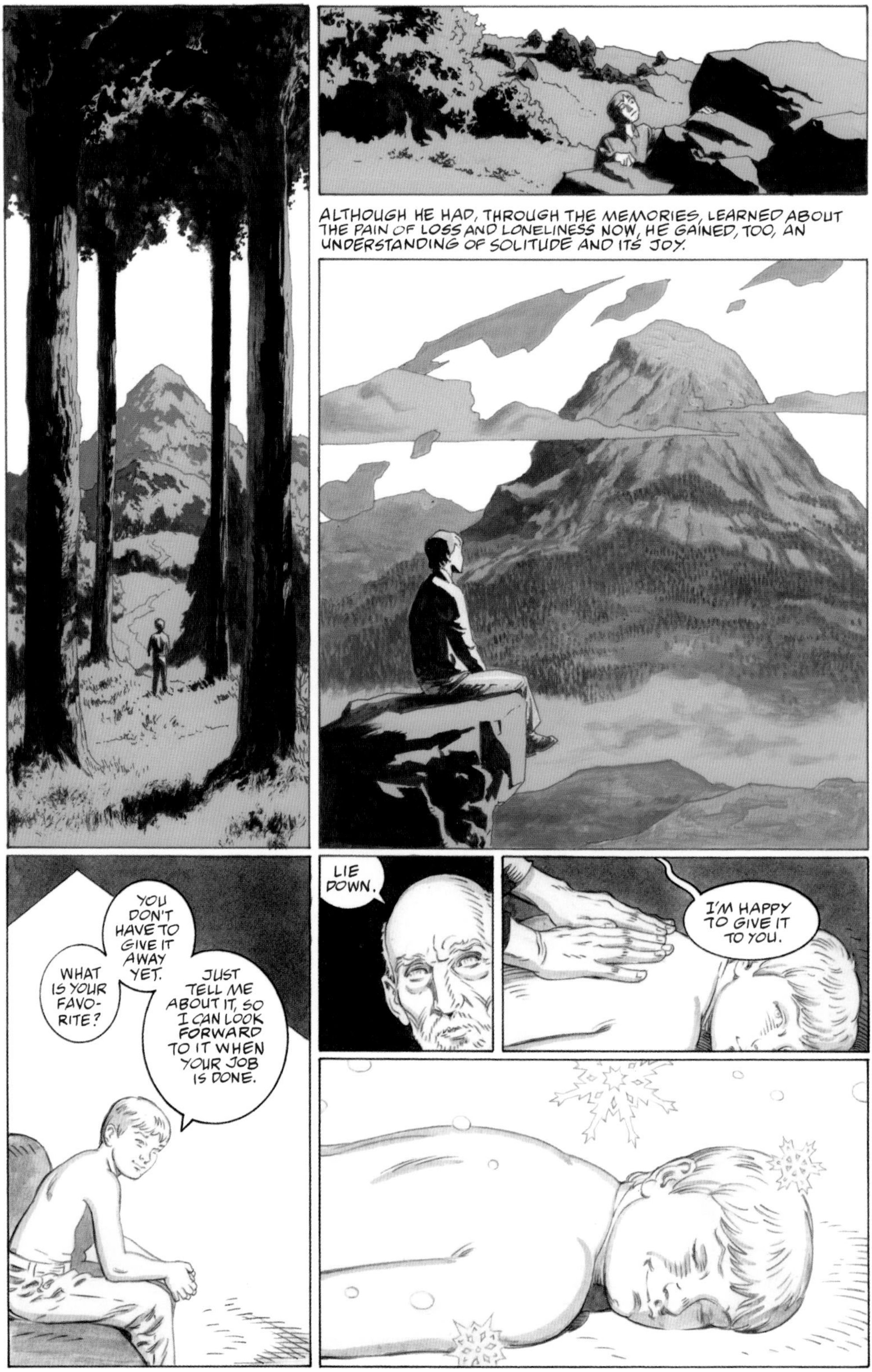
ALTHOUGH HE HAD, THROUGH THE MEMORIES, LEARNED ABOUT THE PAIN OF LOSS AND LONELINESS NOW, HE GAINED, TOO, AN UNDERSTANDING OF SOLITUDE AND ITS JOY.
WHAT IS YOUR FAVORITE?
YOU DON'T HAVE TO GIVE IT AWAY YET.
JUST TELL ME ABOUT IT, SO I CAN LOOK FORWARD TO IT WHEN YOUR JOB IS DONE.
LIE DOWN.
I'M HAPPY TO GIVE IT TO YOU.

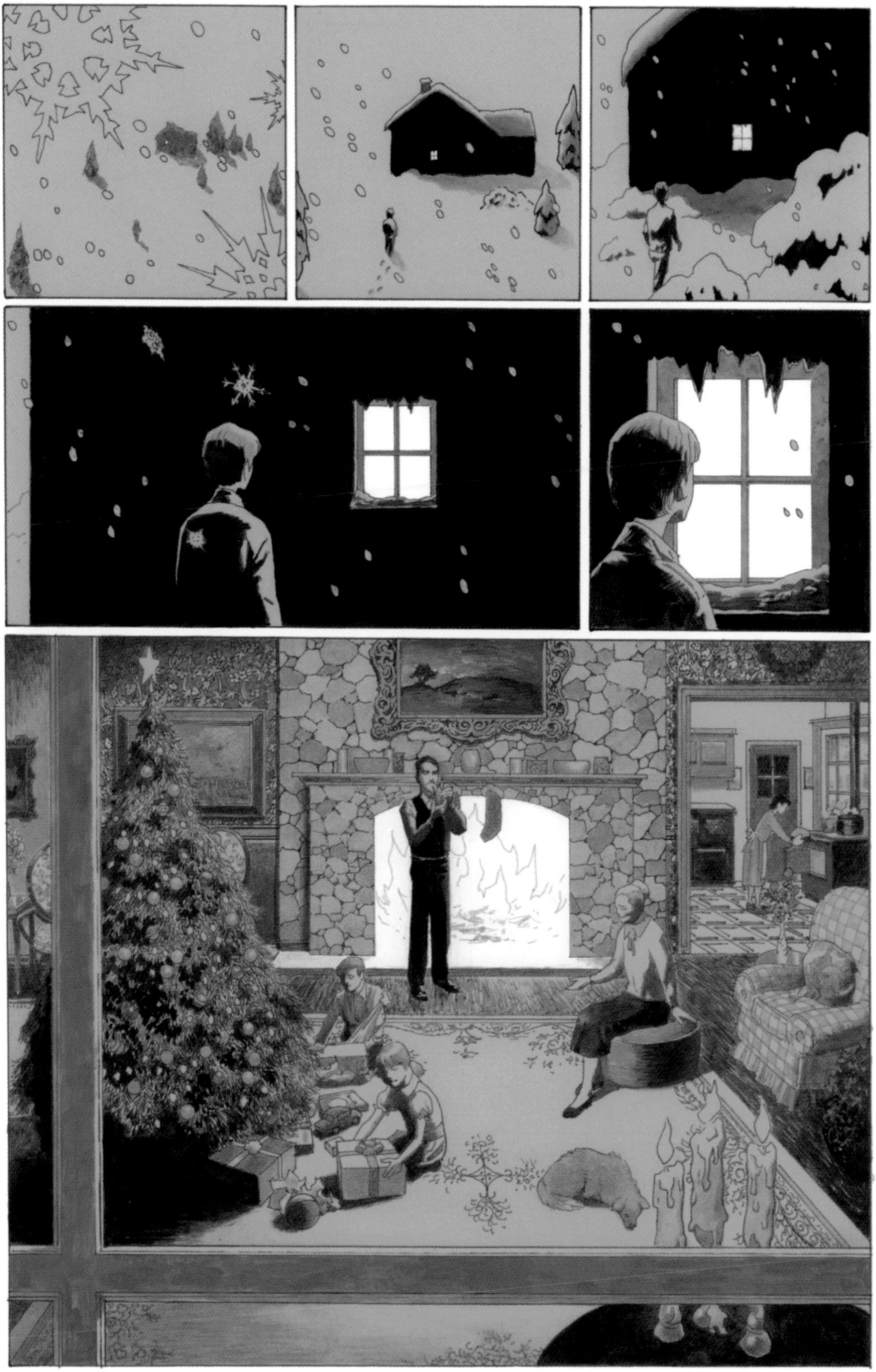

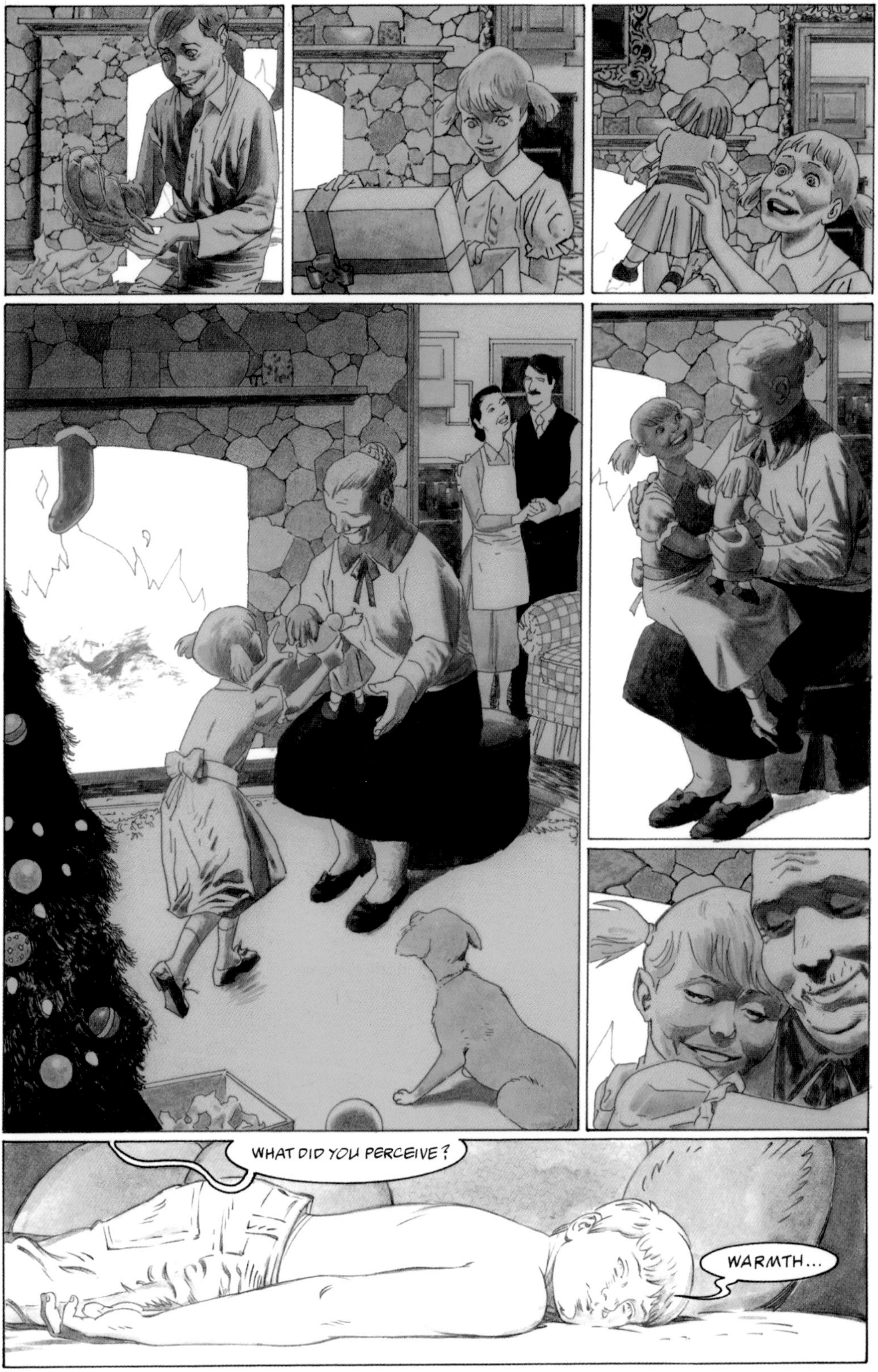
WHAT DID YOU PERCEIVE?
WARMTH...

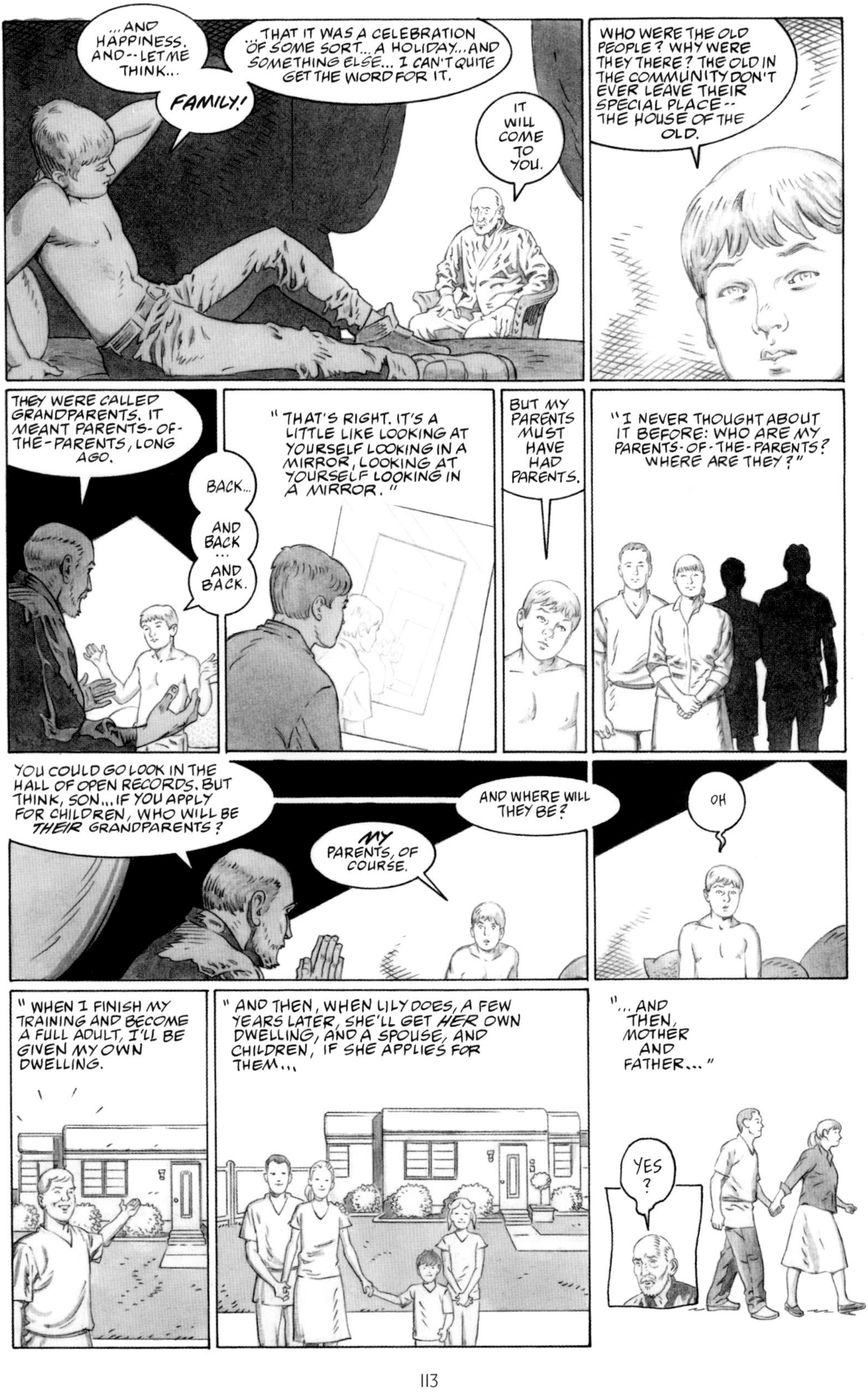
...AND HAPPINESS. AND--LET ME THINK...
...THAT IT WAS A CELEBRATION OF SOME SORT... A HOLIDAY... AND SOMETHING ELSE... I CAN'T QUITE GET THE WORD FOR IT.
FAMILY!
IT WILL COME TO YOU.
WHO WERE THE OLD PEOPLE? WHY WERE THEY THERE? THE OLD IN THE COMMUNITY DON'T EVER LEAVE THEIR SPECIAL PLACE-- THE HOUSE OF THE OLD.
THEY WERE CALLED GRANDPARENTS. IT MEANT PARENTS-OF-THE-PARENTS, LONG AGO.
BACK...
AND BACK...
AND BACK.
"THAT'S RIGHT. IT'S A LITTLE LIKE LOOKING AT YOURSELF LOOKING IN A MIRROR, LOOKING AT YOURSELF LOOKING IN A MIRROR."
BUT MY PARENTS MUST HAVE HAD PARENTS.
"I NEVER THOUGHT ABOUT IT BEFORE: WHO ARE MY PARENTS-OF-THE-PARENTS? WHERE ARE THEY?"
YOU COULD GO LOOK IN THE HALL OF OPEN RECORDS. BUT THINK, SON... IF YOU APPLY FOR CHILDREN, WHO WILL BE THEIR GRANDPARENTS?
MY PARENTS, OF COURSE.
AND WHERE WILL THEY BE?
OH
"WHEN I FINISH MY TRAINING AND BECOME A FULL ADULT, I'LL BE GIVEN MY OWN DWELLING.
"AND THEN, WHEN LILY DOES, A FEW YEARS LATER, SHE'LL GET HER OWN DWELLING, AND A SPOUSE, AND CHILDREN, IF SHE APPLIES FOR THEM...
"...AND THEN, MOTHER AND FATHER..."
YES?

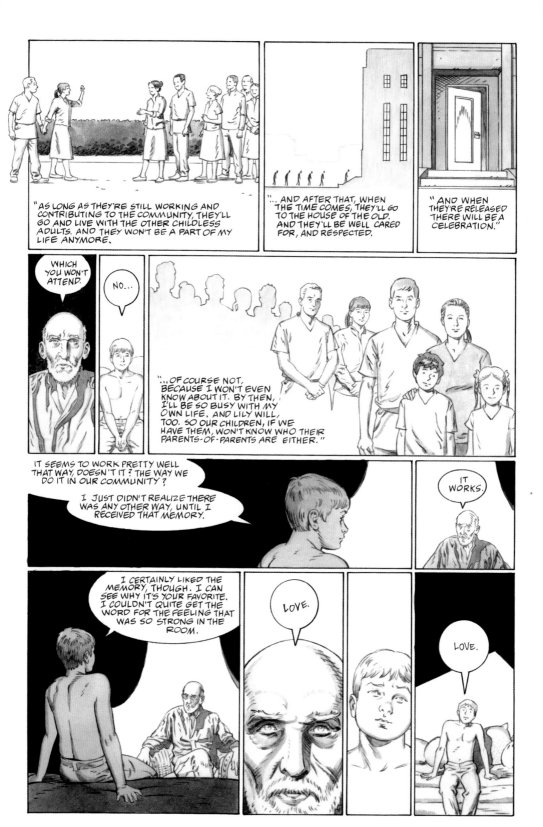

"AS LONG AS THEY'RE STILL WORKING AND CONTRIBUTING TO THE COMMUNITY, THEY'LL GO AND LIVE WITH THE OTHER CHILDLESS ADULTS. AND THEY WON'T BE A PART OF MY LIFE ANYMORE.

"... AND AFTER THAT, WHEN THE TIME COMES, THEY'LL GO TO THE HOUSE OF THE OLD. AND THEY'LL BE WELL CARED FOR, AND RESPECTED.

"AND WHEN THEY'RE RELEASED THERE WILL BE A CELEBRATION."

WHICH YOU WON'T ATTEND.

NO...

"...OF COURSE NOT, BECAUSE I WON'T EVEN KNOW ABOUT IT. BY THEN, I'LL BE SO BUSY WITH MY OWN LIFE. AND LILY WILL, TOO. SO OUR CHILDREN, IF WE HAVE THEM, WON'T KNOW WHO THEIR PARENTS-OF-PARENTS ARE EITHER."

IT SEEMS TO WORK PRETTY WELL THAT WAY, DOESN'T IT? THE WAY WE DO IT IN OUR COMMUNITY?

I JUST DIDN'T REALIZE THERE WAS ANY OTHER WAY, UNTIL I RECEIVED THAT MEMORY.

IT WORKS.

I CERTAINLY LIKED THE MEMORY, THOUGH. I CAN SEE WHY IT'S YOUR FAVORITE. I COULDN'T QUITE GET THE WORD FOR THE FEELING THAT WAS SO STRONG IN THE ROOM.

LOVE.

LOVE.

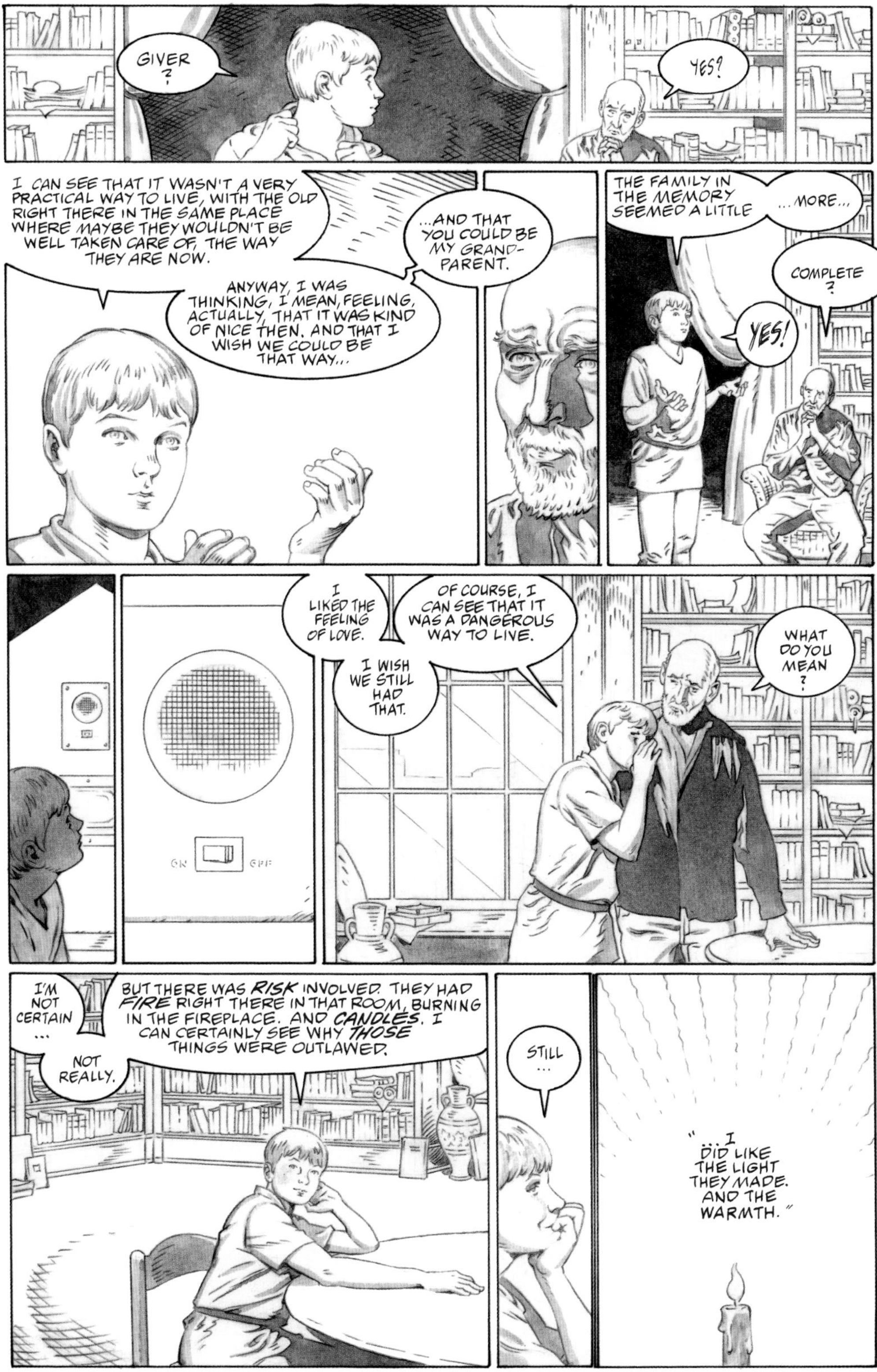
GIVER?
YES?
I CAN SEE THAT IT WASN'T A VERY PRACTICAL WAY TO LIVE, WITH THE OLD RIGHT THERE IN THE SAME PLACE WHERE MAYBE THEY WOULDN'T BE WELL TAKEN CARE OF, THE WAY THEY ARE NOW.
ANYWAY, I WAS THINKING, I MEAN, FEELING, ACTUALLY, THAT IT WAS KIND OF NICE THEN. AND THAT I WISH WE COULD BE THAT WAY...
...AND THAT YOU COULD BE MY GRAND-PARENT.
THE FAMILY IN THE MEMORY SEEMED A LITTLE
...MORE...
COMPLETE?
YES!
I LIKED THE FEELING OF LOVE.
I WISH WE STILL HAD THAT.
OF COURSE, I CAN SEE THAT IT WAS A DANGEROUS WAY TO LIVE.
WHAT DO YOU MEAN?
ON
OFF
I'M NOT CERTAIN...
NOT REALLY.
BUT THERE WAS RISK INVOLVED. THEY HAD FIRE RIGHT THERE IN THAT ROOM, BURNING IN THE FIREPLACE. AND CANDLES. I CAN CERTAINLY SEE WHY THOSE THINGS WERE OUTLAWED.
STILL...
"...I DID LIKE THE LIGHT THEY MADE. AND THE WARMTH."

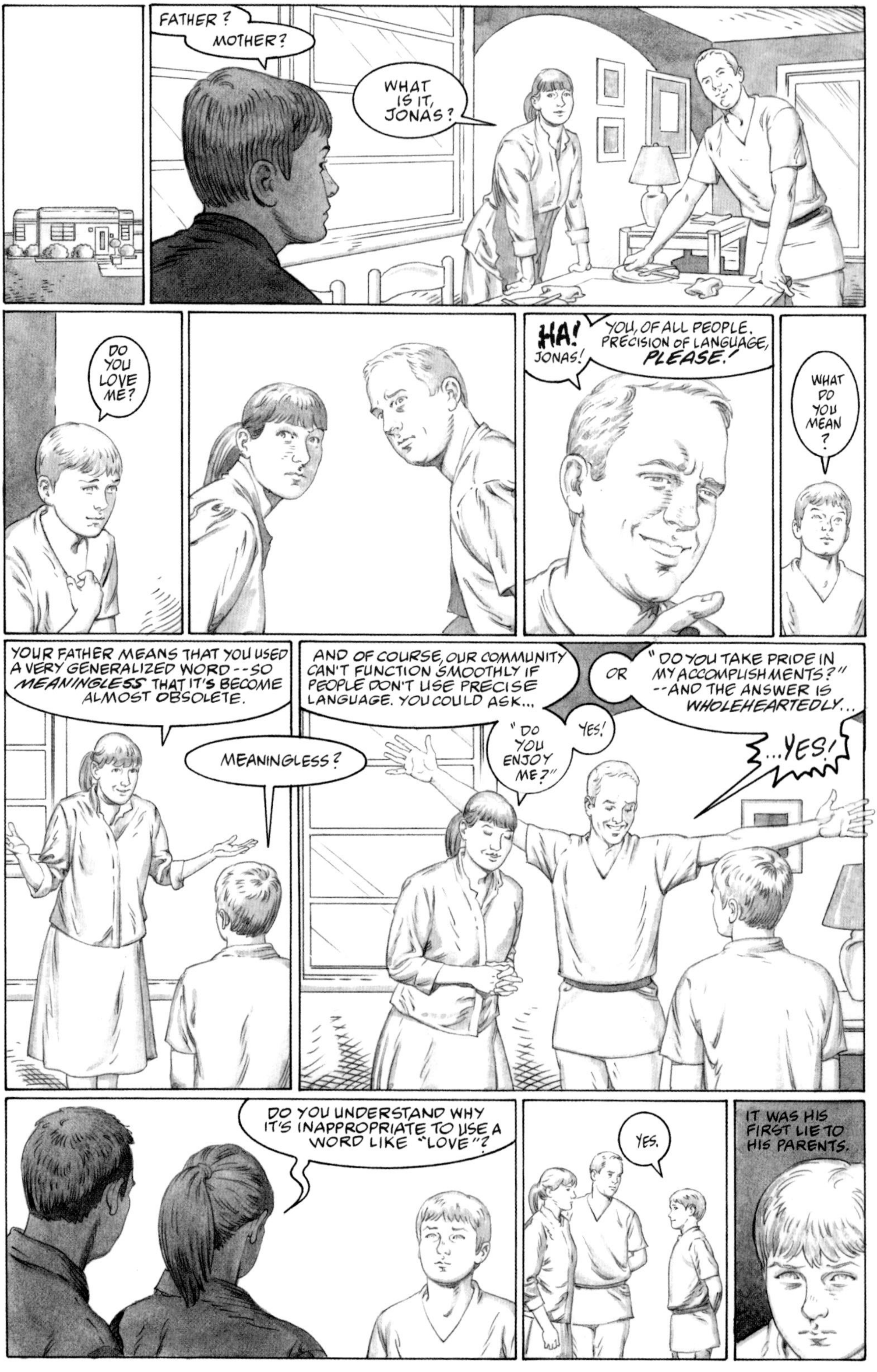

FATHER? MOTHER?
WHAT IS IT, JONAS?
DO YOU LOVE ME?
HA! JONAS!
YOU, OF ALL PEOPLE. PRECISION OF LANGUAGE, PLEASE!
WHAT DO YOU MEAN?
YOUR FATHER MEANS THAT YOU USED A VERY GENERALIZED WORD--SO MEANINGLESS THAT IT'S BECOME ALMOST OBSOLETE.
MEANINGLESS?
AND OF COURSE, OUR COMMUNITY CAN'T FUNCTION SMOOTHLY IF PEOPLE DON'T USE PRECISE LANGUAGE. YOU COULD ASK...
"DO YOU ENJOY ME?"
YES!
OR
"DO YOU TAKE PRIDE IN MY ACCOMPLISHMENTS?" --AND THE ANSWER IS WHOLEHEARTEDLY...
...YES!
DO YOU UNDERSTAND WHY IT'S INAPPROPRIATE TO USE A WORD LIKE "LOVE"?
YES.
IT WAS HIS FIRST LIE TO HIS PARENTS.

THE CRIB WAS IN HIS ROOM AGAIN. AFTER GABE HAD SLEPT SOUNDLY IN JONAS'S ROOM FOR FOUR NIGHTS, HIS PARENTS HAD PRONOUNCED THE EXPERIMENT A SUCCESS.

GABRIEL?

HE CAN BE UPGRADED IN THE NURTURING CENTER, NOW THAT HE'S SLEEPING.

AND HE CAN BE OFFICIALLY NAMED AND GIVEN TO HIS FAMILY IN DECEMBER.

BUT WHEN HE WAS TAKEN AWAY, HE STOPPED SLEEPING AGAIN, AND CRIED IN THE NIGHT.

SO, HE WAS BACK IN JONAS'S SLEEPINGROOM.

THINGS COULD CHANGE, GABE.

THINGS COULD BE DIFFERENT. I DON'T KNOW HOW, BUT THERE MUST BE SOME WAY FOR THINGS TO BE DIFFERENT.

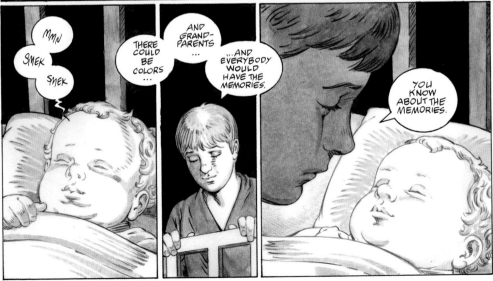

MMN

SMEK

SMEK

THERE COULD BE COLORS ...

AND GRAND-PARENTS ...

...AND EVERYBODY WOULD HAVE THE MEMORIES.

YOU KNOW ABOUT THE MEMORIES.

EACH NIGHT HE GAVE MEMORIES TO GABRIEL: MEMORIES OF BOAT RIDES AND PICNICS IN THE SUN, SOFT RAINFALL AND DANCING BAREFOOT ON THE LAWN.

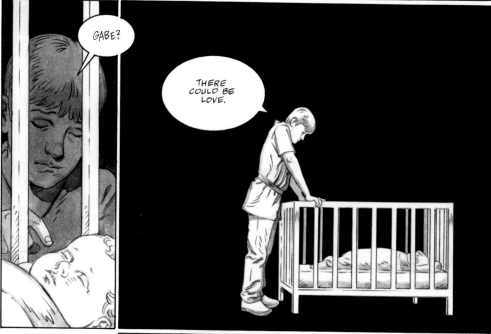

GABE?

THERE COULD BE LOVE.

THE NEXT MORNING, FOR THE FIRST TIME, JONAS DID NOT TAKE HIS PILL.

118

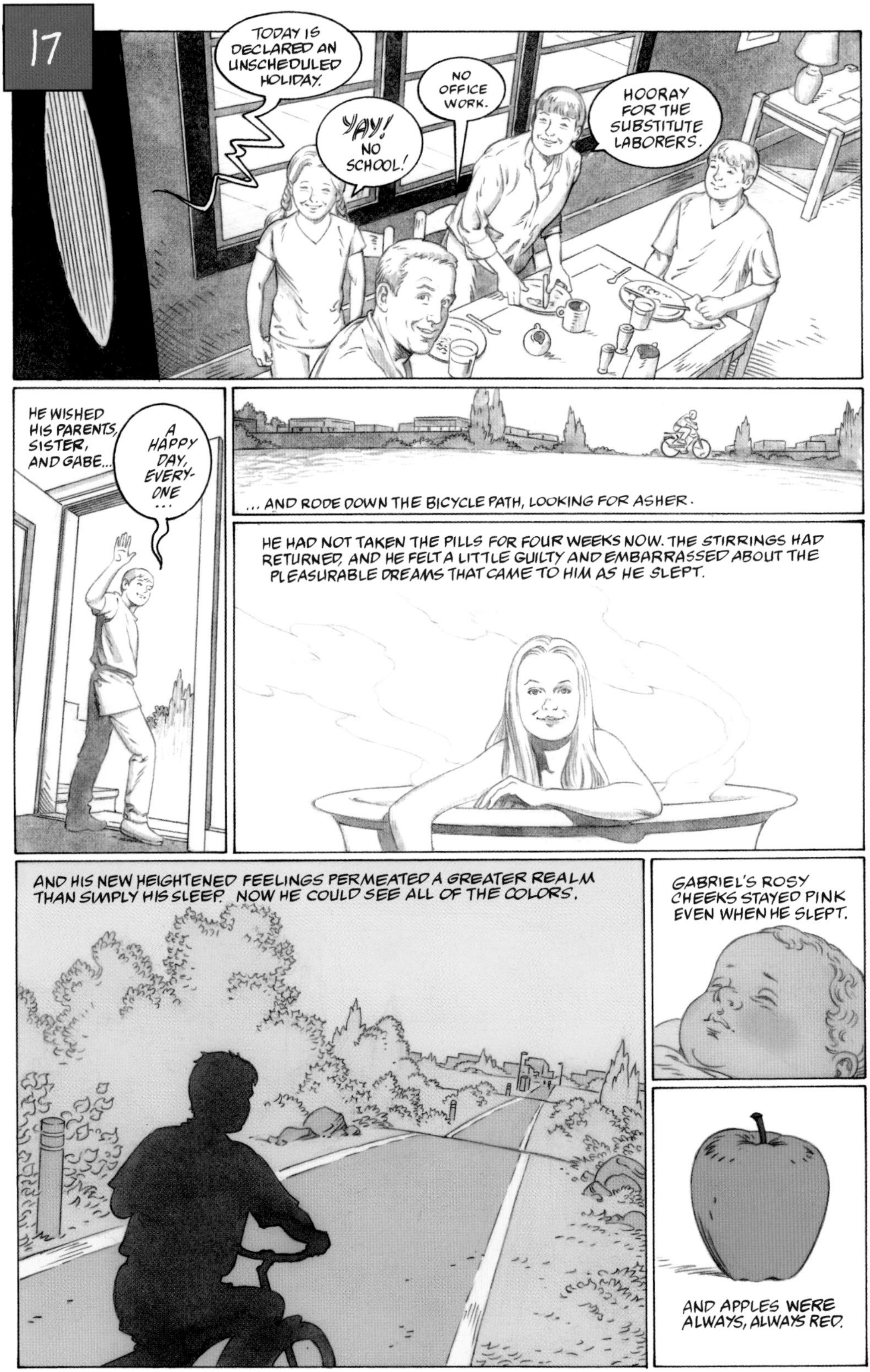
17
TODAY IS DECLARED AN UNSCHEDULED HOLIDAY.
YAY! NO SCHOOL!
NO OFFICE WORK.
HOORAY FOR THE SUBSTITUTE LABORERS.
HE WISHED HIS PARENTS, SISTER, AND GABE...
A HAPPY DAY, EVERYONE . . .
... AND RODE DOWN THE BICYCLE PATH, LOOKING FOR ASHER.
HE HAD NOT TAKEN THE PILLS FOR FOUR WEEKS NOW. THE STIRRINGS HAD RETURNED, AND HE FELT A LITTLE GUILTY AND EMBARRASSED ABOUT THE PLEASURABLE DREAMS THAT CAME TO HIM AS HE SLEPT.
AND HIS NEW HEIGHTENED FEELINGS PERMEATED A GREATER REALM THAN SIMPLY HIS SLEEP. NOW HE COULD SEE ALL OF THE COLORS.
GABRIEL'S ROSY CHEEKS STAYED PINK EVEN WHEN HE SLEPT.
AND APPLES WERE ALWAYS, ALWAYS RED.

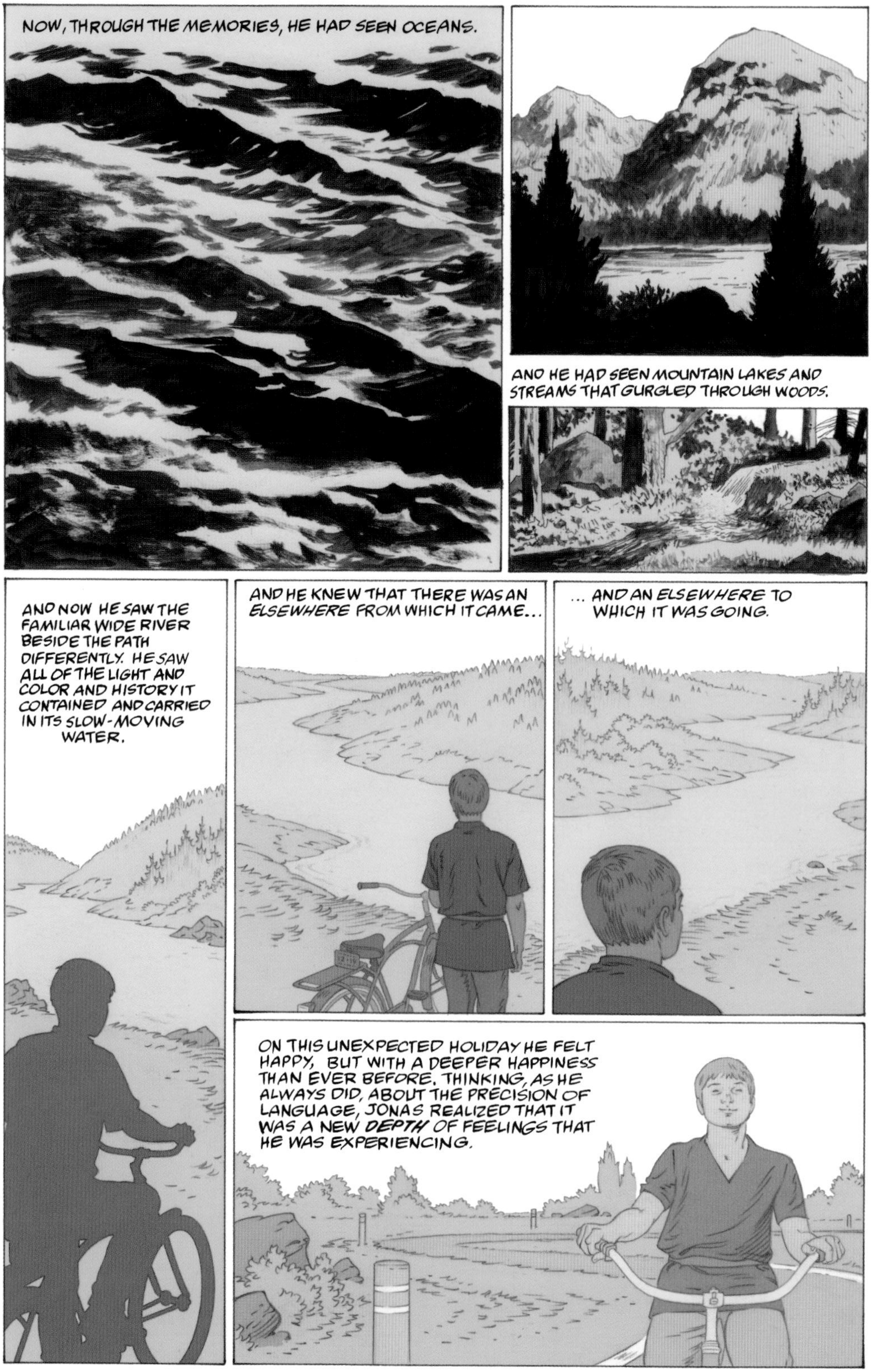
NOW, THROUGH THE MEMORIES, HE HAD SEEN OCEANS.
AND HE HAD SEEN MOUNTAIN LAKES AND STREAMS THAT GURGLED THROUGH WOODS.
AND NOW HE SAW THE FAMILIAR WIDE RIVER BESIDE THE PATH DIFFERENTLY. HE SAW ALL OF THE LIGHT AND COLOR AND HISTORY IT CONTAINED AND CARRIED IN ITS SLOW-MOVING WATER.
AND HE KNEW THAT THERE WAS AN ELSEWHERE FROM WHICH IT CAME...
... AND AN ELSEWHERE TO WHICH IT WAS GOING.
ON THIS UNEXPECTED HOLIDAY HE FELT HAPPY, BUT WITH A DEEPER HAPPINESS THAN EVER BEFORE. THINKING, AS HE ALWAYS DID, ABOUT THE PRECISION OF LANGUAGE, JONAS REALIZED THAT IT WAS A NEW DEPTH OF FEELINGS THAT HE WAS EXPERIENCING.

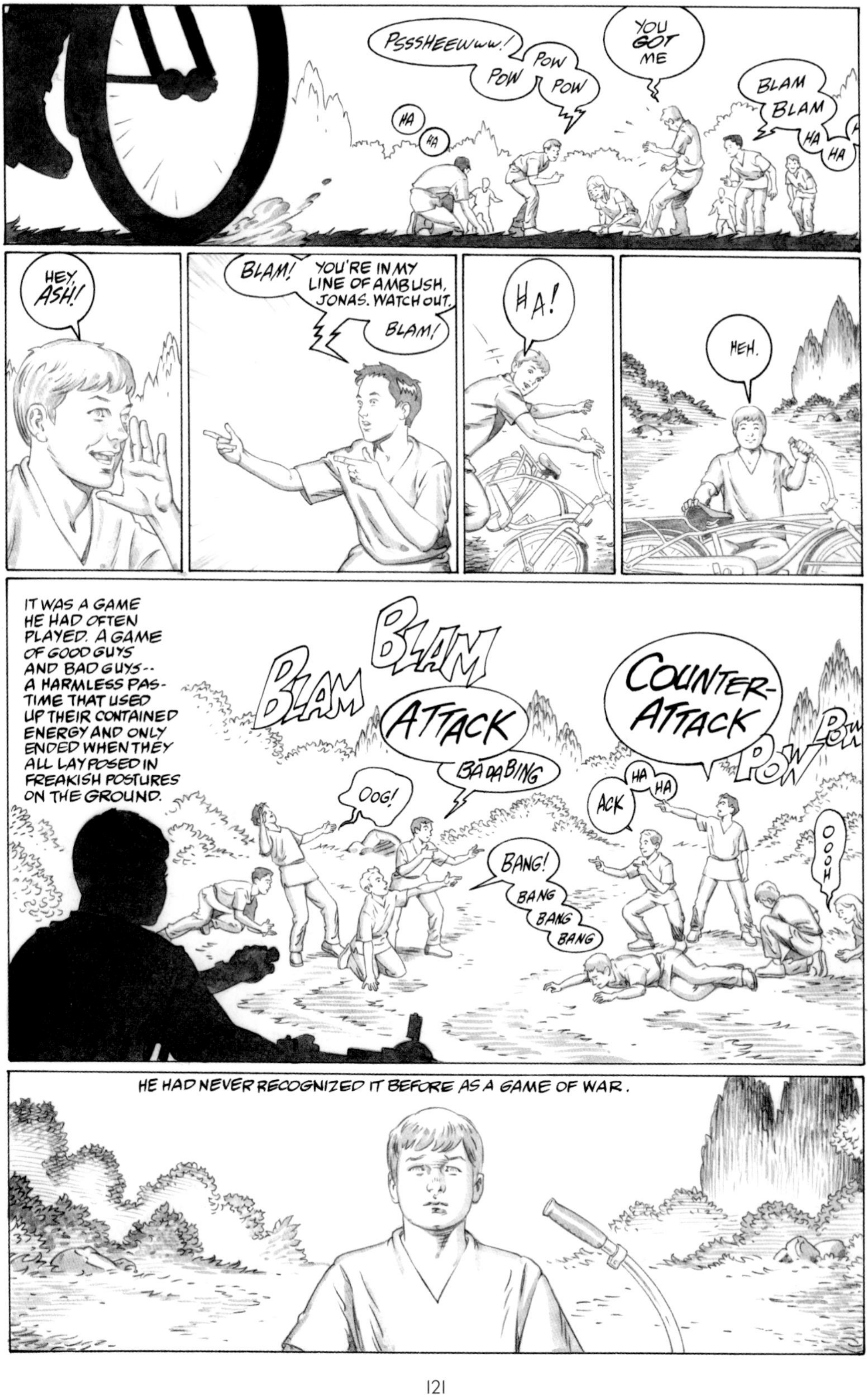
PSSSHEEWWW!
POW POW POW
HA HA
YOU GOT ME
BLAM BLAM
HA HA
HEY, ASH!
BLAM!
YOU'RE IN MY LINE OF AMBUSH, JONAS. WATCH OUT.
BLAM!
HA!
HEH.
IT WAS A GAME HE HAD OFTEN PLAYED. A GAME OF GOOD GUYS AND BAD GUYS-- A HARMLESS PASTIME THAT USED UP THEIR CONTAINED ENERGY AND ONLY ENDED WHEN THEY ALL LAY POSED IN FREAKISH POSTURES ON THE GROUND.
BLAM
BLAM
ATTACK
BA DA BING
OOG!
COUNTER-ATTACK
POW
HA HA
ACK
BANG!
BANG BANG BANG
OOOH
HE HAD NEVER RECOGNIZED IT BEFORE AS A GAME OF WAR.

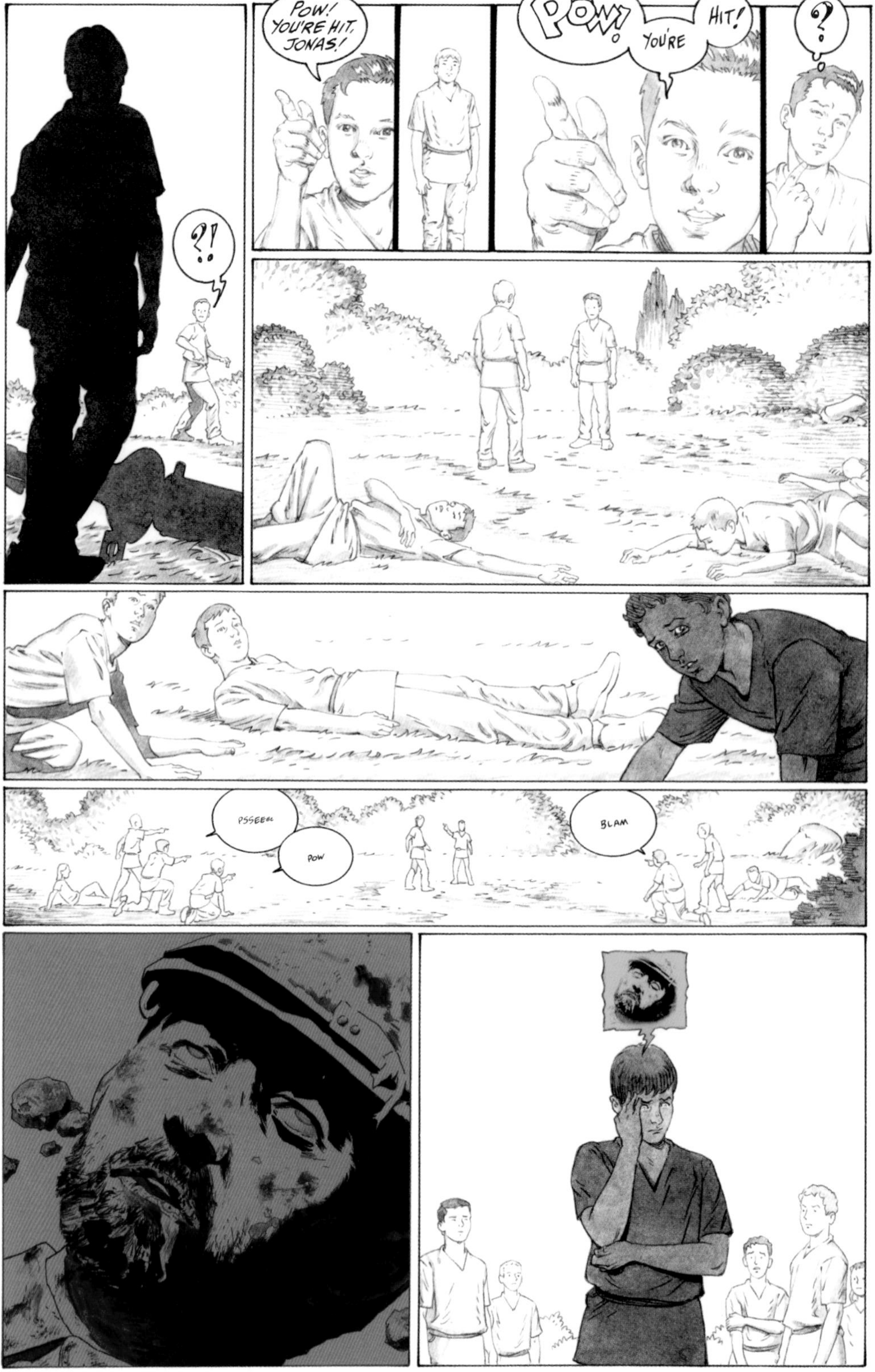

?!
POW! YOU'RE HIT, JONAS!
POW!
YOU'RE
HIT!
?
PSSEEE
POW
BLAM

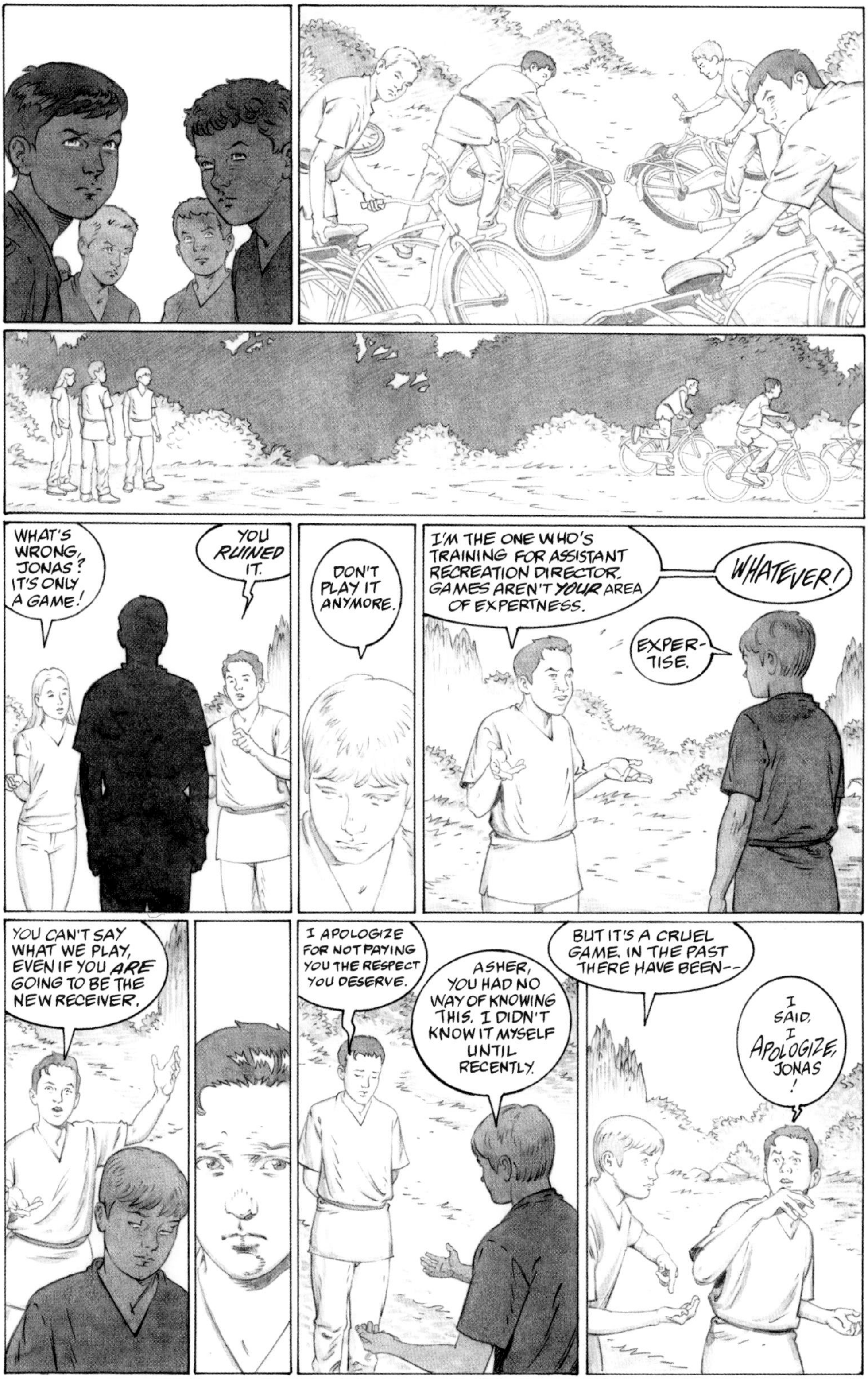
WHAT'S WRONG, JONAS? IT'S ONLY A GAME!
YOU RUINED IT.
DON'T PLAY IT ANYMORE.
I'M THE ONE WHO'S TRAINING FOR ASSISTANT RECREATION DIRECTOR. GAMES AREN'T YOUR AREA OF EXPERTNESS.
EXPERTISE.
WHATEVER!
YOU CAN'T SAY WHAT WE PLAY, EVEN IF YOU ARE GOING TO BE THE NEW RECEIVER.
I APOLOGIZE FOR NOT PAYING YOU THE RESPECT YOU DESERVE.
ASHER, YOU HAD NO WAY OF KNOWING THIS. I DIDN'T KNOW IT MYSELF UNTIL RECENTLY.
BUT IT'S A CRUEL GAME. IN THE PAST THERE HAVE BEEN--
I SAID, I APOLOGIZE, JONAS!

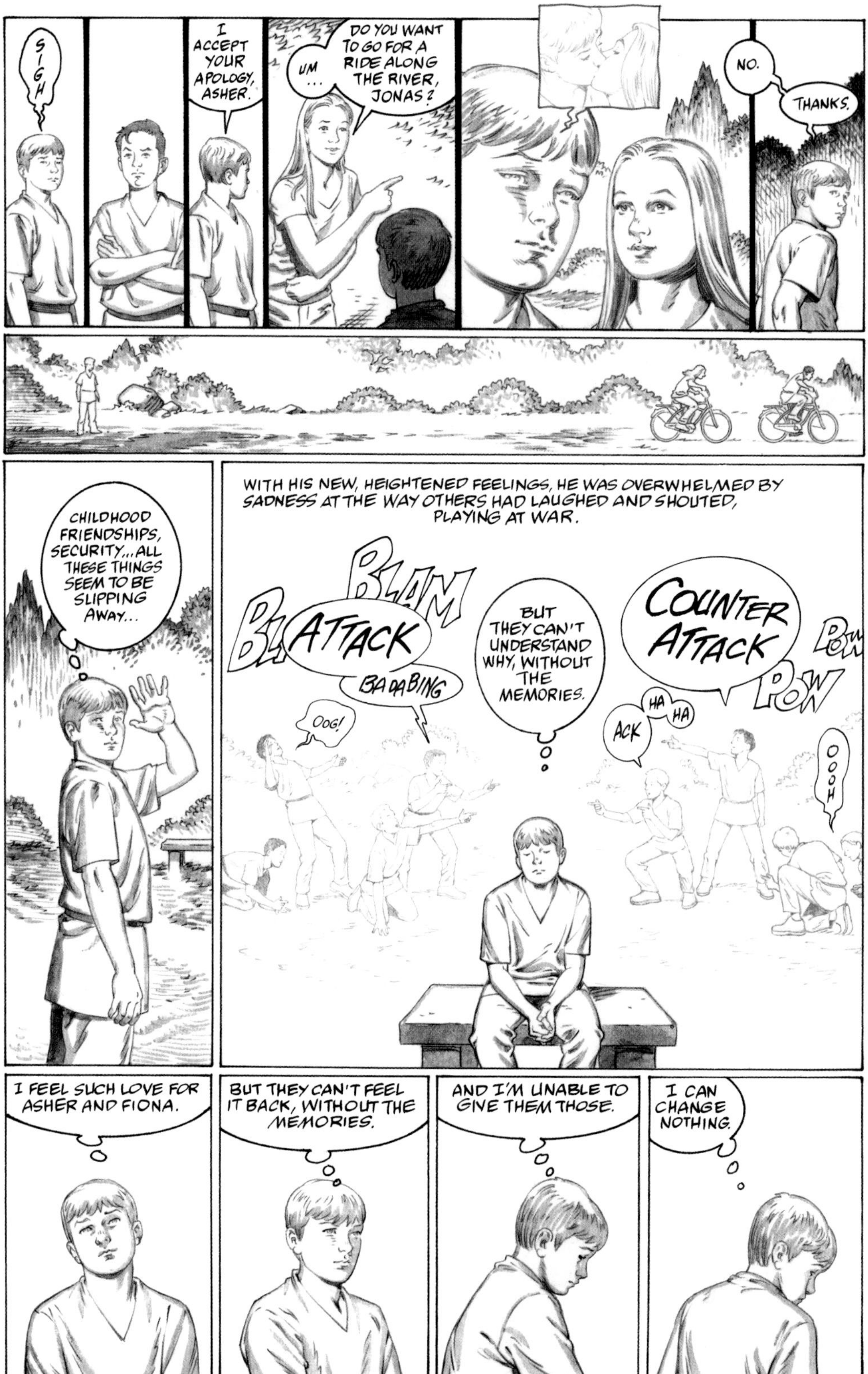
SIGH
I ACCEPT YOUR APOLOGY, ASHER.
UM ...
DO YOU WANT TO GO FOR A RIDE ALONG THE RIVER, JONAS?
NO.
THANKS.
CHILDHOOD FRIENDSHIPS, SECURITY... ALL THESE THINGS SEEM TO BE SLIPPING AWAY...
WITH HIS NEW, HEIGHTENED FEELINGS, HE WAS OVERWHELMED BY SADNESS AT THE WAY OTHERS HAD LAUGHED AND SHOUTED, PLAYING AT WAR.
BLAM
ATTACK
BADABING
OOG!
BUT THEY CAN'T UNDERSTAND WHY, WITHOUT THE MEMORIES.
COUNTER ATTACK
POW
ACK
HA
HA
OOOH
I FEEL SUCH LOVE FOR ASHER AND FIONA.
BUT THEY CAN'T FEEL IT BACK, WITHOUT THE MEMORIES.
AND I'M UNABLE TO GIVE THEM THOSE.
I CAN CHANGE NOTHING.

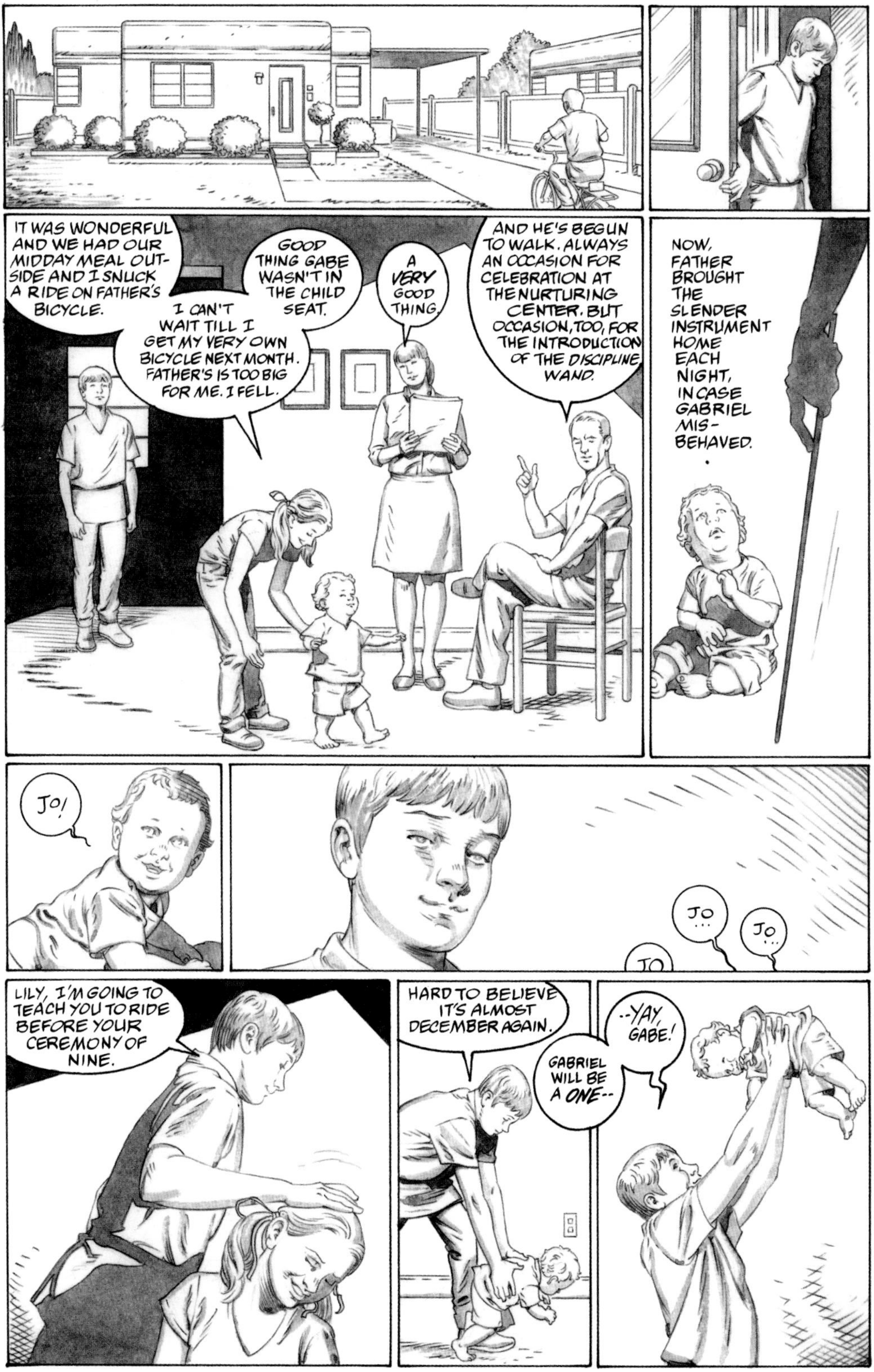
IT WAS WONDERFUL AND WE HAD OUR MIDDAY MEAL OUTSIDE AND I SNUCK A RIDE ON FATHER'S BICYCLE.
I CAN'T WAIT TILL I GET MY VERY OWN BICYCLE NEXT MONTH. FATHER'S IS TOO BIG FOR ME. I FELL.
GOOD THING GABE WASN'T IN THE CHILD SEAT.
A *VERY* GOOD THING.
AND HE'S BEGUN TO WALK. ALWAYS AN OCCASION FOR CELEBRATION AT THE NURTURING CENTER. BUT OCCASION, TOO, FOR THE INTRODUCTION OF THE *DISCIPLINE WAND.*
NOW, FATHER BROUGHT THE SLENDER INSTRUMENT HOME EACH NIGHT, IN CASE GABRIEL MISBEHAVED.
JO!
JO...
JO...
JO
LILY, I'M GOING TO TEACH YOU TO RIDE BEFORE YOUR CEREMONY OF NINE.
HARD TO BELIEVE IT'S ALMOST DECEMBER AGAIN.
GABRIEL WILL BE A *ONE*--
--YAY, GABE!

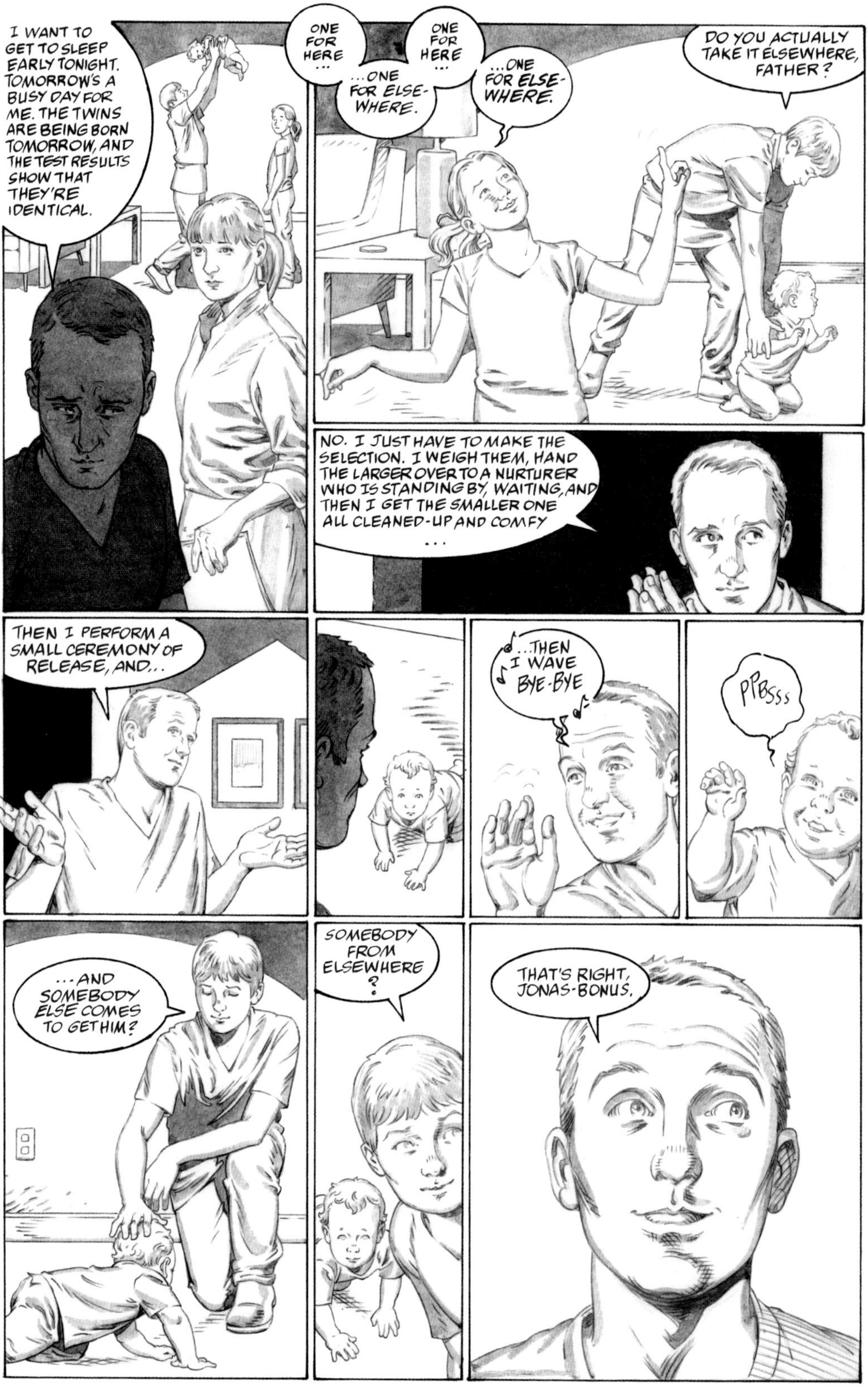
I WANT TO GET TO SLEEP EARLY TONIGHT. TOMORROW'S A BUSY DAY FOR ME. THE TWINS ARE BEING BORN TOMORROW, AND THE TEST RESULTS SHOW THAT THEY'RE IDENTICAL.
ONE FOR HERE ...
...ONE FOR ELSE-WHERE.
ONE FOR HERE ...
...ONE FOR ELSE-WHERE.
DO YOU ACTUALLY TAKE IT ELSEWHERE, FATHER?
NO. I JUST HAVE TO MAKE THE SELECTION. I WEIGH THEM, HAND THE LARGER OVER TO A NURTURER WHO IS STANDING BY, WAITING, AND THEN I GET THE SMALLER ONE ALL CLEANED-UP AND COMFY ...
THEN I PERFORM A SMALL CEREMONY OF RELEASE, AND...
...THEN I WAVE BYE-BYE
PPBsss
...AND SOMEBODY ELSE COMES TO GET HIM?
SOMEBODY FROM ELSEWHERE?
THAT'S RIGHT, JONAS-BONUS.

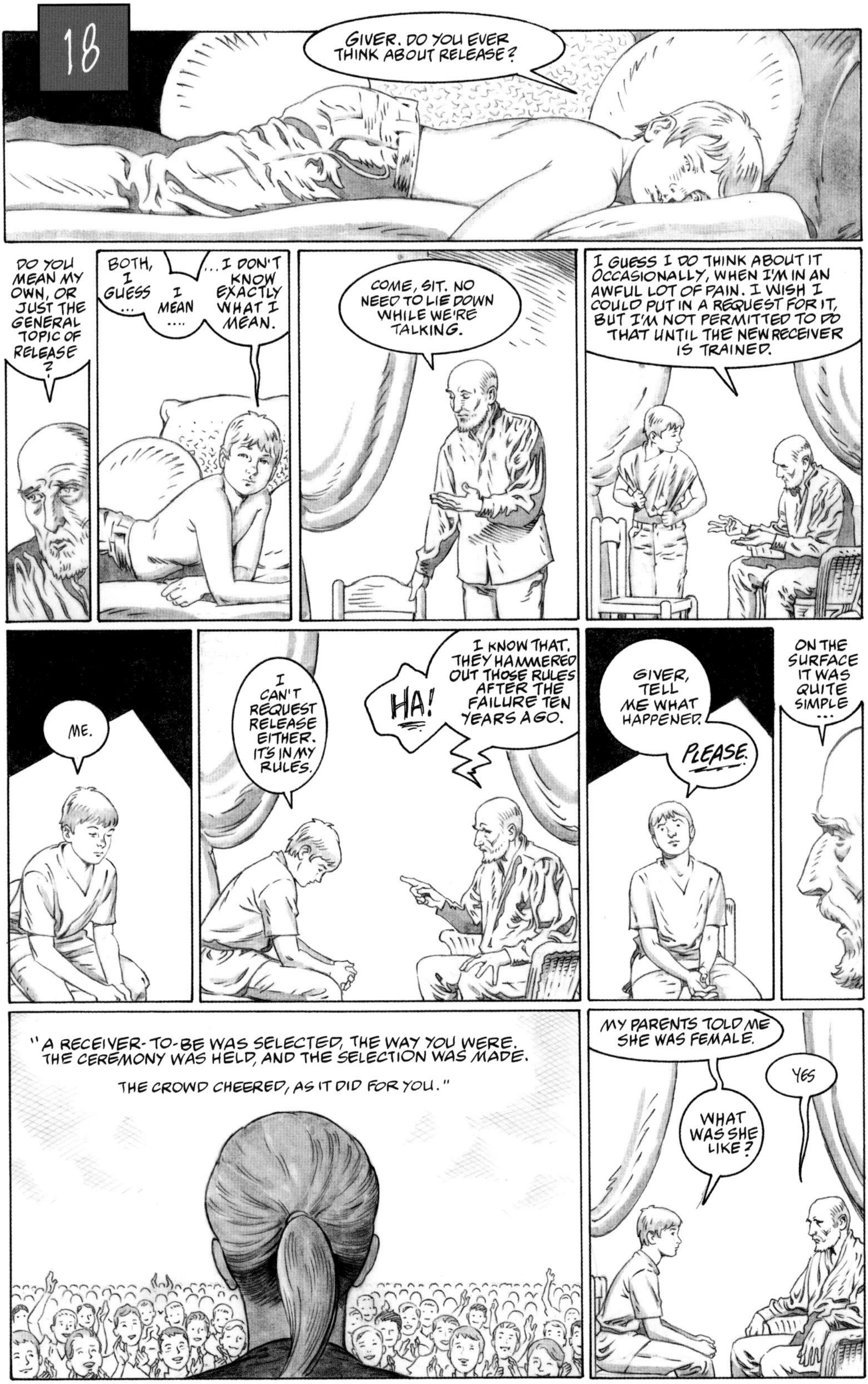
18
GIVER. DO YOU EVER THINK ABOUT RELEASE?
DO YOU MEAN MY OWN, OR JUST THE GENERAL TOPIC OF RELEASE?
BOTH, I GUESS ...
I MEAN ....
... I DON'T KNOW EXACTLY WHAT I MEAN.
COME, SIT. NO NEED TO LIE DOWN WHILE WE'RE TALKING.
I GUESS I DO THINK ABOUT IT OCCASIONALLY, WHEN I'M IN AN AWFUL LOT OF PAIN. I WISH I COULD PUT IN A REQUEST FOR IT, BUT I'M NOT PERMITTED TO DO THAT UNTIL THE NEW RECEIVER IS TRAINED.
ME.
I CAN'T REQUEST RELEASE EITHER. IT'S IN MY RULES.
HA!
I KNOW THAT. THEY HAMMERED OUT THOSE RULES AFTER THE FAILURE TEN YEARS AGO.
GIVER, TELL ME WHAT HAPPENED.
PLEASE.
ON THE SURFACE IT WAS QUITE SIMPLE ...
"A RECEIVER-TO-BE WAS SELECTED, THE WAY YOU WERE. THE CEREMONY WAS HELD, AND THE SELECTION WAS MADE.
THE CROWD CHEERED, AS IT DID FOR YOU."
MY PARENTS TOLD ME SHE WAS FEMALE.
YES
WHAT WAS SHE LIKE?

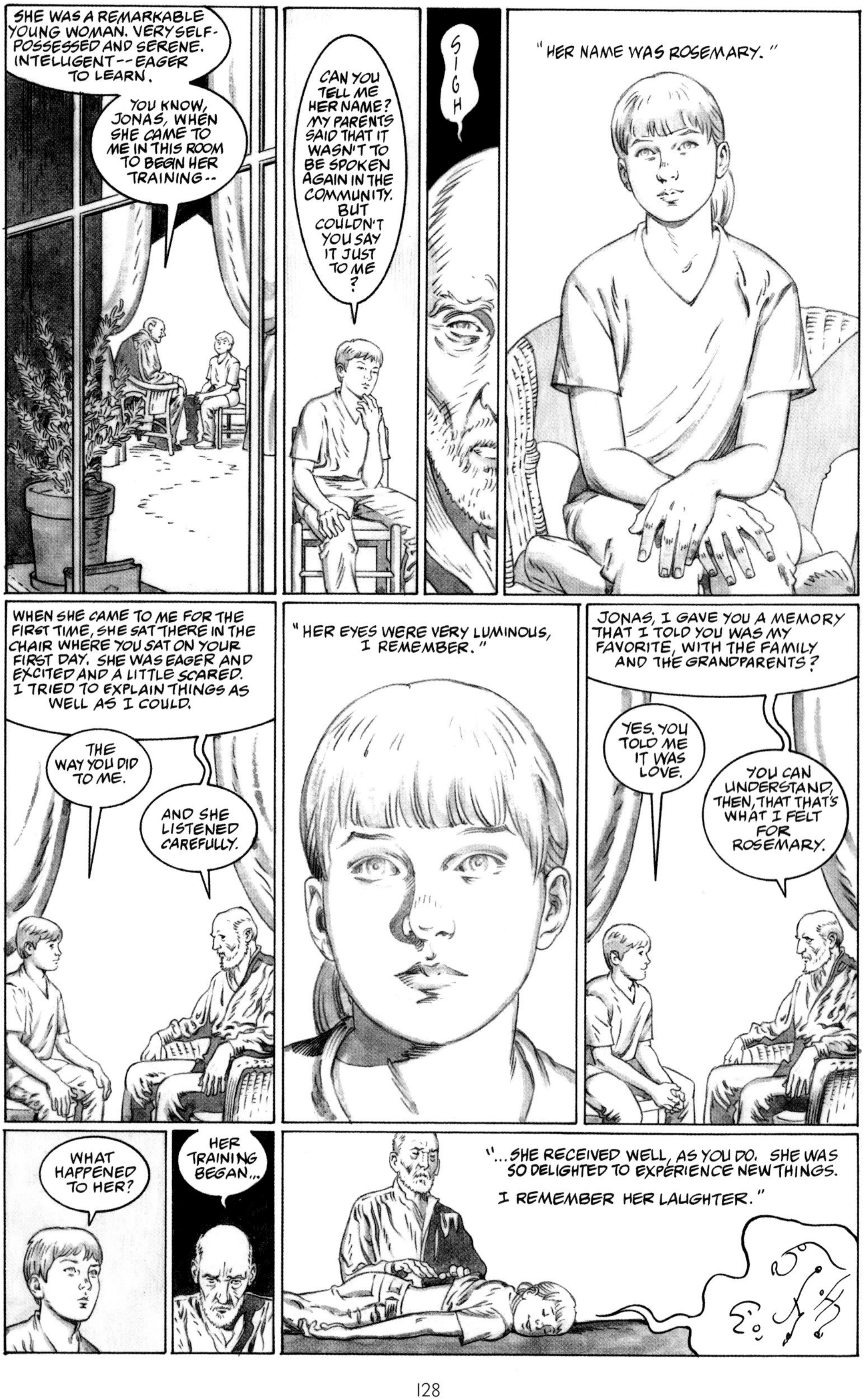
SHE WAS A REMARKABLE YOUNG WOMAN. VERY SELF-POSSESSED AND SERENE. INTELLIGENT-- EAGER TO LEARN.
YOU KNOW, JONAS, WHEN SHE CAME TO ME IN THIS ROOM TO BEGIN HER TRAINING--
CAN YOU TELL ME HER NAME? MY PARENTS SAID THAT IT WASN'T TO BE SPOKEN AGAIN IN THE COMMUNITY. BUT COULDN'T YOU SAY IT JUST TO ME?
SIGH
"HER NAME WAS ROSEMARY."
WHEN SHE CAME TO ME FOR THE FIRST TIME, SHE SAT THERE IN THE CHAIR WHERE YOU SAT ON YOUR FIRST DAY. SHE WAS EAGER AND EXCITED AND A LITTLE SCARED. I TRIED TO EXPLAIN THINGS AS WELL AS I COULD.
THE WAY YOU DID TO ME.
AND SHE LISTENED CAREFULLY.
"HER EYES WERE VERY LUMINOUS, I REMEMBER."
JONAS, I GAVE YOU A MEMORY THAT I TOLD YOU WAS MY FAVORITE, WITH THE FAMILY AND THE GRANDPARENTS?
YES. YOU TOLD ME IT WAS LOVE.
YOU CAN UNDERSTAND, THEN, THAT THAT'S WHAT I FELT FOR ROSEMARY.
WHAT HAPPENED TO HER?
HER TRAINING BEGAN...
"...SHE RECEIVED WELL, AS YOU DO. SHE WAS SO DELIGHTED TO EXPERIENCE NEW THINGS.
I REMEMBER HER LAUGHTER."

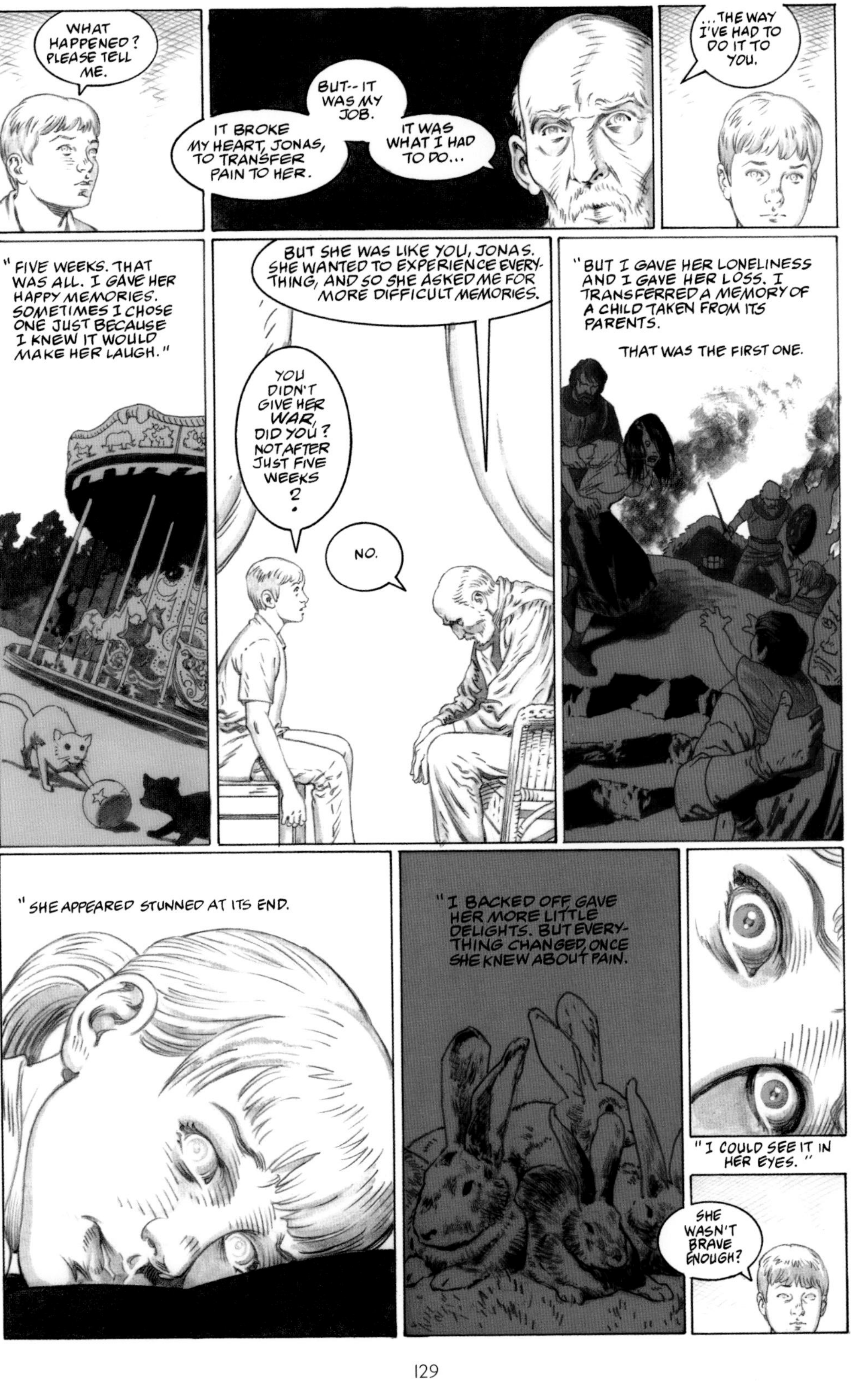
WHAT HAPPENED? PLEASE TELL ME.
IT BROKE MY HEART, JONAS, TO TRANSFER PAIN TO HER.
BUT-- IT WAS MY JOB.
IT WAS WHAT I HAD TO DO...
...THE WAY I'VE HAD TO DO IT TO YOU.
"FIVE WEEKS. THAT WAS ALL. I GAVE HER HAPPY MEMORIES. SOMETIMES I CHOSE ONE JUST BECAUSE I KNEW IT WOULD MAKE HER LAUGH."
BUT SHE WAS LIKE YOU, JONAS. SHE WANTED TO EXPERIENCE EVERY-THING, AND SO SHE ASKED ME FOR MORE DIFFICULT MEMORIES.
YOU DIDN'T GIVE HER WAR, DID YOU? NOT AFTER JUST FIVE WEEKS?
NO.
"BUT I GAVE HER LONELINESS AND I GAVE HER LOSS. I TRANSFERRED A MEMORY OF A CHILD TAKEN FROM ITS PARENTS.
THAT WAS THE FIRST ONE.
"SHE APPEARED STUNNED AT ITS END.
"I BACKED OFF, GAVE HER MORE LITTLE DELIGHTS. BUT EVERY-THING CHANGED, ONCE SHE KNEW ABOUT PAIN.
"I COULD SEE IT IN HER EYES."
SHE WASN'T BRAVE ENOUGH?

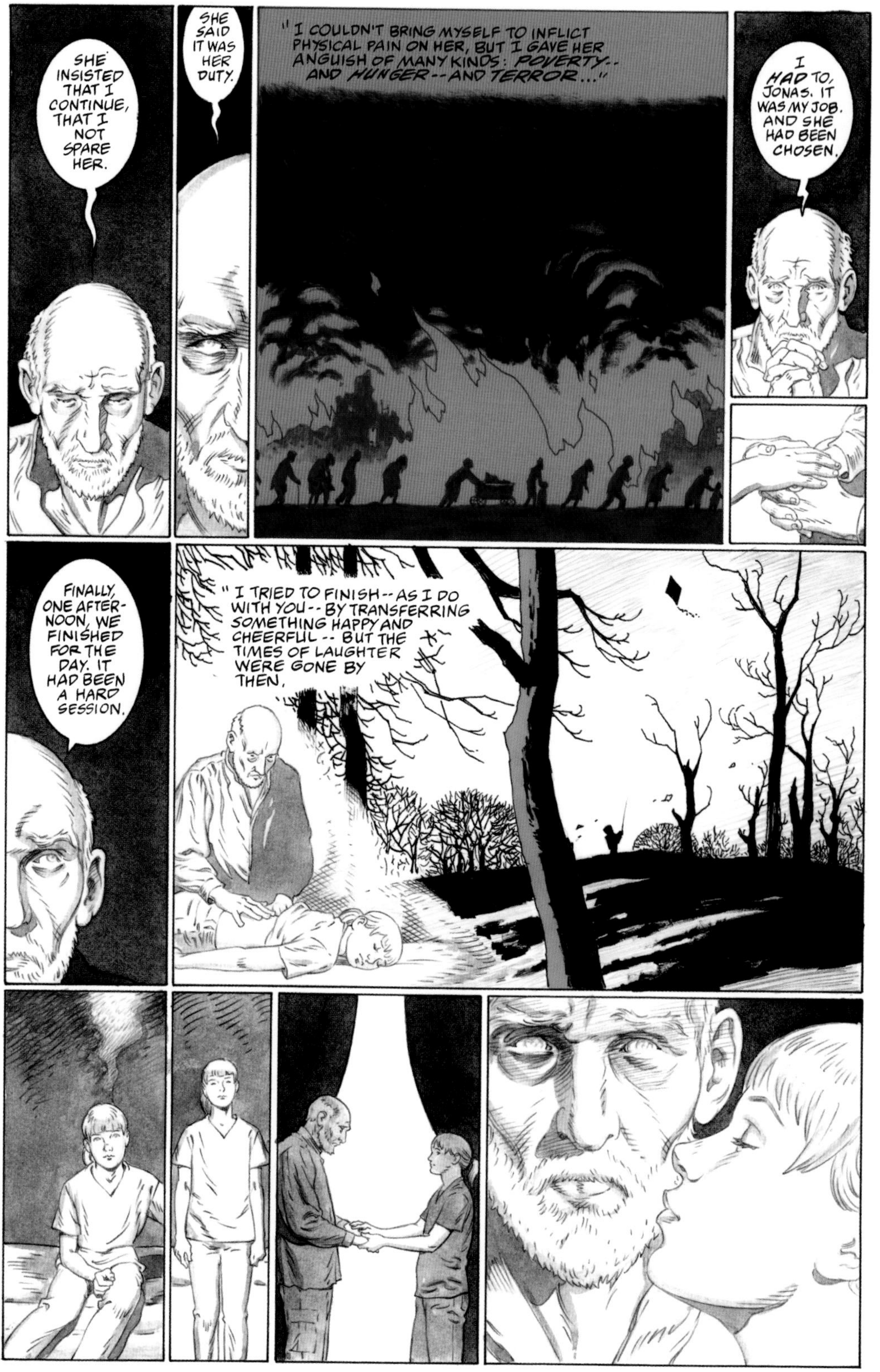
SHE INSISTED THAT I CONTINUE, THAT I NOT SPARE HER.
SHE SAID IT WAS HER DUTY.
"I COULDN'T BRING MYSELF TO INFLICT PHYSICAL PAIN ON HER, BUT I GAVE HER ANGUISH OF MANY KINDS: POVERTY-- AND HUNGER--AND TERROR..."
I HAD TO, JONAS. IT WAS MY JOB. AND SHE HAD BEEN CHOSEN.
FINALLY, ONE AFTERNOON, WE FINISHED FOR THE DAY. IT HAD BEEN A HARD SESSION.
"I TRIED TO FINISH--AS I DO WITH YOU--BY TRANSFERRING SOMETHING HAPPY AND CHEERFUL--BUT THE TIMES OF LAUGHTER WERE GONE BY THEN.

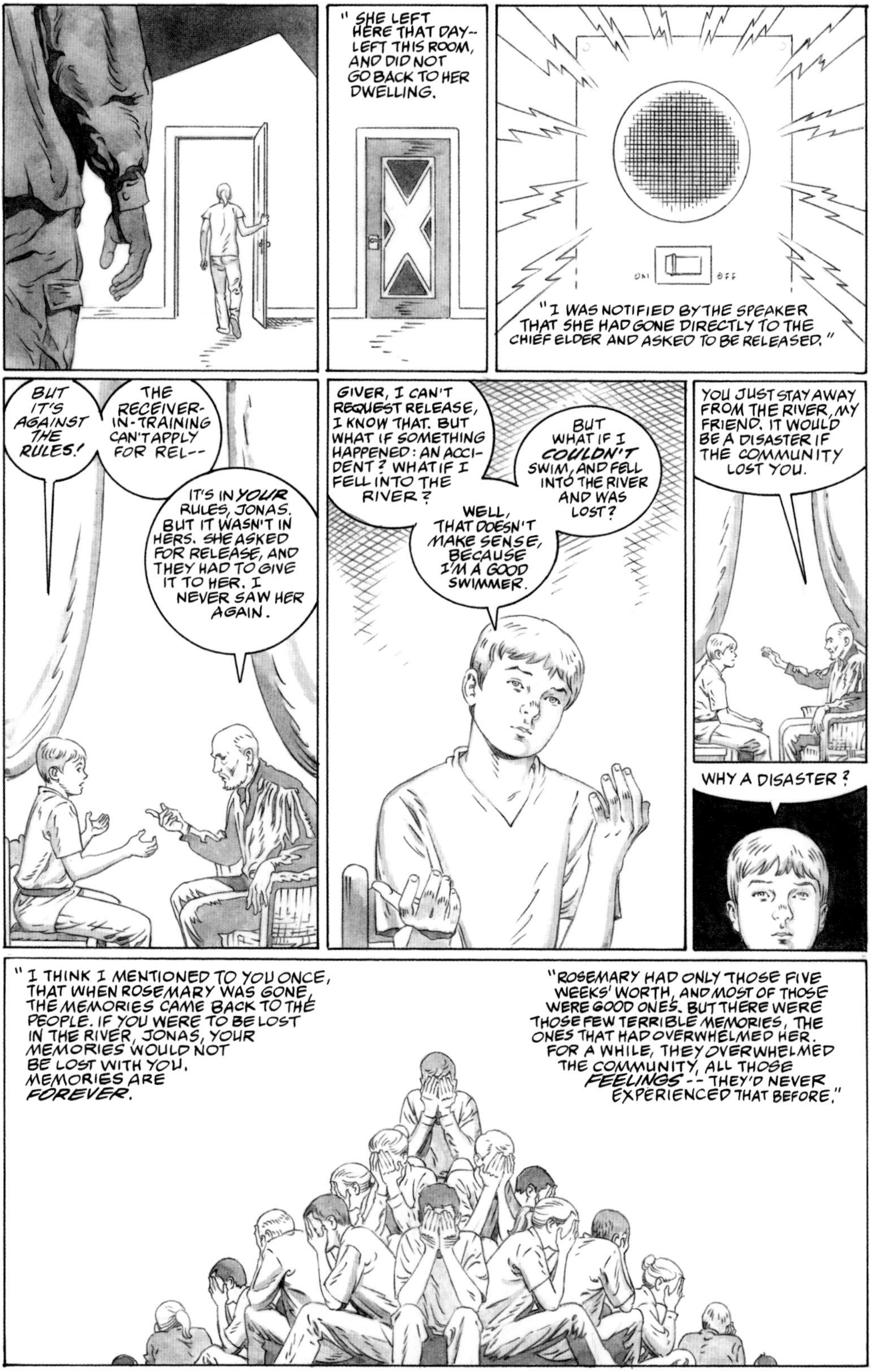
"SHE LEFT HERE THAT DAY-- LEFT THIS ROOM, AND DID NOT GO BACK TO HER DWELLING.
ON OFF
"I WAS NOTIFIED BY THE SPEAKER THAT SHE HAD GONE DIRECTLY TO THE CHIEF ELDER AND ASKED TO BE RELEASED."
BUT IT'S AGAINST THE RULES!
THE RECEIVER-IN-TRAINING CAN'T APPLY FOR REL--
IT'S IN YOUR RULES, JONAS. BUT IT WASN'T IN HERS. SHE ASKED FOR RELEASE, AND THEY HAD TO GIVE IT TO HER. I NEVER SAW HER AGAIN.
GIVER, I CAN'T REQUEST RELEASE, I KNOW THAT. BUT WHAT IF SOMETHING HAPPENED: AN ACCIDENT? WHAT IF I FELL INTO THE RIVER?
BUT WHAT IF I COULDN'T SWIM, AND FELL INTO THE RIVER AND WAS LOST?
WELL, THAT DOESN'T MAKE SENSE, BECAUSE I'M A GOOD SWIMMER.
YOU JUST STAY AWAY FROM THE RIVER, MY FRIEND. IT WOULD BE A DISASTER IF THE COMMUNITY LOST YOU.
WHY A DISASTER?
"I THINK I MENTIONED TO YOU ONCE, THAT WHEN ROSEMARY WAS GONE, THE MEMORIES CAME BACK TO THE PEOPLE. IF YOU WERE TO BE LOST IN THE RIVER, JONAS, YOUR MEMORIES WOULD NOT BE LOST WITH YOU. MEMORIES ARE FOREVER.
"ROSEMARY HAD ONLY THOSE FIVE WEEKS' WORTH, AND MOST OF THOSE WERE GOOD ONES. BUT THERE WERE THOSE FEW TERRIBLE MEMORIES, THE ONES THAT HAD OVERWHELMED HER. FOR A WHILE, THEY OVERWHELMED THE COMMUNITY, ALL THOSE FEELINGS -- THEY'D NEVER EXPERIENCED THAT BEFORE."

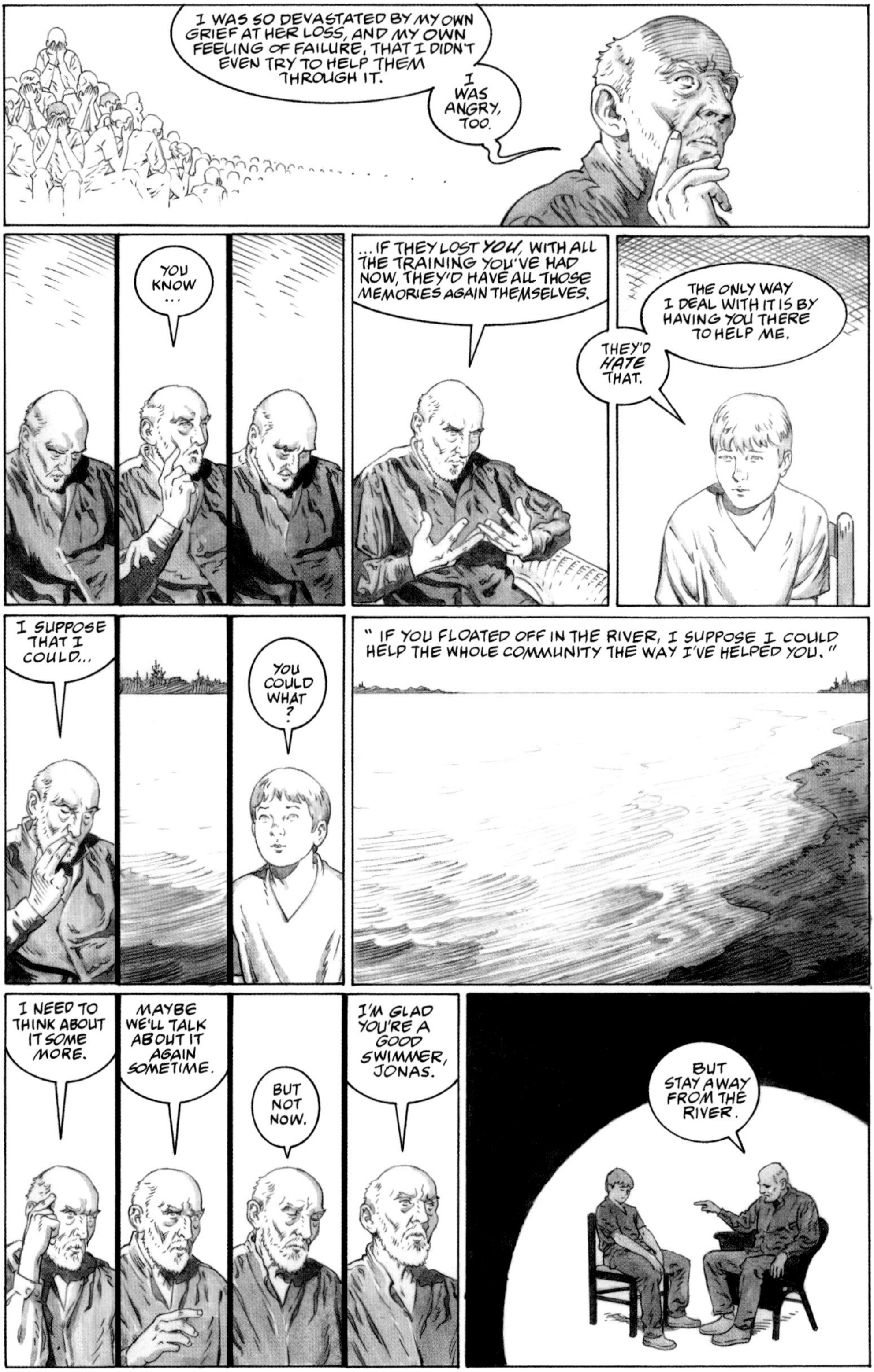
I WAS SO DEVASTATED BY MY OWN GRIEF AT HER LOSS, AND MY OWN FEELING OF FAILURE, THAT I DIDN'T EVEN TRY TO HELP THEM THROUGH IT.
I WAS ANGRY, TOO.
YOU KNOW . . .
. . . IF THEY LOST YOU, WITH ALL THE TRAINING YOU'VE HAD NOW, THEY'D HAVE ALL THOSE MEMORIES AGAIN THEMSELVES.
THEY'D HATE THAT.
THE ONLY WAY I DEAL WITH IT IS BY HAVING YOU THERE TO HELP ME.
I SUPPOSE THAT I COULD...
YOU COULD WHAT ?
" IF YOU FLOATED OFF IN THE RIVER, I SUPPOSE I COULD HELP THE WHOLE COMMUNITY THE WAY I'VE HELPED YOU. "
I NEED TO THINK ABOUT IT SOME MORE.
MAYBE WE'LL TALK ABOUT IT AGAIN SOMETIME.
BUT NOT NOW.
I'M GLAD YOU'RE A GOOD SWIMMER, JONAS.
BUT STAY AWAY FROM THE RIVER.

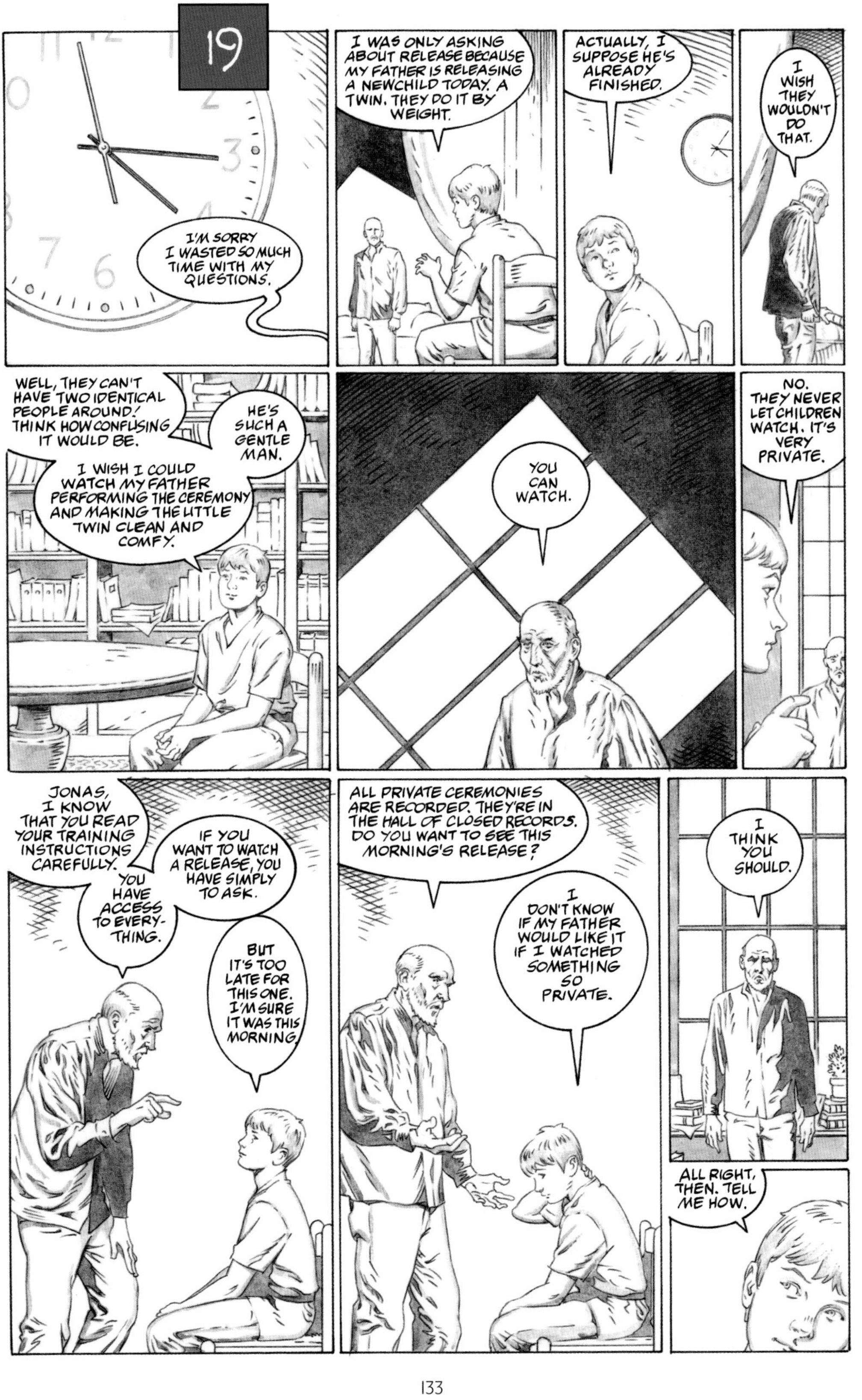
19
I'M SORRY I WASTED SO MUCH TIME WITH MY QUESTIONS.
I WAS ONLY ASKING ABOUT RELEASE BECAUSE MY FATHER IS RELEASING A NEWCHILD TODAY. A TWIN. THEY DO IT BY WEIGHT.
ACTUALLY, I SUPPOSE HE'S ALREADY FINISHED.
I WISH THEY WOULDN'T DO THAT.
WELL, THEY CAN'T HAVE TWO IDENTICAL PEOPLE AROUND! THINK HOW CONFUSING IT WOULD BE.
HE'S SUCH A GENTLE MAN.
I WISH I COULD WATCH MY FATHER PERFORMING THE CEREMONY AND MAKING THE LITTLE TWIN CLEAN AND COMFY.
YOU CAN WATCH.
NO. THEY NEVER LET CHILDREN WATCH. IT'S VERY PRIVATE.
JONAS, I KNOW THAT YOU READ YOUR TRAINING INSTRUCTIONS CAREFULLY.
YOU HAVE ACCESS TO EVERY-THING.
IF YOU WANT TO WATCH A RELEASE, YOU HAVE SIMPLY TO ASK.
BUT IT'S TOO LATE FOR THIS ONE. I'M SURE IT WAS THIS MORNING.
ALL PRIVATE CEREMONIES ARE RECORDED. THEY'RE IN THE HALL OF CLOSED RECORDS. DO YOU WANT TO SEE THIS MORNING'S RELEASE?
I DON'T KNOW IF MY FATHER WOULD LIKE IT IF I WATCHED SOMETHING SO PRIVATE.
I THINK YOU SHOULD.
ALL RIGHT, THEN. TELL ME HOW.

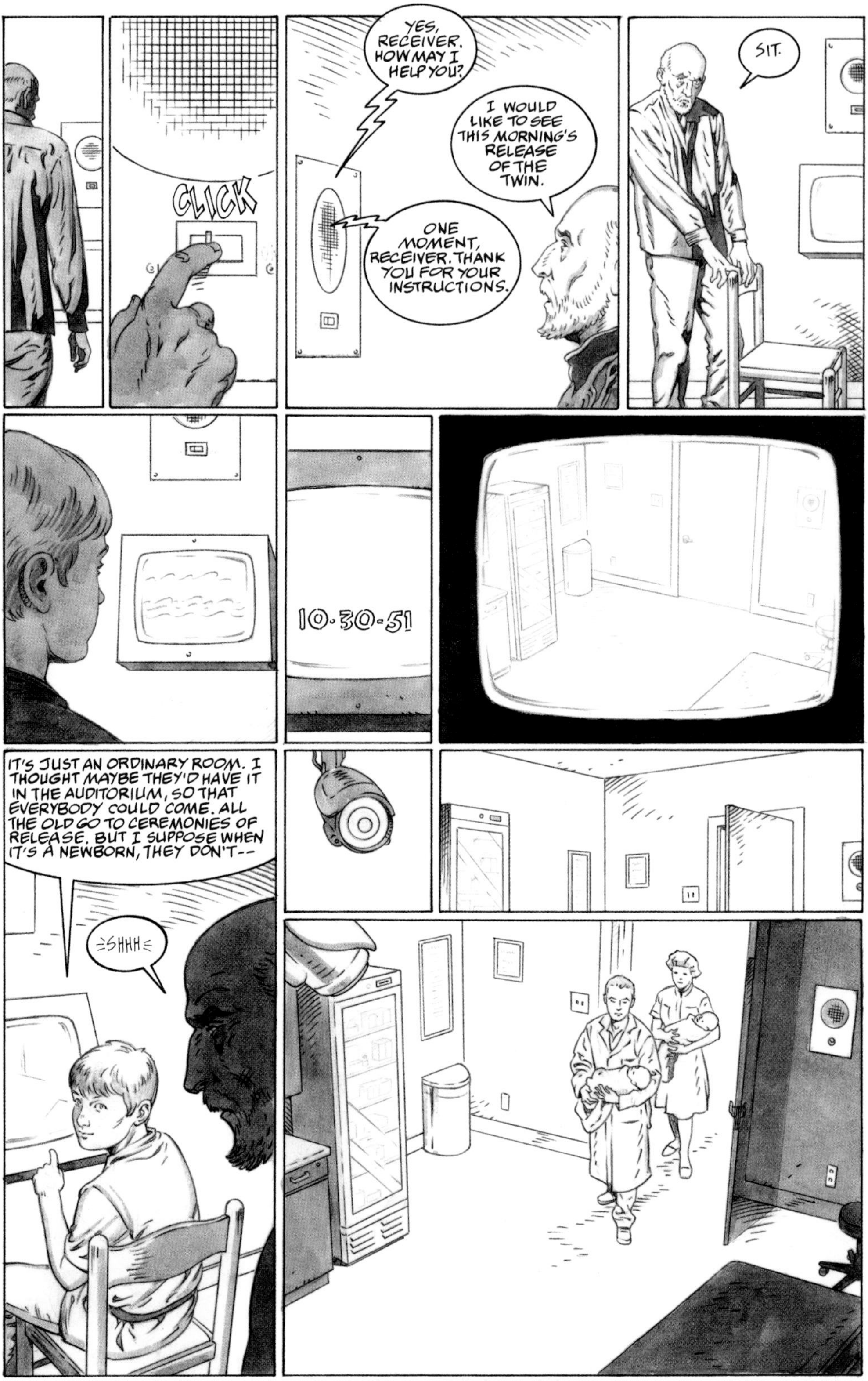
CLICK
YES, RECEIVER. HOW MAY I HELP YOU?
I WOULD LIKE TO SEE THIS MORNING'S RELEASE OF THE TWIN.
ONE MOMENT, RECEIVER. THANK YOU FOR YOUR INSTRUCTIONS.
SIT.
10-30-51
IT'S JUST AN ORDINARY ROOM. I THOUGHT MAYBE THEY'D HAVE IT IN THE AUDITORIUM, SO THAT EVERYBODY COULD COME. ALL THE OLD GO TO CEREMONIES OF RELEASE. BUT I SUPPOSE WHEN IT'S A NEWBORN, THEY DON'T--
SHHH

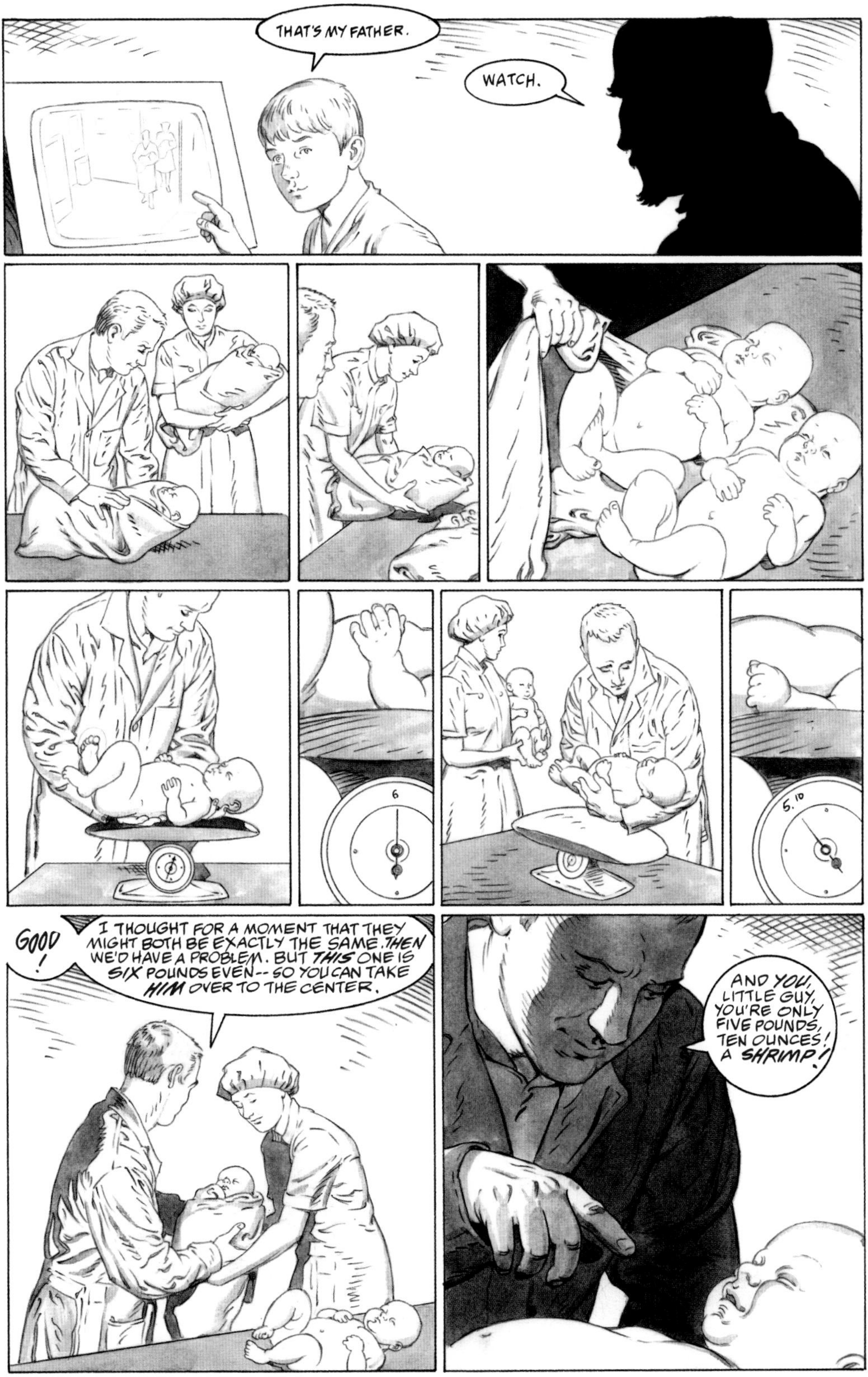
THAT'S MY FATHER.
WATCH.
6
5.10
GOOD!
I THOUGHT FOR A MOMENT THAT THEY MIGHT BOTH BE EXACTLY THE SAME. THEN WE'D HAVE A PROBLEM. BUT THIS ONE IS SIX POUNDS EVEN-- SO YOU CAN TAKE HIM OVER TO THE CENTER.
AND YOU, LITTLE GUY, YOU'RE ONLY FIVE POUNDS, TEN OUNCES! A SHRIMP!

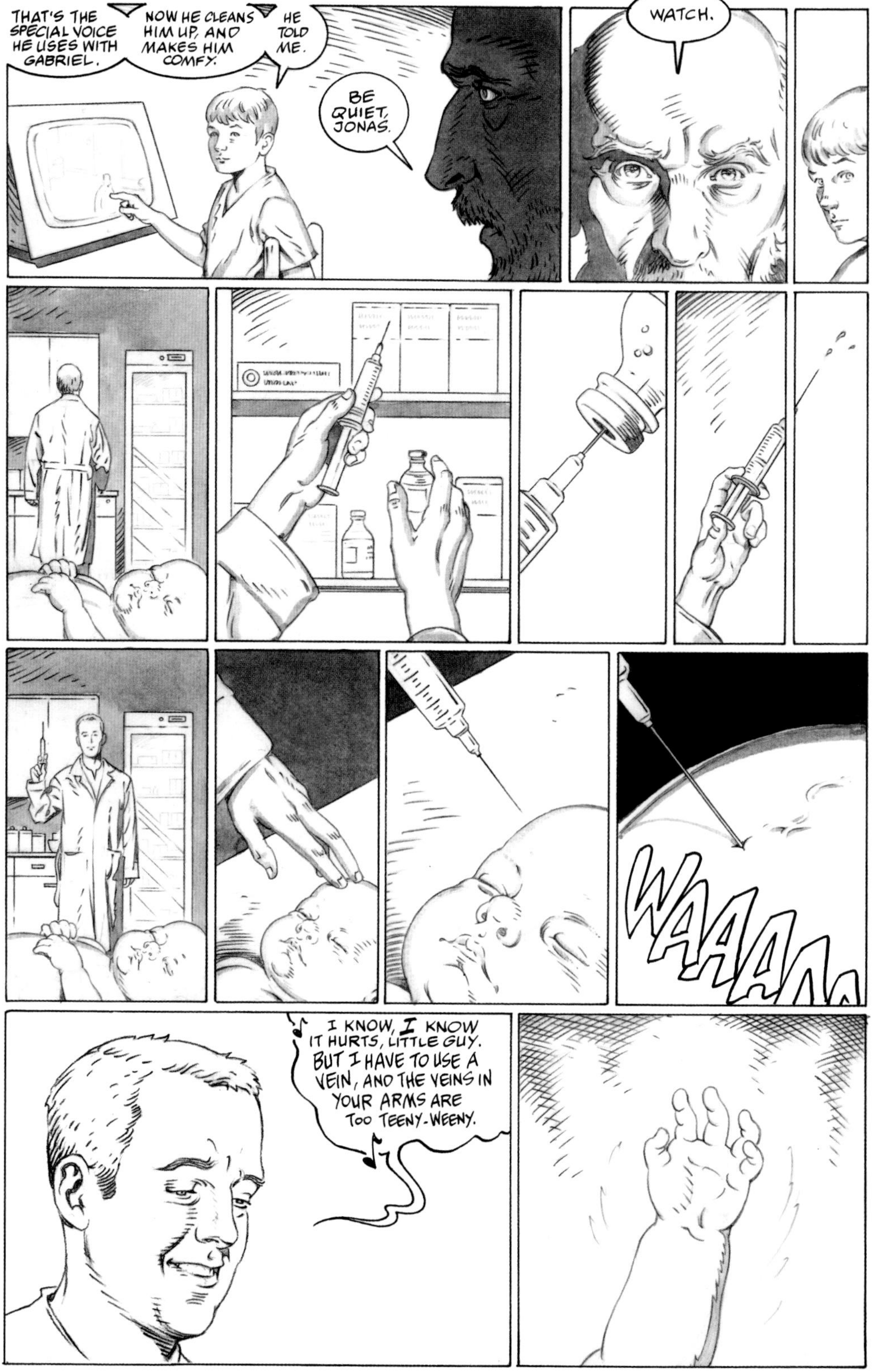
THAT'S THE SPECIAL VOICE HE USES WITH GABRIEL.
NOW HE CLEANS HIM UP, AND MAKES HIM COMFY.
HE TOLD ME.
BE QUIET, JONAS.
WATCH.
WAAAA
I KNOW, I KNOW IT HURTS, LITTLE GUY. BUT I HAVE TO USE A VEIN, AND THE VEINS IN YOUR ARMS ARE TOO TEENY-WEENY.

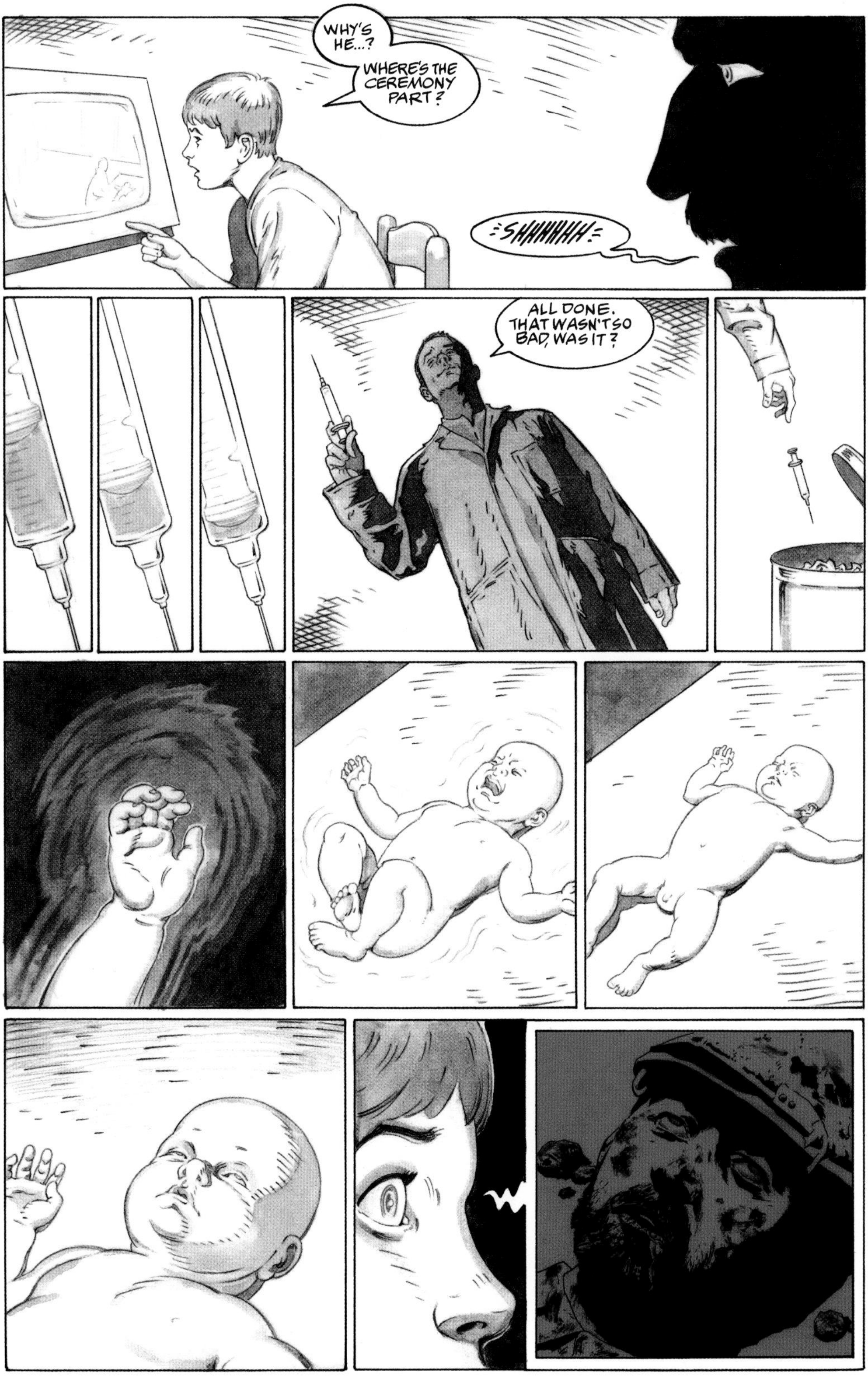
WHY'S HE...?
WHERE'S THE CEREMONY PART?
SHHHHHH
ALL DONE. THAT WASN'T SO BAD, WAS IT?

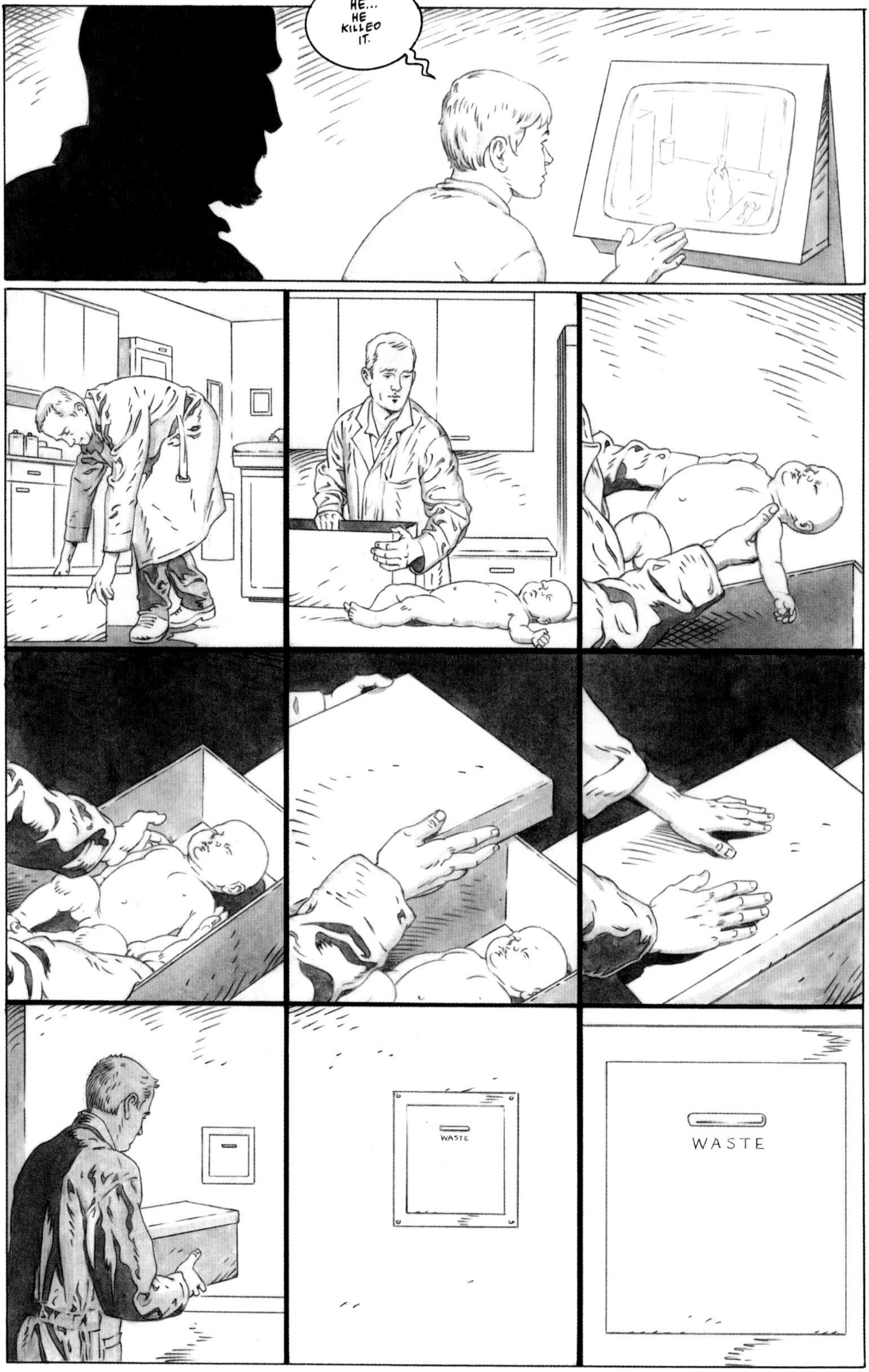
HE... HE KILLED IT.
WASTE
WASTE

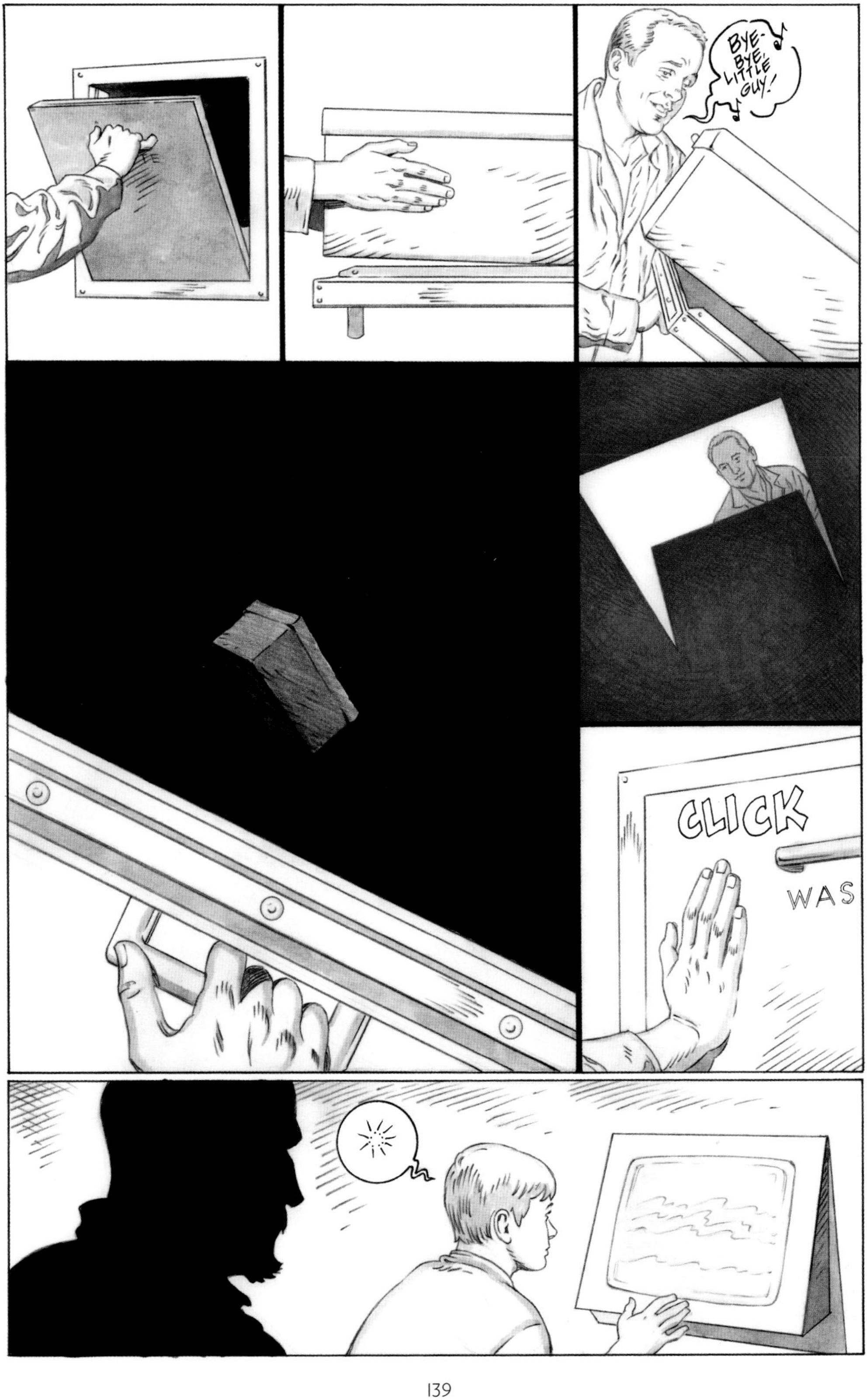
BYE-BYE, LITTLE GUY!
CLICK
WAS

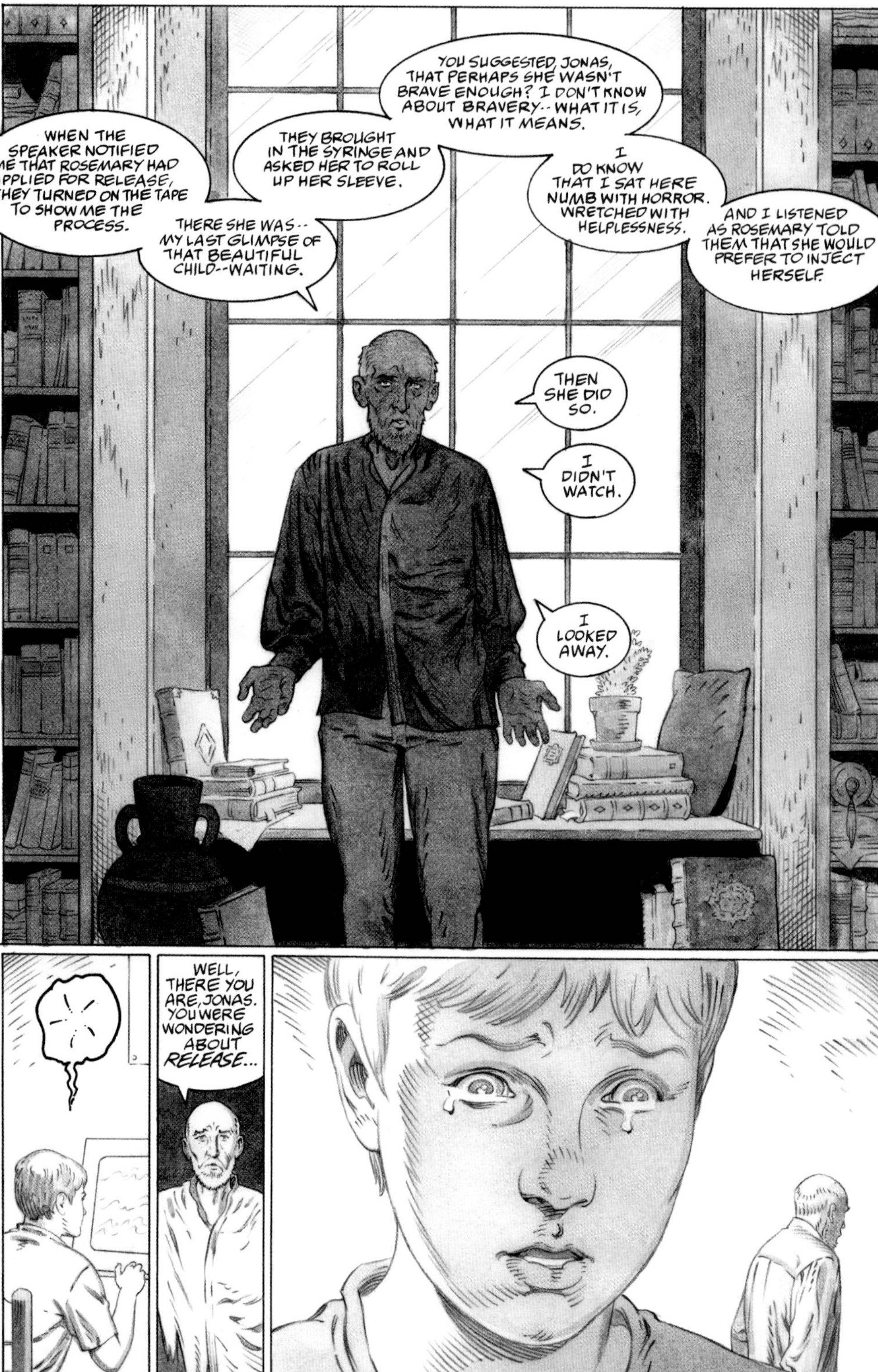

WHEN THE SPEAKER NOTIFIED ME THAT ROSEMARY HAD APPLIED FOR RELEASE, THEY TURNED ON THE TAPE TO SHOW ME THE PROCESS.
THERE SHE WAS-- MY LAST GLIMPSE OF THAT BEAUTIFUL CHILD--WAITING.
THEY BROUGHT IN THE SYRINGE AND ASKED HER TO ROLL UP HER SLEEVE.
YOU SUGGESTED, JONAS, THAT PERHAPS SHE WASN'T BRAVE ENOUGH? I DON'T KNOW ABOUT BRAVERY-- WHAT IT IS, WHAT IT MEANS.
I DO KNOW THAT I SAT HERE NUMB WITH HORROR. WRETCHED WITH HELPLESSNESS.
AND I LISTENED AS ROSEMARY TOLD THEM THAT SHE WOULD PREFER TO INJECT HERSELF.
THEN SHE DID SO.
I DIDN'T WATCH.
I LOOKED AWAY.
!
WELL, THERE YOU ARE, JONAS. YOU WERE WONDERING ABOUT *RELEASE*...

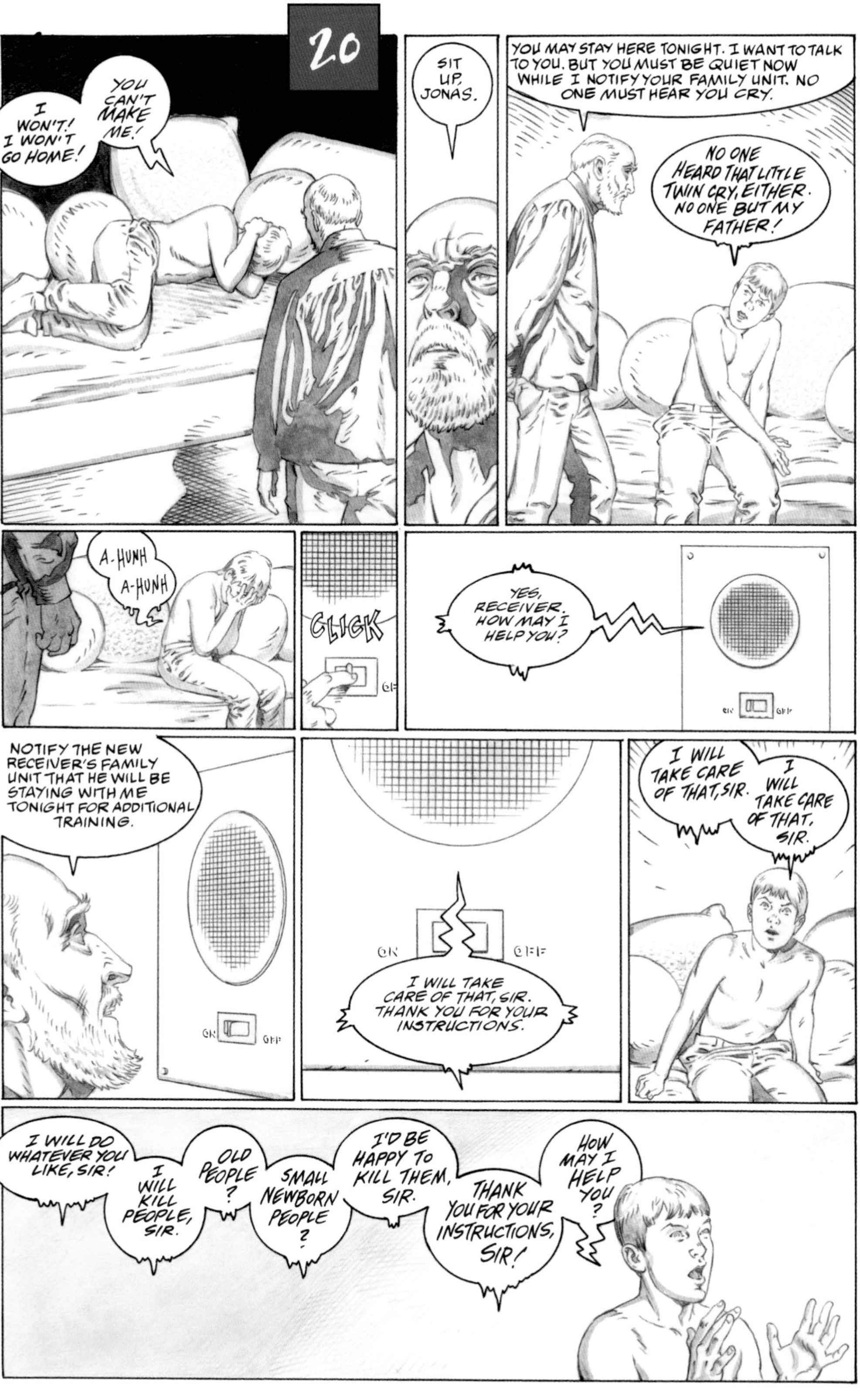
20
I WON'T! I WON'T GO HOME!
YOU CAN'T MAKE ME!
SIT UP, JONAS.
YOU MAY STAY HERE TONIGHT. I WANT TO TALK TO YOU. BUT YOU MUST BE QUIET NOW WHILE I NOTIFY YOUR FAMILY UNIT. NO ONE MUST HEAR YOU CRY.
NO ONE HEARD THAT LITTLE TWIN CRY, EITHER. NO ONE BUT MY FATHER!
A-HUNH A-HUNH
CLICK
YES, RECEIVER. HOW MAY I HELP YOU?
NOTIFY THE NEW RECEIVER'S FAMILY UNIT THAT HE WILL BE STAYING WITH ME TONIGHT FOR ADDITIONAL TRAINING.
ON OFF
I WILL TAKE CARE OF THAT, SIR. THANK YOU FOR YOUR INSTRUCTIONS.
I WILL TAKE CARE OF THAT, SIR.
I WILL TAKE CARE OF THAT, SIR.
I WILL DO WHATEVER YOU LIKE, SIR!
I WILL KILL PEOPLE, SIR.
OLD PEOPLE?
SMALL NEWBORN PEOPLE?
I'D BE HAPPY TO KILL THEM, SIR.
THANK YOU FOR YOUR INSTRUCTIONS, SIR!
HOW MAY I HELP YOU?

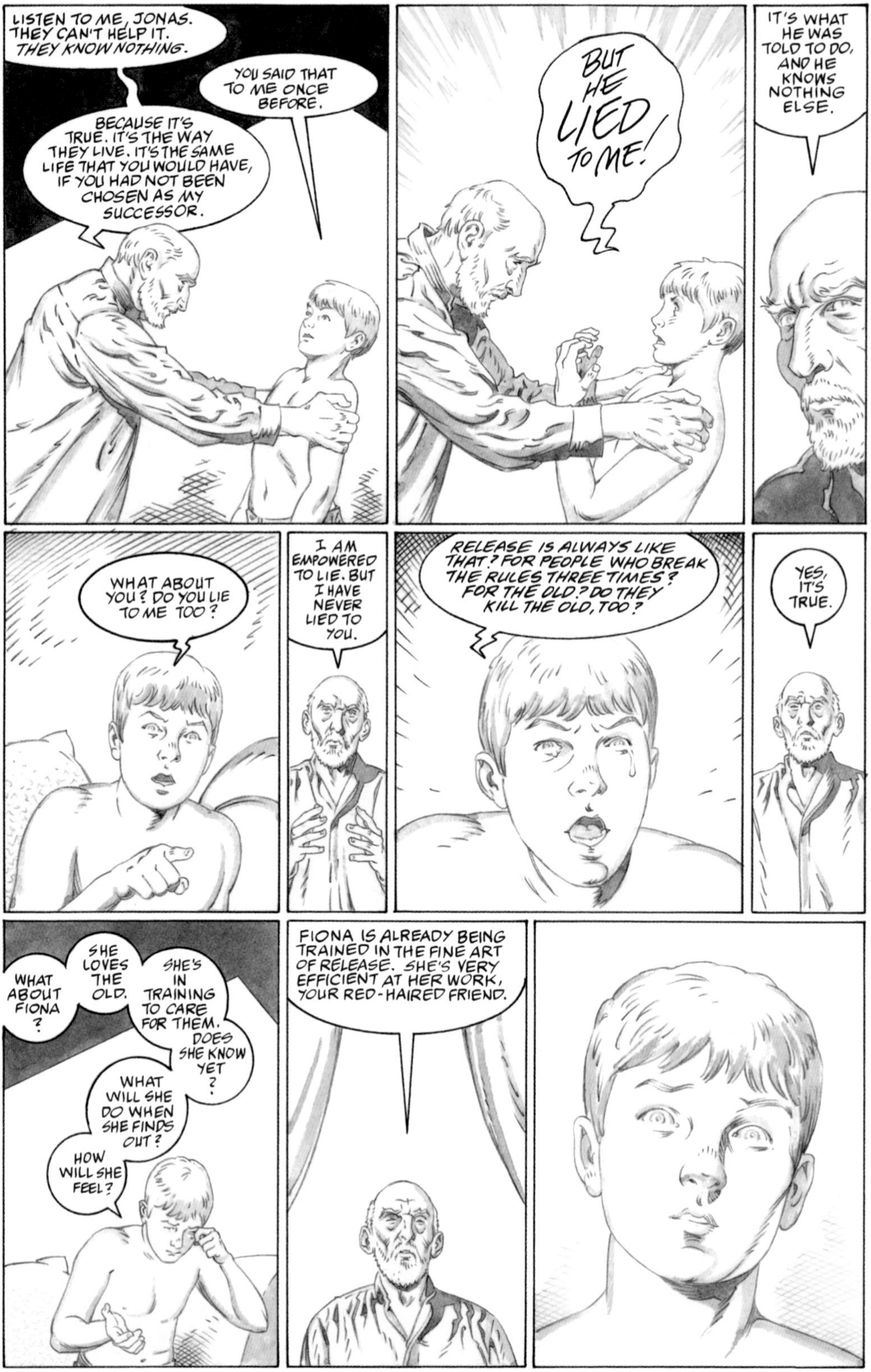
LISTEN TO ME, JONAS. THEY CAN'T HELP IT. *THEY KNOW NOTHING.*
YOU SAID THAT TO ME ONCE BEFORE.
BECAUSE IT'S TRUE. IT'S THE WAY THEY LIVE. IT'S THE SAME LIFE THAT YOU WOULD HAVE, IF YOU HAD NOT BEEN CHOSEN AS MY SUCCESSOR.
BUT HE LIED TO ME!
IT'S WHAT HE WAS TOLD TO DO, AND HE KNOWS NOTHING ELSE.
WHAT ABOUT YOU? DO YOU LIE TO ME TOO?
I AM EMPOWERED TO LIE. BUT I HAVE NEVER LIED TO YOU.
RELEASE IS ALWAYS LIKE THAT? FOR PEOPLE WHO BREAK THE RULES THREE TIMES? FOR THE OLD? DO THEY KILL THE OLD, TOO?
YES, IT'S TRUE.
WHAT ABOUT FIONA?
SHE LOVES THE OLD.
SHE'S IN TRAINING TO CARE FOR THEM.
DOES SHE KNOW YET?
WHAT WILL SHE DO WHEN SHE FINDS OUT?
HOW WILL SHE FEEL?
FIONA IS ALREADY BEING TRAINED IN THE FINE ART OF RELEASE. SHE'S VERY EFFICIENT AT HER WORK, YOUR RED-HAIRED FRIEND.

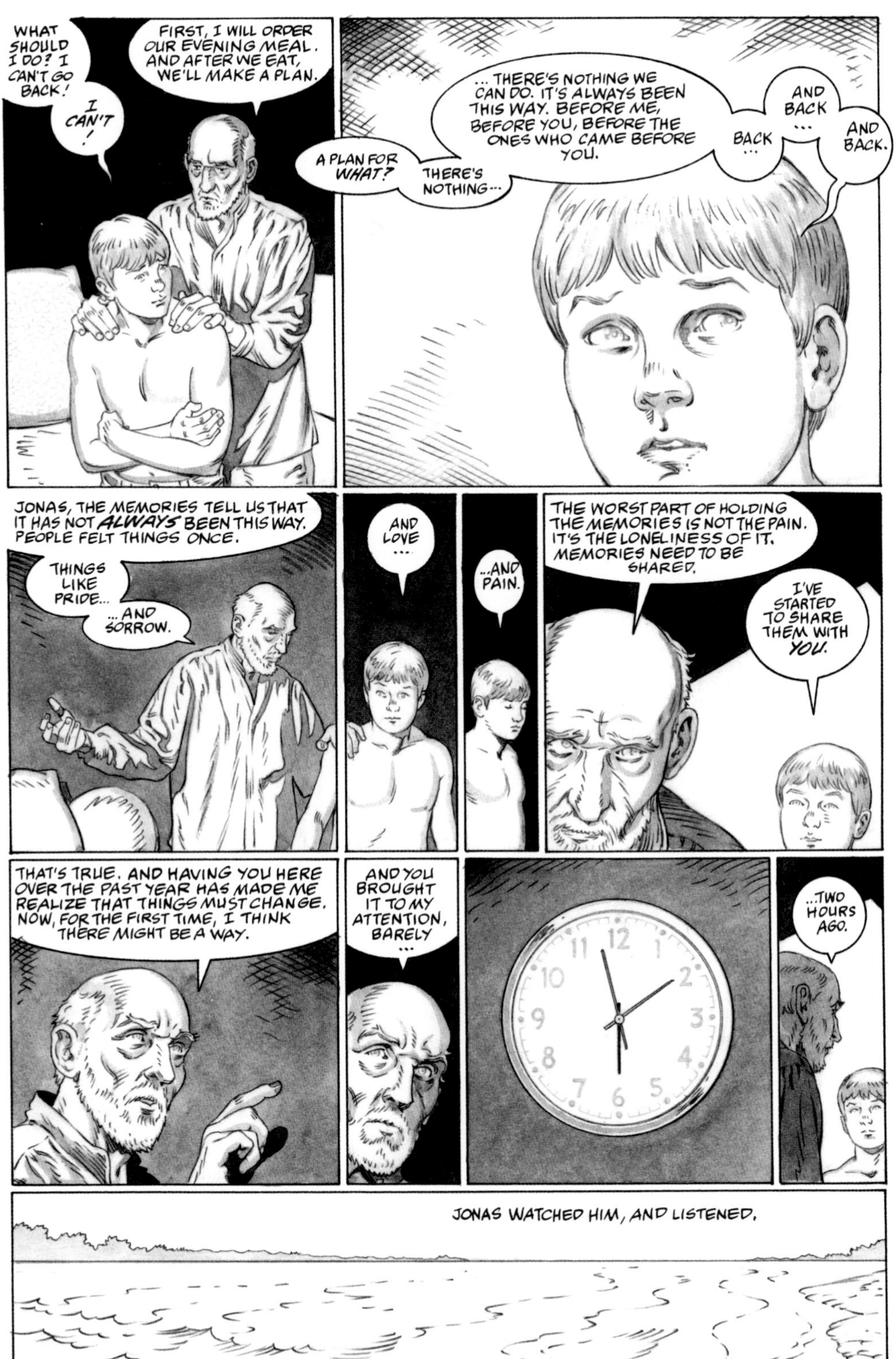
WHAT SHOULD I DO? I CAN'T GO BACK!
I CAN'T!
FIRST, I WILL ORDER OUR EVENING MEAL. AND AFTER WE EAT, WE'LL MAKE A PLAN.
A PLAN FOR WHAT?
THERE'S NOTHING...
... THERE'S NOTHING WE CAN DO. IT'S ALWAYS BEEN THIS WAY. BEFORE ME, BEFORE YOU, BEFORE THE ONES WHO CAME BEFORE YOU.
BACK...
AND BACK...
AND BACK.
JONAS, THE MEMORIES TELL US THAT IT HAS NOT ALWAYS BEEN THIS WAY. PEOPLE FELT THINGS ONCE.
THINGS LIKE PRIDE...
...AND SORROW.
AND LOVE...
...AND PAIN.
THE WORST PART OF HOLDING THE MEMORIES IS NOT THE PAIN. IT'S THE LONELINESS OF IT. MEMORIES NEED TO BE SHARED.
I'VE STARTED TO SHARE THEM WITH YOU.
THAT'S TRUE. AND HAVING YOU HERE OVER THE PAST YEAR HAS MADE ME REALIZE THAT THINGS MUST CHANGE. NOW, FOR THE FIRST TIME, I THINK THERE MIGHT BE A WAY.
AND YOU BROUGHT IT TO MY ATTENTION, BARELY...
...TWO HOURS AGO.
JONAS WATCHED HIM, AND LISTENED.

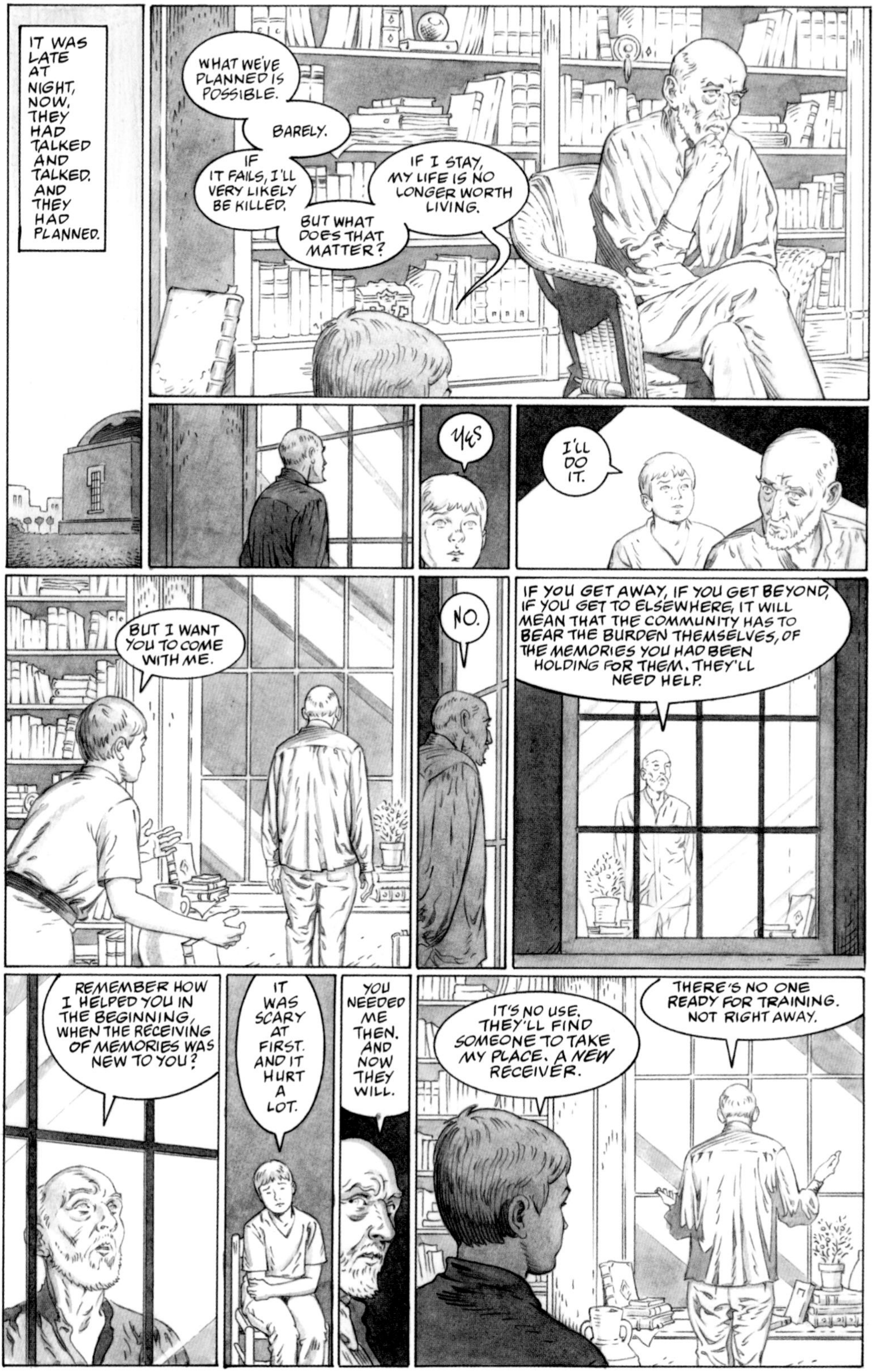
IT WAS LATE AT NIGHT, NOW, THEY HAD TALKED AND TALKED. AND THEY HAD PLANNED.
WHAT WE'VE PLANNED IS POSSIBLE.
BARELY.
IF IT FAILS, I'LL VERY LIKELY BE KILLED.
BUT WHAT DOES THAT MATTER?
IF I STAY, MY LIFE IS NO LONGER WORTH LIVING.
YES
I'LL DO IT.
BUT I WANT YOU TO COME WITH ME.
NO.
IF YOU GET AWAY, IF YOU GET BEYOND, IF YOU GET TO ELSEWHERE, IT WILL MEAN THAT THE COMMUNITY HAS TO BEAR THE BURDEN THEMSELVES, OF THE MEMORIES YOU HAD BEEN HOLDING FOR THEM. THEY'LL NEED HELP.
REMEMBER HOW I HELPED YOU IN THE BEGINNING, WHEN THE RECEIVING OF MEMORIES WAS NEW TO YOU?
IT WAS SCARY AT FIRST. AND IT HURT A LOT.
YOU NEEDED ME THEN. AND NOW THEY WILL.
IT'S NO USE. THEY'LL FIND SOMEONE TO TAKE MY PLACE. A NEW RECEIVER.
THERE'S NO ONE READY FOR TRAINING. NOT RIGHT AWAY.

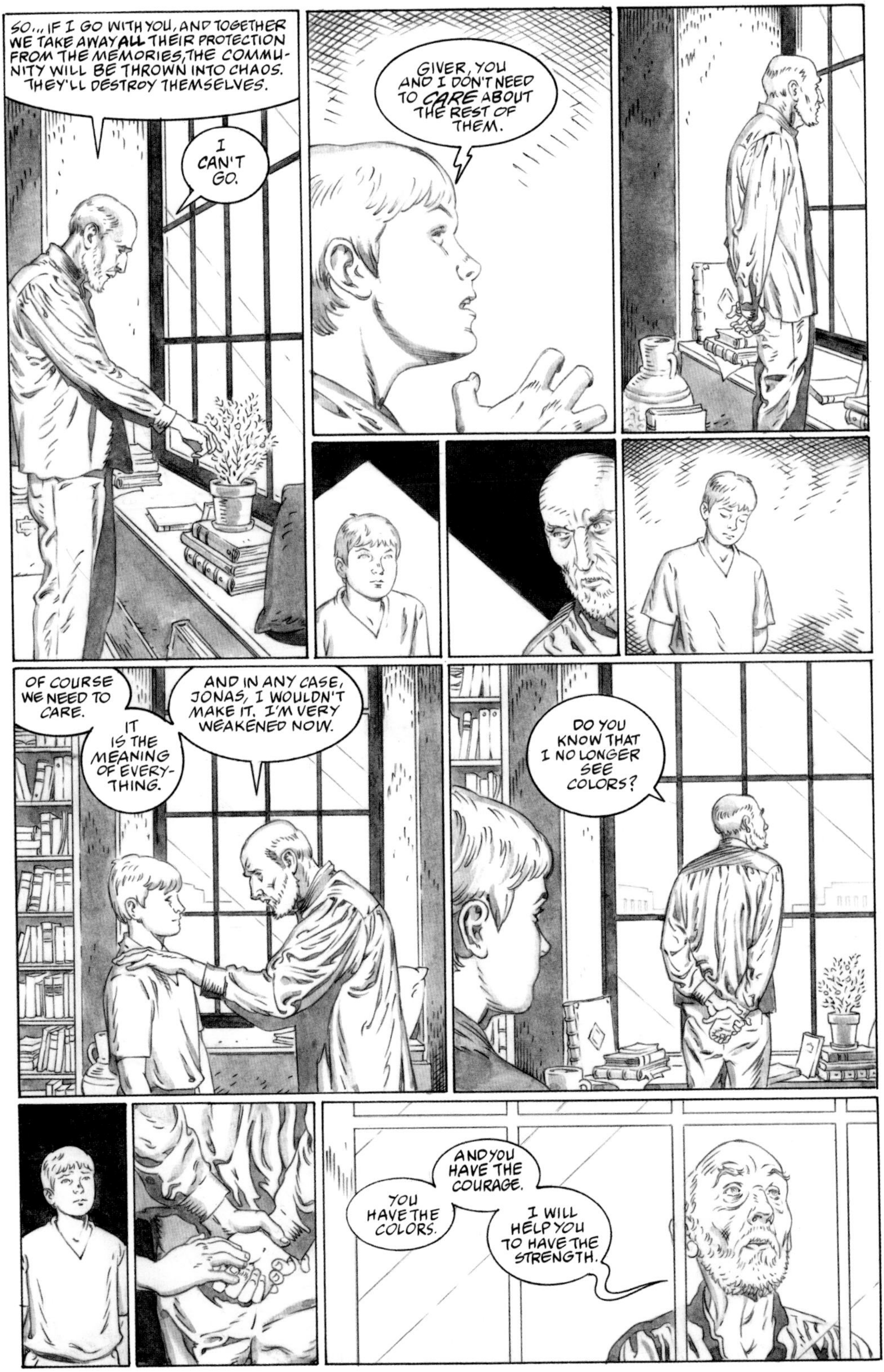
SO... IF I GO WITH YOU, AND TOGETHER WE TAKE AWAY ALL THEIR PROTECTION FROM THE MEMORIES, THE COMMUNITY WILL BE THROWN INTO CHAOS. THEY'LL DESTROY THEMSELVES.
I CAN'T GO.
GIVER, YOU AND I DON'T NEED TO CARE ABOUT THE REST OF THEM.
OF COURSE WE NEED TO CARE.
IT IS THE MEANING OF EVERYTHING.
AND IN ANY CASE, JONAS, I WOULDN'T MAKE IT. I'M VERY WEAKENED NOW.
DO YOU KNOW THAT I NO LONGER SEE COLORS?
YOU HAVE THE COLORS.
AND YOU HAVE THE COURAGE.
I WILL HELP YOU TO HAVE THE STRENGTH.

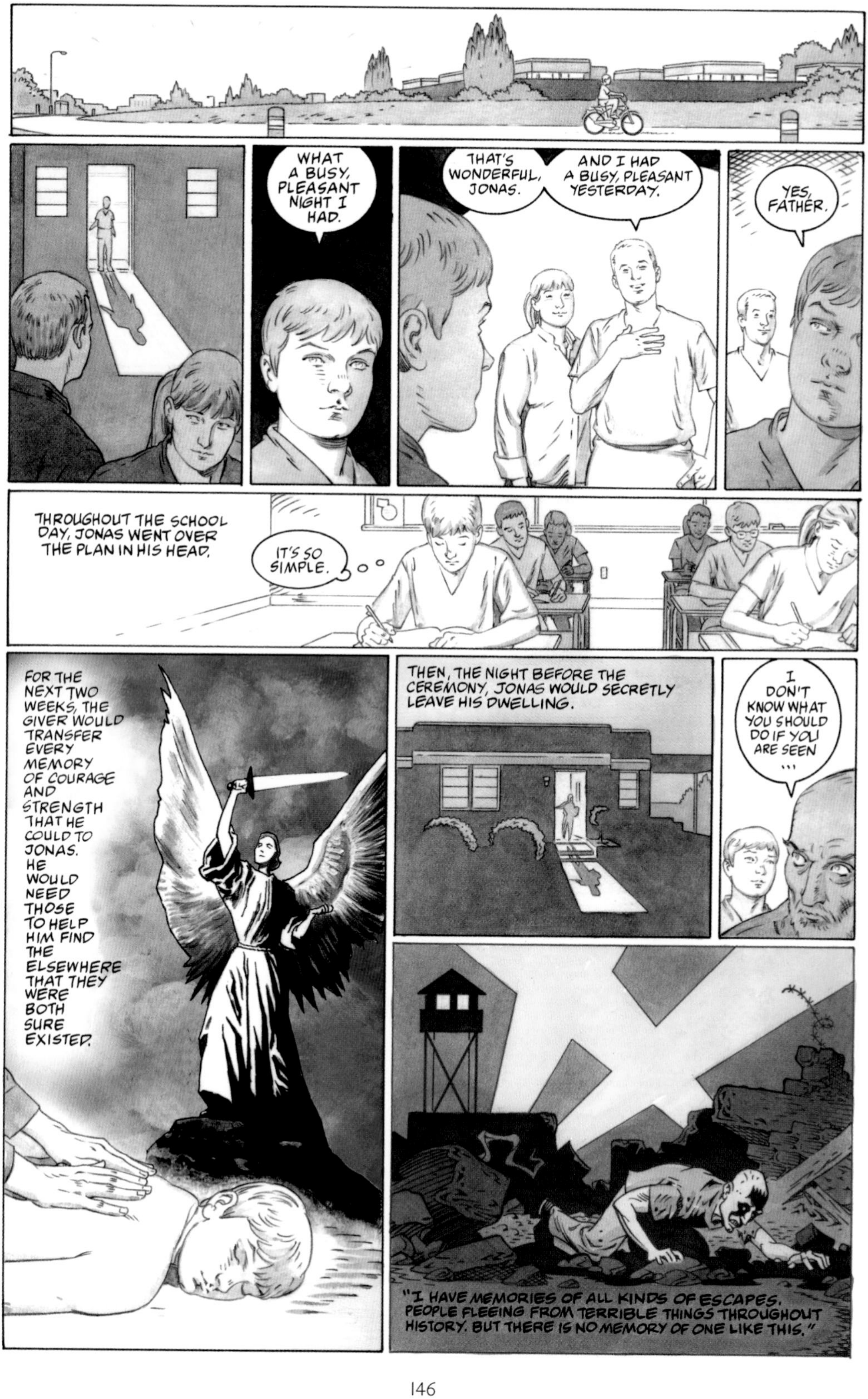
WHAT A BUSY, PLEASANT NIGHT I HAD.
THAT'S WONDERFUL, JONAS.
AND I HAD A BUSY, PLEASANT YESTERDAY.
YES, FATHER.
THROUGHOUT THE SCHOOL DAY, JONAS WENT OVER THE PLAN IN HIS HEAD.
IT'S SO SIMPLE.
FOR THE NEXT TWO WEEKS, THE GIVER WOULD TRANSFER EVERY MEMORY OF COURAGE AND STRENGTH THAT HE COULD TO JONAS. HE WOULD NEED THOSE TO HELP HIM FIND THE ELSEWHERE THAT THEY WERE BOTH SURE EXISTED.
THEN, THE NIGHT BEFORE THE CEREMONY, JONAS WOULD SECRETLY LEAVE HIS DWELLING.
I DON'T KNOW WHAT YOU SHOULD DO IF YOU ARE SEEN ...
"I HAVE MEMORIES OF ALL KINDS OF ESCAPES. PEOPLE FLEEING FROM TERRIBLE THINGS THROUGHOUT HISTORY. BUT THERE IS NO MEMORY OF ONE LIKE THIS."

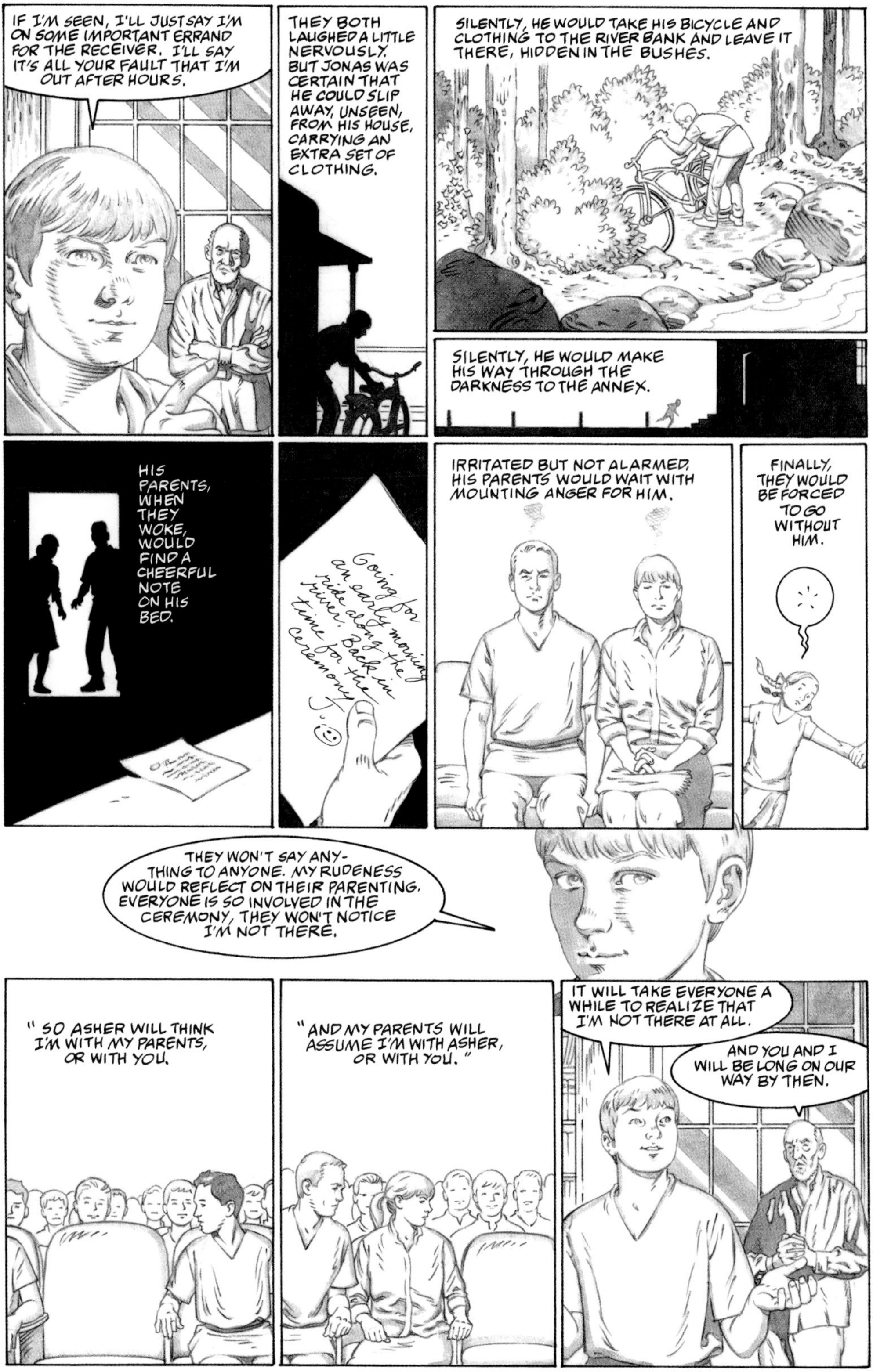
IF I'M SEEN, I'LL JUST SAY I'M ON SOME IMPORTANT ERRAND FOR THE RECEIVER. I'LL SAY IT'S ALL YOUR FAULT THAT I'M OUT AFTER HOURS.
THEY BOTH LAUGHED A LITTLE NERVOUSLY. BUT JONAS WAS CERTAIN THAT HE COULD SLIP AWAY, UNSEEN, FROM HIS HOUSE, CARRYING AN EXTRA SET OF CLOTHING.
SILENTLY, HE WOULD TAKE HIS BICYCLE AND CLOTHING TO THE RIVER BANK AND LEAVE IT THERE, HIDDEN IN THE BUSHES.
SILENTLY, HE WOULD MAKE HIS WAY THROUGH THE DARKNESS TO THE ANNEX.
HIS PARENTS, WHEN THEY WOKE, WOULD FIND A CHEERFUL NOTE ON HIS BED.
Going for an early morning ride along the river. Back in time for the ceremony. J.
IRRITATED BUT NOT ALARMED, HIS PARENTS WOULD WAIT WITH MOUNTING ANGER FOR HIM.
FINALLY, THEY WOULD BE FORCED TO GO WITHOUT HIM.
THEY WON'T SAY ANYTHING TO ANYONE. MY RUDENESS WOULD REFLECT ON THEIR PARENTING. EVERYONE IS SO INVOLVED IN THE CEREMONY, THEY WON'T NOTICE I'M NOT THERE.
"SO ASHER WILL THINK I'M WITH MY PARENTS, OR WITH YOU.
"AND MY PARENTS WILL ASSUME I'M WITH ASHER, OR WITH YOU."
IT WILL TAKE EVERYONE A WHILE TO REALIZE THAT I'M NOT THERE AT ALL.
AND YOU AND I WILL BE LONG ON OUR WAY BY THEN.

IN THE EARLY MORNING, THE GIVER WOULD ORDER A VEHICLE AND DRIVER. HE VISITED THE OTHER COMMUNITIES FREQUENTLY, MEETING WITH THEIR ELDERS, SO THIS WOULD NOT SEEM TO BE AN UNUSUAL UNDERTAKING.

WHEN THE DRIVER AND VEHICLE ARRIVED, HE WOULD SEND THE DRIVER ON SOME BRIEF ERRAND AND, DURING HIS ABSENCE, HELP JONAS HIDE IN THE STORAGE AREA OF THE VEHICLE.

THE CEREMONY WOULD BEGIN, BUT BY THEN, JONAS AND THE GIVER WOULD BE ON THEIR WAY.

BY MIDDAY, JONAS'S ABSENCE WOULD BECOME APPARENT, AND WOULD BE A CAUSE FOR SERIOUS ALARM. SEARCHERS WOULD BE SENT OUT INTO THE COMMUNITY.

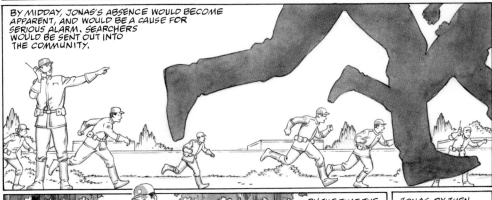

BY THE TIME THE BICYCLE AND CLOTHING WERE FOUND, THE GIVER WOULD BE RETURNING.

JONAS, BY THEN, WOULD BE ON HIS OWN, MAKING HIS JOURNEY *ELSEWHERE*.

THE GIVER, ON HIS RETURN, WOULD FIND THE COMMUNITY IN A STATE OF CONFUSION AND PANIC.

HE WOULD GO TO THE AUDITORIUM, WHERE THE PEOPLE WOULD BE GATHERED STILL.

HE WOULD MAKE THE SOLEMN ANNOUNCEMENT THAT --

JONAS HAS BEEN LOST IN THE RIVER!

HE WOULD IMMEDIATELY BEGIN THE CEREMONY OF LOSS.

JONAS! JONAS!

JONAS   JONAS   JONAS

JONAS

TOGETHER, THEY WOULD LET JONAS'S PRESENCE IN THEIR LIVES FADE AWAY...

JONAS
JONAS
JONAS
JONAS
JONAS
JONAS
JONAS
JONAS

...UNTIL HE WAS NO MORE THAN AN OCCASIONAL MURMUR, AND THEN...

JONAS
JONAS
JONAS

...BY THE END OF THE LONG DAY, GONE FOREVER, NOT TO BE MENTIONED AGAIN.

THEIR ATTENTION WOULD TURN TO THE OVERWHELMING TASK OF BEARING THE MEMORIES THEMSELVES. THE GIVER WOULD HELP THEM.

149

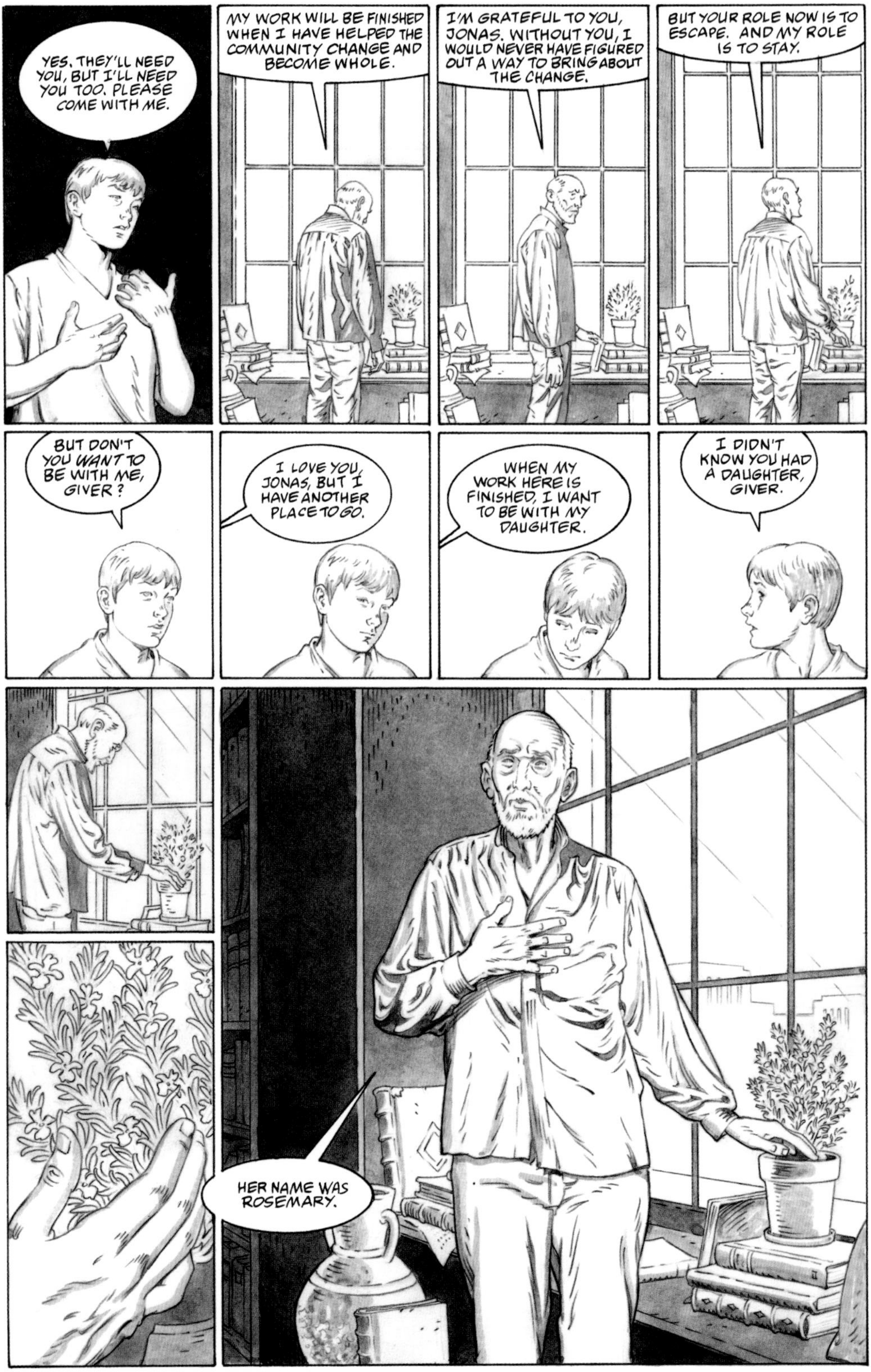
YES. THEY'LL NEED YOU, BUT I'LL NEED YOU TOO. PLEASE COME WITH ME.
MY WORK WILL BE FINISHED WHEN I HAVE HELPED THE COMMUNITY CHANGE AND BECOME WHOLE.
I'M GRATEFUL TO YOU, JONAS. WITHOUT YOU, I WOULD NEVER HAVE FIGURED OUT A WAY TO BRING ABOUT THE CHANGE.
BUT YOUR ROLE NOW IS TO ESCAPE. AND MY ROLE IS TO STAY.
BUT DON'T YOU *WANT* TO BE WITH ME, GIVER?
I LOVE YOU, JONAS, BUT I HAVE ANOTHER PLACE TO GO.
WHEN MY WORK HERE IS FINISHED, I WANT TO BE WITH MY DAUGHTER.
I DIDN'T KNOW YOU HAD A DAUGHTER, GIVER.
HER NAME WAS ROSEMARY.

21

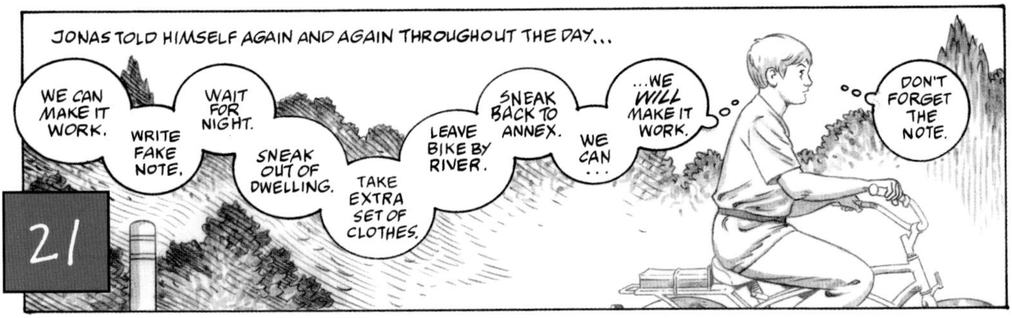
JONAS TOLD HIMSELF AGAIN AND AGAIN THROUGHOUT THE DAY...
WE CAN MAKE IT WORK.
WRITE FAKE NOTE.
WAIT FOR NIGHT.
SNEAK OUT OF DWELLING.
TAKE EXTRA SET OF CLOTHES.
LEAVE BIKE BY RIVER.
SNEAK BACK TO ANNEX.
WE CAN . . .
...WE *WILL* MAKE IT WORK.
DON'T FORGET THE NOTE.

BUT THAT EVENING EVERYTHING CHANGED.
ALL OF IT--ALL THE THINGS THEY HAD THOUGHT
THROUGH SO METICULOUSLY--

-- FELL APART.

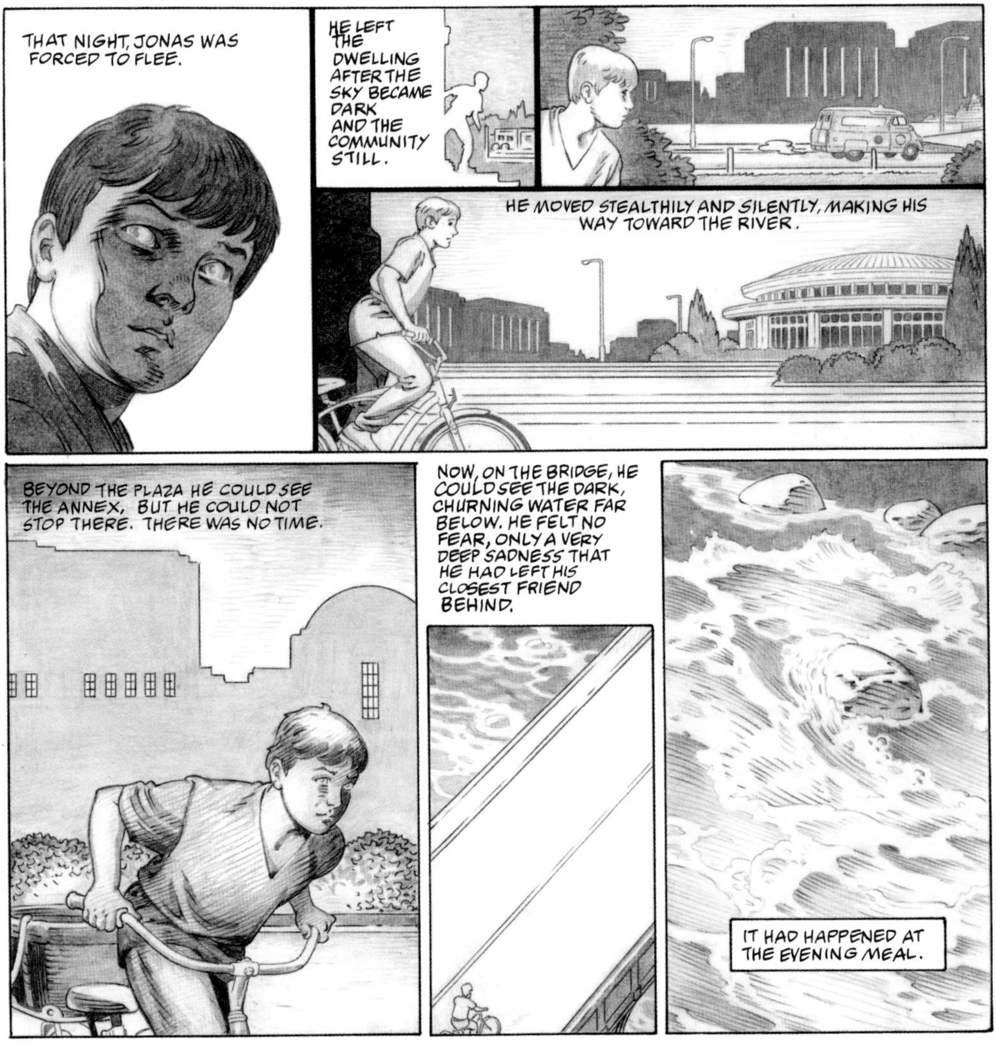
THAT NIGHT, JONAS WAS FORCED TO FLEE.
HE LEFT THE DWELLING AFTER THE SKY BECAME DARK AND THE COMMUNITY STILL.
HE MOVED STEALTHILY AND SILENTLY, MAKING HIS WAY TOWARD THE RIVER.
BEYOND THE PLAZA HE COULD SEE THE ANNEX, BUT HE COULD NOT STOP THERE. THERE WAS NO TIME.
NOW, ON THE BRIDGE, HE COULD SEE THE DARK, CHURNING WATER FAR BELOW. HE FELT NO FEAR, ONLY A VERY DEEP SADNESS THAT HE HAD LEFT HIS CLOSEST FRIEND BEHIND.
IT HAD HAPPENED AT THE EVENING MEAL.

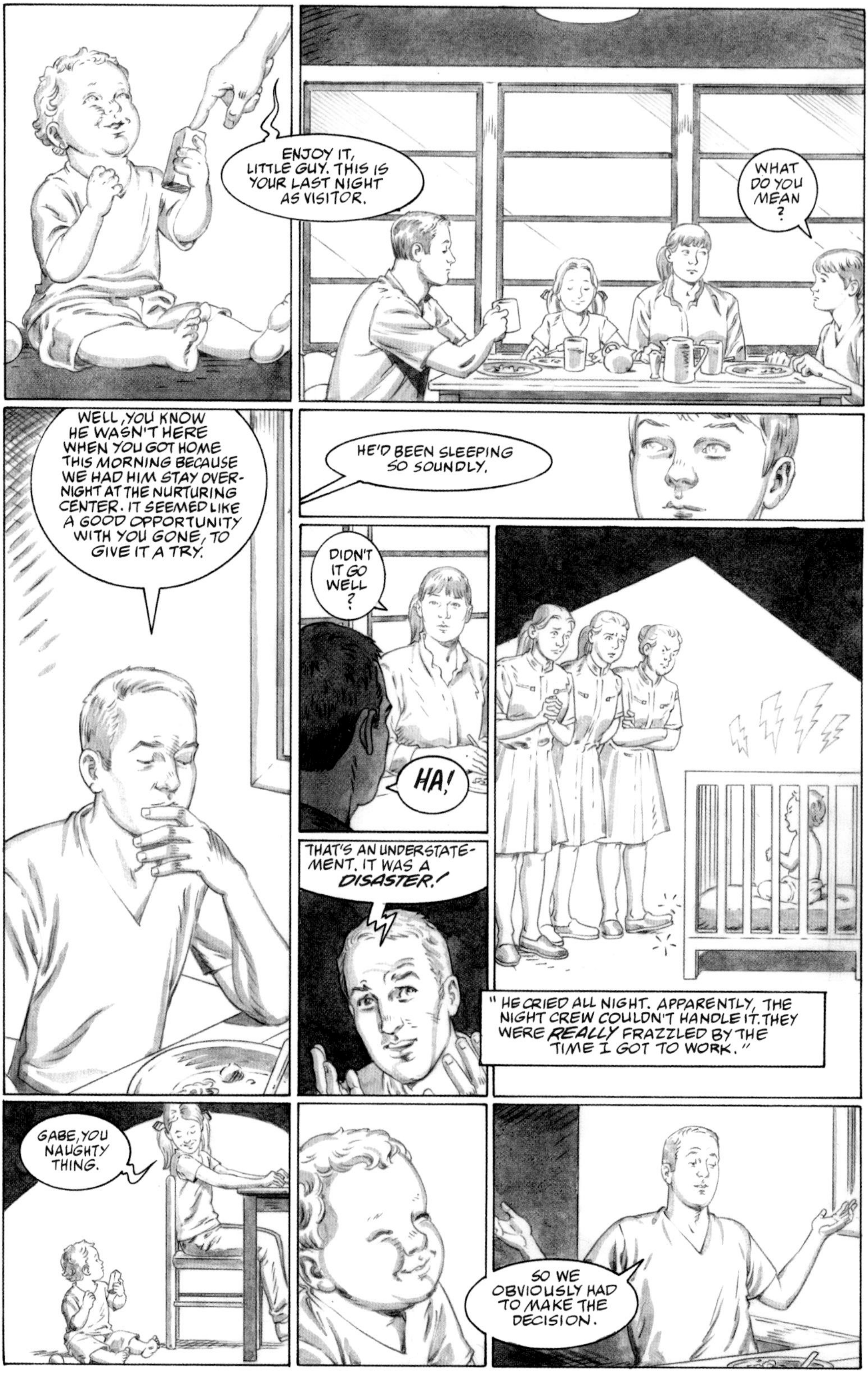
ENJOY IT, LITTLE GUY. THIS IS YOUR LAST NIGHT AS VISITOR.
WHAT DO YOU MEAN?
WELL, YOU KNOW HE WASN'T HERE WHEN YOU GOT HOME THIS MORNING BECAUSE WE HAD HIM STAY OVER-NIGHT AT THE NURTURING CENTER. IT SEEMED LIKE A GOOD OPPORTUNITY WITH YOU GONE, TO GIVE IT A TRY.
HE'D BEEN SLEEPING SO SOUNDLY.
DIDN'T IT GO WELL?
HA!
THAT'S AN UNDERSTATE-MENT. IT WAS A DISASTER!
"HE CRIED ALL NIGHT. APPARENTLY, THE NIGHT CREW COULDN'T HANDLE IT. THEY WERE REALLY FRAZZLED BY THE TIME I GOT TO WORK."
GABE, YOU NAUGHTY THING.
SO WE OBVIOUSLY HAD TO MAKE THE DECISION.

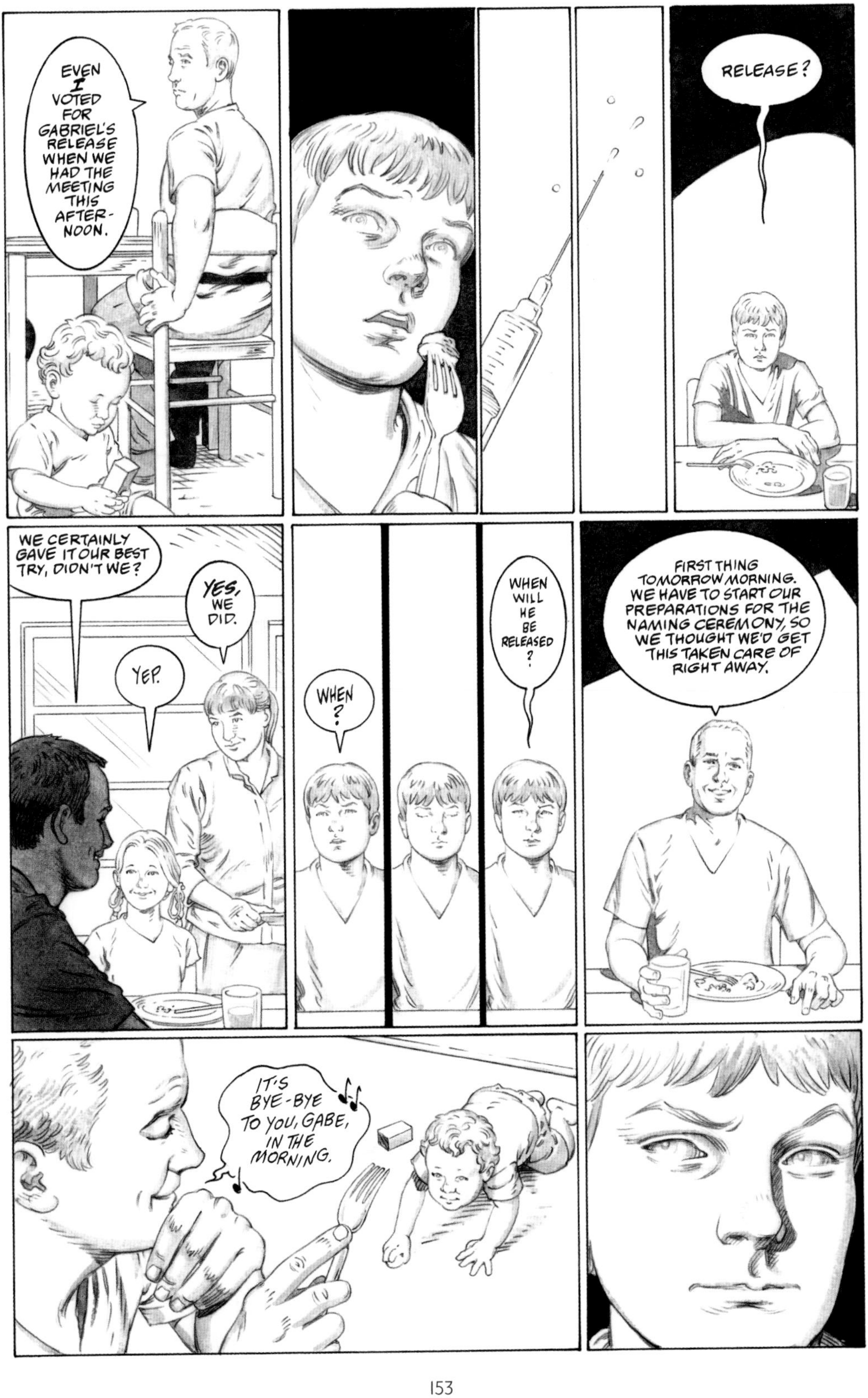
EVEN I VOTED FOR GABRIEL'S RELEASE WHEN WE HAD THE MEETING THIS AFTER-NOON.
RELEASE?
WE CERTAINLY GAVE IT OUR BEST TRY, DIDN'T WE?
YES, WE DID.
YEP.
WHEN?
WHEN WILL HE BE RELEASED?
FIRST THING TOMORROW MORNING. WE HAVE TO START OUR PREPARATIONS FOR THE NAMING CEREMONY, SO WE THOUGHT WE'D GET THIS TAKEN CARE OF RIGHT AWAY.
IT'S BYE-BYE TO YOU, GABE, IN THE MORNING.

JONAS REACHED THE OPPOSITE SIDE OF THE RIVER. THE COMMUNITY WHERE HIS ENTIRE LIFE HAD BEEN LIVED LAY BEHIND HIM NOW. AT DAWN, THE ORDERLY, DISCIPLINED LIFE HE HAD ALWAYS KNOWN WOULD CONTINUE AGAIN, WITHOUT HIM.

THE LIFE WITHOUT COLOR, PAIN, OR PAST.

IT WAS NOT SAFE TO SPEND TIME LOOKING BACK. HE THOUGHT OF THE RULES HE HAD BROKEN SO FAR.

FIRST, HE HAD LEFT THE DWELLING AT NIGHT.

A MAJOR TRANS-GRESSION.

SECOND, HE HAD ROBBED THE COMMUNITY OF FOOD.

A VERY SERIOUS CRIME.

THIRD, HE HAD STOLEN HIS FATHER'S BICYCLE.

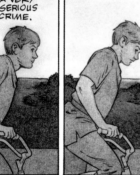

BUT IT WAS NECESSARY BECAUSE IT HAD THE CHILD SEAT ATTACHED TO THE BACK.

AND HE HAD TAKEN GABRIEL, TOO.

THAT NIGHT, BEFORE HE LEFT, HE TRANSMITTED TO GABE THE MOST SOOTHING MEMORY HE COULD.

HE KNEW HE HAD THE REMAINING HOURS OF THE NIGHT, BEFORE THEY WOULD BE AWARE OF HIS ESCAPE.

SO HE RODE HARD, WILLING HIMSELF NOT TO TIRE AS THE MINUTES AND MILES PASSED,

THERE HAD BEEN NO TIME TO RECEIVE THE MEMORIES HE AND THE GIVER HAD COUNTED ON OF STRENGTH AND COURAGE.

SO HE RELIED ON WHAT HE HAD ...

...AND HOPED IT WOULD BE ENOUGH.

HE CIRCLED THE OUTLYING COMMUNITIES, THEIR DWELLINGS DARK. GRADUALLY, THE DISTANCES BETWEEN COMMUNITIES WIDENED, WITH LONGER STRETCHES OF EMPTY ROAD.

HIS LEGS ACHED AT FIRST.

THEN, AS TIME PASSED, THEY BECAME NUMB.

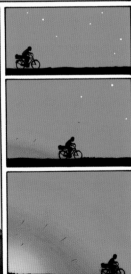

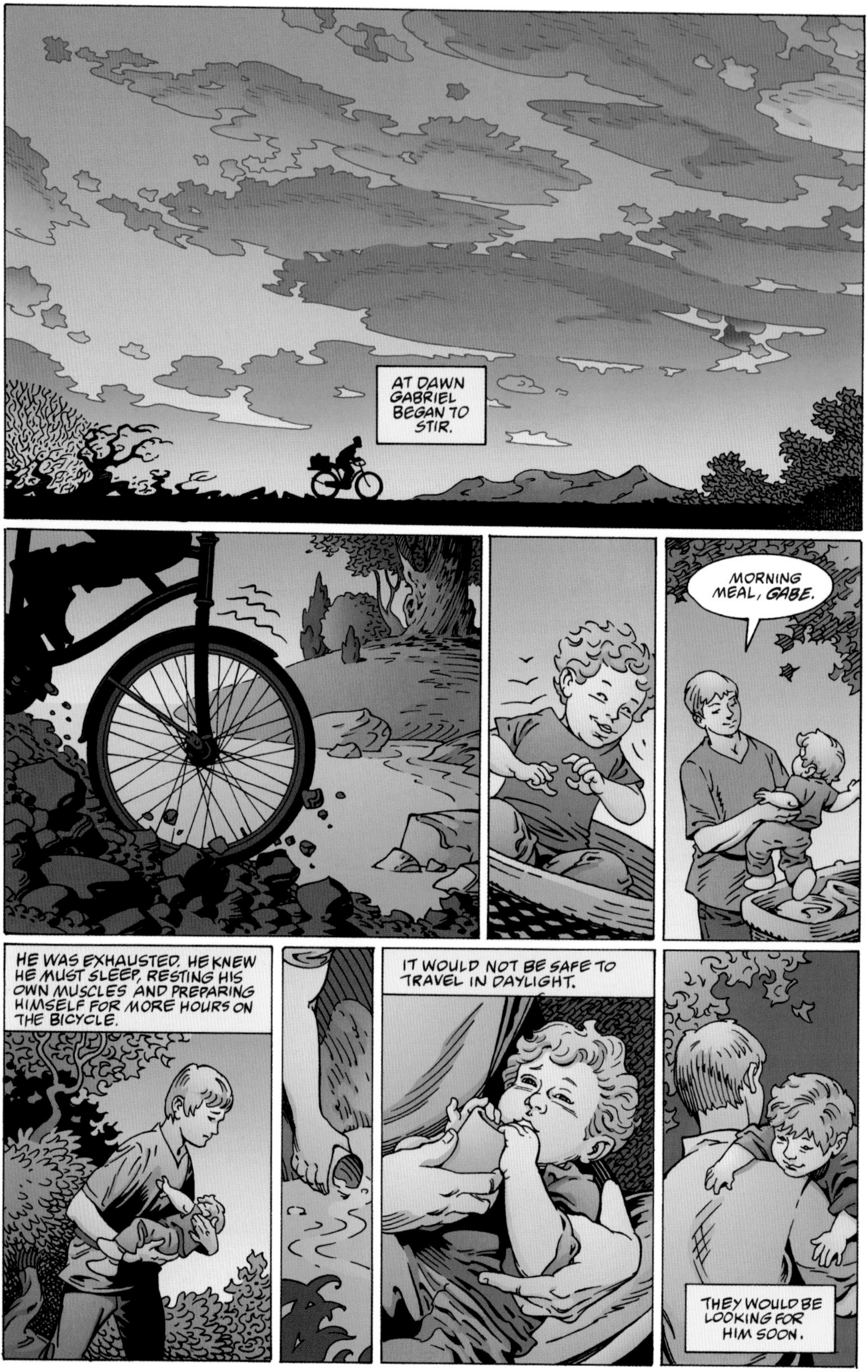
AT DAWN GABRIEL BEGAN TO STIR.
MORNING MEAL, GABE.
HE WAS EXHAUSTED. HE KNEW HE MUST SLEEP, RESTING HIS OWN MUSCLES AND PREPARING HIMSELF FOR MORE HOURS ON THE BICYCLE.
IT WOULD NOT BE SAFE TO TRAVEL IN DAYLIGHT.
THEY WOULD BE LOOKING FOR HIM SOON.

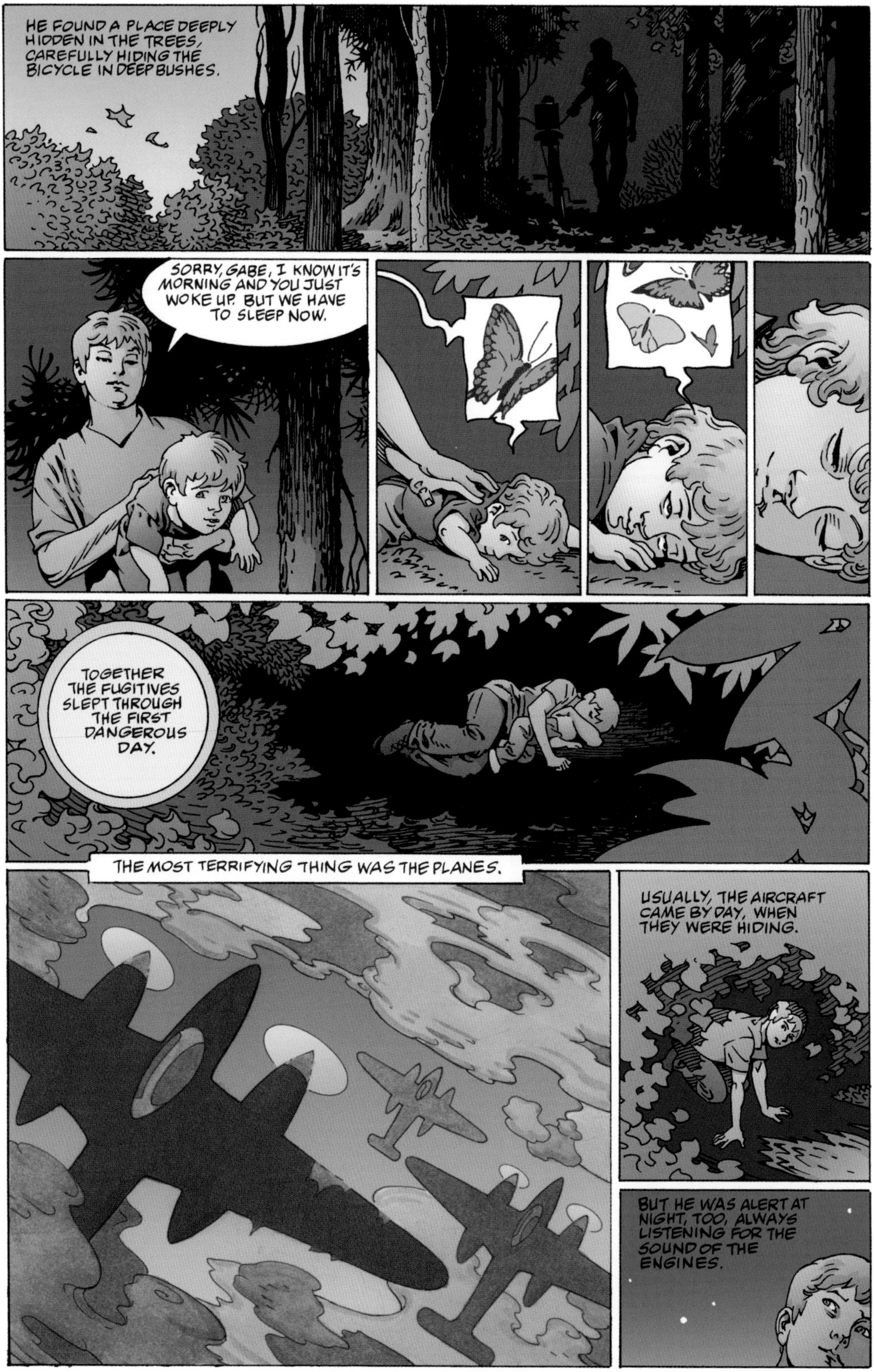
HE FOUND A PLACE DEEPLY HIDDEN IN THE TREES, CAREFULLY HIDING THE BICYCLE IN DEEP BUSHES.
SORRY, GABE, I KNOW IT'S MORNING AND YOU JUST WOKE UP. BUT WE HAVE TO SLEEP NOW.
TOGETHER THE FUGITIVES SLEPT THROUGH THE FIRST DANGEROUS DAY.
THE MOST TERRIFYING THING WAS THE PLANES.
USUALLY, THE AIRCRAFT CAME BY DAY, WHEN THEY WERE HIDING.
BUT HE WAS ALERT AT NIGHT, TOO, ALWAYS LISTENING FOR THE SOUND OF THE ENGINES.

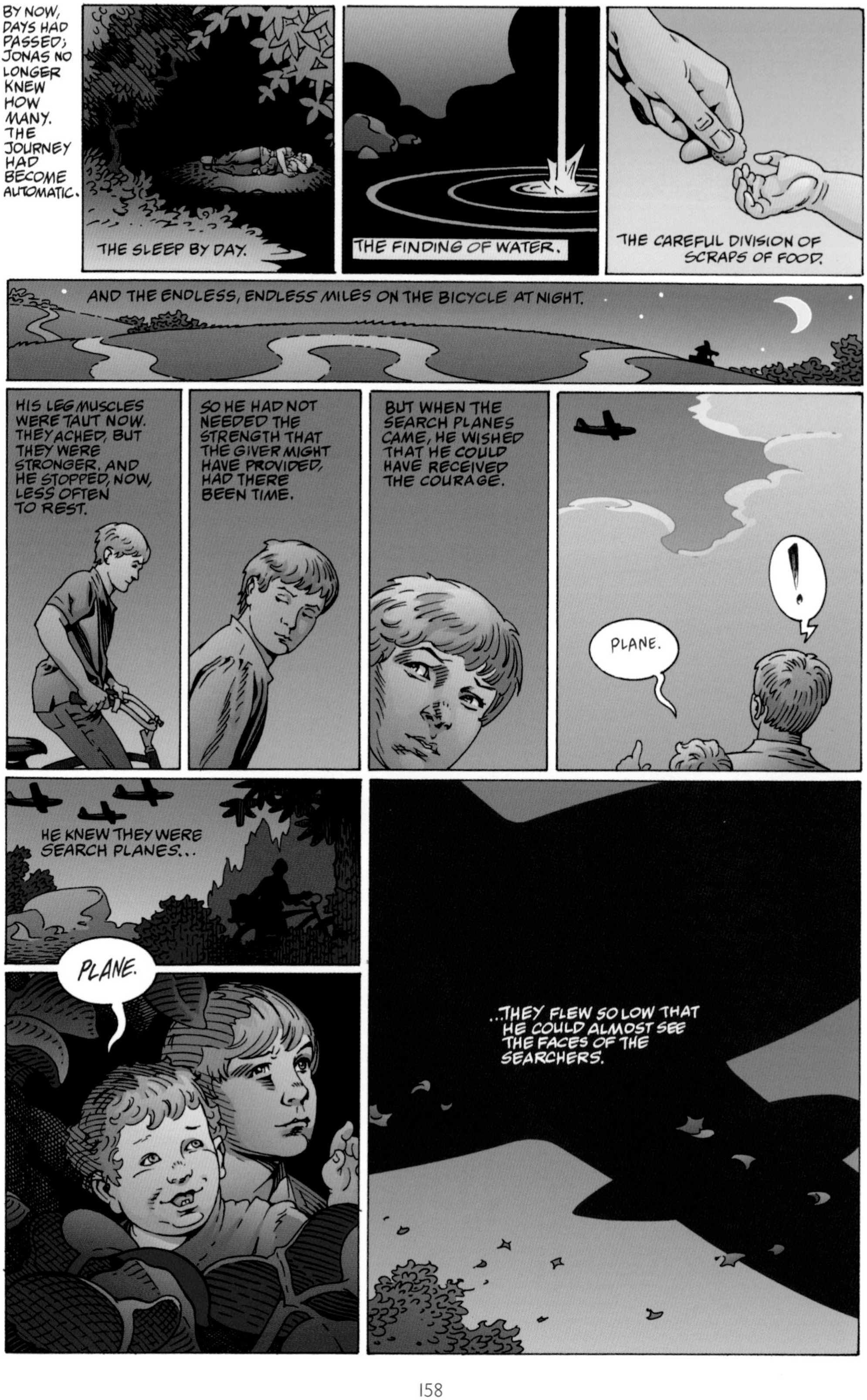
BY NOW, DAYS HAD PASSED; JONAS NO LONGER KNEW HOW MANY. THE JOURNEY HAD BECOME AUTOMATIC.
THE SLEEP BY DAY.
THE FINDING OF WATER.
THE CAREFUL DIVISION OF SCRAPS OF FOOD.
AND THE ENDLESS, ENDLESS MILES ON THE BICYCLE AT NIGHT.
HIS LEG MUSCLES WERE TAUT NOW. THEY ACHED, BUT THEY WERE STRONGER. AND HE STOPPED, NOW, LESS OFTEN TO REST.
SO HE HAD NOT NEEDED THE STRENGTH THAT THE GIVER MIGHT HAVE PROVIDED, HAD THERE BEEN TIME.
BUT WHEN THE SEARCH PLANES CAME, HE WISHED THAT HE COULD HAVE RECEIVED THE COURAGE.
PLANE.
!
HE KNEW THEY WERE SEARCH PLANES...
PLANE.
...THEY FLEW SO LOW THAT HE COULD ALMOST SEE THE FACES OF THE SEARCHERS.

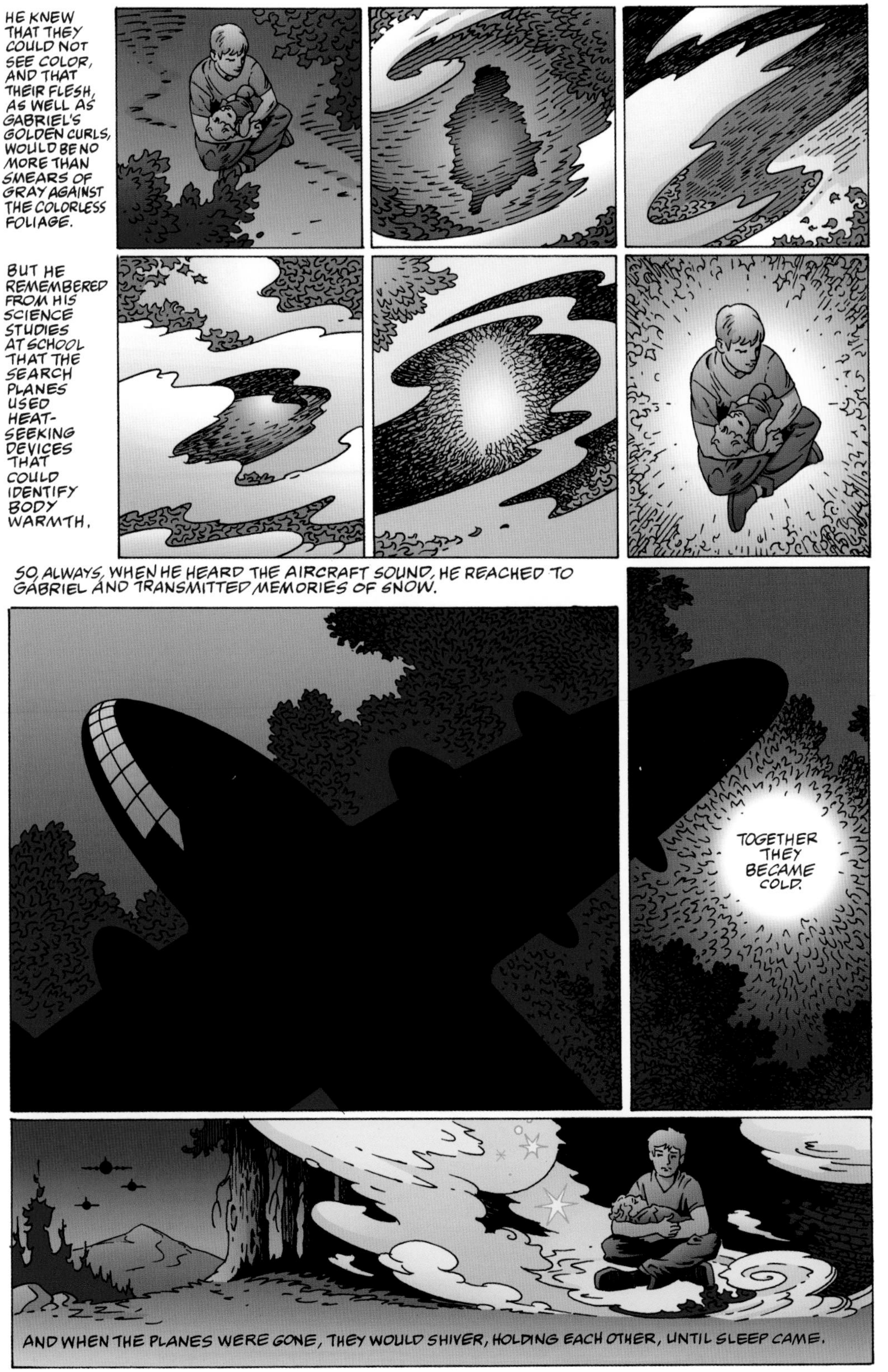
HE KNEW THAT THEY COULD NOT SEE COLOR, AND THAT THEIR FLESH, AS WELL AS GABRIEL'S GOLDEN CURLS, WOULD BE NO MORE THAN SMEARS OF GRAY AGAINST THE COLORLESS FOLIAGE.
BUT HE REMEMBERED FROM HIS SCIENCE STUDIES AT SCHOOL THAT THE SEARCH PLANES USED HEAT-SEEKING DEVICES THAT COULD IDENTIFY BODY WARMTH.
SO, ALWAYS, WHEN HE HEARD THE AIRCRAFT SOUND, HE REACHED TO GABRIEL AND TRANSMITTED MEMORIES OF SNOW.
TOGETHER THEY BECAME COLD.
AND WHEN THE PLANES WERE GONE, THEY WOULD SHIVER, HOLDING EACH OTHER, UNTIL SLEEP CAME.

SOMETIMES, URGING THE MEMORIES INTO GABRIEL, JONAS FELT THEY WERE MORE SHALLOW, A LITTLE WEAKER THAN THEY HAD BEEN. IT WAS WHAT HE AND THE GIVER HAD PLANNED: THAT AS HE MOVED AWAY FROM THE COMMUNITY, HE WOULD SHED THE MEMORIES AND LEAVE THEM BEHIND FOR THE PEOPLE.

BUT NOW, WHEN HE NEEDED THEM, WHEN THE PLANES CAME, HE TRIED HARD TO CLING TO WHAT HE STILL HAD, OF COLD, AND TO USE IT FOR THEIR SURVIVAL.

HE PEDALED THROUGH THE NIGHTS, THROUGH ISOLATED LANDSCAPE, NOW, WITH THE COMMUNITIES FAR BEHIND AND NO SIGN OF HUMAN HABITATION AROUND HIM, OR AHEAD.

HE WAS CONSTANTLY VIGILANT...

...LOOKING FOR THE NEAREST HIDING PLACE, SHOULD THE SOUND OF ENGINES COME.

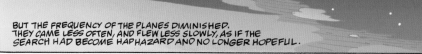BUT THE FREQUENCY OF THE PLANES DIMINISHED. THEY CAME LESS OFTEN, AND FLEW LESS SLOWLY, AS IF THE SEARCH HAD BECOME HAPHAZARD AND NO LONGER HOPEFUL.

FINALLY, THERE CAME AN ENTIRE DAY AND NIGHT WHEN THEY DID NOT COME AT ALL.

160

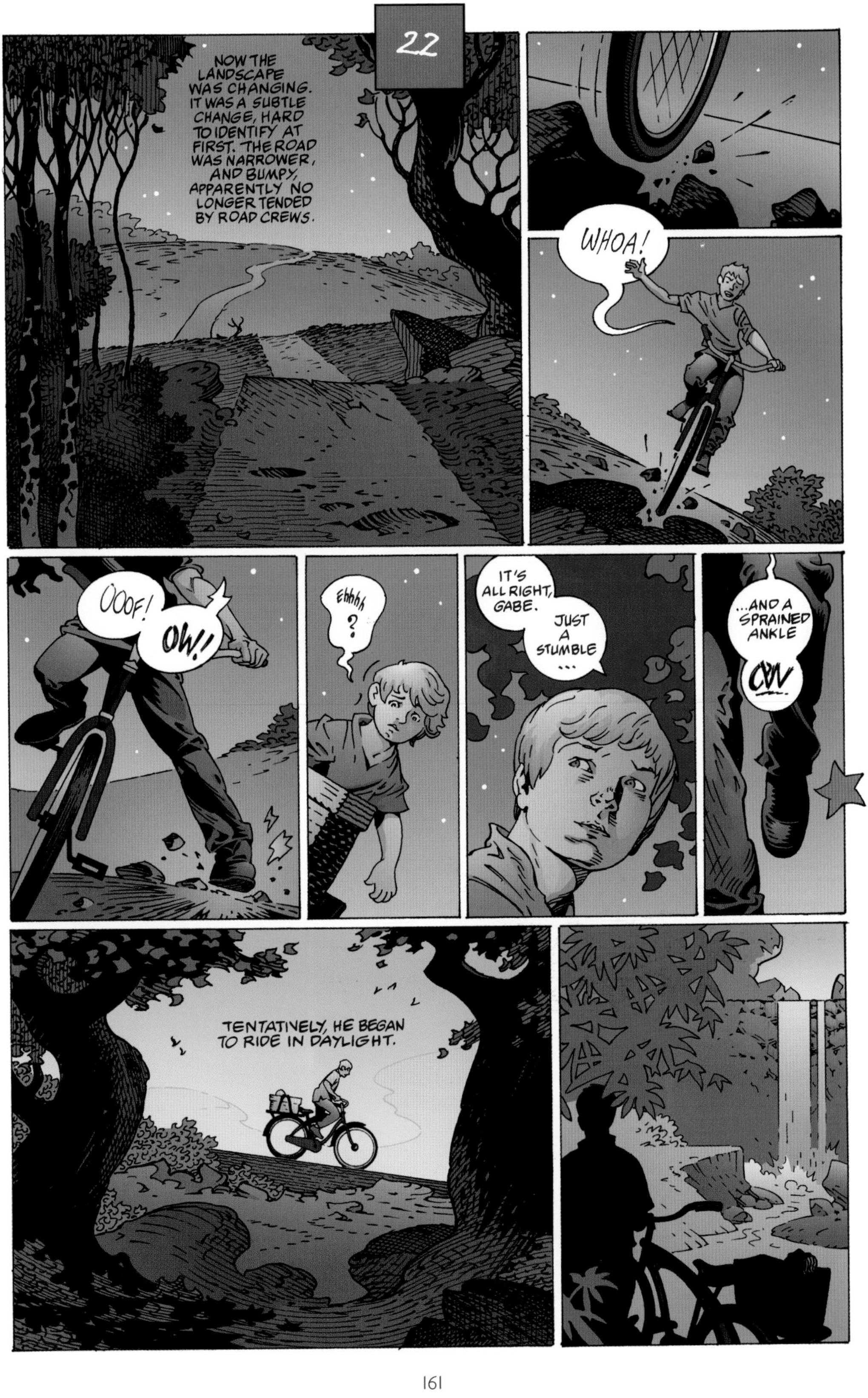
22
NOW THE LANDSCAPE WAS CHANGING. IT WAS A SUBTLE CHANGE, HARD TO IDENTIFY AT FIRST. THE ROAD WAS NARROWER, AND BUMPY, APPARENTLY NO LONGER TENDED BY ROAD CREWS.
WHOA!
OOOF!
OW!!
Ehhhh ?
IT'S ALL RIGHT, GABE.
JUST A STUMBLE ...
...AND A SPRAINED ANKLE
TENTATIVELY, HE BEGAN TO RIDE IN DAYLIGHT.

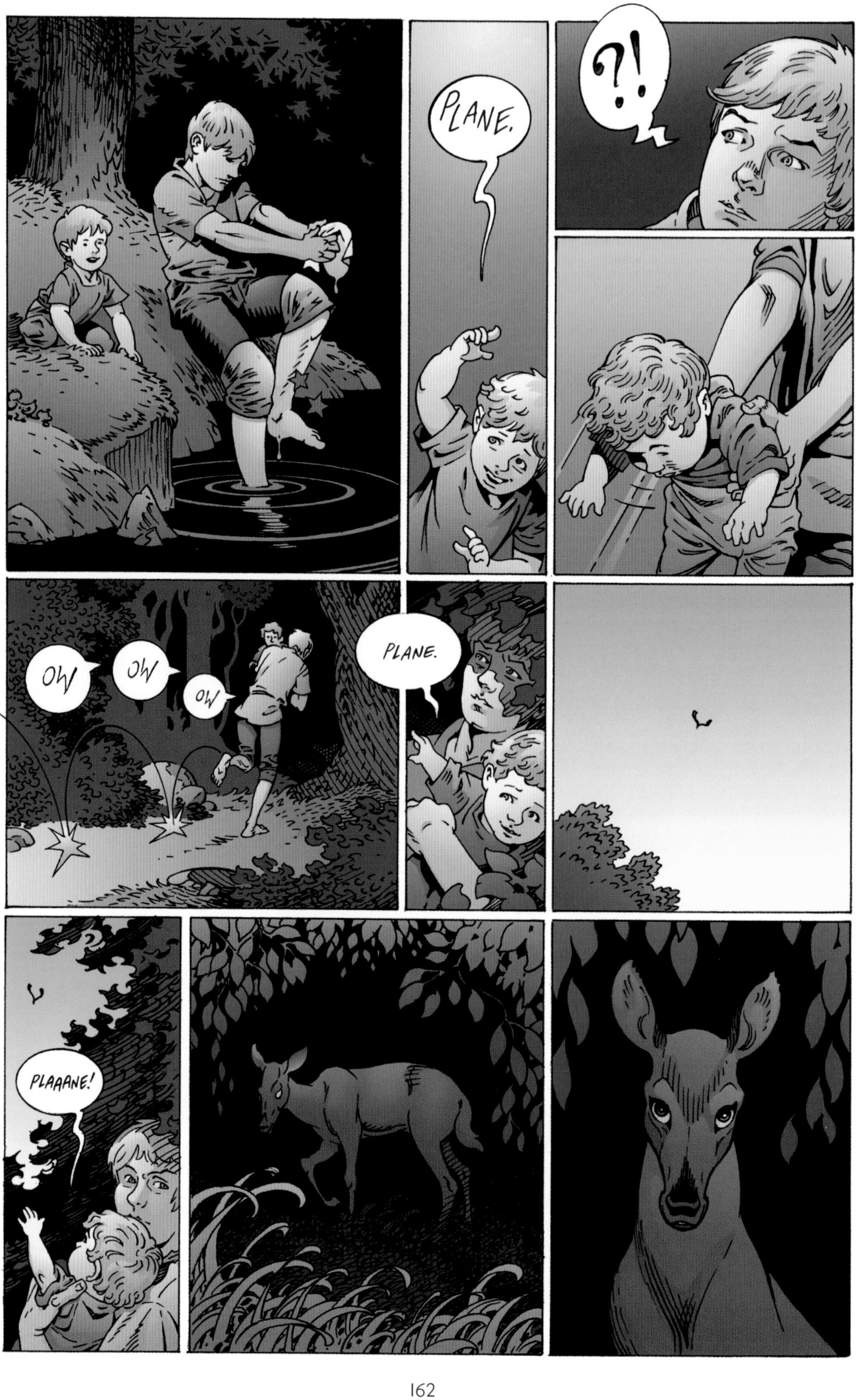
PLANE.
?!
OW
OW
OW
PLANE.
PLAAANE!

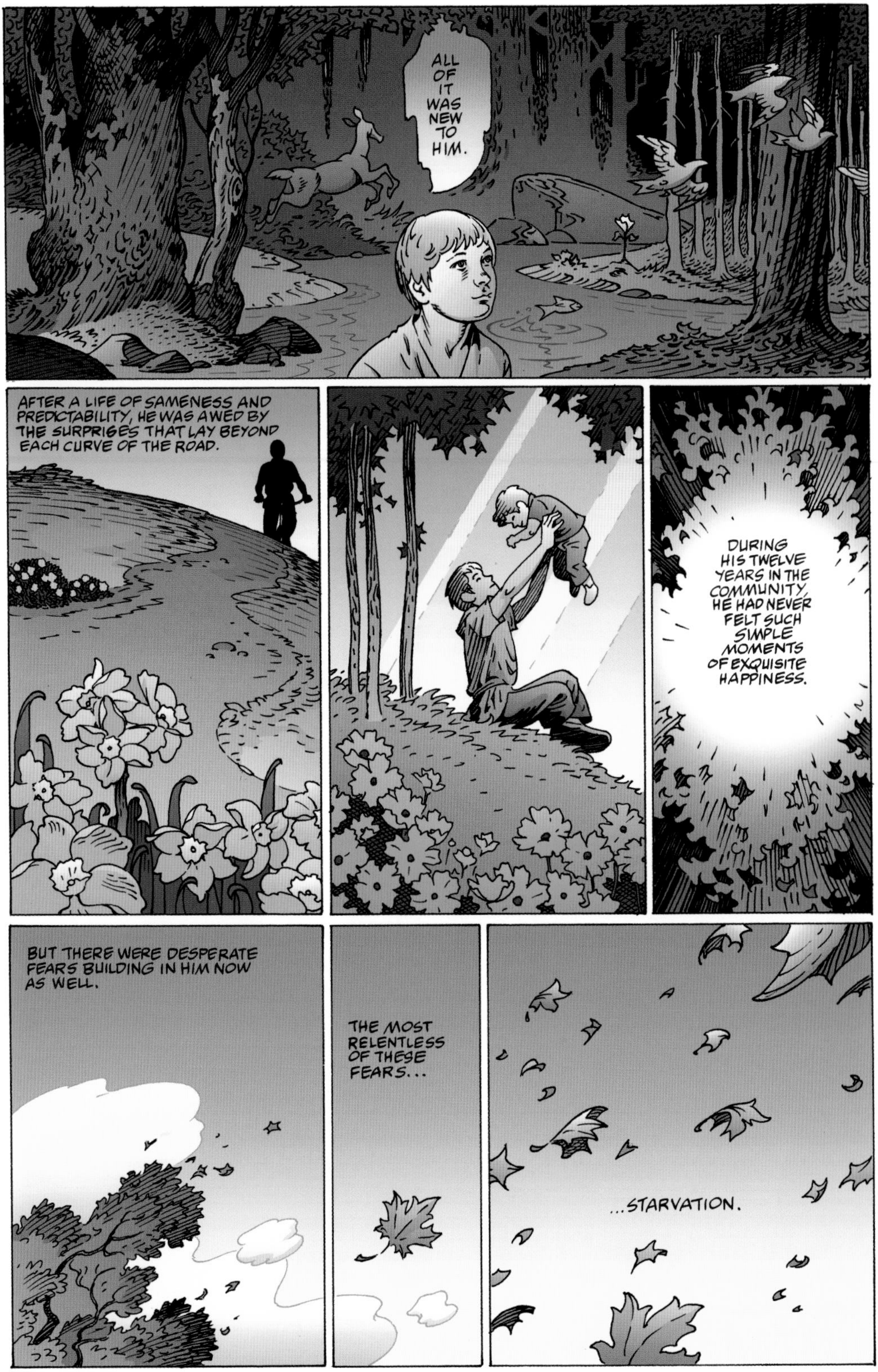
ALL OF IT WAS NEW TO HIM.
AFTER A LIFE OF SAMENESS AND PREDICTABILITY, HE WAS AWED BY THE SURPRISES THAT LAY BEYOND EACH CURVE OF THE ROAD.
DURING HIS TWELVE YEARS IN THE COMMUNITY, HE HAD NEVER FELT SUCH SIMPLE MOMENTS OF EXQUISITE HAPPINESS.
BUT THERE WERE DESPERATE FEARS BUILDING IN HIM NOW AS WELL.
THE MOST RELENTLESS OF THESE FEARS...
...STARVATION.

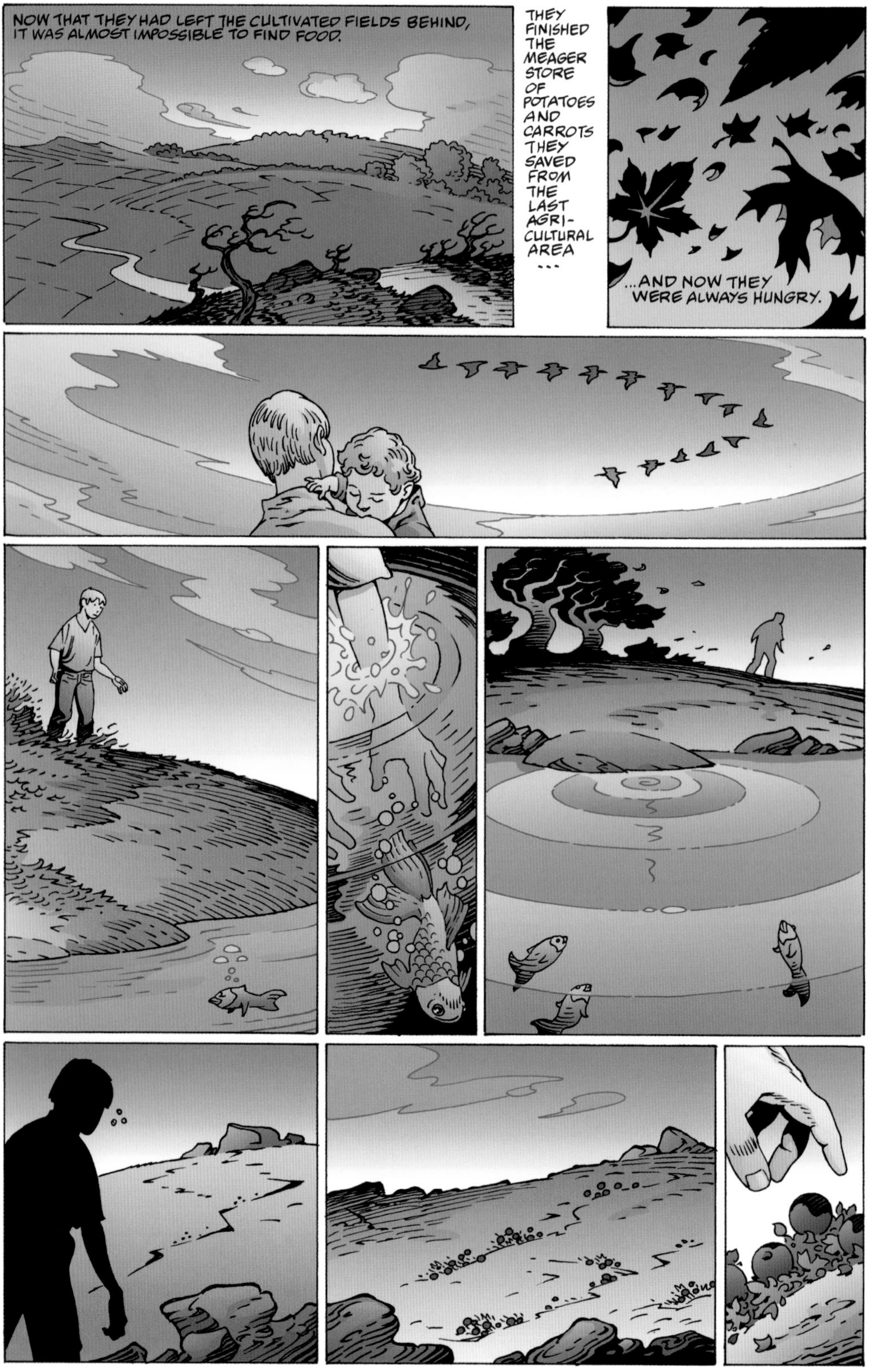
NOW THAT THEY HAD LEFT THE CULTIVATED FIELDS BEHIND, IT WAS ALMOST IMPOSSIBLE TO FIND FOOD.
THEY FINISHED THE MEAGER STORE OF POTATOES AND CARROTS THEY SAVED FROM THE LAST AGRI-CULTURAL AREA ...
...AND NOW THEY WERE ALWAYS HUNGRY.

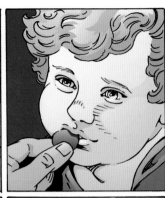

JONAS REMEMBERED, SUDDENLY AND GRIMLY, THE TIME IN HIS CHILDHOOD WHEN HE HAD BEEN CHASTISED FOR MISUSING A WORD.

I'M STARVING!

YOU ARE *NOT* STARVING.

YOU HAVE NEVER *BEEN* STARVING.

YOU WILL NEVER *BE* STARVING.

IF I HAD STAYED IN THE COMMUNITY I WOULD NOT BE STARVING.

IT'S AS SIMPLE AS THAT.

ONCE, I WANTED A CHOICE.

THEN, WHEN I HAD A CHOICE, I MADE THE WRONG ONE: THE CHOICE TO LEAVE,

AND NOW I'M STARVING.

BUT IF I'D STAYED ...

"IF I HAD STAYED, I WOULD HAVE STARVED IN OTHER WAYS. I WOULD HAVE LIVED A LIFE HUNGRY FOR FEELINGS...

"...FOR LOVE."

HOUSE OF THE OLD

AND GABRIEL?

"FOR GABRIEL THERE WOULD HAVE BEEN NO LIFE AT ALL."

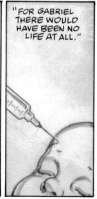

SO THERE HAS NEVER REALLY BEEN A CHOICE.

166

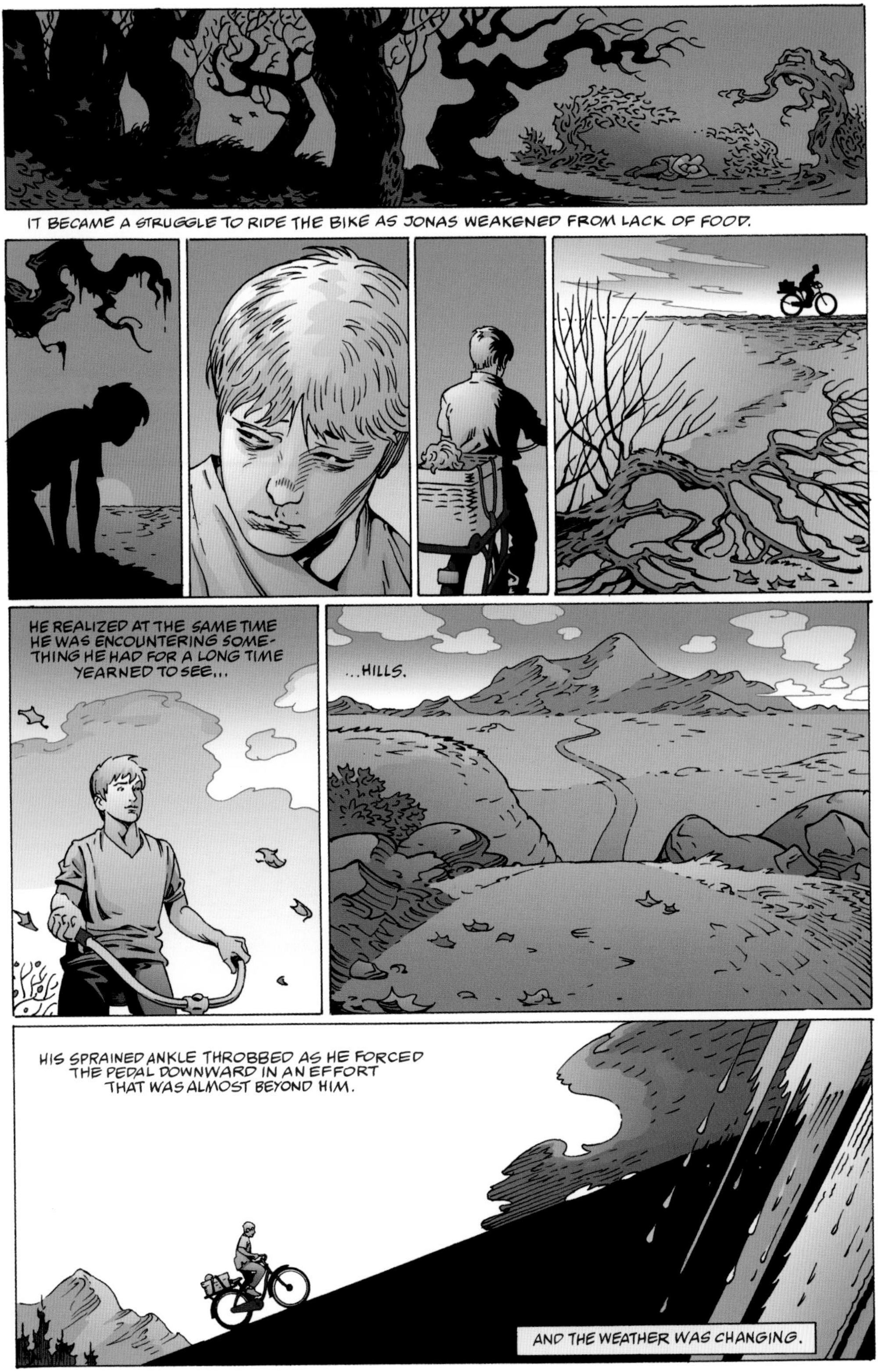
IT BECAME A STRUGGLE TO RIDE THE BIKE AS JONAS WEAKENED FROM LACK OF FOOD.
HE REALIZED AT THE SAME TIME HE WAS ENCOUNTERING SOMETHING HE HAD FOR A LONG TIME YEARNED TO SEE...
...HILLS.
HIS SPRAINED ANKLE THROBBED AS HE FORCED THE PEDAL DOWNWARD IN AN EFFORT THAT WAS ALMOST BEYOND HIM.
AND THE WEATHER WAS CHANGING.

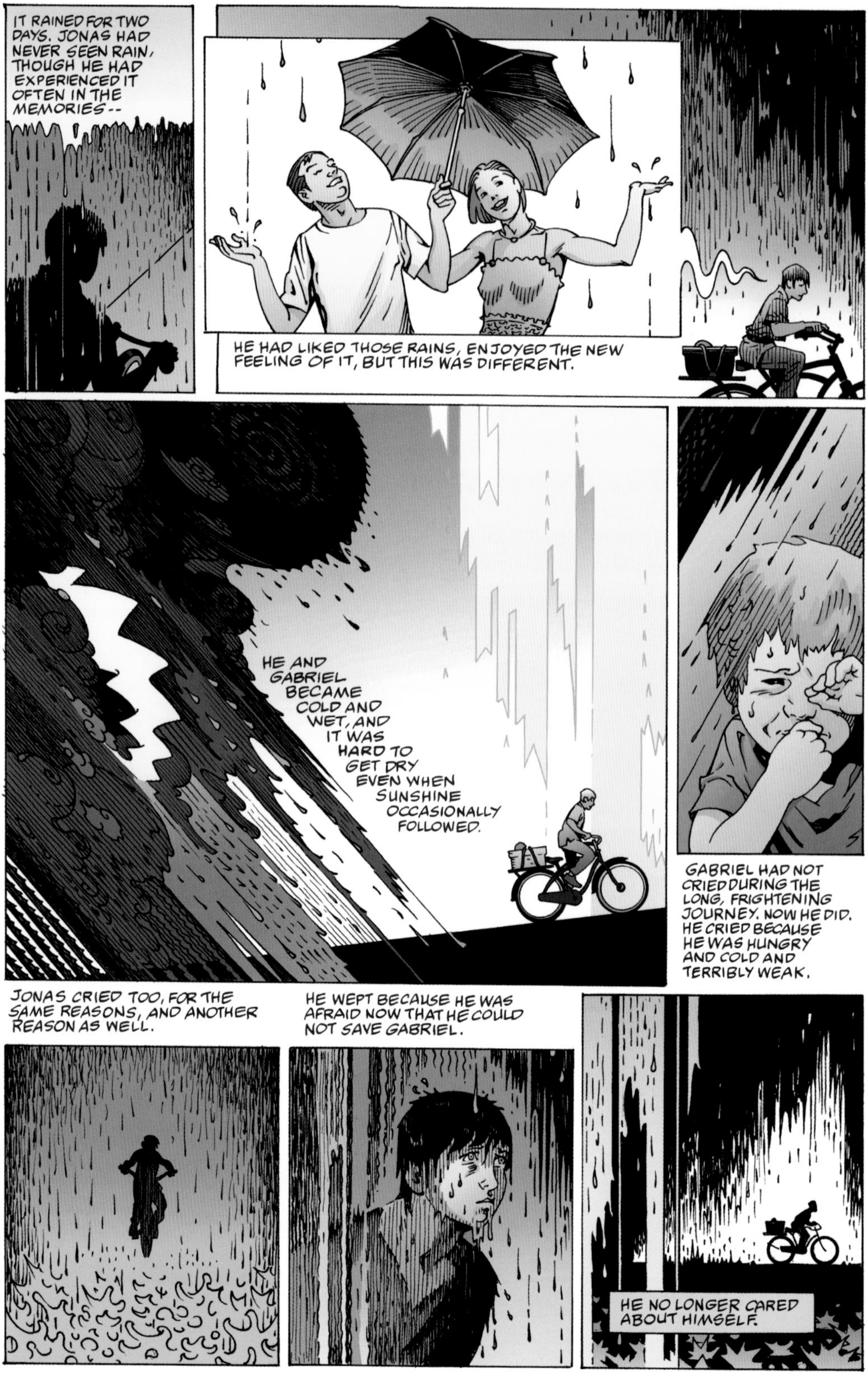

IT RAINED FOR TWO DAYS. JONAS HAD NEVER SEEN RAIN, THOUGH HE HAD EXPERIENCED IT OFTEN IN THE MEMORIES--
HE HAD LIKED THOSE RAINS, ENJOYED THE NEW FEELING OF IT, BUT THIS WAS DIFFERENT.
HE AND GABRIEL BECAME COLD AND WET, AND IT WAS HARD TO GET DRY EVEN WHEN SUNSHINE OCCASIONALLY FOLLOWED.
GABRIEL HAD NOT CRIED DURING THE LONG, FRIGHTENING JOURNEY. NOW HE DID. HE CRIED BECAUSE HE WAS HUNGRY AND COLD AND TERRIBLY WEAK.
JONAS CRIED TOO, FOR THE SAME REASONS, AND ANOTHER REASON AS WELL.
HE WEPT BECAUSE HE WAS AFRAID NOW THAT HE COULD NOT SAVE GABRIEL.
HE NO LONGER CARED ABOUT HIMSELF.

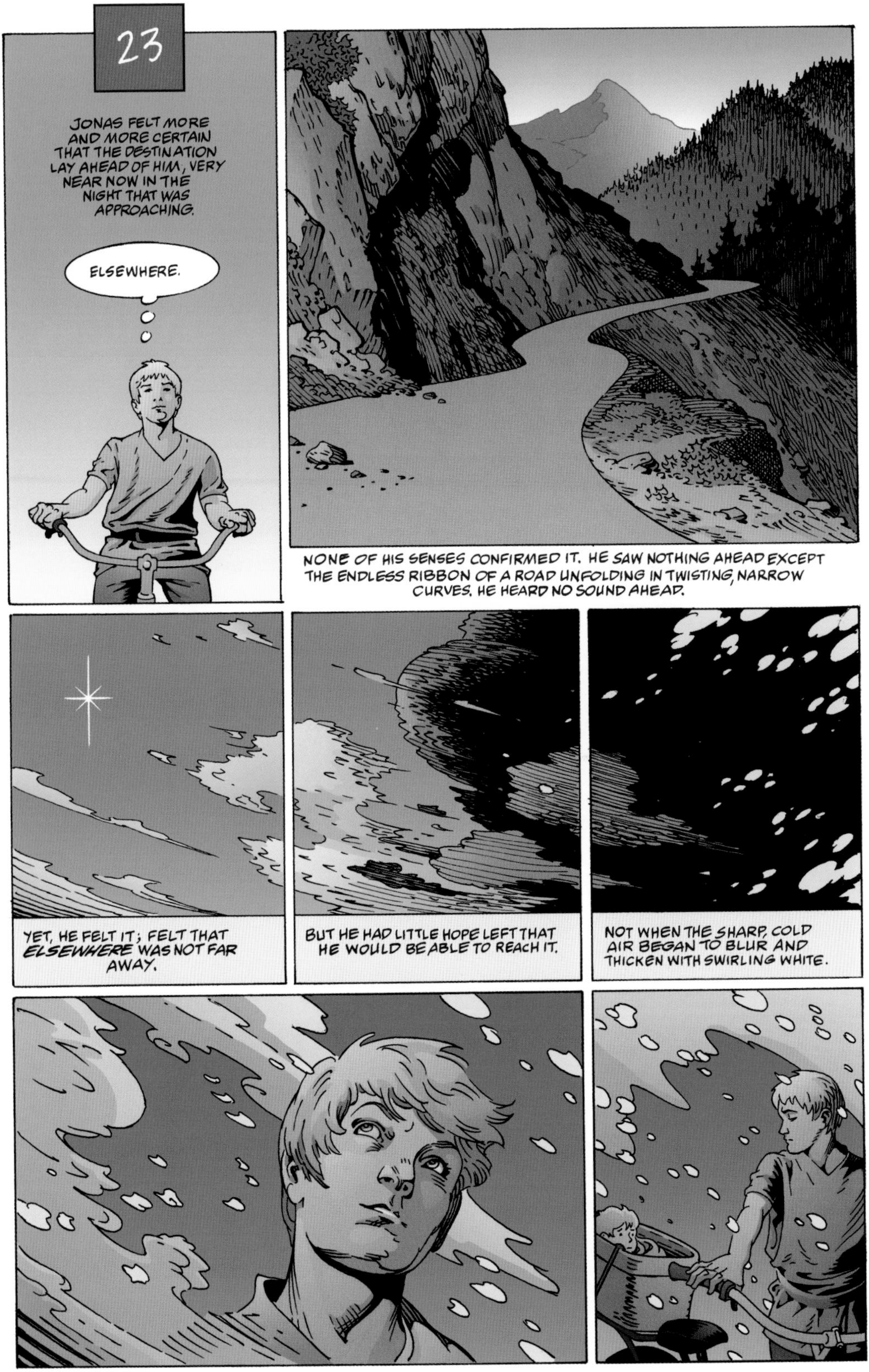
23
JONAS FELT MORE AND MORE CERTAIN THAT THE DESTINATION LAY AHEAD OF HIM, VERY NEAR NOW IN THE NIGHT THAT WAS APPROACHING.
ELSEWHERE.
NONE OF HIS SENSES CONFIRMED IT. HE SAW NOTHING AHEAD EXCEPT THE ENDLESS RIBBON OF A ROAD UNFOLDING IN TWISTING, NARROW CURVES. HE HEARD NO SOUND AHEAD.
YET, HE FELT IT; FELT THAT *ELSEWHERE* WAS NOT FAR AWAY.
BUT HE HAD LITTLE HOPE LEFT THAT HE WOULD BE ABLE TO REACH IT.
NOT WHEN THE *SHARP*, COLD AIR BEGAN TO BLUR AND THICKEN WITH SWIRLING WHITE.

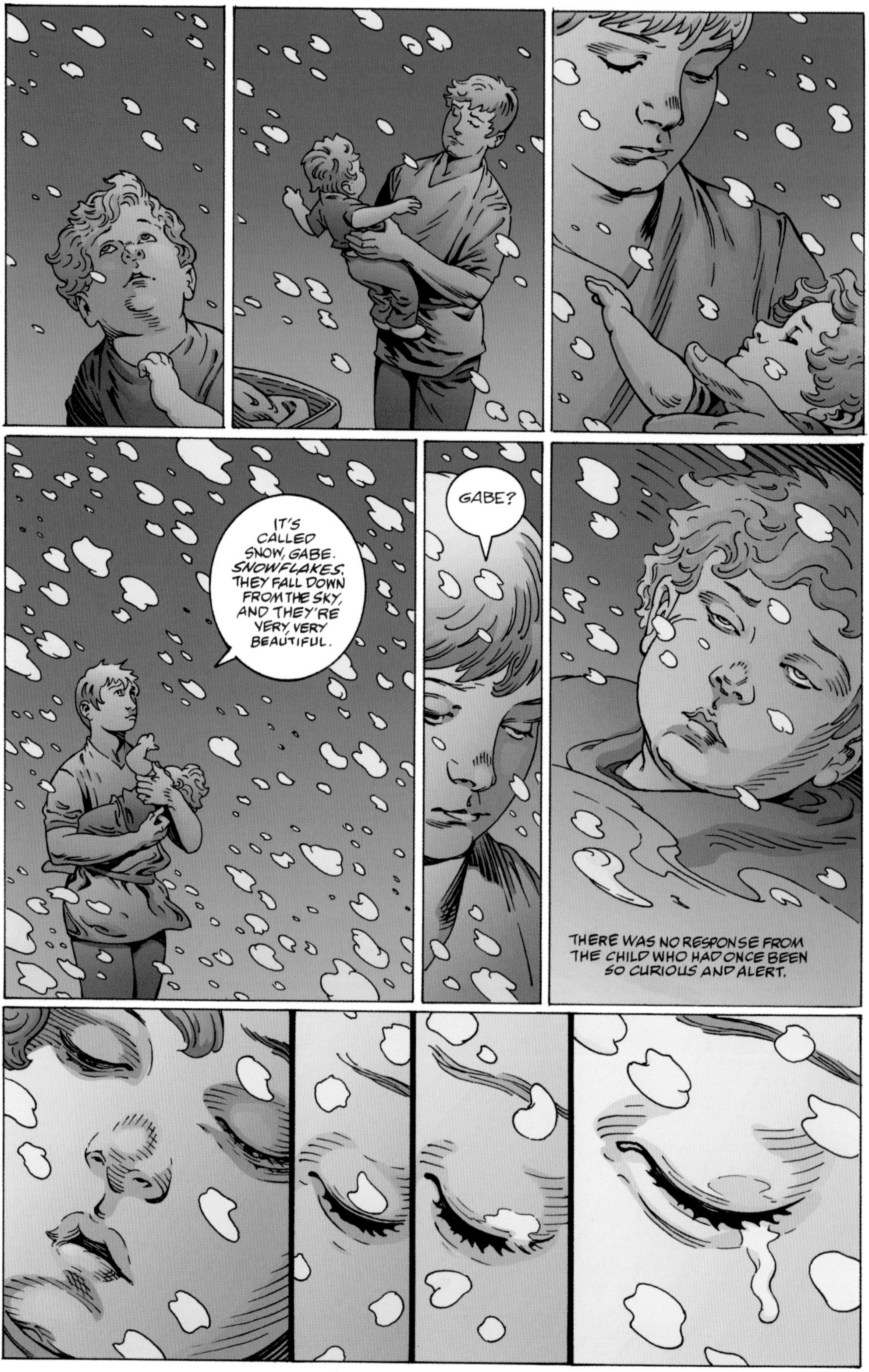
IT'S CALLED SNOW, GABE. SNOWFLAKES. THEY FALL DOWN FROM THE SKY, AND THEY'RE VERY, VERY BEAUTIFUL.
GABE?
THERE WAS NO RESPONSE FROM THE CHILD WHO HAD ONCE BEEN SO CURIOUS AND ALERT.

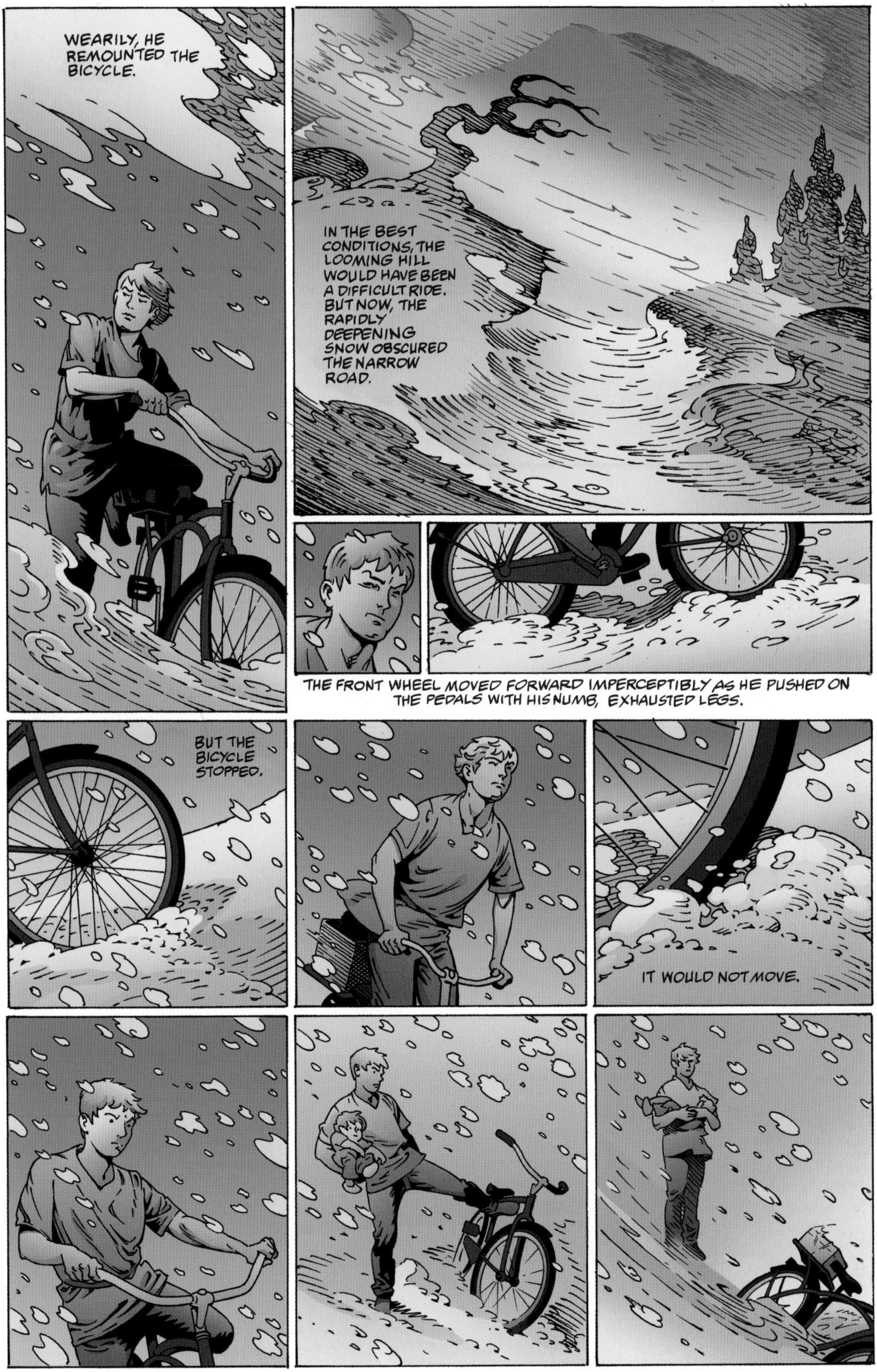
WEARILY, HE REMOUNTED THE BICYCLE.
IN THE BEST CONDITIONS, THE LOOMING HILL WOULD HAVE BEEN A DIFFICULT RIDE. BUT NOW, THE RAPIDLY DEEPENING SNOW OBSCURED THE NARROW ROAD.
THE FRONT WHEEL MOVED FORWARD IMPERCEPTIBLY AS HE PUSHED ON THE PEDALS WITH HIS NUMB, EXHAUSTED LEGS.
BUT THE BICYCLE STOPPED.
IT WOULD NOT MOVE.

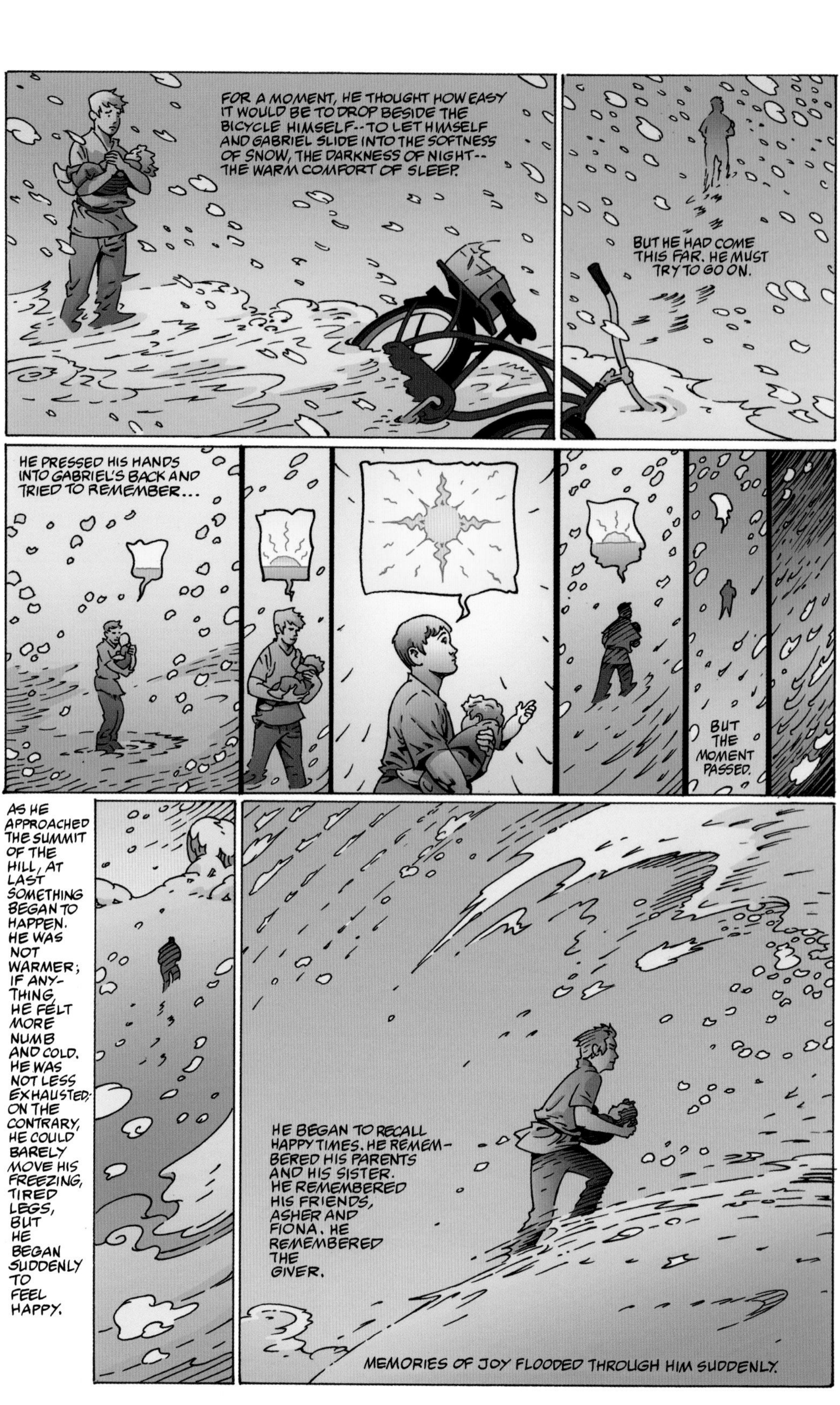
FOR A MOMENT, HE THOUGHT HOW EASY IT WOULD BE TO DROP BESIDE THE BICYCLE HIMSELF--TO LET HIMSELF AND GABRIEL SLIDE INTO THE SOFTNESS OF SNOW, THE DARKNESS OF NIGHT-- THE WARM COMFORT OF SLEEP.
BUT HE HAD COME THIS FAR. HE MUST TRY TO GO ON.
HE PRESSED HIS HANDS INTO GABRIEL'S BACK AND TRIED TO REMEMBER...
BUT THE MOMENT PASSED.
AS HE APPROACHED THE SUMMIT OF THE HILL, AT LAST SOMETHING BEGAN TO HAPPEN. HE WAS NOT WARMER; IF ANY-THING, HE FELT MORE NUMB AND COLD. HE WAS NOT LESS EXHAUSTED; ON THE CONTRARY, HE COULD BARELY MOVE HIS FREEZING, TIRED LEGS, BUT HE BEGAN SUDDENLY TO FEEL HAPPY.
HE BEGAN TO RECALL HAPPY TIMES. HE REMEM-BERED HIS PARENTS AND HIS SISTER. HE REMEMBERED HIS FRIENDS, ASHER AND FIONA. HE REMEMBERED THE GIVER.
MEMORIES OF JOY FLOODED THROUGH HIM SUDDENLY.

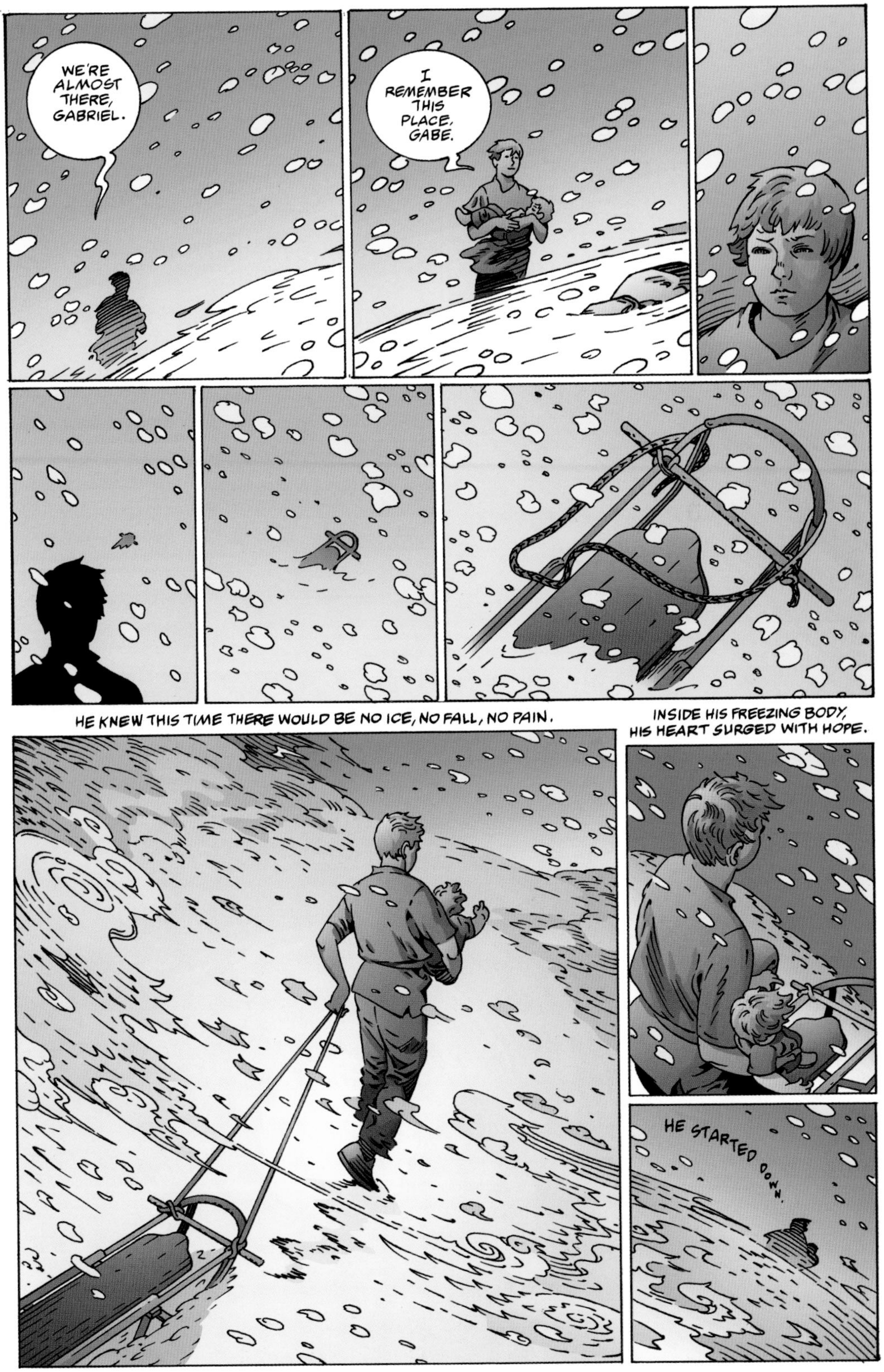

WE'RE ALMOST THERE, GABRIEL.
I REMEMBER THIS PLACE, GABE.
HE KNEW THIS TIME THERE WOULD BE NO ICE, NO FALL, NO PAIN.
INSIDE HIS FREEZING BODY, HIS HEART SURGED WITH HOPE.
HE STARTED DOWN.

JONAS FELT HIMSELF LOSING CONSCIOUSNESS, AND WITH HIS WHOLE BEING WILLED HIMSELF TO STAY UPRIGHT ATOP THE SLED, CLUTCHING GABRIEL, KEEPING HIM SAFE.

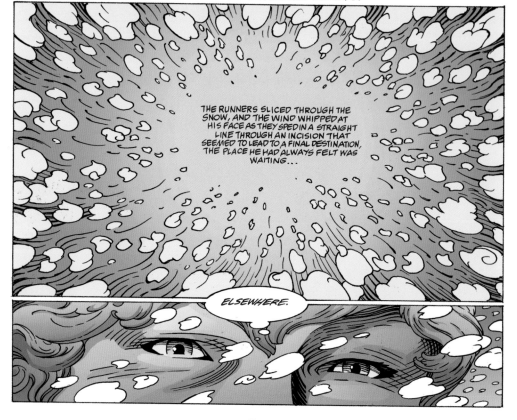

THE RUNNERS SLICED THROUGH THE SNOW, AND THE WIND WHIPPED AT HIS FACE AS THEY SPED IN A STRAIGHT LINE THROUGH AN INCISION THAT SEEMED TO LEAD TO A FINAL DESTINATION, THE PLACE HE HAD ALWAYS FELT WAS WAITING...

ELSEWHERE.

AND ALL AT ONCE HE COULD SEE LIGHTS, AND HE RECOGNIZED THEM NOW. HE KNEW THEY WERE SHINING THROUGH THE WINDOWS OF ROOMS, THAT THEY TWINKLED FROM TREES IN PLACES WHERE FAMILIES CREATED AND KEPT MEMORIES, WHERE THEY CELEBRATED LOVE.

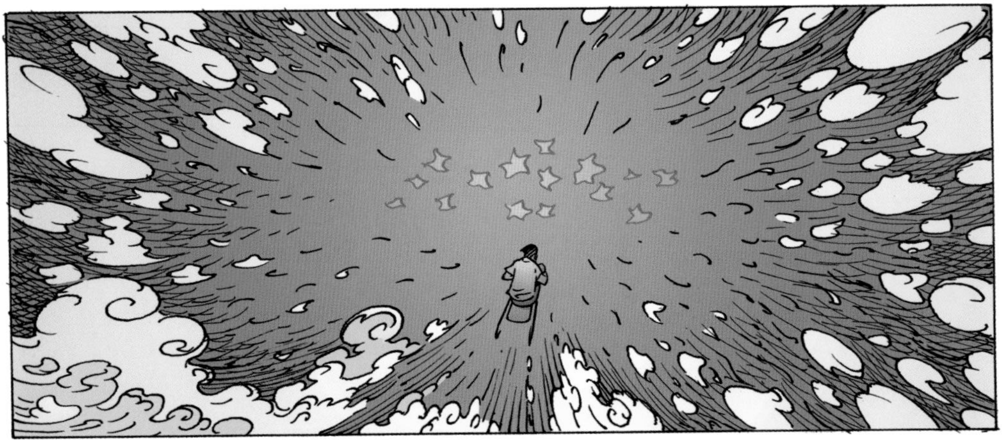

SUDDENLY, HE WAS AWARE WITH CERTAINTY AND JOY THAT BELOW, AHEAD, THEY WERE WAITING FOR HIM; AND THAT THEY WERE WAITING, TOO, FOR THE BABY.

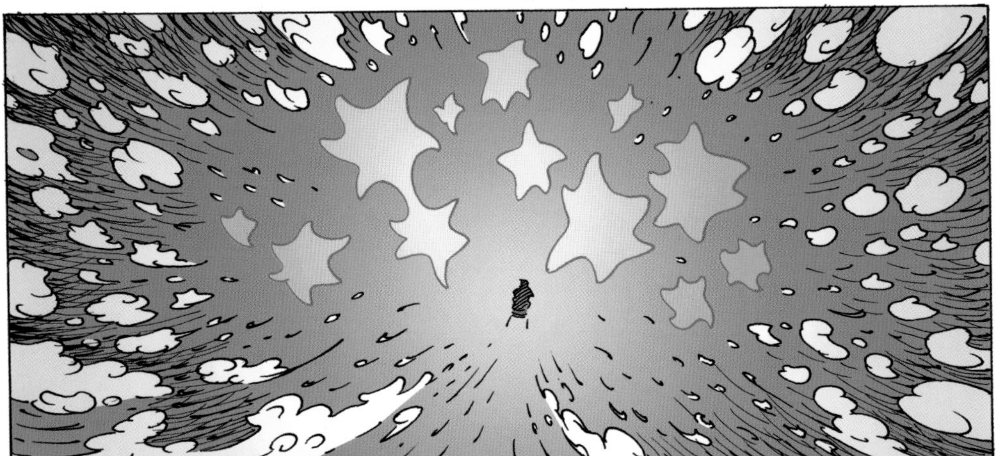

FOR THE FIRST TIME, HE HEARD SOMETHING HE KNEW TO BE MUSIC.

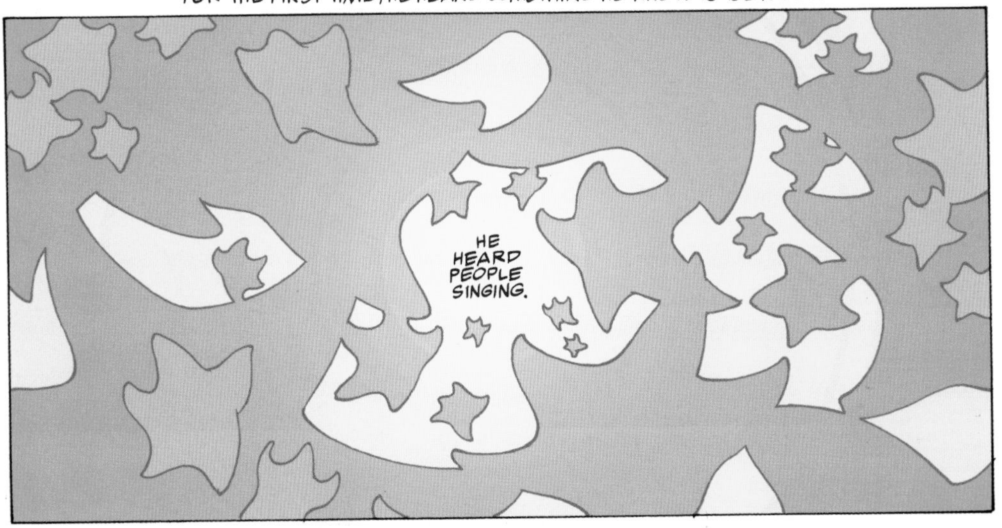
HE HEARD PEOPLE SINGING.

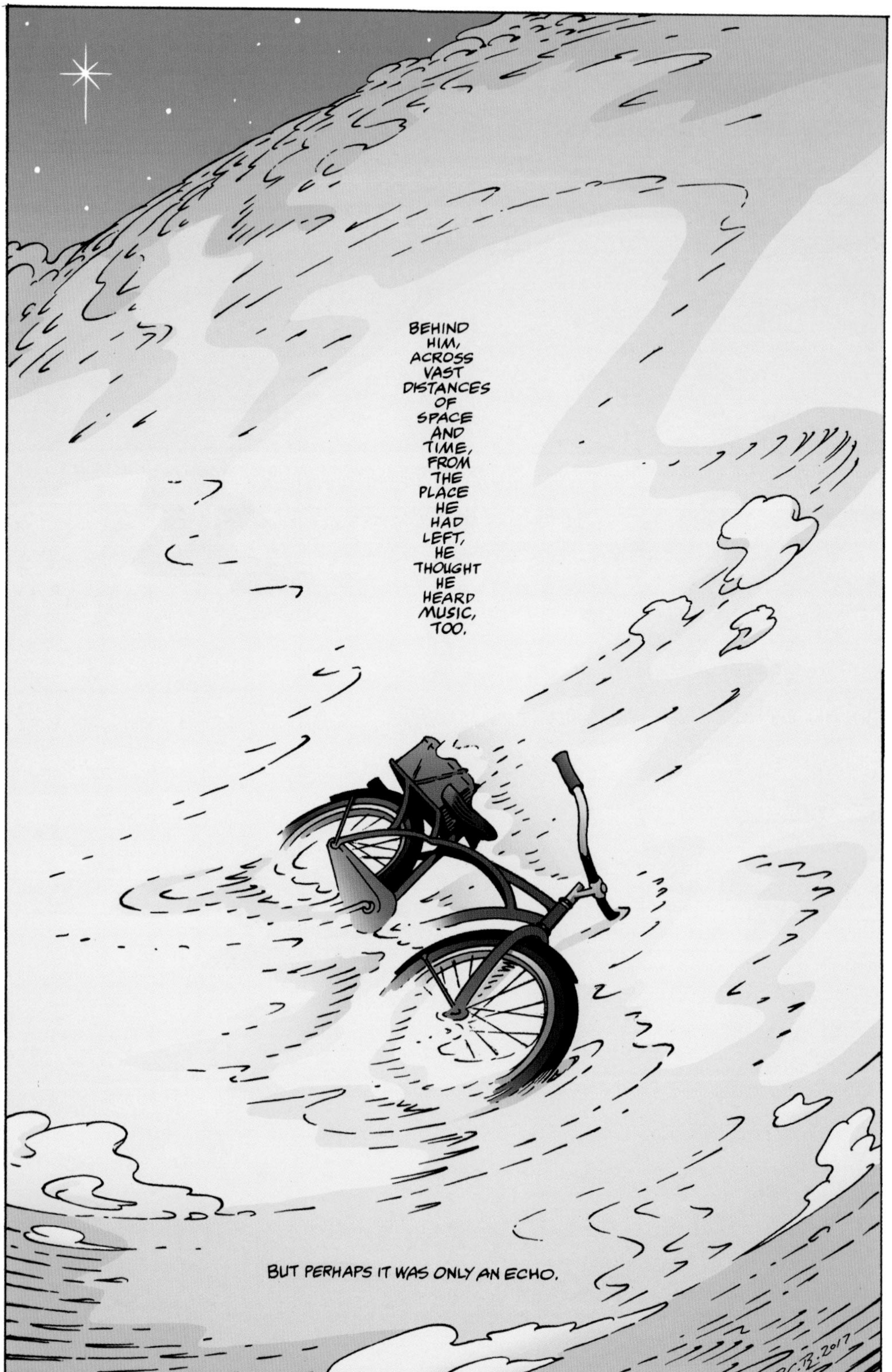
BEHIND HIM, ACROSS VAST DISTANCES OF SPACE AND TIME, FROM THE PLACE HE HAD LEFT, HE THOUGHT HE HEARD MUSIC, TOO.
BUT PERHAPS IT WAS ONLY AN ECHO.
P.C.R. 2017

A Conversation with the
Creators of *The Giver* Graphic Novel

LOIS LOWRY

P. Craig Russell's graphic novel adaptation is the latest stop on a journey that has seen many manifestations of *The Giver*. Do you have a favorite interpretation or version other than the original text?

I can't really say that I have a favorite. But I do like Eric Coble's dramatic stage version. I've seen it performed many times . . . and every time it's different, even though the script remains the same . . . because of different set and costume designers. It's always fascinating to me to see those creative imaginations at work.

Is there anything in this graphic novel version of *The Giver* that surprised you? Or gave you a new perspective on the story you hadn't considered before?

I can't say it's surprising, really; but it was interesting to see the scene where Jonas bathes the old woman, Larissa, in the House of the Old. The theater, the movie, and the opera have all avoided including that scene because of the difficulties it presents. But Russell made it very touching and poignant, I think.

Did you have any input on the illustrations? Do you have a favorite scene from this book?

No, no input from me! And I think it's wise in general that writers and illustrators don't intrude upon each other. I'd have been MUCH too inclined to say "Why don't you do it this way? Or that way?" Not my job!

I have a number of favorite scenes from the book; one would be when Jonas receives the vision of Christmas and family.

Over the years, *The Giver* has been read by millions of people—children and adults—and many fans have spoken or written to you. What do you think fans will get out of the graphic novel that they might not have gotten from the original book?

I don't think fans/readers will necessarily get anything *new* from the graphic novel to *The Giver*; it adheres so very closely to the original. But I think they'll get an enhanced enjoyment from seeing the depictions of scenes that they have already seen in their own minds.

Of course, some of the audience will be coming to the book for the first time in the graphic form. But I'm guessing that most of them will already have read it. So there will be a feeling of familiarity and recognition for them.

Do you read graphic novels? Do you have a favorite?

I certainly did when I was a kid! We called them comic books then, of course. And my favorite wasn't an action hero (though I did enjoy Captain Marvel), but rather a sturdy little girl with curly hair and a funny hat named Little Lulu. I adored her. Looking back on her today, I admire my own taste, because Lulu was smart and funny and something of a feminist, even in the 1940s, before any of us had heard that word.

In the world of *The Giver,* there is very little time for creative pursuits, and the community doesn't emphasize the arts. What do you think society loses by neglecting the creative arts?

As far as I'm concerned, the world comes to an end when art and music and literature are lost. The creative arts are the way we come to terms with our own existence. Nietzsche said, "We possess art lest we perish from the truth."

P. CRAIG RUSSELL

Had you read *The Giver* before you were approached about this project? What were your first impressions?

When I was first approached with the offer to do a graphic novel version of *The Giver*, the book was new to me. When *The Giver* appeared on the scene in the early '90s, I was way past its target age and so was unaware of its enormous popularity and impact. But I said I'd give it a read, and a copy was sent to me. I couldn't put it down and I didn't have to come to the end before I knew I wanted to do it.

What was your first step in creating this graphic novel? Was there any image that immediately came to you when you thought about taking on the project?

My first step in any adaptation after reading the book is to tear all the pages out. I then place two facing pages facedown on a copy machine and copy them onto 11" x 17" paper. This gives me enormous margins in which I can make thumbnail sketches and notes. Then it's a slow process of chipping away at it by underlining and sometimes streamlining dialogue and cutting out descriptive passages that are made redundant by the pictures. Some pictures immediately jump to mind and claim real estate on the page, while other scenes resist visualization. If those resistant scenes can be solved, they frequently are the most interesting in the book.

Throughout *The Giver,* Jonas begins to see color in a world that has previously appeared black and white. How did you want to approach this unique challenge for the graphic novel?

The ideas in the book are, of course, what are most important about it, but it was the great visual, theatrical coup of the sunrise in a colorless world halfway through Chapter 21 that sealed the deal for me. Prior to that was the challenge of making a black-and-white world interesting. My solution was to not do it in black and white. I feared basic black and white would simply look like a graphic novel without the budget for color. So I relied on a technique I've used a few times before. I drew, penciled, the book in blue pencil and did the finished, traditional ink line in pencil, with a soft HB lead. I let the blue show through and sometimes even used it to fill in sky or water. I then used ink wash—that is, ink mixed with water—to give various tones of gray to the drawings. This blue/silvery tonal look gave life to the page, while at the same time giving the look of a world without color, that stark black and white would not.

Much like Jonas discovers new emotions as he begins to experience memory and color, readers will discover something new about *The Giver* through your illustrations. What is one thing you hope readers—old and new alike—will discover about *The Giver* through your artwork?

I've always remained exceedingly faithful to the themes and ideas of whatever source material I'm working with whenever I do an adaptation. But at the same time, whenever you use source material to produce a new work of art, whether you're turning a short story into a film, a play into an opera, or a novel into a graphic novel, these new works have to succeed by the dictates of their new form. In other words, your final work has to be judged as a successful film, opera, or graphic novel. Lois Lowry's ideas remain intact and, I hope, are strongly sustained in this adaptation. What I hope the new reader brings away from it is an appreciation of the range and capabilities of this visual form and its potential to convey abstract ideas visually.

Was there a scene in *The Giver* that was particularly challenging to bring to life visually?

I always talk about the challenge of those pages I call "scenes without pictures." Scenes that have no dialogue where I can show characters engaged in conversation and no overt action to stage. In *The Giver,* the challenge was in showing the transfer of memories, such as Jonas transferring warmth to Gabriel, in a visual way. For this I used the traditional word "balloon" or "bubble" to hold the image, the balloon pointer showing which character was holding the thought, and then slowly retracted that pointer and slowly advanced it toward the receiver of the thought. A solution that's much simpler and clearer to look at than it is to explain.

How do you visualize a world of Sameness in an interesting way? How do you make a gray world visually exciting?

Utilizing the plasticity of panel design helped bring visual stimulation to the page, even as the world within the varying panel shapes retained its cookie-cutter definition. And Lowry's slow introduction of color in Jonas's brief glimpses of red kept anticipation alive of brighter things to come.

I avoided the temptation to draw a future world "futuristically." Nothing looks more dated, more of its time, than a vision of the future seen thirty years later. Instead I went backwards and placed the community in something of a retro '50s world or even further back with the Miami-style Art Deco houses.

In the world of *The Giver,* there is very little time for creative pursuits, and the community doesn't emphasize the arts. What do you think society loses by neglecting the creative arts?

The Giver in its very quiet way is one of the most terrifying stories I've ever read, fully deserving a place on the shelf next to *1984* or *Animal Farm*. I suspect it will be the first graphic novel I've worked on for which there will be cries to remove it from the shelves. I've seen those lists of books. I'll be in good company.